Prai

"Yasmine Gal
—Sherrily

"Erotic and darkly bewitching . . . a mix of magic and passion."
—Jeaniene Frost, *New York Times* bestselling author

"Yasmine Galenorn is a hot new star in the world of urban fantasy."
—Jayne Ann Krentz, *New York Times* bestselling author

"Yasmine Galenorn is a powerhouse author; a master of the craft who is taking the industry by storm, and for good reason!"
—Maggie Shayne, *New York Times* bestselling author

"Spectacularly hot and supernaturally breathtaking."
—Alyssa Day, *New York Times* bestselling author

"Simmers with fun and magic."
—Mary Jo Putney, *New York Times* bestselling author

"Yasmine Galenorn's imagination is a beautiful thing."
—Fresh Fiction

"Galenorn's gallery of rogues is an imaginative delight."
—*Publishers Weekly*

"Pulls no punches . . . [and] leaves you begging for more."
—Bitten by Books

*continued*

# FLIGHT
## FROM
# MAYHEM

## YASMINE
## GALENORN

BERKLEY BOOKS, NEW YORK

# BERKLEY

**An imprint of Penguin Random House LLC**
**375 Hudson Street, New York, New York 10014**

FLIGHT FROM MAYHEM

A Berkley Book / published by arrangement with the author

ISBN: 9780425272169

PUBLISHING HISTORY
Berkley mass-market edition / August 2016

PRINTED IN THE UNITED STATES OF AMERICA

10  9  8  7  6  5  4  3  2  1

Cover art by Tony Mauro.
Cover design by Danielle Mazzella di Bosco.
Interior text design by Laura K. Corless.

Penguin
Random
House

Dedicated to
Jo Yantz, a great friend, and a great workout partner.

*Greed is so destructive. It destroys everything.*

—EARTHA KITT


*Violent predators are not like the rest of us.*

—SUSAN ESTRICH

# ACKNOWLEDGMENTS

I always say the same thing during acknowledgments, but truthfully, these people keep me going each book. I owe thank-yous to a great many people. My editor at Berkley, Kate Seaver. My agent, Meredith Bernstein. My husband—Samwise Galenorn—and our four cats. My assistants, Jennifer Price and Andria Holley. Friends who listen to me vent—Jo and Maura, Carol and Vicki. All so very helpful in a business that just as easily eats you up and spits you out as offers you the chance to do what you love.

To my spiritual guardians—Mielikki, Tapio, Ukko, and Rauni—I give my thanks and devotion.

To all my loyal readers who buy my books to support my habit of writing—thank you. I hope you continue to love the stories, and I hope to continue to write them!

You can find out information about all my books and work on my website, galenorn.com.

# CHAPTER 1

The wind blew through my hair, streaming it back under the helmet as the massive engine purred between my legs, vibrating through my entire body. I gripped Alex's waist with my hands, my breasts pressing against his back as we leaned into the turn. His body was icy even through his butt-hugging jeans and snug leather jacket. He smelled like bay rum, and by now, I knew that scent all too well. I knew every curve of his body—six weeks of steady sex had ensured that.

We were headed toward the new 520 Bridge. As we neared the floating bridge that stretched out for over a mile, crossing the lake that separated Seattle from the Greater Eastside, I could feel the call of the water—a deep, sensual recognition that washed through my core, making me ache for its depths. The water and I had a special connection, seeing that I was a blue dragon and my very nature was connected to the life-affirming liquid. But tonight we weren't headed to the beach so I could swim. No, it was party time.

I wasn't sure exactly where we were going, but apparently Bette was in charge of it, and that was all Alex would tell me. "Unless you've been to one of Bette's parties, you've never been to a party."

With that less-than-comforting thought ringing in my head, I had swung onto the back of his Suzuki Hayabusa and held on as we roared out into the April night, under a heavy cloud cover. As we wove through the silent city streets, Alex deftly maneuvered the rumbling machine through the labyrinth of roads. It occurred to me that Seattle must have been planned out by some drug-crazed cartographer who randomly decided to have one-way streets change direction at major intersections.

As we gobbled up the miles, the streets grinding beneath the bike's wheels, I glanced up at the pale shadow of the moon. She was gleaming from behind the cloud cover, two days past full. By the time we crossed the bridge, the wind was churning the water to splash up and over the edge. To our left, the specter of the old bridge was awaiting deconstruction. It had been decommissioned only a month ago, a dark silhouette that had become outdated and dangerous. There was a one-in-twenty chance the 520 would go down, floundering to the bottom, if the area had another major earthquake. And the chances of a major earthquake in Seattle were *when*, not if.

We passed a car that had stalled out, and then we were over Lake Washington and coming up on Bellevue. We were headed to a private residence on Lake Sammamish in Redmond. Not Bette's house—she lived in a houseboat at the Gasworks Marina—but her current beau's home. Apparently he was some genius software engineer at a startup that had put down roots in the area. High tech was king here, and this was the land of Microsoft, Starbucks, and money.

I inhaled another breath of Alex's cologne. It was comforting—familiar in a world that was still so alien to me. In my realm, I had nothing like this. In my world, I was an outcaste, pariah. Here, I mattered. At least in some small way, I—and what I could do—made a difference to people.

We leaned into the gentle curve of the exit as we swung off the 520 freeway and onto West Lake Sammamish Parkway NE. As we passed through the suburbs and then past Marymoor Park, we came to a fork in the road, where the parkway split off into Bel-Red Road. We veered left, keeping on the parkway, as we curved toward Lake Sammamish. A few minutes later we swung onto NE 38th Street and down to the end, to the neighborhood next to Idylwood Park.

To the left sat a row of houses, and we pulled into the driveway of the last one before reaching the lakeshore. A string of cars filled the drive. I gazed up at the house. It was huge—one of what were commonly called McMansions, or starter castles, around these parts—and it had its own private beach access.

As Alex idled the motor, then switched it off, I removed my helmet, shaking my hair free. I swung off the bike, hopping aside, as Alex put down the kickstand and then joined me. We hung the helmets over the handles of the bike and—as I ordered my hair to straighten itself and smooth out the frizz—we headed for the private beach.

Alex wrapped his arm around my waist. One thing I'd say for him—he made an attentive boyfriend. I wondered for the umpteenth time why Glenda had let him get away. He was a handful when it came to stubbornness, but in the six weeks we had been going out, I had never once felt neglected. In fact, in some ways, the attention was overwhelming. Togetherness was fun, but too much togetherness left me chafing.

At six one, Alex had me beat by an inch. His wheat-colored hair was tousled and shoulder length, and his eyes were pale—frosty as an autumn morning. Handsome in a scruffy, rugged way, he also happened to be a vampire. He also happened to be my boss and parole officer, so to speak.

"Where is everybody?" I glanced around, looking for the party site.

"Down at the water's edge. Bette said they had a bonfire going." His arm still encircling my waist, we headed down the sloped road leading to the shore. There was a gate—of course. Around here, it seemed like everything fun was gated away from the public, for private amusement only. But the gate was open and the sound of laughter filtered up from behind the foliage-thick hedges barring our view.

Within a couple of minutes we found ourselves on the lakeshore. Sure enough, Bette was there, manning the massive grill covered with dogs and burgers. The smells set my stomach to grumbling. Because I couldn't shift form unless I was underwater, and therefore couldn't just fly off to catch and eat a cow every now and then, I found that I had to eat every day, several times a day, just like humans. If I let more than a few hours go by, I was hungry again. That had been one of the most surprising discoveries when I came Earthside.

"I'm going to find Ralph. Go say hello to Bette for us." Alex gave me a slap on the ass and meandered off into the crowd.

I was slowly getting used to being around crowds. I'd been a loner most of my life, and in the Dragon Reaches, where the population was sparse and I could go for days without seeing anybody, being a loner meant truly being alone. I glanced around, finally steeling myself to wander through the crowd of strangers over to Bette. But the next moment, a familiar voice intruded into my thoughts.

"Hey, Shimmer!"

I turned to find Ralph standing there, his Flying Horse energy drink in his hand. The man consumed caffeine like a crazed jackrabbit. He smiled, but I could tell something was unsettling him. The longer I was around others, the more I realized that I was somewhat of an emotional barometer. It was a blue dragon thing, though I hadn't realized it extended beyond my fellow dragons. I wasn't entirely comfortable with the fact that I could walk into a room and sense that Ralph was irritated at his family, or that Bette was hungering to jump her current boy toy of the month.

Ralph nodded me off to the side. He was around five eight and lanky, with brownish black hair and John Lennon glasses, tinted dark. Good-looking in a geek-chic way, Ralph was also a certified computer genius and a werewolf. Over the past few weeks, his crush on me had abated, especially since Alex and I had gotten together, and now the awkwardness had passed.

"Shimmer, I'm worried about Bette. Where's Alex?" He craned his neck. "I thought I saw you come in together."

"We did, but he took off toward . . . hell, I don't know where he went. Is Chai here yet?"

Chai was my best friend. A djinn, he had followed me when I got exiled from the Dragon Reaches. He said it was to see the sights, but I knew he wanted to keep an eye on me. He was a good sort, though—like all djinns—he was unpredictable, and he had settled in as my roommate. On the plus side, he did a great job of keeping the place spotless. He also significantly cut down on the heating bill by radiating enough heat when it got chilly to create an ambient temperature. On the downside . . . well, there *wasn't* a downside.

Ralph shook his head. "Not that I know of. Anyway, Bette's putting on a good show for the public, but I caught her crying earlier, and you know how often *that* happens. When I asked her what was wrong, she pretended she had an eyelash in her eye, but those were real tears."

The tone of his voice told me enough that he wasn't exaggerating. I glanced over at the Melusine, wondering how to approach her. Bette was friendly as all get-out, but she was closemouthed when it came to her own vulnerabilities, and she knew how to ward off anybody who got too close to touchy subjects.

Right now, she was flipping burgers onto a plate that Dent, her current boy toy, was holding. Ralph had told me in private that Dent was a poser—that he really wasn't all that good at his job but was able to fake his way through. But poser or not, he and Bette had fun, and that was all that mattered.

"I'll corner her and see if I can find out what's going on." But at that moment, my attention was violently yanked away when Alex's voice thundered over the murmuring of the crowd.

"I swear if you don't get your ass away from me, woman, I'm going to put the fang to you!"

What the hell? I glanced at Ralph, who shook his head. We jogged in the direction of the outburst and as we threaded our way through the crowd and out into the open, I froze.

"Oh crap." I face-palmed, shaking my head. "I don't want to deal with this right now."

"You and every other sane person on this planet," Ralph muttered.

There, standing in front of Alex, one hand on her hip, shaking a finger in Alex's face, was the pleather-clad, red-haired succubus who I had hoped might have fallen off the face of the earth. Alex's ex-girlfriend, Glenda. And Glenda was no Glinda. She was a harpy-tongued bitch, rather than a saccharine-sweet witch, all right.

"You're pond scum, Alex Radcliffe. You're a bottom-feeder. Cocksucker! Motherfucker!"

Alex stared at her, his look flashing between amusement and irritation. "To think I used to kiss that mouth. Glenda, what did you expect? It was a mutual breakup, in my opinion, but it was far too long in coming. Face it, we're done. We were done *years* ago, but neither one of us had the courage to let go. It was time we said good-bye. You weren't happy, and neither was I."

He shifted, darting away from her shaking finger. But his casual tone seemed to just fuel her fire.

"I should have drained you—I should have sucked your chi

down to the core." Her voice had risen higher than I thought possible. Now, everybody was staring at them.

I sidled away, not wanting to draw her attention, but that was a hope gone to hell in a handbasket as I accidentally bumped against one of the guests. In trying to both keep my footing and steady the man I had knocked off balance, I overcompensated in the other direction and wavered, teetering on one foot. In slow motion, like in the movies, I went careening into the pool, gasping as I sank deep beneath the chlorinated brine that masqueraded as water. As I kicked my way to the surface, sputtering, I saw that every head had turned to stare at me.

Alex had an incredulous look on his face. Then, before I could make a move to get out of the pool, he began to laugh, slapping his thigh. "Oh, Shimmer, bless you for breaking up this little farce of a tête-à-tête. I needed that laugh. Get out of there, woman, and dry yourself off."

Glenda gave him a seething look. "How dare you ignore me?" Her hand met his cheek, the slap echoing through the air.

Alex stopped laughing. His eyes turned a dangerous shade of crimson and he let out a low hiss. "Don't you *ever* strike me again, Glenda. Not if you value your breath. I put up with your tantrums for too long, but no more. Hit me again at risk of your life. *Do you understand?*"

Ten seconds flat turned the easygoing expat Aussie into a deadly predator. *Everybody* took a step back at his words.

Glenda's eyes widened. "This isn't over, Radcliffe," she said, but now her voice was shaking, the anger turning to fear. As she swung around, I pulled myself out of the pool and began to wring out my hair, the scent and taste of chlorine making me queasy. "And *you* . . . you'd better hope we never cross paths in a dark alley. I blame you! You encouraged him. I knew from the start that's what you were out to do."

I stared at her, my own temper flaring. A cold breeze

rushed through me. "You need to rethink your words, Glenda. You may be a succubus, but let me remind you . . . you know what I am." I wasn't in the habit of revealing my nature in front of humans—it wasn't good common sense.

A cruel smile crossed Glenda's face. Apparently, she realized the same thing because very deliberately, she locked my gaze, then snorted. "You're just a neutered dragon."

As whispers began to race through the crowd, I took a step toward her. I had to defuse the potential damage she had just caused.

"Call me a dragon lady, will you? You're the bitch here."

She stiffened, but before I could drag her skinny-ass self over to the pool and throw her in, Chai appeared. Over seven feet of gorgeous, muscled golden body, with a jet black high ponytail and sea foam–colored eyes, the djinn cut a formidable figure. He was wearing a form-fitting V-neck tee and jeans. I envied him his ability to create wardrobe out of wishes—he could wear anything he wanted without worrying about the cost. But right now, clothes were the last thing on his mind.

He leaned over Glenda, and she actually cowered back. "If you ever threaten my little sister again, I will personally stuff you in a bottle, seal it shut, and toss you out on the Ocean of Agony. Do you understand?"

Glenda let out an audible gulp, fear washing across her face. "I was just about to leave."

"Then, may I suggest you go *now*?" Chai's voice was barely above a whisper, but somehow it seemed a far worse threat than if he had been yelling.

Glenda whirled on her stiletto heels, marching off. She didn't say another word—not even a mumble. Alex and Chai watched her go, both with grim expressions on their faces. I shivered as Ralph handed me a towel. Bette hurried over, Dent by her side.

"Are you okay, Shimmer? I'm sorry you took an unexpected dip." Dent seemed perfectly amiable, if a little bland.

"I don't know if I have anything that will fit you, except a terry-cloth robe, but if you want to change into that, we can wash and dry your clothes while you wait."

I ran the towel over my hair, squeezing it to dry it as much as possible. "Thanks, I'd appreciate that."

Alex touched my elbow. "I'm so sorry about Glenda. She's a real . . . well, she's got a temper on her and it looks like she's decided to blame me for the breakup. But I wonder why she waited until now?"

"I know why. She found out we're together. She doesn't want you, but she doesn't want anybody else to have you, either." I shook my head. "She's a real winner, that's for sure."

Bette cocked her head. "Follow me. Dent, take over the burgers, would you? I'll show Shimmer to the bathroom where she can shower and dry her hair while I find her a robe. Chlorine leaves a nasty residue." She linked her arm through mine and began to steer me toward the path leading up to the house, leaving Ralph, Alex, and Chai to discuss Glenda's inopportune appearance.

"You okay, sugar?" Bette was the chain-smoking, leather-clad, curse-like-a-sailor grandmother I never had. Clad in leopard-print jeggings and a chartreuse V-neck bodysuit, she was wearing a black leather jacket over the top. She was loud and nasal, with a bouffant so high it rivaled Marge Simpson's. I was confounded by how she managed to navigate on her platform CFM pumps. But Bette had become a good friend over the months, and she had introduced me to several delightful Earthside delicacies, like See's Candies—though I didn't have much of a sweet tooth—and dripping, oozy fast-food cheeseburgers.

I nodded. "Yeah, I am. Glenda had better watch out, though, or Alex will take her down. He's a gentleman, but not when threatened. And she crossed that line tonight."

"You aren't spoiling for a catfight, are you?" She glanced around to make certain we weren't being overheard, then lowered her voice so that it was barely a whisper. "Because honey, I know you're a dragon, but Glenda's mean as a junk-yard dog, and she's got a lot of tricks up her sleeve. She wouldn't hesitate to fight dirty." Bette sounded so concerned that I wanted to hug her.

"No. I'm not spoiling for a fight at all. I'd be happier if she just disappeared." I paused, then remembered what Ralph had said. "Bette, I'm going to just come out and say it. We're friends. Ralph told me he thought something was wrong, and now that we're away from that crowd out there, I can sense it, too. What's going on? Your smile is pretty much plastered on right now." Now that I was standing next to her and every-body else was out of the way, I could tell that she was upset over something. The emotion radiated off her in waves. "Are you upset at Dent?"

She blinked. "Dent? Why would I be? No, he's just a little bit of fun and flirt right now. We both know that. But . . . now that you mention it, I *am* worried, but it's not about me. I have a friend I'm thinking may be in trouble."

"Ralph? Alex?"

"No, no one you know." She led me into a large bedroom that was decked out in black and white, with potted palms as one of the few accent colors. The floors were dark hard-wood. Everything felt out of a designer magazine. Bette darted into an enormous walk-in closet, then returned with a thick, plush terry-cloth robe. It was a pale shade of blue.

"My favorite color."

"There's a bathroom through that door. Take a shower and warm up, get the chlorine off you. And on the vanity, you'll find a blow dryer so you can dry your hair. If you need anything, let me know. There are clean towels on the side of the vanity. I'll wait out here."

I wanted to ask about her friend but decided that it could wait till I got the chlorine off me. I hated the stuff, and it didn't like me much either. I seemed to react to it. Sadly, my reaction was strong enough that it put the kibosh on me puttering around in swimming pools. But two weeks ago,

I'd discovered a saline pool nearby and signed up for a membership at the gym just so I could go swimming. Of course, it wouldn't do to turn into a dragon in the pool—it wasn't really big enough, anyway, but it felt good just to immerse myself in the water.

I slipped out of my wet clothes, kicking them to one side. As I stepped under the warm stream of water, I let out a long breath, stretching so that it pounded on my back. The bath gel was honeysuckle scented—no doubt Bette's rather than Dent's. I lathered up, soaping away the stink of the chlorine. The chemical didn't exactly burn my skin, but a pale rash rose up when I went too long without washing after it touched any significant portion of my body.

As I scrubbed under the streaming water, I frowned.

Glenda's arrival nagged at me. I wasn't seriously worried she would hurt me. Regardless of my temporary limitations, I could still beat the crap out of her, though I doubted my water magic would affect her in any significant way. But the fact that she had decided to show up at a party and pick a fight in public . . . that was troubling.

She obviously hadn't moved on, and considering the way she had used Alex like a whipping boy, I had the feeling that she was finding it difficult to dig up anybody else who would put up with both her temper and her inborn need to fuck every man she saw. Succubi weren't cut out for relationships. Neither were incubi. And yet some of them—against all odds—kept trying.

After I finished, I stepped out of the shower and wrapped my towel around me. It was so plush and thick that I checked the label—I wanted towels like this. Noting the brand, I wrapped another around my hair. As I padded over to the vanity, I saw that Bette had taken away my wet clothes and had laid out the blow dryer and the robe. I dried off, then slid into the robe and tied it tight.

Leaning on the counter, I stared at myself in the mirror. Six months ago, I had been sent Earthside. Exiled, for a crime that I fully admitted to. The alternative was to stay in the Dragon Reaches and let Greanfyr—the white dragon I had stolen from—hunt me down and execute me. And if he did, nobody would raise a wing to stop him, given my persona non grata status.

As I softly ordered my hair to untangle itself, the shimmering streaks of blue and purple gleamed among the dark strands. They were natural. They indicated who—or rather, *what*—I was, and were as much a part of me as was my tattoo. My ink was a reminder to me that I existed. That I belonged, even though everybody else said I didn't. A blue dragon, the tattoo coiled up from my waist with the tail curling near my hip. The dragon slinked up my right side, surrounded by waves, curling up so that the neck and head coiled over my right shoulder and down my arm, with more ocean waves along the side.

I flipped on the blow dryer, the heat warming me as I instructed my hair to section out, holding itself away from my head while I aimed the blowing air at it. That was one lovely thing about being a dragon—my hair had a mind of its own and I could make it behave however I wanted with just a blink of a thought. Which was why when the Wing-Liege cut it to my midback, the pain had been overwhelming. Our hair was a part of our body, a part of our mane when we were in dragon shape, and unlike that of humans and Fae, it had nerve endings and could register pain and pleasure. Touching Alex's skin with my hair gave me a thrill, even as having someone yank on it could hurt like a son of a bitch.

As the hair fell into place, smoothing softly against my head in clean, gleaming lines, I began to shake off the evening. Earlier, I had been uneasy about coming to the party. I had thought it was just because I would have to face a bunch of strangers and pretend to be Fae—my cover was that of a water Fae. A nymph, to be exact. Humans didn't really know about dragons, and we aimed to keep it that way as much as possible. But something had set me on edge, and now I wondered if I had been anticipating Glenda showing up.

When my hair was dry and smooth, I slid my feet into the plush terry slippers Bette had left for me and headed into the bedroom to find her sitting there, checking her phone, with a worried frown on her face. She glanced up as I sat down beside her.

"All washed up and clean?"

"Yeah, the chlorine is off my skin, so I should be fine. Now tell me what's going on. Did you get some bad news?" I leaned back in the chair, thoroughly enjoying the soft sinking feeling of the cushions.

Bette looked about ready to say no, but then she paused. "I'm not sure if it's bad news or not. That's the problem. I told you I'm worried about a friend, right?"

She seemed reluctant to say anything, which meant she wasn't at all sure on what she was chewing on. I knew Bette and she was never reticent with her opinions unless she truly wasn't sure what she thought about something.

I nodded. "Right. Why don't you tell me, and we can talk it over and decide if it's bad news?" I motioned to the robe. "I really don't feel like wandering around in a group of strangers wearing nothing but a bathrobe. Plus it will give them time to change the subject to something other than Glenda, Alex, and me. I just hope that Ralph and Alex can quash the dragon rumor."

Grinning, I stuck my feet up on the ottoman and settled back, thinking that—given furniture this comfortable—I'd consider hanging out with Dent, too.

Bette lit up a cigarette and, as usual, let it dangle off her lip. I was about to ask if Dent let her smoke inside but then saw a few ashtrays scattered around, which meant he probably smoked, as well. Bette was no fool—she never got involved with nonsmokers or teetotalers who might try to curb her habits. But she was also gracious enough to refrain from lighting up in my house, or over at Ralph's, and she kept her smoke downwind.

She inhaled deeply, then blew out a ring pretty and perfect enough to make even a dragon jealous. As she gave me a little shrug and put her own feet up, she said, "All right. I hate breaking secrets. Oh, it's nothing earthshaking, but, fuck a duck, this has been eating me up. I don't know if you realized that I volunteer at the Supe Community Action Council once a week. I teach an art class there."

I stared at her. It was hard to imagine Bette doing anything of the sort. But I kept my mouth shut.

"So, a lot of my students tend to be elderly Fae—mostly Earthside. They're . . . think of them like the great-aunt who lives in the upstairs attic. They've lost enough strength and vitality to lack confidence, but they're still in fairly good health. Which means another few hundred years to go, but they aren't ready to die just yet."

I knew very little about how the Fae aged. My kind tended to keep to themselves for the most part. It was mostly due to arrogance but, regardless of the cause, there were few dragons who took an interest in the outside world. Or outsiders. We tended to be an insular race.

Bette puffed on her cigarette. "So, the problem is this: I have a student there, a friend really. Her name is Marlene, and she's one of the Woodland Fae. She's a lovely woman, but she's drifting, really. When the Fae get as old as she is, especially the nature Fae, they tend to get a bit . . ." She looked like she was trying to find a polite word for what she was thinking.

Ever helpful, I said, "Balmy?"

A nod, then: "Yeah, balmy sums it up. Marlene and I get together and play poker once every couple of weeks. We watch movies, and take walks in her garden because she's too old to go out in the wild anymore, but I keep an eye on her, you know? Make certain that she's eaten lately and isn't just sitting in the garden, dozing during the rain."

I sighed. In my realm, when dragons reached that age, they slept in their dreyeries until they never woke up again. They were treated by their families as sleeping gods, ancestors to be venerated and waited on. But among humans—and some of the Fae—the aging ones were treated with less respect and often just left on their own, discarded like used tissue.

"I understand. You make sure she's okay, and that's a good thing, Bette. But what's the problem?"

"Marlene told me a few days ago that she's dating a young man. I was surprised—she's no Melusine, after all. And she's never mentioned wanting to explore that side of her life again. In fact, I thought she was pretty much over any interest in anything but pottering around. But she told me he makes her feel young, and that he romances her." A dark look flashed through her eyes. "I don't trust him, Shimmer. Marlene's a lovely woman but she's not a cougar, and she's very, very wealthy."

I blinked at that. Vampires tended to accumulate wealth. The Fae? Some of them did, but Woodland Fae weren't that interested in material goods, especially the Earthside ones.

"So you think this guy is looking for a sugar mama?"

Bette croaked out a laugh. "Pumpkin, I think he's out to get what he can. I can't come out and tell Marlene what I think, though—it would hurt her feelings terribly. So I'm thinking I should just bite the bullet and find out what I can behind the scenes. I'll ask Ralph to use his know-how to see what we can dig up about the guy. I need his last name, though, and she hasn't given it to me. I'm supposed to meet her for lunch tomorrow. Would you join us? I know you can read emotion, even though you try to hide it."

I stared down my nose at her. "Oh, really?" Even though she was spot-on, it surprised the hell out of me to hear that she knew. I hadn't mentioned it to anybody but Alex. But then, he and Bette were thick as thieves and for all I knew, she was privy to our entire relationship.

"Shimmer, you've been working with us for almost seven months. By now, you should know that there aren't any secrets in the office." She cackled then and puffed on her cigarette again before tamping it out in one of the ashtrays. "Which is why I can tell you this: Glenda? She's not done with the pair of you. I'd expect trouble from that little bitch, because honey, you cross a succubus? You've got a mess of worms on your plate."

And with that lovely thought filling my head, I agreed to have lunch with Bette and Marlene the next day. But even as Bette brought me my clothes—now clean and dry—all I could think of was Glenda, the bad and brazen, and what revenge she might be planning.

# CHAPTER 2

One thing about working the night shift, it left my days free. Because I was a dragon, even in my human shape I needed far less sleep than most people. In fact, usually five hours was plenty, and I could run on four without a problem if it wasn't night after night.

Alex dropped me off. Glenda's appearance had put a damper on the rest of the evening and the awkward silence between us begged for an argument, so we both decided to let it rest. Chai was already home by the time I climbed off the back of the motorcycle. He was out in the yard, working under the cover of darkness using the glow of a faint light he had conjured to see by as he weeded the flower beds. We had discovered his inner gardener and, within a few weeks of him moving in as my roommate, my yard was the prettiest one on the block.

He stood as I came up the sidewalk. "Door's unlocked, and I left a plate of chicken on the counter." He dusted his hands on his jeans. "You need to talk, Little Sister?"

Chai was like that. We had a bond, and he could sense when I was upset and vice versa. We had always been aware of the connection, but once he moved in, the strength became obvious. Now he followed me into the house, which was spotless. I had never been dirty or a slob, but Chai was a neat-freak and the house was always clean.

I wandered over to the aquarium that took up two thirds of the long wall in my living room. I had a variety of fish swimming in it, meandering this way and that. Coolray came up to the glass and pressed a tentacle to it. Everybody said jellyfish had no minds, but I knew better. They might not have brains like humans or dragons, or even like octopi, but they had a sentience that existed outside the norm. Over the years, I had been able to tap into it. I pressed my hand against the glass and whispered, "Hello," and Coolray zoomed to the top of the tank and then down again. That was the way he usually greeted me.

As I watched the water, I began to breathe easier. Being in my home, with the aquarium, always calmed me down. It was my safe haven, and even though I lived in the infamous Greenbelt Park District—the most haunted area of Seattle—I always felt like my house had a buffer around it, repelling all spooks and spirits. And it had a good security system to repel the other miscreants.

Chai came up behind me and pressed his hands against my shoulders, kissing the top of my head. "Something bothering you, Little Sister?"

I shrugged. "Glenda, for one. I really didn't expect her to show up like that. And I have a nasty feeling she's not done with Alex and me yet. I really don't want to deal with her."

"Unfortunately, relationships are messy and most come with some form of baggage."

I had dated around some—even here, Earthside. In fact, when I first arrived, I took to dating a half-demon, half-Titan named Carter. He was a demigod, really, when I thought about it. And I had discovered that, as wonderful a friend he was to have, he was far too dark and intense for me to endure as a boyfriend.

A thought struck me. "Do you think . . . am I . . . maybe I'm not cut out to be in a relationship? I don't like mess. I don't like complications."

"You just don't like dealing with people because you don't know how. You've always been a loner, Shimmer. At the orphanage you had to fend for yourself. You didn't dare trust anybody to help you out, because chances were you'd be let down. And ever since then, you've been fending for yourself."

I sucked in a slow, deep breath. He was right. "I couldn't trust that anybody would care enough to come through in a pinch."

"See? I think that—for you—it feels easier when you only have yourself to worry about. You're just going through the growing pains most people . . . be they dragon or human . . . go through when they learn how to interact with others. You're just coming to it far later than most. And seriously? It's not easy, whether you're trying to cope with a lover's baggage, or a friendship that might be going through a bumpy spot." He wrapped his arms around me for a quick hug. "Now go eat something. You only picked at your food at the party."

"You're like a fussy mother hen, you know that?" I grinned up at him, my worries sliding away. Chai was always good at helping me see things in a clearer light. "And, by the way, I love hanging out with you. I don't feel out of place. Humans are pretty short, especially human women. And so are the Fae. I always feel like I'm one of the tallest ones in the room."

"True, but around me, you're short and petite and easy to hug. And yes, I *am* a fussy mother hen. So do as I say and eat." He steered me into the kitchen, where I found a plate of chicken waiting. Fried chicken. I loved fried chicken, had developed a passion for it, in fact.

As I ate, licking my fingers, Chai poured me a glass of milk and cut me a slice of cherry pie, pushing them across the table to me. I wiped my mouth with a napkin, then told him about Bette's friend.

"I'm having lunch with them today. I'm not sure if Bette's just being overprotective, or what she expects me to find out. I sense emotion, but I can't read minds." I toyed with the last bite of the pie. There was something about cherries that intrigued me. They had such a bright pop of color and flavor. Back in the Dragon Reaches, my diet had been mostly meat—cows here and there, a horse . . . other creatures that ventured into the highlands. But being stuck in human form most of the time meant I ate human food, and it had begun to dawn on me that really, humans and Fae had it one up on dragons with variety and flavors.

"She's worried about a friend. She's reaching out to you, so help her however you can. She probably doesn't expect anything from you except maybe a confirmation that she should be worried, or a reassurance that she's imagining things." Chai tilted his head to the side, leaning back in the chair. "Just be honest with her, and walk softly. She's a blunt old broad, yes, but I have the feeling—from what you've told me—that this worries her more than she's letting on. She needs you to be supportive."

Listening, I finished the last bite and stared at the plates. All that was left were the bones.

Chai had brought me another gift besides not feeling alone in the house—one that was invaluable. He was helping me understand how to best bridge the chasm that seemed to exist between me and others. I was learning how to interact without feeling like the proverbial bull in a china shop.

"Got it. Thanks, Chai." I glanced at the clock. It was eight A.M. already? "I thought it was seven."

"Nope. Eight."

I carried my plates over to the counter and rinsed them off. I was due to meet Bette and Marlene at noon, which gave me a few hours of free time—one fewer than I'd expected, but what the hell. Ralph had begged out of my driving lesson that morning, so that was off the calendar. I was due to take my test in a week or so, and finally, I wouldn't have to rely on anybody to drive me anywhere.

Feeling oddly at loose ends, I headed outside. My neighbors to the right were up; I could tell by the lights on in their house. We didn't really know each other, especially since I worked nights and they worked during the day. Other than Charles and Linda, I really didn't know anybody else on the street. Most of the houses stood empty. While the housing boom was in full force again, people just steered clear of the weathered, ghostly homes, as if the energy pushed them back saying, *No, leave us to our restless sleep.*

I wandered across the street. A run-down two-story house sat opposite mine, abandoned, with an overgrown lot that was well on its way to becoming a jungle. The fence was weathered and falling apart, the pickets no longer white nor upright. A huge old weeping willow was budding out—though the leaves were still a few weeks away. And everywhere, waist-high grass filled the yard. I looked for the for-sale sign and finally found it, buried under a thatch of thistle that had overgrown the signpost, but the sign was old and so faded I couldn't read the number on it. Gingerly avoiding the prickly plant, I skirted it and entered through the broken gate. I wasn't sure what about the house attracted me, but something had caught my attention.

As I slowly snooped around the yard, I saw an old swing attached to a thick willow branch. The chains were a little rusty, but it looked sturdy, so I sat down on the board and quietly pushed myself back and forth, letting the energy of the yard settle around me.

At the Lost and Foundling, we had never had toys. We had been given recreational time, especially when we were little, but it had been regimented and structured, geared toward competitive games. I had always longed to run off, to play by myself, but we were forced into team sports and forced to focus on winning. The handlers claimed that they did so for the good of the orphans—that if we weren't taught to compete, we would die when we were released, unable to stand up for ourselves against the harshness of a world that refused to acknowledge our presence. I remembered one day in particular, when the enormity of being the only person I could count on crashed in on me.

It was on a day they called Benefactor's Day . . .

"What's your name?"

We were in human form, standing at attention in the vast Grand Hall of the Lost and Foundling. We had lined up in our natural form, for inspection. The Benefactor wanted to see how well we shifted, so we were ordered to transform so she could see how we had learned our lessons.

I never had a problem with shifting shape, but the girl two spots down the line always had difficulty. She never wanted to be in human form, and her transformations were sloppy, usually ending up with her sprawled on the ground. I didn't really like her—she had a hot temper and was always starting fights—but I didn't dislike her enough to wish her what was coming next.

Stumble shifted, clumsily at best, the last to attempt the maneuver. It didn't go so well. She made it into human form but went sprawling at the Benefactor's feet, right onto her nose.

Benefactor Tris changed shape along with Ser-Rigel, the director of the Lost and Foundling. The Ser looked royally pissed as Stumble picked herself up off the floor and slowly came to attention. I could tell she was shaking, and she had good reason. To embarrass the orphanage in front of a Bene-factor? Unacceptable. And punishments for screwing up were harsh. The Ser glared at her, but he said nothing. It was not his place to speak until the Benefactor pronounced judgment.

"I see you have not yet managed to take her in hand. I believe we discussed this one the last time I visited." Benefactor Tris's words echoed in front of all of us, her voice ricocheting through the chamber. I shuddered. That the Ser was getting rebuked, and in front of the orphans, meant trouble all the way down the line.

"Stumble seems to have difficulty with even easy tasks. She is a quarrelsome girl." The Ser glared at Stumble, who had gone white as a sheet. That she was a white dragon made her even more pale, and for once, I felt downright sorry for her. She couldn't help having a testy temper—she was a white, after all, and her inability to shift easily? Not really her fault. Some dragons were just slower than others.

"Then perhaps we should find her something to do that requires very little in the way of basic skills. She's not even fit for a scullery drudge, given her inability to handle rudimentary tasks. And given her age, she's not likely to grow out of it. We might as well channel our resources into those who can become productive in our society. After all, I don't offer you donations in order for you to waste them on the ineffectual." Benefactor Tris glanced up and down the line at the rest of us. "The rest seem responsive enough, though I don't like the surly look on the blue's face there."

I sucked in a deep breath but then realized she was talking about the blue dragon next to me. When the Benefactors paid a visit, it was best to be as bland and pleasant as possible. Stand out too much and you could find yourself in a mess. Too pretty and you might end up a concubine in some lecherous dragon's dreyerie. Too bright and you would be forced into whatever work they wanted you to do. Too stupid and you ended up culled . . . which meant you were cast out—until full grown—and that usually meant an early death.

The blue dragon the Benefactor had pointed to immediately hung his head, trying to appear repentant. He was a troublemaker, all right, but he wasn't stupid.

With a huff, Benefactor Tris turned back to the Ser. "Take

this . . . Stumble . . . and sell her to the stockyards. They can put her to work shoveling dung, and she might fetch a price that will repay some of the food she's eaten here." And with that, the Benefactor moved toward the door. "Come, we'll discuss the waning half of the year in your office."

Ser-Rigel turned to us and motioned for us to bow. We did, in unison. Even Stumble managed it, though tears were streaking down her cheeks. As the adults left, leaving us dragonettes to our own devices, a small group of the tougher, crueler orphans gathered around Stumble.

*"Dung-heap! Dung-heap!"*

*"You might as well shovel shit, seeing that you're in a pile of it!"*

As the chanting continued, Stumble dropped to the floor, weeping loudly. I pushed my way through the milling orphans until I was facing the loudest bully. He was another white, of course. *That figured.* Whites had nasty tempers and were usually quick to cruelty.

"Leave her alone."

"What did you say to me?" He turned, looming over me. He was tall for his age and was going to be a bruiser.

"I said, leave her alone. She's already facing enough hell, without *you* picking on her." I folded my arms across my chest, staring him down.

"You going to make me back off, Blue-baby?" He snorted. "Shimmer, don't mess with me. Don't even try."

I pushed him then, shoving him back against the others who had joined in teasing Stumble.

"Never try to tell me what to do, Dom. I don't take orders very well." And then we were at it, rolling around on the floor in a scuffle. I whipped him across the face with my hair and he yelled as the strands left long welts on his skin. As he tried to punch me in the stomach, the door opened and Ser-Rigel returned, this time without the Benefactor.

He took one look at our scuffle and motioned for two of

the older dragonettes to separate us. As they dragged us apart, the Ser took in the situation. He walked over to Dom and smacked him upside the head a good one.

"Quit causing trouble. No egos here, not for your likes. Remember: you are a *foundling*. You are an *orphan*, which means you are nothing. Until you grow to an age where you can give back to society, all you are is a leech on resources. You have no heritage, therefore you do not exist. You are here by the grace of the Benefactors who fund this organization. Your only existence is physical. You have no name. You have no standing. Never let me catch you acting as though you even *think* you have a right to be here." He paused, then added, "Twenty days' work detail in the Grand Hall. You can scrub the floors. Perhaps it will teach you a little of the humility that should be second nature to you by now. Quarters—and speak not lest I decide you should be sold to the stockyards along with the girl."

Dom's eyes flashed, but he bowed curtly, then turned and stormed out of the room. Ser-Rigel watched him go, then—without even glancing at me—said, "You know fighting is forbidden. Even in defense of others. But . . . it's late and I have no more interest in this matter. To your quarters without dinner, girl."

As I bowed, then silently headed toward the door, I heard him speaking softly to Stumble. I wasn't sure what he said to her, but her tears stopped and—as I gave a tiny glance over my shoulder—I saw her being led away. That was the last we ever saw of Stumble. The next day she was gone, to the stockyards to a lifetime of shoveling out stalls in the vast cattle reserve where so much of our food was raised.

Over the next few days, I thought about her, and thought about how with a single word, our lives—the lives of all the orphans—could be snuffed out. We were nothing. We didn't exist. We had no lineage, no heritage. And if we weren't strong and flexible, we wouldn't make it to graduation. I remembered this, right through the day I walked through the gates of the Lost and Foundling for the last time. I never looked back.

A sudden gust brought me back to the present. I glanced at the sky. We were due for rain, but it seemed to be holding off for the moment. Wondering what had drawn me to the house, I jumped off the swing and headed up to the house itself. As I clattered up the stairs, the porch bowed dangerously under my weight and a board cracked. I lightly jumped to a safer spot as the rotten wood splintered, leaving a hole where I had been standing. With a shrug, I reached out for the doorknob and was surprised to find it was unlocked. I pushed open the door and cautiously peeked inside.

The house was old, that much was clear—it had to have been built in the 1930s or so. I slipped into the hallway and tried the switch. No electricity. I wasn't sure why I had expected there to be. The foyer was narrow, with a room leading off to either side, and the hallway continued, widening to include a staircase going up.

I peeked inside the room to the right. There was almost no furniture—a chair or two had been left behind. The bay window overlooked the porch and the front yard. Must have been a parlor, I thought as I walked into the room, my boots echoing on the hardwood. Or a sitting room. A fireplace with a stone mantel was all boarded up, but from what I could tell, it had been lovely in its time. Otherwise the room was empty, and I quietly closed the door behind me.

The room to the left of the front door led into what appeared to be an office. The desk was still there—old wood, dull from years of dust. The chair behind it had once been leather but was full of holes where mice had chewed through it. Again, the windows in this room faced the front of the house. The hardwood continued. I knelt, examining the boards. Solid, beneath the wear and tear. If someone were to refinish them, they might actually be pretty.

Feeling bolder, and still pressured to explore, I returned to the hallway and passed by the staircase. A door to the left opened beneath the stairs. In the dim light, I could see a staircase leading down. Probably the entryway to the basement. Feeling disturbed—something didn't feel right down there—I quickly closed the door and headed down the hall. Another door to the right proved to be a second living area, and another door beneath the stairs led to a two-piece powder room.

The end of the hall opened up into the kitchen. It was a large kitchen. Huge, in fact, with enough space for a giant farm table that sat to one side. I looked around, suddenly aware of another presence in the room with me. I could hear the clatter of forks against china, a slip of laughter here and there, and the smell of cinnamon filled the air. Shaking my head, I sat down at the table, wondering what was going on.

A hand brushed my shoulder and I jumped.

"Hello? Is anybody here?" I glanced around nervously but could see no one. But the sound of laughter grew—it was lazy laughter, happy sit-around-the-fire-and-talk laughter that stopped abruptly as a sudden breeze gusted past me and I shivered. As I turned, I saw a silhouette by the kitchen sink, and as I watched, the form grew solid, shimmering into sight.

She was in her late sixties, I thought—maybe a little older—wearing a pale blue housedress with a floral apron over it. The apron was full, with a bib. The woman had pale silver hair and a smile on her face, and she was wiping her hands on a dish towel. She was also staring straight at me, and the hairs on the back of my neck stood up on alert. She could see me, and she knew I could see her.

I cleared my throat. The ghosts on our last big case had been mostly terrifying, but there had also been one ghost—a sad young woman—who I had felt sorry for, more than anything.

"Well, if you aren't going to say hello, I will." The ghost gave me a cheery smile. "Even though you are sitting in my kitchen, unasked."

Startled, I jumped to my feet. "I'm sorry. I didn't think anybody lived here." And then I realized how ridiculous that sounded. Nobody did live here. At least, nobody who was alive.

She laughed. "Nobody does, not anybody from your side of the veil. And yes, before you ask, I know very well that I'm dead. What's your name? I'm Mary."

I stammered. I'd never met a talkative spirit before. Especially one who realized she was a ghost. "My name's Shimmer. I'm your neighbor from across the street. I moved in a few months ago." I paused, then added, "I just noticed this house today . . . really . . . and it . . . for some reason I wanted to come see it."

Mary brushed a hand across her forehead, pushing a curl of silver hair out of the way. "Oh, I know why. I was feeling lonely today and wishing I had someone to talk to. And . . . I wanted to meet you. You must have picked up on it." Her eyes were twinkling. "I never would have thought there were dragons in the world. Not when I was alive. Everything seemed so small . . ." She paused, blinking. "I can't quite remember it, to be honest. My life, that is."

A feeling of wonder and loneliness swept over me. I slowly edged my way back into the chair, still keeping on edge but breathing more slowly after the initial panic. "Why do you stay, then? Why not move on?"

Once again, the duck of the head and a faint look of confusion. "I don't rightly . . . I protect this house. It was my house, and there are evil creatures in the world. Evil spirits. I protect this place from the shadows that seek to claim it."

I had never thought that ghosts might battle against their own. I nodded slowly. "Not long ago, my friends and I fought against a creature who was holding a number of spirits trapped. It wasn't a spirit or ghost, but it could control those of your world."

"There are those creatures around. They're dangerous, and they lurk in dark shadows. They haunt abandoned houses and long-forgotten forts. Sometimes, they see beacons that attract them." She raised her head, giving me a questioning look. "You . . . you and your fiery friend over there . . . you shine like a beacon in the night. I know you're a sensitive. An empath. So I projected the need for you to come here, and you sensed it."

She sat down at the table on the opposite side. "This was my home, you know. I love this house, and I lived here from the time I was a bride . . . My husband, Leroy, passed away. He had . . . he was unwell. We had a passel of children. They were my joy. Especially my baby boy . . ." Again, her voice drifted. "But they didn't want this house. I don't know where they are now. I keep hoping they'll come back so I can say good-bye one last time."

I wanted to make her feel better, to give her something to hold on to. "What do you want from me? Is there anything I can do?"

She set the translucent tea towel to one side, then gently folded her hands on the table. "Yes, there is. Buy this house. Keep it safe. Make it a home again. It may not look like it right now, but this house has a heart. It has my heart in it. I cannot think of seeing it fall to a developer. Or crumble away."

I started to protest—I already owned a house and wasn't really in the market for a new one—but then I stopped. Obviously, she was concerned about the energy in the area. "Why haven't you nudged anybody else who has looked at this house to buy it? Haven't you found anybody else you could contact?"

She let out a long sigh that sounded like wind through dried corn husks. "No, every time someone came in the house who I thought might be able to hear me, something drove them off. Something outside in the backyard—or maybe it's the neighbor's yard. I don't know. I can't leave the house. When I returned, after . . . I don't know where I was. But I woke up and found myself here, and I can't leave. Not even if I wanted to. Some force keeps me here."

That didn't sound right. I frowned and leaned back, folding

my arms across my chest. "I'll see what I can find out. Maybe there's something my friends and I can do to help you. I can't make any promises, but I'll look into it. Meanwhile, I have a house, but what about if I can find somebody who would love and take care of the place? Maybe someone who can help to hold the negative spirits at bay?" I had no idea who the hell I was talking about, but it seemed like a possibility that either Bette or Ralph or Alex would know someone who might be in the market for a haunted house.

Mary regarded me quietly for a moment, then nodded. "It's worth a try. Follow me." She stood and led me out of the kitchen. She didn't seem to be walking so much as float- ing, and it suddenly occurred to me that I was palling around with a ghost in an abandoned house. Yeah, my life wasn't exactly turning out to be how I'd expected it to be.

She led me along the hallway, to the door under the stairs leading into what appeared to be the basement. As she motioned for me to open it, I hesitated.

"Are you sure you want to go down there?" I stared at the gaping darkness. Once again, the energy unsettled me and I wasn't sure exactly why.

"I hid money down there when I was alive." Mary was right next to me now, urging me on. She was standing to my left, and even though she was insubstantial, I was beginning to feel a little hedged in. I glanced at her. Now that she was up close and personal, something seemed off. Maybe it was the glint in her eyes, maybe it was some sensation that was just begin- ning to creep through me, but the friendly old grandmother suddenly reminded me of the wolf out of "Little Red Riding Hood."

I jerked back, but not before she reached out. Her hand slammed me into the stairwell, though I didn't feel her actual fingers, just the force behind the shove. I lurched forward and would have fallen down the stairs had I not caught myself on the railing. I whirled around in time to see Mary cringing as a dark shadow loomed up and over her. She looked terrified, trying to shake it off like she might shake off a cloak that had wrapped around her.

I took that moment to leap back, away from the steps, and though I couldn't do much, I gathered what water molecules there were in the air around us and solidified them into a thin spate of rain that pelted down into the hallway. While there was no way the water would hurt the creature who was attacking Mary, I did manage to startle it and the shadow let go, vanishing as I stared at it. A very ghostly Mary leaned against the wall, wincing as she rubbed her head.

"What the hell was that?" I pointed to the basement, yelling.

She let out a soft moan. "He doesn't want anybody to buy this house and land. He hounds me, and I run from him. And then I fight back, and he comes back stronger."

And right there, I decided enough was enough. I might not be able to clear an entire district, but I wanted my section of the neighborhood back. And if it took working with a brigade of friendly ghosts, so be it—that was what I'd do.

"I'm going to find help. I'll be back. And we'll do our best to get someone in here who knows what they're doing when it comes to ghosts."

And with that, I headed toward the front door, wondering just how I was going to keep my promise. I might not be an exorcist, and I sure as hell wasn't a miracle worker, but I was stubborn and I was a dragon. It wasn't in my nature to let anybody else win out over me. Mary laughed behind me, a light, musical note that stuck in my memory long after I shut the door behind me and returned to my own house.

# CHAPTER 3

It occurred to me that Stacy—one of the few friends I had made in Seattle—might want to move in across the street, but then I shut that idea down real fast. For one thing, she already had a house that had been in her family for some time. For another, Stacy lived with her mother, who was disabled and unable to work, and she also helped provide for her little brother. The last thing she needed in her life were spooks and spirits. In fact, we had been supposed to get together for breakfast the next day, but when I got home from Mary's house, there was a message on my answering machine from her begging off due to a cold.

I let out a sigh. "Damn it." I really liked Stacy. She was one of the few humans who knew I was a dragon. After the first "Oh, shit," she had shrugged it off and that was that.

I told Chai about what had happened at the house. "You don't want to live over there, do you?" I leaned forward, a hopeful look plastered on my face.

He stared at me for a moment. "Seriously? You are

seriously asking me that?" With a snort, he added, "Thank you very much, but I'm not interested in fending off nasty spirits. Although I admit, living in this area, we're bound to run into them." He paused, then softly said, "You know who would be perfect for the house? Tonya."

Tonya Harris was a witch we had met while up in Port Townsend on a case. But she had a shop up there, and that was her home. "I doubt she's going to move down here to set up business." But the thought had lodged itself in the back of my mind and I found myself turning it over as I showered again before getting dressed for my lunch with Bette and Marlene.

I glanced out the window. The sky was overcast and it looked like rain. Which meant something that wouldn't plaster itself to my body if I got caught in a sudden downpour. I picked a simple V-neck sweater and a pair of black jeans, then slid a pale blue Windbreaker over the top. As I zipped it up and grabbed my purse, Chai cocked his head to one side.

"Have fun. I might meander across the street and meet Mary myself."

I paused. He sounded like a man with a plan. Or should I say, a djinn with a plan? "Just don't be rude. She's perfectly nice and I don't want her run out of here. Not that I think you could—she seems to be trapped. I think that whoever . . . *whatever* . . . that shadow was has her pinned in there."

Chai squinted, shading his eyes with his hands as he stared at the house across the street. "I'm not fond of those who imprison others." The cryptic note in his voice made me leery, but I decided to leave well enough alone. Bette would be by in a few minutes to pick me up for the lunch with Marlene. I headed out on the porch to wait.

As I stood there, staring quietly at Mary's house, I found myself thinking about Chai's idea. True, Tonya did have a home and a life in Port Townsend, but I could easily see her in this house, bringing it back to life with her witchy ways.

At that moment, Bette pulled up in her 1967 Chevy Impala. She had tricked it out as a lowrider, and I half expected the cops to stop us every time I rode with her. I dashed down the steps as a flurry of raindrops let loose, spattering against the sidewalk. I darted between them, yanking open the passenger door as I slipped inside the car.

Bette was chain-smoking, as usual, and she winked at me. "How's it hanging, girl?"

I fastened my seat belt—no sane person rode anywhere with Bette without a seat belt—and let out a long sigh. "Weird. That's how it's going." As we headed toward the restaurant, I told her what had happened in Mary's house.

She snorted. "You have to be careful with ghosts. Never can tell what they're up to, and half the time they aren't what you think they are. My bets are on Mary to be in cahoots with the shadow creature. Then again, I could be wrong. I knew a wonderful spirit years back—named Connie. She had been killed in a car wreck back in New York, when Alex and I first came to America. That was when cars weren't as safe as they are now."

As she spoke, she swerved to miss a garbage truck backing out of an alley. I grimaced, clutching the door handle, but she didn't seem to notice.

"Oh yeah, what happened?"

"She went off the road and plowed into a brick wall. She'd been at a speakeasy. We arrived the year that Prohibition ended, but we were here for a few heated months before the law was repealed. Anyway, she had enough bathtub gin in her to drown a sailor. Connie was our neighbor. I remember going outside that night—it was sweltering in the city during the summer. No A/C back then. Anyway, so she came lurching up the sidewalk, bloody and roughed up. I ran out to help her, only to realize she was already dead. Her spirit hung around for quite a while after that, but her ghost always seemed a bit giddy, like the gin had never quite worn off."

I stared at Bette. A *drunk* ghost? "You have some of the weirdest stories, woman."

"You haven't heard the half of them. Not yet."

"Why don't you buy the house across the street? You'd be a fun neighbor and I can't see any ghost getting one up on you." I was only half-joking. Bette would make an awesome neighbor.

But she shook her head. "No, girl. I love my houseboat and there's no way in hell you're getting me to live on dry land. I tried that with Alex and it never worked. We were roommates when we first arrived over here on the West Coast, though our relationship was dead and over in terms of any hanky-panky."

I smiled softly. The pair were the best of friends. That was one reason Glenda had broken up with Alex. She insisted he give up his friendship with Bette and there was no way in hell that would ever happen. I was glad that he had stood his ground. Anybody who would give up a friendship that had lasted over a hundred years for a bitchy girlfriend—or boyfriend—wasn't the kind of lover I wanted to be involved with.

"I'm not Glenda. You don't ever have to reassure me, Bette." I spoke softly, but she caught the nuance.

She gave me a sideways glance as we turned into a parking lot by a Bonnie's—a chain diner endemic to the Pacific Northwest that had recently sprung up everywhere. The cigarette was ready to fall off her lip, but she somehow managed to keep hold of it for a final puff before stabbing it out in the ashtray. "Shimmer, you're a good girl. Don't even start with the 'I'm a dragon' bit. I'm older than you are, so don't even go there."

I wasn't sure how old I was. Dragons had long, long lives—well longer than the Fae, for the most part, but she was right in that I was young for my kind. I had probably wandered the Dragon Reaches for a couple of thousands of years, Earthside years that is, but I was still new to the world in comparison to most of my Dragonkin brethren.

"I just never want you to worry. I have no idea what will happen with Alex and me—we're still testing the waters in our relationship, and frankly, I'm skittish enough to want to take it slow. Hell, if Glenda weren't such a bitch and she wanted to still be friends with him, I wouldn't care."

I pushed open my door and swung out into what was now a downpour. As Bette and I hustled inside, I noticed she was wearing a new zebra-print pair of stretch pants, along with a sparkling black sequined top. Her leather jacket hung open over the top, and her hobo bag was as big as a backpack. Given I knew she never traveled without her iPad, two packs of cigarettes, a notepad, a water bottle, and a small box of cookies, as well as makeup and every other necessity to womankind, the size of her purse made sense. She was wearing sunglasses and a sheer pink scarf tied under her chin to protect the ever-present bouffant from the rain.

When we were inside, she pulled off her sunglasses and glanced around, frowning. "I don't see Marlene, but that doesn't mean she's not here." As a waitress came up, Bette told her we were meeting a friend and the girl let us meander around, looking for her. After a few minutes, Bette was satisfied Marlene hadn't arrived yet and so we took a booth near the door so she could easily find us when she arrived.

I opened the menu, though every diner I had been in seemed to serve the same variations in food—Americana spread across the nation. Food guaranteed to be the same wherever you went, so you never had to worry about what you were getting.

"I'll start with a chocolate shake, please. With whipped cream on top?" I had developed a love for the frothy drinks. It didn't matter to me what flavor they were; as long as it was liquid ice cream with whipped cream and a cherry on top, I was happy.

Bette grinned. "You just can't get enough of those, can you?"

I shook my head. In the past week, during our lunch break—which would be a late-night snack for most people—I had ordered a shake with my delivery of whatever else I might want. "You've got me there."

She ordered coffee and a large cola.

I glanced around. The diner was filled with the lunch crowd. It had been a while since I had eaten out at this time. Usually, by now I was curled up on the sofa, watching TV while I waited to doze off for the few hours I needed to sleep. After the waitress brought our drinks, I frowned and glanced at the clock.

"She knows where to meet us, right?"

"Right. I think I'll give her a call. She might be stuck in traffic." Bette pulled out her phone and dialed while I sucked down my milkshake. A moment later, she set down her phone, frowning at it. "She's not answering. That's strange. As old world as she can be, Marlene never goes anywhere without her phone."

"Maybe she's driving and can't answer?" I motioned to the waitress. "Another?"

"No, I think something's wrong." Bette was usually pretty laid-back, so the frantic tone in her voice set me on alert. She wasn't prone to hysterics.

"Do you want to drop by her place and see if everything is okay?" I called the waitress back. "Make that to go, please."

Bette nodded. "We'll give it five more minutes, till your shake is ready, and if she hasn't shown up by then, I'd appreciate it if you'd come check things out with me."

The waitress brought my shake and we paid for our drinks. Bette ordered a dozen doughnuts to go and then we headed back to her car. I stuffed a cinnamon-covered doughnut in my mouth and stuck my shake in the cup holder, next to Bette's refill. As we pulled out of the parking lot, I could tell that the Melusine was fretting. She might be a tough old broad, but she cared about her friends more than most people cared about their families.

Marlene lived in a house near the arboretum. It was a single-story bungalow, small and cozy and pretty, with a garden that had been allowed to grow gracefully wild. The moment we stepped off the sidewalk and onto the walkway up to the house, a sense of peace flowed over me, like soft silk trailing past. The driveway was empty. If she was home, someone else had her car.

"I can tell one of the Woodland Fae live here." I kept my voice down—it seemed proper. No shouting, no swearing. This land was tended to by a steward of the planet and unless somebody was as thick as a brick, I had the feeling they wouldn't be able to shake off the feeling of being watched by every tree and bush. As we quietly approached the front door, Bette tensed up. I tried to tune into what she was feeling, but the moment I opened myself up, a deluge of fear and anger swept over me and I let out a cry, dropping to my knees at the sudden assault of emotion.

"Bette!" I winced, rubbing my forehead.

She spun, then crouched down beside me. "Shimmer, what is it? Do you need me to call a doctor?"

I shook my head, trying to drive back the spikes that felt like they were jabbing me from every which way. "I don't know what it is. I was trying to sense whatever I could and . . ."

A soft look of understanding stole over the Melusine. "You've become an empath—I suspected as much last night. I'll bet you've always had the ability, but it never opened itself up before. And now, you're having to come to terms with it. Pull back, girl. Pull those feelers back and it should help some."

I wasn't sure what she meant, but I tried to do as she suggested and, after a moment, I could think again. But even though I was feeling better, I also knew that something had happened here. Something to desperately upset the beings who were rooted on this lot.

"Bette, something horrible happened here—and recently. I'm worried about your friend. The trees, the plants, I think they're all upset, though I can't communicate directly with them. If there were a stream or the like running through the area, that would be a different matter."

Bette frowned and pushed the doorbell. The buzzer rang, a soft hollow chime from inside the house, but nobody was answering. She rang again. Still no answer. With a look at me—I nodded—she tried the door. It was unlocked.

"Do you think we should call the cops?" I hesitated to just barge in. If something had gone wrong, then I didn't want to destroy any evidence.

"Maybe . . . why don't we take a look inside? If we find her hurt, we'll call the medics. If we find anything else . . . we'll call the police." She took out a handkerchief and softly pushed the door open, and I realized she wasn't taking a chance on mucking up any fingerprints. With a cautious glance inside, she stepped through the door and I followed.

We entered the living room. The house was cozy, that much I could tell right off. Plants covered the bookshelves and walls. And a long-haired black cat let out a mew and came running up to us, crying anxiously. Bette picked up the fluffy creature, petting it softly.

"Hey there, Snookums. Where's Marlene? Hmm? Where's your mama?" She flashed a glance over her shoulder at me. "This is Snookums, and he seems awfully upset. He usually won't come up to strangers. Me, he tolerates, because by now he knows me, but that he came running out with you here, too? Unusual." She stopped, then pointed. "Marlene's purse."

I followed her direction. There, on the floor, lay a purse. It was a pretty leather satchel, open, with the contents strewn around. I slowly walked over and knelt down, staring at it. The latch on it had been broken, as if someone had been in a great hurry and had trouble getting it open. Once again, a ripple of fear raced up my back. Motioning for Bette to stay where she was, I crossed to a partially open door on the other side of the room, and leaned in. A bedroom—Marlene's by the look of it. The sheets were partially ripped off the bed. There was a jewelry armoire and it had been tipped over, with the drawers scattered around the floor. The closet door was half off its hinges. Still no sign of Marlene, though.

Quickly, I made my way back to Bette. "We need to get out of here and call Chase."

"Look in the kitchen, first?" Bette was pleading with me, I could hear the fear behind her words.

Grimly, I nodded and crossed to the opening that led into the dining area and the galley kitchen. I glanced around. Nothing. Dirty dishes on the counter, but not a lot of them.

There was another door at the end of the kitchen and I cautiously approached. I grabbed a potholder that was on the counter to turn the knob, trying not to wipe off any prints that might be on the handle. The laundry room came into sight, as well as a door leading to the backyard. Nothing in the laundry seemed off, so I peeked out the door. The yard and patio were small, but everything looked normal, from the scrollwork chairs and glass-topped table sitting on red brick, to the tidy little herb garden. But even so, once again the sense of fear and anger and worry hit me. This time I managed to keep it at bay, while stumbling back into the house.

I returned to the living room, where Bette was comforting the yowling cat.

"She's nowhere in sight. If it weren't for her purse, I'd say she just got a late start. Her car's not in the driveway, though." I hadn't seen any car in the drive when we pulled up.

Bette shook her head. "True, it isn't. But see, near her purse? Her key chain's there, and her car key is on it. So whoever has her car has their own key to it. Or they hot-wired it." She buried her face in Snookums's fur. "I'm afraid, Shimmer. I'm afraid something happened to her."

"I'll call Chase." I softly crossed to the phone and put in the call to the Faerie-Human Crime Scene Investigation Unit. The FH-CSI was run by a detective named Chase Johnson. I didn't know him very well, but he was father to a baby girl, I gathered, with the Elfin Queen. There was some big to-do over the fact, but I knew very little about it. What I knew best about him was that he ran the police unit set up to deal with Otherworld visitors.

I had the phone number on speed dial, thanks to Alex's insistence. A voice came on the line, a Yugi Brinker. With a glance at Bette, who nodded me on, I said, "This is Shimmer, from the Fly by Night Magical Investigations Agency. I'm calling in regard to our concern over a friend who has gone missing. She's one of the Woodland Fae—elderly— and we have reason to be concerned over her safety."

Officer Brinker promised to send someone over within the next half hour, and so Bette and I settled in to wait. She found Snookums's bowl—which was empty and looked like it hadn't been filled that morning—and fed him from the bag of cat food sitting on the counter. He started to purr as he tore into the food. I watched.

"Humans and Fae love cats, don't they?"

"Not all of them, but a lot, yes. Why?"

"I've just never had much experience with the animals. I think I like them better than dogs. Dogs are messy." I tilted my head, watching Snookums scarf down the food. After a few minutes, he finished and ran back over to Bette, sprawling at her feet as if he knew she would protect him. He was licking one paw as the doorbell rang.

"I'll get it." I motioned for Bette to stay there and answered the door. It was a man in uniform. He was pale and tall, slight with neatly trimmed dark hair.

"I'm Officer Hancock, from the FH-CSI? Someone reported a missing person?" His eyes were gleaming and I recognized right off that he wasn't human. I wasn't sure what he was, but human? Definitely not.

"My name is Shimmer. I'm the one who called. Please, come in." I led him into the living room where Bette stood. "This is Officer Hancock."

"I think we've met, a few months ago, when Alex was working on a case for Were-mates, Inc." Bette inclined her head. "Bette, if you remember? I'm the receptionist at the—"

"I remember, ma'am." The cop nodded, a friendly smile emerging from his taciturn expression. "And thank you again, for helping us with that case. What seems to be the problem?"

Bette ran down the facts that we knew of. Marlene was supposed to meet us for lunch, she never showed, we dropped by, found her apartment out of order—especially in the bedroom, her purse on the floor, the jewelry armoire overturned. All the pertinent pieces.

He jotted down everything, and then as we waited, he knelt down by the purse. He took a picture of it, then gathered up everything while wearing a pair of latex gloves, bagging the purse and its contents. Then he looked in the bedroom. After a while he returned.

"I'm going to call in the forensics team, see if we can find any source of blood or other possible evidence. If it weren't for the purse and the jewelry case, I'd say she may have gone off on her own and forgot to say anything. But those two facts . . . we'll have to see what we can find out. Do you know if she has any family in the area?"

Bette shook her head. "No, she transplanted herself from up north a ways, she told me, and I have no idea who she might be related to. The only person I know about is a younger boyfriend. In fact, I was rather suspicious about him but never got a chance to meet him. I think she called him Doug but that's all I remember." She gave the cop one of our office cards as well as her home number. "Listen, is it okay if I take her cat with me? He seems lonely and I don't want to just leave him here. I'll leave a note for her—"

"Go ahead, but I suggest you don't leave a note, not just

yet. Better not to advertise your presence until we figure out what happened to her." He called in the forensics unit while we found the cat carrier and managed to stuff Snookums—who wasn't making it easy—into the box. As Bette snapped the latch shut, she motioned for me to get the cat food. She elicited a promise from Officer Hancock to call her if they found any traces of blood or anything, and we headed out to her car.

As we sat in the front seat, the cat wailing from the carrier in the backseat, I glanced at the yard again. The plants who lived there were afraid and upset. They knew something had happened. I had mentioned my impressions to the cop, and he had written it down, but I had no clue how seriously they would take me. Finally, Bette lit up a cigarette.

"You can't smoke that around the cat." I pulled it out of her mouth and tamped it out. "He doesn't get a choice."

"Well, I can't keep him at my place then, because I sure can't quit smoking cold turkey, not after all these years."

Sighing, I gave a little shrug. "Fine, I'll take him. What do I need in order to take care of a cat?"

"Cat box, litter, scoop, food, dishes, toys . . ." Bette let out a snort. "This is going to go ever so well. I just . . . oh well, at least you'll have Chai at your place. He might be able to keep you and the cat from throttling each other."

"What do you mean by that?" I glared at her.

"Just . . . oh, wait till you have him at home. I think you're in for a surprise." And with that, she gunned the motor and we were off to the pet store.

# CHAPTER 4

By the time I got Snookums situated and fell asleep, Chai was cooing over him and I was frustrated. The cat was going nuts in front of my aquarium and I half expected him to hurl himself against the glass in pursuit of the fish. But finally he seemed to calm down and I decided I could chance going to bed. Snookums was sitting patiently, eyeing the swimming fish with a hungry glare. I made sure he had plenty of food and water, and Chai promised to get his litter box set up, and so I traipsed into my bedroom, stripped, and fell into an exhausted sleep.

When the alarm went off, I opened my eyes to see a pile of fur. Granted it was pretty fur, but fur nonetheless. As I squinted myself awake, I realized that Snookums was curled up beside me, breathing softly. I stared at the creature, then hesitantly ran my hand over his back. He shifted and started to purr, and his fur felt silky against my fingers. I stroked him again and he shifted onto his back, stretching out to show his belly. With a laugh, I blew on it softly, then bounced up and began to dress.

I had already taken two showers in the past twenty-four hours, and while I could happily stay under the water for days, I really didn't have the time for another. I slid into my bathing suit—I was hoping to find time for a swim, and maybe wearing my suit would bring me luck on that—then jammed myself into my jeans and slipped on a sleeveless black tank top. Brushing my hair back into a ponytail, I sat down on the bed to slide my feet into a pair of ankle boots and zip them up. We worked Sunday nights and took Fridays off, depending on what our caseload was like.

"You coming?" I asked the cat, but he ignored me in favor of the bed, so I gave him a ruffle on the head, then dashed downstairs.

Chai was there, holding out a massive sausage-cheese muffin in one hand, my purse in the other. "Eat."

I slung the purse over my shoulder and jammed the sandwich in my mouth as I glanced up at the clock. I had overslept and Bette would be here to pick me up any minute. "Cat's up on my bed," I said around the mouthful of bread, sausage, and cheese. "Can you feed him and keep an eye on him?"

Chai nodded, a sly grin on his face. "I like cats."

"He's yours until we find Marlene." And then, blowing him a quick kiss, I headed out the door as Bette's unmistakable, absolutely obnoxious horn sounded. It was raining like crazy, and I tried to protect the rest of my sandwich as I dashed down the porch steps and yanked the door open, sliding inside.

Bette gave me a pale grin. "Chai takes care of you, doesn't he?"

"Chai's like a brother to me." I polished off the rest of the sandwich and licked my fingers, then burped. Surprised by the sudden belch, I rolled my eyes. "Spicy sausage."

"Yes, I'll bet Chai has a spicy sausage." Bette snorted.

"That's not what I meant—" I stopped, realizing she was teasing me. It still took me some time to figure out when somebody was joking, but I was getting better about not rising to every jape.

But her smile was short lived. She cleared her throat. "There's been no sign of Marlene. I called the FH-CSI before I came over to pick you up. They've been asking around, and the last thing they figured out is that she talked to someone last night, at around ten P.M. I'm not sure who it was, but they have her cell phone records. Apparently, she sounded nervous, according to whoever they were talking to, but she insisted that everything was all right."

"Her neighbors know anything?"

Bette shook her head. "No, except the boyfriend—Douglas Smith—was around for about three weeks. He hasn't been seen today. The police have an APB out on him as a person of interest, though with a name like that and nothing else to go on, it's not going to be easy to find him." She edged into the parking lot next to the building the Fly by Night Magical Investigations Agency was in.

Alex had bought the three-story brick walk-up some years back. He had left it almost in pristine condition, repairing it in the style in which it had been built. A red neon sign glowed in the front window with the agency name on it, and as we headed into the building, the sound of our shoes echoed on the tile. The main offices of the agency were housed on the main floor, though old files were kept upstairs in the archives. To be honest, I hadn't gone exploring the rest of the building because I felt it really was none of my business.

Now, as we approached the half door with the frosted window that led into the waiting room, I turned to Bette. "What else is in the building? I know archives and old case files, but this is a huge building and we seem to only take up the main floor."

She laughed. "Oh, Alex has a number of secrets, *chérie* . . .

Some of the rooms are empty. Others, well, let's just say that he keeps what he wants to in them. Don't go prowling around, though. You might not always like what you find. Even though I will guarantee you there's nothing illegal on the premises, you just don't go prying into another person's secrets without good reason."

I frowned, not sure if I liked her answer. But I didn't have time to think it over because, as we entered the room, we found Alex and Ralph sitting in the waiting room, talking to a lovely young woman. She couldn't have been more than nineteen, with red hair that was caught back in a braid. She was frowning, biting her lip as Alex and Ralph seemed to be lighting into her for something.

"What's going on?" Bette sauntered over.

The girl glanced up at her, looking grateful to see us. She started to stand, but Alex motioned for her to sit down. He nodded me over to his side and slid his arm around my waist, giving me a quick kiss. I still felt odd about him kissing me in the office, but it wasn't like we were hiding anything.

"You're just in time. Bette, will you start a new file for this young woman? Her name is Lydia Wagner. She's our newest client." He gave the girl a look that told me he wasn't exactly thrilled about the case. "Lydia, this is Shimmer. She's one of our detectives, and my girlfriend as you might have noticed. And that's Bette, our receptionist."

Lydia murmured a "Nice to meet you" that sounded anything but genuine, and she stared back at the floor. Puzzled, I caught Ralph's eye, but he just shook his head.

Bette hustled behind the counter and started a new case file. "Lydia, dear, just come over to the desk and let me get some information from you."

Alex cleared his throat. "When you're done, please send her into the office. Ralph, Shimmer, get your things and join us." He turned and stomped away. I hadn't seen him seem so grumpy since . . . well . . . since Glenda had shown up at the party the night before.

Ralph pushed me into my office and shut the door behind me. "If you haven't noticed, Alex is in one hell of a mood, and it doesn't help that we've got ourselves a live one. Lydia's nice, but stupid as all get out. Not unintelligent, just a world-class idiot."

I scrambled to get out my iPad, my notebook, and a pen that worked. My office was small, but at least it had a window looking out to the alley that was guarded by reinforced iron bars. Alex had encouraged me to decorate it as I wanted, so I had plastered the walls with pictures of the ocean and sea-shore, and—most recently—one of Chai and me clowning around down at the docks. I had introduced him to Pike Place Market, and he loved going down there to hang out with the street vendors and performers.

"What's with her? And why's Alex so grumpy?"

"Glenda sent a message." He glanced over his shoulder, making certain that the door was still shut. "I was here early, working on some new software for the system, and I heard something in the outer office. I knew the doors were locked, so it had to be someone with a key. Which Glenda apparently still has, because when I got out there, she was just leaving. She snickered and told me to tell Alex she had left him a gift. I decided to take a look, just in case she decided to booby-trap his office, and sure enough, she left him a gift all right. An absolutely gorgeous silver stake sitting on his desk."

I grimaced. That it was a stake was bad enough, but a *silver* one? That was adding insult to injury. "At least she didn't leave it rigged up to stab him, but I'd say that's a clear threat."

And the kicker was, if she made good with it, nobody would convict her. Vampires had no legal rights and could be murdered without recrimination from the courts. While the Seattle Vampire Nexus was working on putting a stop to that, vamp-hate groups were numerous, and the religious fervor was a small but vocal—and active—minority.

"Yeah. He came in when I was examining it, making sure it wasn't triggered with a spell or anything of that nature. I had to tell him about it—this wasn't something I could just keep quiet. What if she tries for blood next time?" He cleared his throat. "She's persona non grata around here, obviously, but you should be careful, too. She's not happy with either of you."

I nodded, realizing that being in a relationship meant you were saddled with baggage no matter what—whether it was your own past or your partner's past. "I will be. Meanwhile, is there a way to get that key back from her?"

"No, but Alex has a locksmith coming out tonight to change the locks. And the building is warded against anybody just popping in. I don't know if you knew that."

I nodded. "Vaguely, though it was never clearly explained to me. Somebody named Ysella?"

Ralph motioned for me to follow him. "We'd better get in there, and yes. Ysella's a sorceress. She's Fae, and she hires herself out as a warding expert for a number of people. We met her through Carter. Let's go, or Alex will chew our heads off."

We filed into his office. He glanced at Ralph, then at me as we took our seats next to Lydia. She seemed a bit cowed, and I felt rather sorry for her. Alex could be intimidating when he wanted to be, and right then, he wasn't in a very diplomatic mood.

I leaned forward. "Lydia, I'm Shimmer. Would you like a cup of coffee, or some water or something?"

She gave me a grateful smile. "Thanks, coffee would be great. No cream, one sugar."

I quickly exited. Bette swiveled around in her chair as I poured the coffee and added the sugar. "The girl's terrified, or looks it," I said. "Oh, and I don't know if Ralph told you, but Glenda was here. She left a silver stake for Alex. Locksmith will be here to change the locks pretty soon."

"I found out about it. Alex is madder than a hornet and

has every right to be. I'll keep an eye on things out here, then. You'd better get back in there." She waved me off.

I hurried back in, handing Lydia her coffee, as I gave Alex a concentrated look to say, *Lighten up, dude.*

He stared at me for a moment, then relented. "I'm sorry, Miss Wagner. I had a rather unpleasant surprise waiting for me when I arrived at the office this evening. I don't mean to take it out on you. Please, accept my apologies for my behavior." When he wanted to, Alex could pull off the boyish rogue act pretty easily, and Lydia bought it up. He genuinely meant it—Alex wasn't a player at all—but the stake had obviously unnerved him.

Lydia ducked her head and flashed us all a smile. "That's all right. My day hasn't been too great either. That's why I'm here. I need your help."

"Shimmer, when you and Bette arrived, Lydia was telling Ralph and me that she's set something in motion that she can't control. She's a witch. Lydia, why don't you elaborate now that we're all here?"

I pulled out my notebook and pen, as Ralph set up his iPad to record the conversation. "Please, go ahead when you're ready."

Lydia swallowed, hard. "I really fucked up. I was practicing opening gates—portals. And I let something through that I couldn't control. I can't send it back and it's loose in the city now."

I groaned. "What did you summon?"

"This morning I was out in Wedgewood Park, and I opened a gateway to the realm of Fire. I invoked a salamander. I was just hailing it, I didn't mean for it to enter through the gate, but one barged through anyway. I just was trying to . . . salute it, I guess. Anyway, it broke through, destroyed the gate behind it, and ran off into the park. It's about the size of a giant crocodile or Komodo dragon. I tried to follow it, but the damn thing is fast. If we don't find it and send it back, it's going to do some damage."

I rubbed my forehead. I knew something about salamanders, thanks to Chai, who came from the realm of Fire himself. They were magical beasts and they had voracious appetites. And they had no compunction about eating people, pets, or anything else that fit in their mouths.

"Great. When was this?" Alex leaned back, shaking his head. "And what on earth were you doing opening a gateway to the realm of Fire?"

"Around five this afternoon. And it was part of my lessons. I'm an apprentice with a witch who lives out near Talamh Lonrach Oll—the Fae Sovereign Nation. Only I wasn't supposed to do it on my own. I was supposed to be supervised, but I thought there wouldn't be any harm to it. I haven't told her yet." She grimaced. "She's going to be so pissed. I thought, if I could find the salamander first and send it back . . ."

Alex finally broke into a light laugh. "She might go easier on you? Oh, girl, we all try that one—depending on what mess we've gotten ourselves into. Sometimes it works, sometimes it doesn't. Fine. We'll help you. We need a retainer of two hundred dollars, though."

I glanced at the girl's clothes. They were clean and neat, but not really in style, and her shoes were scuffed. I could sense the conflict running through her. "That two hundred would probably be part of your rent money, wouldn't it?"

She bit her lip, but shook her head. "No, but it's my electricity money and bus fare for the month. I was hoping . . . you might take payments?"

I shot Alex a long look. He rolled his eyes, but shrugged.

"Fine. You can pay us ten dollars a month till it's paid off. How about that?"

As she nodded, a grateful smile on her face, he motioned for her to go with Ralph. "I want you to give Ralph all the information on where exactly you were, and when this all happened. He'll fill out a payment form for you to sign. Then we'll do what we can to track down the critter. Now go on."

As he shooed her out of the office, with Ralph following her, I closed the door behind them and turned back to Alex.

"You did the right thing."

He let out a snort but pushed back his chair and motioned for me to join him. I slid behind the desk, facing him as I straddled his lap. Our lips met, and his soft, chill touch registered against my own warm skin. As his tongue slid between my lips, he wrapped his arms around my waist, his hands slipping under my shirt to caress my back. I moaned gently, leaning in, my arms around his neck as the kiss wound on and on. I wanted him—here, now.

Alex pulled away. In a ragged voice: "Lock the door."

I jumped up and hurried over to the door, locking it. But he was at my back, pressing my breasts against the cool re-inforced steel as his lips brushed the back of my neck. I managed to turn around, breathless, my back to the door, and reached down, fumbling for his buckle as he unzipped my jeans. In a flurry of movement, I slid my hand down the front of his pants and wrapped my hand around him. He was thick and hard, and all I could think of was how much I wanted him inside me. My breath short, I gave him a slow squeeze, and—as he moaned—pushed him away as I leaned down to take off my boots and kick off my jeans.

The moment I was free of them, Alex pinned me against the door again, and I wrapped my legs around his waist as he cradled my butt. My breasts ached, and I yanked up my shirt. While holding me fast with one hand, he reached for my breast with his other and kneaded the flesh, his fingers pinching my nipple and sending a sharp ache of pleasure knifing through me.

"I wish I could stay with you when sunrise comes." He pressed his lips against mine, crushing my mouth with his, catching my lip on one of his fangs. A drop of blood welled up and his eyes grew wide as he flicked it away with his tongue, but he didn't press the issue.

My stomach was a barrel of knots as I whispered, "Fuck me before we're interrupted."

"You want it, love? You want me in you, all hard and sweaty?"

I let out a low laugh. "You don't sweat. Get your cock inside me, Radcliffe."

Alex shifted, and I slid onto him, my legs still wrapped around his waist. He began to grind against me, his thick, hard shaft driving me back against the door as we rattled it with our rhythmic thumping. I let out a low groan as he filled me full, and then—before I knew what he was doing—we were on the floor and he was above me, shifting as he drove deeper and deeper.

I closed my eyes, the tidal wave of sensation taking me out of myself, out of my head. Everything except his touch melted away. His mouth on my breasts, his body sliding against mine—that cool, icy feel of him deep inside me, stoking my need. My hands were on his back, his muscles taut beneath my fingers as I drew him closer, my breasts pressing against his chest as his hips swiveled until it felt like he was in the very center of my core. He reached down with one hand, fingering me, and the room began to spin as my thoughts vanished and everything became a wash of desire. I tried to catch my breath but couldn't—the hunger was so deep and the ache so vast—and then, like sea foam crashing against the shore, I came, cresting as the wave filled my need.

Alex let out a low moan, his back arching, and then he slumped in my arms, still deep within me, and softly kissed my nose. "My woman."

I shifted beneath him, kissing him gently. Those two words made me vaguely uncomfortable and yet . . . they made me feel needed. After a moment, I sucked in a long breath and let it out slowly.

"I suppose we had better get dressed. I'm pretty sure Ralph's done with Lydia by now."

"You always have to be so logical." But he slowly pushed himself away, then rolled over and let out a satisfied snicker. "Think Ralph might have an eye for the girl?"

"Not really. Ralph will find somebody, don't you worry about that." I sat up, then pushed myself to my feet. I hadn't planned for sex, but Alex had a box of wet wipes in his desk and I quickly cleaned up, then dressed again as he pulled up his pants and fastened his belt. "I'm not that comfortable, you know. Having sex here. It doesn't feel . . . appropriate."

"Romantic, aren't you?" But his voice was light, and the bad mood seemed to have passed. "You're right, and really— this shouldn't happen. We should keep it professional at the office. But, damn it, Shimmer. You're so . . . I don't know. Every time I'm around you, all I can think about is how much I want you." He stroked my arm, then leaned over to kiss me again, this time gently and on the cheek. His eyes met mine, and for a moment, it felt like I was seeing myself reflected in his gaze—lovely and turbulent and slightly wanton. "I like being with you. I like being around you."

I paused. The tone in his voice felt almost poignant and set my stomach to quivering. But all I said was, "Practicality can be a good thing. I learned that the hard way in the Dragon Reaches." I kissed him on the nose, and then—making sure everything looked neat and tidy—I unlocked the door. As we headed out to the waiting room, I saw Ralph sitting with Lydia in the conference room.

He flashed us a look that told me he knew exactly what we'd been up to, but said nothing except, "I have all of the information we need from Lydia. I'm going to make certain she gets back to her car all right, and then we should start searching for this creature. From what she tells me, salamanders can be very dangerous."

The sex haze drained away posthaste. "Yeah, she's right."

At that moment, the locksmith arrived and Bette took him in hand. Ralph walked Lydia out to her car, while Alex and I glanced over the info that he had taken from her.

Wedgewood Park was near a cemetery. Which meant . . . fresh bodies, possibly, which might just be attractive to a big fiery lizard.

"We should check the Wedgewood Cemetery. Lizards can be scroungers. While you pull up the coordinates on that, I'm going to call Chai and see if he has any advice. If anybody knows anything about salamanders, it's going to be him." I headed into my office. Truth was, I needed to regroup. As much as I loved my time with Alex, if I didn't get a handle on what our personal rules were, it was going to drive me crazy. This was the third time we'd had sex at the office, and I swore it would be the last. While I wasn't shy or embarrassed, I didn't want to make Bette, or Ralph, or any clients uncomfortable.

Plus, there was another fact I couldn't ignore.

Alex was my boss, and essentially my parole officer. And now, my lover. Things had gotten convoluted very quickly. Hell, I barely knew how I felt about being Earthside, let alone suddenly in a relationship. I had never had a boyfriend in my life, though I had plenty of temporary lovers. No dragon worth his station would ever have considered me as relationship material given my lineage.

I shut the door to my office and dropped into the chair behind my desk. As I swiveled around, staring out into the dark alley, it occurred to me that I had no clue what the hell I was doing. I had no long-term plans. I didn't even know what I would do if they reinstated me to the Dragon Reaches when my time Earthside was over. Even though the Wing-Liege had promised me some sort of standing if I came through this all right, the fact was, I'd always be an orphan and outcaste to the people who mattered. Unless I found my parents—which seemed as far away as the moon. I had left the Lost and Foundling determined to seek out whatever information I could on them. Centuries later, I still had no clue. But then . . . what if I happened to make friends with a dragon who could look into things for me? I knew a couple of dragons who lived in town. And at least one of them had a great deal of standing in the Dragon Reaches.

The whirl of thoughts was cut short by the jangle of my phone. I glanced at it. Chai.

"Just the person I wanted to talk to, my friend." I put him on speaker so I wouldn't have to pop in the earbud. I hated that thing.

"I'm cleaning out your refrigerator. When I get done, you won't have any food left—it's all pretty rank. Don't you ever get around to tossing out old stuff?" Chai let out a snort. "So you might want to go shopping unless you're willing to let me fill the fridge after I've cleaned it."

"All you ever want is spicy food and I don't like it." That was the truth, too. Spicy food stirred up my stomach and not in a good fashion. Not only did it give me heartburn, but it made me feel gassy and I would puff smoke if I burped loud and deep enough. All dragons did, even if we couldn't breathe flame in human form. "I'll go shopping later. Bette will take me, I guess. Listen, I was going to call you anyway. I need to ask you a question. What do you know about salamanders?"

"They're lizards?" Chai sounded preoccupied.

"I *know* they're lizards. I mean the ones from the Elemental plane of Fire. We've apparently got one loose and running around the city, and now we need to go find it and send it back to its own plane. How would we go about searching for such a creature?"

Somehow, I had my doubts that Alex had thought that far ahead yet. Lydia as good as told us she couldn't banish it back to where it came from, and none of us could. Which meant we were going to need either a higher-powered sorceress, or . . .

"Say, Chai . . ."

He let out an exasperated sigh. "Yeah, yeah. I know. You need help. You can't ask me. The djinn thing. I'll be down there as soon as I wash out the shelves here. Remind Alex, Bette, and Ralph not to ask for my help. By now they seem to have it down, but you never know when somebody's going to slip." And with that, the line went dead.

Satisfied—Chai could help us all he wanted as long as we didn't ask for it—I set my phone down. At least one thing was going right. And I kept that thought until I stepped out into the outer office to find Bette weeping at her desk, where Chase Johnson—director of the FH-CSI—stood, looking uncomfortable.

# CHAPTER 5

Bette turned to me, swiveling her chair around. "They found her. They found Marlene." Her face crumpled, and I realized I had never seen Bette when she was sad. She might be pissed or irritated or even just contemplative, but in the time I had worked for the agency, I had never seen her look this upset.

By *found*, I assumed they meant *body*. I turned to the detective. "Dead?"

"I'm afraid so. Homicide. And this is the tip of a much bigger problem." He motioned to Alex. "I need to discuss something in private with you and your team. When you're ready . . ." Alex locked the door and turned the CLOSED sign around. Wordlessly, Bette looked up at him and he moved to her, wrapping his arms around her shoulders and kissing the top of her head gently. The gesture made me want to cry—she looked so bereft.

Chase cleared his throat, and Alex helped Bette stand.

"We'll meet in the lunchroom. Shimmer, will you escort the detective there? Bette and I'll be along in a moment."

Ralph followed me, with Chase following him. I led them into the lunch room, where I motioned to the coffeepot. "Would you like a cup of coffee, Detective?"

He nodded. "I can fix it myself, thank you."

I glanced down the hall. Alex was talking to Bette and I could sense the connection between them. It went back years, and I was glad he was here for her. I let them be. "Detective Johnson—"

"Please, call me Chase." He nodded, not smiling, and the lines on his forehead told me he had seen far too much over the years. "You're . . . Shimmer, right?"

I nodded. Then, because I wasn't sure how much he knew, but I knew he was tight with the D'Artigos, I added, "You probably should know that I'm a dragon, Chase."

He nodded, a faint smile creeping around the corners of his lips. "I already knew that, Shimmer. I keep close tabs on the Supe community. But thank you for making certain that I was informed."

"How bad is it?" I nodded toward the door. "Marlene?"

The smile vanished. "Bad, I'm afraid. It's pretty ugly." He added cream and sugar to his coffee, then sat down to wait. A moment later, Bette and Alex joined us. Bette had dried her tears and now she slumped down in a chair beside me.

"So, let's hear it. I'm ready." Bette stared at Chase, a resolute look on her face. "I'm older than you think. Older than Shimmer here. So don't worry about shocking me. I just . . . didn't expect her to be dead."

Chase toyed with his cup, then leaned forward, resting his elbows on the table. "We have a problem. I think we have a serial killer on the loose."

Bette's eyes grew wide. Alex let out a grunt.

"Your friend Marlene is the latest in a series of murders that all follow the same MO. We found her car on the side of the road, and . . . what was left of her was in the trunk." He grimaced.

"What . . . was left of her?" Ralph blanched.

Chase sucked in a deep breath. "Her eyes were missing, along with her tongue. We've had three other murders like this—all elderly Fae. All have been killed away from home, and all have been found in the trunks of their own cars, missing their eyes and tongues. Their bank accounts have been wiped out, and any jewelry and small, expensive items have been missing from their houses. In Marlene's case, when you contacted us earlier this morning, we discovered that she should have had close to thirty thousand dollars' worth of jewelry in her house—and we can't find any of it. We checked her bank accounts and they were cleared out this morning, early when the bank opened. She had over one hundred thousand dollars in her savings."

"Do you know who emptied them? You can't just take that much money out of an ATM." Alex frowned, sitting back and crossing his arms.

"That's the thing—the bank camera? The film shows Marlene entering the lobby and conducting the transaction. She asked for her funds in a cashier's check two days ago, and they had it ready for her this morning. The film from the first transaction places her there, too, so we know it was her. But the kicker is, the coroner placed her death to be sometime during the night."

"So it couldn't be her at the bank, unless she has a twin." I frowned. "You said there were several other murders?"

"Yes, and in every case, we have the murder victim clearing out their account, when they were unquestionably . . . already dead." Chase swallowed, hard. "We're at a loss. I've worked with Supes for years now. Hell, I'm even a small part elf myself—I found that out not long ago. But this has us stumped. And we can find nobody who has a connection to all four of the murders."

"You mean that none of the victims have any friends in common?" Ralph frowned. "That seems unlikely."

"Oh, they have friends in common, but everybody has an alibi. We even thought maybe that some necromancer animated the bodies, but a reanimated corpse wouldn't be able to pass for normal at the bank—not if they were zombies or ghouls." Chase let out a long sigh. "I wondered, since you personally know one of the victims, if you might know anything else about what was going on in her life. Detectives—and those who work for them—often make better witnesses than civilians."

Bette nodded, lighting up a cigarette. "She was talking a lot about a new boyfriend. A boy toy. Douglas Smith. I told your men about him and they put out an APB on him."

"Right. We haven't been able to trace him anywhere. And the name doesn't ring a bell with any of the other victims' families. However . . ." Chase paused. "We do have a potential connection. All of the other victims had recently become romantically involved with new liaisons. We have a list of names to check out. We're thinking maybe there's a ring of thieves—well, murderers now—targeting specific wealthy, elderly Fae." He pulled out a little notebook from his suit jacket and opened it. "I was wondering if any of these names ring a bell."

"Let's hear them." Bette leaned forward, and Alex reached out to pat her gently on the shoulder.

"Mary Little."

"Mary? A woman?"

"Yes, as far as we know, she had recently become involved with an elderly forest Fae gentleman named Victor Goldwater. He lived out near Mount Rainier and was found in the trunk of his car, on Aurora Boulevard. Again, his eyes and tongue were missing. He was worth over two hundred thousand dollars." Chase slapped the notebook on the table. "Damn it. This just makes me fucking sick."

"There are some pretty sick people out there." Alex

glanced over at me, giving me a soft smile. "Shimmer, you doing okay?"

"I've seen some rough stuff in my life, too. Yeah, I'm all right."

Bette shook her head. "Don't recognize the name, not at all. But Victor . . . I knew him, or rather, I was acquainted with him. What about the other two?"

"Wisteria te Verisa, from Otherworld. Had at least a couple hundred thousand in gold jewelry—all gone. Her neighbor said she had recently become involved with a man named Ralph Savage."

Again, Bette shook her head. "No . . . no bells on Savage, but Wisteria, yes."

"Lissel Hansburg, Earthside Fae from Norway. Older woman, recently dating a man named Kort Vanderberg. Worth one hundred and fifty thousand."

"Lissel, yes. Kort, nothing." Bette's lips were tight, pale. "All four of the victims frequented the Supe Community Action Council. I met them all there."

I pulled out my notepad. "So, we have four victims, all killed in the same manner, and with the same mutilations. All four were elderly Fae recently involved with a younger person—none of them the same person. Are we sure that the names weren't changed?"

"But there were two women, and two men," Bette asked, then stopped. "Though good makeup and dresses can do wonders for some guys, I guess."

"I think . . . we've got descriptions from Lissel and Wisteria's friends. The guy doesn't sound remotely the same in the looks department. No, I think we're dealing with a ring, with four different partners who have found a lucrative, albeit deadly, avocation." Chase let out a sigh. "Did you *see* this Douglas, by chance? Marlene doesn't seem to have had many friends and we have no description of him."

Bette shook her head. "Sadly, no. I wish I had taken her up on her invitation to go to dinner with them, now." She paused. "But that doesn't explain how the four victims showed up at their banks to clear out their accounts after they were killed."

"No, it doesn't. Will you keep your ear to the door?" Chase sucked down the rest of his coffee. "I really don't know what to do. We have dusted every one of their houses for prints and damn if we haven't found a thing out of place. Everything checks out—well, we're still working the prints from Marlene's house."

"How long of a time frame has this been going on? Are they all like a blitz attack?" Alex was looking perturbed. "Something's not tracking at all for me, and I can't put my finger on it."

"That's the curious thing. No. These murders have taken place over the past six weeks. First was Wisteria. Then Victor, then Lissel, and now Marlene." Chase shrugged.

"And where did they live? Ralph, can you pull up a map and let's chart their houses."

Ralph nodded. "Let's go into the conference room so I can do it on the Holo."

I frowned. I'd seen his baby, the Holo, in action a couple of times and I still found it fascinating. Ralph was a genius, and he had created a number of gadgets that had patents pending on them. We made full use of them. Most of them were too sophisticated for the agency's needs, but now and then something struck just the right chord.

We followed him into the conference room, where he moved to a lectern at the back of the room and within minutes, a full-size map of the area appeared in brilliant topographical imagery on the clear plastic screen at the front of the room. We could draw on the screen with dry-erase markers, or Ralph could use a stylus and a touch screen to do so.

Chase let out an appreciative whistle. "Whoa . . . I want one of these."

Ralph let out a laugh. "Glad you like it."

"I'm serious. This is dynamite. What can you do with it?"

"Let's show you. Give me the addresses of the victims." Ralph tapped away on a keyboard as Chase read him off the four addresses. Within a few seconds, four sections on the map began to glow with a gentle red light. Ralph zoomed out so that all four residences were in view, but we were also seeing a close-up view of them on the sides of the map. "Let me triangulate their coordinates to see if we have any sort of a pattern."

A moment later, a series of lines connected the houses, but there wasn't any sort of pattern that seemed to show itself. The mileage between them flashed on the upper left hand of the screen, but that didn't seem to show any correlation, either. None of them were in the same city proper. Marlene was in Seattle, Wisteria had been up in Belles-Faire, Victor had been out by Mount Rainier, and Lissel lived in Renton.

"I've got nothing." Ralph stared at the screen, then went back to tapping the keys. "Nothing in terms of numerological connections—the addresses themselves don't follow a pattern. What about their races? They all seem to be different types of Fae."

"Right." Chase frowned. "That's one link. So far, all of them have been Fae, but three were Earthside. Wisteria was an Otherworld citizen who had moved here to be near her granddaughter who came over here last year. No Weres, so far. No vamps. No other Supes. Nothing but Fae."

"I wonder if that's chance, or deliberate." I played with my pen, staring at the map. "So we have nothing to connect the murders, except the victims were all elderly Fae, and they had money. We have four suspects, none of whom you can find—"

"It's not just that we can't find these people. It's that they don't *exist*. Oh, there are a lot of Doug Smiths, don't get me wrong, but trying to put a finger on anybody who has heard of them since the murders, or has seen any sign of them? Nada." Chase pushed himself to his feet. "I have my hands full with another situation, which just seems to be getting worse and worse, and frankly, my men are spread thin. Which is why I wanted to ask you if you'd be willing to look into this. The department can't afford to outsource much, but we'll do what we can to turn business your way—unofficially—if you can help us figure out what the hell is going on."

I knew this wasn't standard procedure, but I also had figured out that—with the Fae coming out of the closet, along with the other Supes—SOP had gone by the wayside on a number of things. This wasn't old-school law enforcement.

Alex cocked his head to the side, staring at the detective, then gave him a short nod. "Will do. We'll help out pro bono and if you happen to find a few cases that you can send our way, we'd be much obliged. Bette and Marlene were friends. This is the least we can do."

Chase cleared his throat. "I'll have some documents delivered to you. Confidentially, of course."

"I wouldn't have it any other way," Alex said, standing. His eyes twinkled as he held out his hand. "I think we can help each other, and maybe catch us a pack of killers in the process. We'll use utmost discretion."

And with that, he walked Chase to the door, leaving the three of us sitting there.

I reached across the table and took Bette's hands. "You okay, lady?"

She shook her head. "Somehow, I don't think I'm going to be okay for a long time."

Ralph let out a soft sound, then looked back up at the map. "I'll do my best to think of any other correlations that we might be able to make. I'll also run the four Fae through the Werewyx search engine. We know they were all members of the Supe Community Action Council, thanks to Bette. I wonder . . ." He paused.

"What? You have an idea?" Alex reentered the room.

"It's just . . . I wonder if the vamps have had any members go missing? When a vampire is killed, then they turn into dust. There would be nothing for the police to find."

"That's a good catch. I'll check it out right now." Alex rubbed his chin. "Chai's here. Shimmer, you come with me. We'll head over to the Seattle Vampire Nexus and talk to Roman. Ralph, check out the records of the Supe Community Action Council and see if there's any info Chase's men might have missed. Bette, will you fill Chai in on the Wagner issue—the salamander? We need to track the creature down before it unleashes holy hell on Seattle, because you know that's what's going to happen. See if you can find any sign of it. Call us on our cell phones if you catch anything." He motioned to me. "Get your jacket and let's go."

And with that, we were off. As Alex and I headed out to his bike, he tossed me my helmet.

"Do you think we can find these freaks before they take out another victim?" I settled the helmet onto my head, strapping it under the chin. It was the same midnight blue of the bike.

Alex straddled the bike, waiting for me to get on. As I swung on behind him and he started it up, he said, "I don't know, Shimmer. But we're sure as hell going to try." And off we sped, into the Seattle night.

The Seattle Vampire Nexus was in an old mansion that had once belonged to some vampire socialite. The two-acre estate was the hub of vampire happenings. The Seattle Vampire Nexus was an umbrella organization that housed a number of concerns for the Vampire Nation. I knew that Roman, Lord of the Vampire Nation and heir to the throne, basically held court here. Alex had resisted getting involved at first, but when he found out that Roman was trying to create some order that would put humans at ease— as much as they could be around vamps—Alex had gritted his teeth and joined. The SVN was now, essentially, the vampire chamber of commerce.

Vamps had very few rights compared to the other Supes,

and killing a vamp was still legal—not even considered man-slaughter. Legislative activists were trying to change that, but until they did, vamps were sitting ducks for anybody with a grudge against their kind. If they fought back, they could be hunted down without recrimination.

We pulled up to the front, where valets waited. I swung off the bike and Alex followed suit. As we took off our helmets, a valet—who was a vampire, by the look of him—held out a ticket and Alex gave him the keys.

"Not a scratch. You understand?" He glared at the young-ster, who looked like he had been turned before he reached eighteen. That didn't mean much, actually—he could easily be a thousand years old—but he looked barely old enough to vote.

"Got it." The youth swung onto the cycle and eased her around into the parking area.

We dashed up the steps to the door, and Alex pushed through. The building was a bustle of activity, and the main desk—a semicircular affair in black granite—was busy. There were three people in front of us, and Alex grumbled as we took our place in line.

I glanced around. I had been here with him once before, but this was the first time I'd had a chance to really look around. A painting of the royal trio—Lord Roman and his wives, Lady Menolly and Lady Nerissa, who I knew were married to each other as well—graced one wall. It was new and had a warning sign in front of it that the paint was still drying—DON'T TOUCH. A number of vampires were min-gling around, which would have made me nervous if I weren't a dragon. Granted, I couldn't change shape right here and squash the place, but I could do one hell of a lot of damage if I wanted to. I was tough, and while I wasn't trained in martial arts, the fact was I had learned to watch out for myself in the Dragon Reaches. There had been no other choice.

"What are you doing after work?" Alex's question took

me by surprise. My mind had been wandering in a different direction.

"I dunno. Probably going to hang out with Bette. She seems pretty upset. Why?"

"I was thinking we could go out by the water, watch the late-night stars before they fade. We haven't had much time to be alone together during the past few days." It wasn't a complaint, that much I could tell. But his voice was almost wistful, and he sounded lonely.

"Are you okay, Alex?" I knew he couldn't get sick, but maybe there was something else going on back behind those frosty eyes.

He shuffled. "I just . . . Shimmer, when Glenda showed up, I realized how much happier I am with you than I was with her. Even though it's early in our relationship, I was thinking, maybe we could make it exclusive?"

"Oh, wow. I didn't expect that one coming." And I hadn't. Alex didn't strike me as an exclusive sort of guy—at least not considering he had just gotten out of a long-term, very tiring relationship.

"Is it too soon?" He flashed me a boyish grin, the tips of his fangs showing.

Frowning, I tried to think of how to answer him. Was it too soon? Yes. Was it too soon? No. Everything depended on so many varying factors that I wasn't sure how to even begin. But I knew one thing: The lobby of the Seattle Vampire Nexus was not the spot to have the *Where are we going with our relationship* talk.

I bit my lip, trying to plan out what I said so it didn't come out wrong. "I need to think it over, Alex. And I need you to understand that it's not because I want out, or because I don't adore you. You see . . . the thing is, I'm just so new to this. And we—we're just so new *together*. We don't even know if it's working. I mean, I have a lot of fun with you. I like being with you, and when I wake up, the first thing I think about is 'How's Alex?' Don't even think I'm sitting here, wanting to run out and date other men, either. I'm not interested in playing the field. I don't think I'd be very good, coping with more than one man at a time. More than one person, for that matter. But I . . ."

"You need to breathe a little, and you're too polite to say it like that. You need a little space." He didn't look happy—but then again, he didn't look mad. And that was important. I didn't want him thinking he didn't matter to me, because he did.

"Alex, please understand. This is so new to me—I'm far older than you, and in my entire life, I've *never* had any relationship like this. Hell, Carter was hard for me to deal with. But this . . . with you, it's gone to a new level for me. Where, for you, it's . . . a blip." I glanced at the vampire in front of me as he moved to the reception desk. We were now next in line.

Alex blinked. "You think you're a *blip* in my life? That you're just one more notch on my belt? Shimmer, though I've had more relationships than you—a lot more, all right?—that doesn't make this . . . you . . . any less meaningful to me. It's not just sex. I'm not fond of one-night stands."

At that moment, the vampire in front of us veered off to the right and the receptionist—a pale young woman with silver hair and bright blue eyes, which meant she was a newly minted vamp—motioned us up. "How may I direct you?"

Alex frowned, then quickly said to me, "We'll talk about this later. Come on." He took me by the elbow and escorted me across the waiting line, up to the desk. "We need to see Lord Roman—tell him Alex Radcliffe is here, and that I have an important matter to discuss with him. It has to do with possible criminal activity against vampires."

She eyed him quietly for a moment, then tapped her headset and punched a button on the phone. I wasn't paying attention to what she was saying, but a moment later we were being escorted down the hall to a private room. The mansion was old world, with ornate trim, solid wood and marble floors, and textured paint on the walls that reminded me of something Bette had called faux Venetian plaster. I loved the polished, three-dimensional look, although the gold color was a little overwhelming.

As we headed into an office, I steeled myself. I wasn't very familiar with the vampire lord, and I had no doubt the brief few times we had met had fully escaped his notice. But he surprised me when he stood as we entered, nodded at Alex, and gave me a long look.

"Shimmer, well met, Mistress of Dragonkin." He had an effusive way about him that bordered on melodrama but never quite pushed over the edge into corny. As he clicked his heels and bowed, I felt like I should drop into a curtsey, but that would be ridiculous given who I was and my nature. Oh, I could drop low to the floor in front of the Wing-Liege, but it felt awkward and strange to think of doing so around a vampire. The thought that maybe he was making fun of me ran through my head, but again—vampires like Roman didn't waste time on frat-boy idiocies.

"Well met, Lord Roman." In the Dragon Reaches, he would have just made a major faux pas by recognizing me, but I kept my mouth shut. It was nice, for a change, to be greeted civilly. I still wasn't used to how friendly people were to me over Earthside. Hell, if they knew I was a dragon they might not be so friendly, but it wouldn't be because I was an outcaste. It would be because they'd be scared shitless of me.

Roman motioned for us to sit on the opposite side of his desk. "My secretary tells me that you have concerns about criminal activity, Alex? From or against the vampire community?"

Alex shifted in his seat, frowning. "It's a complicated situation. I'm helping . . . someone . . . investigate a case. There have been several murders in the Fae community. I'm thinking Supe serial killer pack—there seem to be several persons of interest. But it occurred to me if they had targeted any vampires for their activities, if they killed their victims, there wouldn't be any bodies left to find. So what I'm trying to ascertain is whether any wealthy vamps have come up missing lately? The victims would most likely be lonely types, possible shut-ins, or recluses who have few friends or who are pining for days gone by."

Roman paused, eyeing us carefully. "I've heard about this through the grapevine. I also understand the FH-CSI is on the job, but from what I gather, they've got their hands full. Another matter that is coming to light is taking all their time right now, but I cannot discuss that. You might be helping them, but if you were, I doubt they'd want that spread around. Is my read on the situation running on track?"

Alex glanced at me, then gave a short nod. "You wouldn't be far off."

Roman's lip curled into a concentrated frown. "I don't think we've had any reports of missing vamps—not from something like this. You say it's a pack of killers?"

Alex shrugged. "It's looking that way, though to be honest, the thought doesn't track well with me. I really don't see that as making much sense. One killer, yes. Two—that happens. But I've found, through the years, that unless it's a government-sanctioned killing squad, anything over two is suspect. Too many members create too many chances that somebody will run their mouth off."

I decided to interrupt. "Could Chase be wrong? I mean, just because all of the victims had new paramours, does it have to mean that they were killed by them? Could it be someone setting it up to look like that? One killer, smart enough to pick victims known to be in new relationships?"

"Or, perhaps a variation." Roman stood, folding his arms and pacing away from his desk. "Remember, there are creatures who can change shape . . . who can take on other forms. I have met a few of them in my time. They tend to be dangerous and unpredictable."

Alex blinked and I could see the "aha" moment sweep over his face. "Of course! Why didn't *I* think of that?"

"Remember, I have been walking this world for over two millennia. I have seen wonders, and I have seen horrors. And all manner of creatures in between." Roman's gaze flashed to me and I felt myself drifting in his frosty stare. I realized—here was someone who had probably been born around the time I had, and yet, he felt so much older. I liked to think of myself as an adult, but truth was, among my kind, my adult life was just really getting under way.

Nodding, Alex said, "That all makes sense. But these shapeshifters—they're a rare breed. They aren't Weres, not like Ralph." Then, he snapped his fingers. "*Doppelgängers*. You're right in that there are other types of these creatures, but doppelgängers are the most common, and most likely to be found around here. I'll bet you anything that's what we're dealing with."

Roman slowly nodded. "I think you're right."

"What's a doppelgänger? I've heard the term, but I'm not terribly familiar with it." I wasn't up on my mythology.

"A doppelgänger is a mutable shifter. They can change form as they like. And they can take on some of the memories of their victims, I think, by consuming the flesh."

A thought struck me—something Chase had said. "Wait! Bette's friend Marlene. She was seen on camera at the bank at a time when she should have been dead."

Alex clapped his hands. "Hot damn, you're right. And so were the others. This has to be the answer." But then he glanced over at Roman, his glee quickly slipping from his face. "Oh hell. That means . . ."

Roman gave him a short nod. "Yes, it does present a problem."

"What? What is it?" Whatever they were thinking was lost on me.

Alex turned to me. "Think about it for a moment. We have a doppelgänger running around. A creature with psychopathic tendencies who can change shape at will. A mutable serial killer." The glee over discovering the answer rapidly drained away. "See what this means? He . . . she . . . *it* . . . could be anywhere. We have no clue who to look for. We don't know what its natural form is, and chances are the creature won't be running around in its birthday suit, anyway. Not if it's smart, and we can be sure that it's fiendishly intelligent."

As the thought settled in—a killer who could change shape at will, who was targeting its victims with a conscious, thoughtful methodology, I began to understand their reaction. "How can we stop it?"

"That's the million-dollar question, love. Roman, if you suspect any vamps of being targeted, let me know, will you?"

Roman stood and ushered us to the door. "Of course. And I'll have my men keep their ears open."

As Alex and I headed out, my thoughts ran to what we were facing. If we were right, not only did this leave us with no clue as to where to look, but at this moment, the creature could be targeting its next victim, ready to begin wooing them to an early death.

# CHAPTER 6

We were too close to sunrise to do much else, so Alex drove me home.

As we sat in the Range Rover in front of my house, he reached out and took my hand. "Shimmer, I want you to know that I'm not going to press you on the question I asked tonight. I just want you to realize how much you already mean to me." He lifted my fingers to his lips and slowly kissed them, one by one. "But I know that you aren't used to this. I understand that you're not sure what you're getting into. And I never want you to feel that—because of the situation—I expect anything out of you. If you were to say to me, 'Alex, back the hell off,' I would." He turned toward me, his gaze searching my face. "You know that, don't you?"

I let out a long breath. "Yes, I do. And thank you. I promise, I'll be straight with you. I'll think about it . . . I just don't want to rush things. I don't want to hurt you, in case I realize I'm not cut out to be anybody's girlfriend. I have no clue who I really am, Alex. Not over here. Back in the Dragon Reaches,

I knew my place. It sucked, but at least there, I knew who I was. Here? There are suddenly so many possibilities." Very softly, I voiced a thought I hadn't wanted to even say aloud. "I don't know if I'm going to *want* to go home after being here. I think . . . I think I could get used to being respected and liked for who I am. I don't feel . . . thrown away . . . here."

He leaned in, his lips touching mine for a long, luxurious kiss. "I know, love. And I realize just how confusing this is for you. I don't want to complicate matters. So, take your time. Answer now, or answer next year. I'll be fine either way." And with that, he stroked my cheek, and I slid out of the car, watching as he drove off. My heart told me to make him smile, agree to be exclusive. My head told me to wait, to not take a chance on hurting him if I realized I couldn't be the person he hoped I could.

As I entered the house, Snookums came running, with Chai right behind him. The cat had something in his mouth and I realized it was one of my favorite scarves. As I watched, Snookums leaped over the back of the sofa, catching Chai off guard. The djinn twisted to keep from barreling into it, tripped, and landed at my feet. My mood shifted and I laughed, reaching over the back of the couch to scoop up the cat, who was kneading a seat cushion while purring and looking mighty proud of himself.

"You're home early. How did it go at the Seattle Vampire Nexus?" Chai rolled over on his side, still on the floor, propping himself up on an elbow.

"Frustrating. We're getting nowhere pretty damned fast, but at least we have an idea. I'll tell you about it while I eat. Any messages?" I headed for the kitchen and Chai leaped to his feet, following behind me.

"You mean did Stacy call? Yeah, her cold has morphed into bronchitis and she's down for the count. I took her a bowl of soup." Stacy had finally met Chai and she knew what he was. Even though she was leery of a lot of the Fae, she had taken to him. People generally did—Chai was a pretty likable guy. But then, all djinns could be charming. That was part of their danger.

"Wonderful, not." I rummaged in the refrigerator, finally coming up with some leftover pizza. I stuck four slices in the microwave and, while they were nuking, I munched on a couple of brownies that had escaped Chai's notice. "So, any clues about the whereabouts of the salamander?"

"Nope. Not at the moment. But I'm working on it. You look tired, Shimmer. What else happened?"

I didn't feel like telling him about Alex's request—that we be exclusive. Chai was protective and he was also on the side of *sleeping with the boss is a bad thing.* He liked Alex, but he hadn't come around to approving of our relationship yet.

"We think we're facing a doppelgänger, and that makes everything just so much worse." Before he could speak, the microwave beeped and I held up my hand. "I'm just tired. Maybe I need some extra sleep. I think I'll take my pizza and go to bed early, for once." Under Chai's watchful eyes, I gathered up my food and a bottle of water and headed toward my bedroom. Surprisingly, I did exactly what I had said I was going to. I polished off the pizza, then slid under the covers and crashed hard.


Bette called and told me to meet her outside early. When she showed up, she hustled me into the car. "Alex called. He said we're to get into the office pronto. No dawdling or stopping for doughnuts. You can bet that something's going on."

By the time we reached the agency, Alex was waiting by Bette's desk, car keys in hand. "We have to get out to the U-District. That salamander has been causing havoc there, and if the FH-CSI is called out on it, Lydia could find herself in trouble. Bette, hold down the fort. Ralph is in his office, trying to figure out some sort of triangulation of coordinates or some such thing. I have no clue, so don't ask." He impatiently glanced at his watch, then at the door leading to Ralph's computer sanctum. We jokingly referred to it as his cyber-fortress.

"I'm going to call Chai. Give me the address and I can send him directly there. He'll be able to help us and he knows enough that I won't have to ask." I grabbed the slip of paper from Alex and stepped to the side. Chai picked up immediately.

"Salamander is on the loose." I cleared my throat. "We're heading out."

"What's the address? I'll meet you there."

I gave him directions. "Be careful. We don't know how strong that thing is." As I hung up and turned back, Alex was halfway to the door.

"He'd better not go and stir up things. Come on, we'll have to take the Range Rover. Get Ralph up here *now*, would you, Bette? We don't have any more time to wait. What the hell do you use to fight a salamander, anyway?" He patted his thigh, then frowned. "Oh bother. Hold on, I need to get Juanita." His voice trailed off as he stomped toward his office to fetch his knife. Juanita was a wicked bowie knife. I wasn't sure if the blade was magical or not, but Alex loved her dearly.

"Chai can probably figure out something to do with the critter." Bette cackled, her cigarette hanging off her lip as she slipped behind the receptionist's desk and punched a button on the intercom. "Wolfie, get your hackles up here. Alex wants to get on the road. Don't forget your jacket—it's chilly out there."

I snickered. Bette teased everybody as much as she mother-henned us, and we all loved it. She was the one constant in this job, and she made coming to work a lot more fun than it would have been otherwise. I leaned over the counter and swiped one of the chocolate Kisses she kept there, popping it in my mouth as I crinkled the foil wrapper between my fingers.

"Earthside has a lot of pluses to be said for it." I grinned. "Candy being one of them."

"I thought you weren't big on sweets." She handed me another.

"I wasn't, but chocolate is growing on me. Alex keeps buying me boxes of it—what's that all about anyway?" I wasn't sure what chocolate had to do with relationships, but he seemed to show up with a box every few weeks.

"Chocolate is to romance, at least among humans, as what . . . oh . . . I have no idea what you dragons do. There's a saying among humans. *Sweets for the sweet.* Chocolate's considered an aphrodisiac, a way to make up for an argument, a mood soother—especially for women. It cures what ails you." She leaned back, puffing on the cig. "I know you've never had much of a relationship before—except with the half-Titan . . . and gods help me, even *I* can't imagine having a go at *him*. You are braver than I, my girl. But seriously, you need to learn about the cultural mores. Have you given Alex any special gifts?"

I frowned. "I'm supposed to give gifts for no reason?" The thought made sense, though it wasn't something I would have thought of on my own. Hell, I didn't even know all the cultural mores of *my own* society, let alone one alien to me.

"Yeah, see, it's kind of a thing here. Tell you what." She leaned in close, lowering her voice. "I happen to know Alex's weak spot. Since he can't eat food or drink, he's developed a weakness for crossword puzzles. He keeps it hidden— doesn't think it's manly, I guess. But truth is, he loves them. Buy him a couple of crossword puzzle books. You'll see."

"Won't he think I've been talking to you?" I still wasn't getting the idea of how a random gift was going to help.

"Not if you tell him you saw them at the bottom of his underwear drawer. That's where he keeps them." She laughed. "*And* that way, he'll think you cared enough to sneak a peek through his things. Alex is an odd duck. He may seem independent, but he's really not all that happy being on his own."

I frowned, thinking about our conversation earlier. "Bette, he asked me if I would consider being exclusive . . . I told him I thought it was too early."

Bette shrugged. "For you, you're probably right. But I'm not surprised he asked. And, he'll probably ask again in a few weeks if you haven't answered. I warn you—eventually, he's going to want to hear a yes. So make up your mind one way or another. But please, don't tell him what he wants to hear just for the sake of shutting him up. Alex has been hurt a lot. If you can't fully give yourself over to the relationship, do the right thing and back out. I don't want to see you break his heart."

I nodded, silently thinking over what she said. She knew Alex better than anyone, and I realized that even though he said he could handle it if I needed to wait, he might be fooling himself.

At that moment, Ralph appeared, jacket in hand. Bette returned to her paperwork, and I grabbed another fistful of Kisses from the bowl. She smacked my hand lightly and I dropped them back onto the counter as she rummaged through a drawer and handed me half a bag.

"Here, take my stash." She glanced up as Alex entered the room.

"Ready to go?" He held up his keys.

"So, we're off to see the Wizard?" Ralph slipped on his jacket.

"Yeah, and the yellow brick road leads directly to a big bad salamander. Let's just hope we can work a little magic that isn't illusion and ship it back to the Elemental plane of Fire before Lydia's blunder goes all Godzilla on the U-District. Chai is on the way there."

And with that, Alex led us out the door, into the night.

* * *

The U-District was so named because it comprised the vast swath of city where the University of Washington sprawled. Composed of sixteen actual colleges and schools, the UW—pronounced "U-Dub"—was also the home of the Huskies, western Washington's beloved favorite college football team. With a massive number of buildings spreading out over block after block of the city, the UW was commonly called one of the "public ivies"—a public version of the Ivy Leagues.

I didn't fully understand the hierarchy of education among humans, but I knew the University of Washington was considered an excellent university, and that they had an incredible medical college. In fact, it was widely accepted that the best place in the world to have a heart attack—and survive—was Seattle. Whether it was the EMTs or the medical facilities, I didn't know, but the city had a good reputation, and the school an even better one.

But a salamander the size of a large, magical Komodo galloping through a bunch of college students wasn't exactly in the same risk category. In fact, it was one of the worst ideas ever. Images of Godzilla—which I'd recently been exposed to thanks to Stacy and her love of old movies— raced through my mind.

As we wound our way into the U-District, my phone rang, startling me. I didn't know many people. Who could be calling me? I glanced at the Caller ID. Tonya? Surprised, but pleased, I answered.

"Hey, good to hear from you!" I poked Alex in the arm as he drove and mouthed, *Tonya*. He nodded back.

"I'll be in town tonight—well, late night, early morning. I thought I'd drop by and say hello." She sounded tired, her voice strained.

"Are you staying long?" I had to admit, after working with her on the peninsula to cope with ghosts and forest wights and all sorts of nasties, I had a newfound respect for humans who worked magic. Plus, I just really liked the woman.

"I'll be there for a couple of days. At least through the week. I have some . . . well, I'll tell you about it when I see you." She sounded even more depressed. My empathy took over. Something was seriously wrong—it echoed through her voice.

"Tonya, are you okay?" I narrowed my brow. "I can tell something's happened."

"You're right, but wait till I get there. I'm coming in on the last ferry, so I'll be in Seattle by around two A.M. I have to find a hotel, but I can meet you for breakfast, if you have the time."

I relayed the info to Ralph and Alex, both of whom immediately began shouting invitations to drop by the office. Ralph grabbed for my phone, but I wrestled it away and brought it back to my ear.

"I take it you heard the guys?"

"Yeah, and tell them I thank them. Feels nice to hear friendly voices who *want* to see me."

Yikes. Something had definitely gone down.

"Come straight to the office when you get in. We should be back by then. Bette will be there if we aren't. Just introduce yourself and tell her we told you to wait for us. And you're not going to a hotel. You'll stay with Chai and me. That's final. So don't even think of looking for a place to check in."

She laughed then—though I could still sense her worry behind the laughter—and agreed.

I stared at my phone, wondering what was wrong. "I miss her. I never thought I'd say that about anybody, especially a human, but it's true." A sudden flare of light in a park up ahead caught my eye. Sliding my phone back into my pocket, I pointed. "What the hell is that?"

"I dunno, but that flash wasn't normal. That's Sakuma

Viewpoint." Alex veered off Boat Street into the parking lot. The small waterfront park overlooking the Lake Washington Ship Canal was barely big enough to hold a couple of benches and a few picnic tables, and it was adjacent to the Boat Street Marina, a one-hundred-slip dock used primarily for long-term moorage.

As Alex brought the Rover to a screeching halt, we slipped out of the car. It wasn't hard to see what had caused the flash—Chai was over near the water's edge, doing his best imitation of a croc wrestler. But instead of a crocodile, he was wrestling with the salamander. Wispy flames flared around them, though I didn't think they were actual fire. I knew Chai well enough to understand that what we were seeing was astral fire—the Elemental form of heat and flame. But even if it wouldn't catch the vegetation alight, it could burn anybody who got in the path of it. Psychic napalm, Chai had once called it.

"Crap. Somehow, I don't think Chai has the upper hand." Ralph stared at the pair.

"I think you're right." I cocked my head. Chai was looking down for the count. The salamander had body-slammed against him and Chai was on the ground. The Elemental beast let out a low rumble. Breathing fire on Chai wouldn't do anything, and I had the feeling the creature knew that, but he could still—"Oh hell!"

The salamander opened its mouth and bit into Chai's massive bicep. The djinn roared, leaping to his feet, bringing the giant fire lizard with him. It held on, but Chai began to spin—faster and faster, rising off the ground into what was quickly becoming a flaming whirlwind. There was a loud noise and the massive salamander went flying.

It landed on the ground in front of us and I jumped back. Alex did the same—fire *could* kill a vampire. Ralph stared at the creature, and the next moment he had turned into a large beautiful white wolf, and then he ran beneath the nearest bush. I didn't blame him in the least. In fact, I scrambled to join him. As Chai—in the guise of his whirling dervish fire tornado—dove for the creature, the salamander let out a loud keening wail. And then it began to vanish, fading to where it was barely visible.

Chai landed on the ground, and the tornado rapidly vanished, leaving the seven-foot tall djinn looking stunned. The next moment, the translucent salamander loped off down the street, out of sight.

"Well, fu—" Alex stopped himself, glancing at me. He had a thing about not swearing in front of women. Quaint, but lovable, and I *did* like the way he respected the women that he met.

"Yeah, I agree." Chai pushed himself to his feet, brushing off his jeans.

Ralph emerged from the bushes, back in his human form. But one look at Chai, who was sporting a bloody arm from the bite of the giant lizard, sent the werewolf to the ground. Ralph face-planted right at the base of Chai's feet.

"That didn't go like we hoped it would." Alex sounded both grumbly and bewildered. He leaned over to make certain Ralph was all right. Ralph mumbled something, then slowly began to open his eyes.

I quickly turned to Chai. "Cover that up." I nodded to his injury.

Chai shrugged, and the next moment a bandage covered the bloody arm. "Ralph needs to get a handle on that little problem of his."

"Yeah, well, tell that to my subconscious," Ralph groaned as we helped him up. "Damn it, not another pair of glasses." His glasses were broken on one side. "I really need to invest in some contacts, except I have an insane fear of touching my eyes. I don't think I could ever put them in. Good thing I always carry a spare pair in my messenger bag."

"You're just one bundle of neuroses, dude." Chai laughed. "Are you all right, though? Glasses can be mended. The body isn't quite so easy to fix."

"I'm fine." Ralph let out a sigh and dusted himself off. "Seriously, I have tried to get help for my problem with blood, but the phobia is so deeply ingrained that my therapist has never been able to make it go away."

Neither Alex nor I had ever asked him what caused it—it seemed like an invasive question. But Chai wasn't as reticent.

"What happened to make you so afraid, Little Wolf?"

Ralph didn't bristle at the nickname. Chai called me Little Sister, and he had taken to calling Ralph Little Wolf with the same familiar fondness. He did *not*, however, call Alex Little Fang, which was probably for the best.

Ralph sighed, then shrugged. "I seldom talk about it, but maybe it's time." He sounded so grim I was about to tell him not to bother. I could feel the tide of emotion swelling up within him and it wasn't pretty. In fact, it was terrifying and stark and I could sense the turmoil that surrounded the problem. But before I could say anything, Ralph led the way back to the car, telling his story as we followed.

"I was barely four years old. My mother left me in the care of an uncle who has a farm out near Snohomish. I was playing with some blocks or something—I don't remember what. I actually don't remember much about that day, except for what happened next."

He opened the backseat and dug through his messenger bag to find the spare pair of glasses, then continued. "My cousin Jonathan was outside, cutting firewood with a chain saw. I idolized Jon. He was fifteen, strong as an ox, smart—and he always took time to explain things to me. Anyway, the next thing I remembered was the sound of Jon screaming. Uncle Sanders ran outside and I followed."

He paused, grimacing. "We saw Jon there, on the ground, bleeding like a fountain. It took me a moment but then I realized that his arm was no longer attached to his body. And then I saw that I was standing next to it, so close that I could reach down and touch the bloody stump. It was like some nightmare where I couldn't wake up, where I couldn't control my actions."

"Cripes, mate. I can just imagine what came next." Alex swung himself into the driver's seat.

"Yeah, pretty much. I poked at the end of it—the part that had been attached to his shoulder. And then, as I stared at the blood on my finger, Jon shrieked again. I've never heard anyone ever sound in so much pain since then. As I watched, Jon convulsed and died. Uncle Sanders was screaming at him—something about 'Don't you dare die on me, son' . . . He was on his knees next to the body. As I stared at the blood on my fingers, something clicked. I realized that the blood had been *inside* Jon . . . that the arm had been *part* of Jon, until a few seconds before. And I fainted. After that—I've never been able to stand the sight of blood. I faint every time."

I could feel the swirl of emotions. "You really idolized your cousin, didn't you?"

"Yeah. And Jon always told me that he'd be there for me. For a long time after the accident, I was terrified he was going to turn into a zombie and come back to get me. I was afraid that he'd tear off my arm, too, so that I'd die." Ralph shook his head. "My parents took me to a therapist—we knew one who was a Were—but it didn't do much good. And I still talk to one now and then, but still . . . The image is too ingrained into my memory. I still see it sometimes, when I see a large pool of blood."

Chai let out a slow whistle. "I wouldn't recommend tackling the problem magically, either. Memory spells can backfire in a big way."

"There are spells to wipe a memory out?" Ralph sounded all too eager, and I flashed Chai a glowering look.

Alex started the car. "Buckle up, everybody. And no, Ralph, you are *not* going to go hunting out a witch to help you with your memories. I'm very sorry about what happened to your cousin, but mate, come on. Messing with your mind? Letting someone go in and rearrange your memories and thoughts? That's not a good idea."

"I suppose you're right." Ralph sounded compliant, but I had the feeling he was still mulling over the idea. There wasn't anything I could say, though.

I stared out the window, thinking about how unfair the world could be to children. And then Ralph's story vanished from my thoughts as I saw a flare-up in the center of the street—the same flash of energy I had seen when we first approached the salamander.

"Got it!" Alex apparently had seen it, too, because he headed in that direction.

As we skidded into a parking space along the narrow sidewalk and clambered out of the Range Rover, I glanced this way and that but couldn't see anything. "Where did it go?"

"Don't bother." Alex pointed to an area in the middle of the street. "See the manhole cover? The damned thing just went down the sewer."

"I'm not going down there." I stared at the gaping hole. The manhole cover looked like it had been twisted—like a penny set on the train tracks.

"Neither am I." Alex glanced back along the street. There were no other cars in sight. "Stay here." He headed toward the manhole. Along the way, he picked up the cover, then cautiously peered down the gaping hole. A moment later he returned to the car.

"See anything?" Ralph leaned forward, seeming eager to change the subject.

"No, but see how it mangled the steel? This tells us one thing: The salamander is insanely strong and dangerous. We can't follow it down there; we don't even know where the sewers lead."

"I think . . . hold on. Let me check something on my iPad." Ralph tapped away and a moment later he grunted. "As I thought—Werewyx lists the sewers in this area as eventually leading into Underground Seattle. Once the salamander finds its way there, there's no telling where it will hide. We need to figure out how to lure it out before we have a hope in hell of catching it."

And with that, Alex handed the manhole cover to Chai, and we headed back to the office.

By the time we got back to the office, Bette had another client waiting. Alex glanced over the form all clients filled out when they first arrived, then motioned the man to follow him back into his office. He didn't say a word to us, but I could tell he was worried.

Bette glanced at me as the door closed behind them. "Trouble?"

"Salamander made it down into the sewer. We lost it. That thing is big and it's dangerous. Chai couldn't stop it." I paused as Ralph waved at Bette, then headed back to his cyber-lair.

Chai watched him go. "Shimmer, keep an eye on Little Wolf. I did not mean to put ideas into his head, but I fear I might have. If he takes it into his mind to hunt up a witch who can wipe memories . . ." When Chai worried about influencing others, I knew that he was serious.

"Yeah, I think maybe you did, too. And Ralph's brilliant. If anybody can dig up a witch who could—and would—attempt a spell like that, he can." I shook my head. "What a memory to carry around."

Bette cleared her throat. "Ralph told you about his cousin, didn't he?"

I nodded. "You knew, then?"

"I have a way, child. I have a way. People tell me things. If I ever decided blackmail was an option, I could be rolling in dough." She arched her eyebrows and stared at Chai. "So I assume *somebody* mentioned something about memory-wiping spells?"

"Unfortunately, I did. I really didn't think about the

ramifications." Chai let out a rumble, then sat down, easing into one of the leather chairs.

I was about to say something when the door opened. Damn, we were busy tonight—we seldom worked on more than a few cases at a time.

The couple who came in looked vaguely familiar, though I knew I hadn't ever met them. But there was something to their facial structure . . . They nodded to me, then turned to Bette. She froze, the smile half-fixed on her face.

"Miss Bette, nice to see you again. Is Ralph around?" The man walked a couple of steps in front of the woman, I noticed, and while her shoulders were back, she made no move to speak.

Bette cleared her throat. "Let me see if he's here. I think he might have just stepped out."

I blinked, not used to Bette lying outright.

She stood, giving me a very slight shake of the head. "Shimmer, watch the desk for me." Her look telling me to keep my mouth shut, she headed toward the back. I swung around behind the counter.

"Won't you have a seat . . ." I trailed off like I'd noticed humans do when they weren't sure of whom they were talking to.

"Pardon me. I didn't mean to be rude. My name is Leon Spangler, and this is my wife, Emily. We're Ralph's parents." He tipped his head to me, taking off his hat.

It took a moment, but then it clicked. Ralph's *parents*. Which meant they were werewolves. The man was burly and big. I could see the muscles straining beneath the work shirt. Emily was wearing a blue dress, tidy and modern but along the modest side. She was pretty but had a look in her eye that told me she was used to running things behind the scenes but never getting the credit. She flashed me a soft smile and I felt an instant camaraderie with her.

"I'm sure Bette will be back in a moment. Please, sit down. That is . . ." I glanced over at the chairs, but Chai was gone. He had gone *poof*, and probably for the best. Were-wolves and magic didn't get along, and djinns were magical creatures through and through. As I cleared my throat, the Spanglers sat down. I had the feeling they weren't going to leave the building without talking to Ralph, no matter whether or not Bette said he was out. No, they'd wait for him.

I was about to offer them coffee when the phone rang. I picked up. It was Chase Johnson.

"Shimmer speaking. I'm afraid you'll have to talk to me, Detective. Alex is in a meeting with a client, and Bette is away from her desk."

Chase mumbled something that I couldn't understand, then said, "We may have another. One of the Fae went missing. He was in the same art class as Marlene at the Supe Community Action Council. The one Bette teaches. And they both belonged to the OBC—the Otherworld Book Club."

I glanced around, looking for a pen. Quickly, so I didn't miss anything, I scribbled down notes as he talked. "Classes . . . book club . . . got it." Then, softly, I laid down the pen. "Detective—"

"Call me Chase, please. Everybody else does."

"Of course. Chase, you're going to want to talk to Alex. We have a possible theory, and I have to say, it's not a pleasant one."

"Theory? All right. And I want to talk to Bette again. Since they all have ties to the Community Action Council, I was hoping she might be able to come up with something that seems out of the ordinary—anything she might have noticed. Can you have her call me when she returns?" He sounded tired—more tired than was good for a human—and I suddenly wanted to reassure him in some way.

"Sure. Listen, we're doing our best. I don't know what we can find out, but trust me, we want this solved and over with. Bette's really upset. She likes these people; they're her friends. And we want to help her, too, so . . . so . . ." My words trailed off. I felt helpless. I wanted so much to soothe their worries—partly because their anxiety shifted around me like waves in the air, unsettling me. But I was quickly coming to realize that I lacked some basic social skills and understanding of how to behave among nondragons, and I didn't like that lack in myself.

"I know, Shimmer. And I appreciate it. I'll talk to you later. Please have Bette give me a call when she can." And with that, he hung up.

I slowly replaced the receiver, staring at the phone. At a loss, I thought about calling Stacy to see how she was. But with bronchitis, that wasn't the best idea. Though she usually kept to a nocturnal schedule because of her jobs, right now, I hoped she was asleep, healing.

And *that* brought me back to thinking about the house across the street and Mary, the ghost. Toying with the pen, I didn't notice that Emily and Leon were suddenly on their feet. I jumped, startled, but then saw that Ralph had entered the waiting room. He motioned for them to follow him into one of the conference rooms.

Bette gave me a quizzical look as I vacated her chair. "Long thoughts?"

"I don't know about long, but lots of thoughts, yes. Just thinking about the murders." As I blurted out the words, I realized that I had just put my foot in my mouth.

But Bette reached out to pat my arm. "I've been around a long time, my dear. Longer than you may imagine. And I've seen a lot of people come and go." For a moment, she sounded more like a grandmother than a biker mama, but then she snickered. "So, Ralph's parents are here. That's going to be fun. *Not.*"

"What do you think they want?"

"I don't know, but every single time they show up, Ralph goes into a funk. I see Chai made himself scarce." Bette lit up another cigarette as she tamped out the one she was just finishing. I grimaced. "I know you hate the smoke, girl, but seriously, you're a dragon. You *breathe fire*. So don't complain to me about my habits."

I grumbled. "I *used* to breathe fire, till they stripped away that power when they took away my power to shift on land. Now, the best I can do is an occasional belch and a wisp of steam. And since I have to be underwater in order to shift form, my fire can't do much except make a burst of hot bubbles to kill a few fish." Suddenly, I wanted nothing more than to go swimming. To shed my human skin and dive deep. "Bette, do you think Alex would mind terribly if I ducked out for a swim?"

"I don't know, but he seems in a somber mood—I'd ask him before taking off anywhere."

"Where are you planning on going?" Alex asked as the door to his office opened. The new client followed him, but within seconds, the man barged out the door. Alex handed Bette the intake form. "Shred. He won't be requiring our services after all."

"Problem, chile?"

"Wanted me to spy on his wife. Said he wanted to make certain she didn't know about his mistress. I don't see that as fair play."

One thing I liked about Alex—he had a sense of honor. It might be a little skewed, but it was definitely there. I stretched. "I was wondering if you'd mind if I take off for a swim. I need to be in the water—it's calling me tonight."

He glanced at the calendar. "It's been a while, hasn't it?"

I nodded. "Yeah, a couple of weeks. I'm feeling restless." When I was out of the water too long, I started getting antsy and it eventually led to discomfort and pain.

"Go then. I can't drive you, though. I have a lot of paperwork I need to finish. Ralph could, I suppose . . . or Bette." He glanced over at Bette. "Why don't you take her, darlin'? She needs the water and I think . . ." He stopped, but I knew what he was thinking. When Bette had found out about

Marlene, the news had been a shock. Maybe she and I could talk while we were out.

I knew Bette must be feeling the same way, because instead of arguing that somebody needed to watch the desk, she nodded. "All right, precious. Ralph's busy with his parents, anyway." She pushed back her chair and stood. I was sliding into my coat when the office door slammed open.

Glenda was standing in the doorway, her eyes narrowed, with a vicious grin on her face. She tossed something into the room, laughed, and then vanished. The next moment, a pungent odor filled the room, along with a massive amount of smoke. The smoke alarm immediately began to screech. Swearing loudly, Alex dove for the security system. He punched in a code, but the phone rang and Bette snatched it up.

"No, we don't have a fire—someone dropped a smoke bomb in our office. Everything is fine. Do *not* send the fire department." She sounded pissed out of her mind.

My first thought was to open the windows. Barred on the outside, the bulletproof glass opened inward. I yanked open the ones nearest me as Ralph and his parents stumbled out of the conference room. Ralph took in what was happening and immediately joined me in trying to clear out the room.

Mrs. Spangler began to cough, and Bette hustled her toward the exit. Leon Spangler followed as Ralph and I finished opening every window we could reach.

Alex motioned to Bette. "The fans in the conference and break room—let's get them set up, woman." They moved in unison, hurrying to drag out the massive fans that kept the office cool during summer days so it wouldn't be sweltering at night, since there was no A/C and the walk-up had a closeted feel to it. After a few moments, the smoke began to clear. Ralph went to check on his parents, who were standing in the main foyer of the building. Bette punched a button to lock the outer door to the building.

"Anybody who wants in can ring the bell," she said.

Another ten minutes and everything was under control and we were all back in the office.

"Damn that bi— woman." Alex was fuming. I had never seen him quite so angry. "It's one thing to come growling at me at a party, but to invade my business and cause this kind of havoc? For all she knows, one of my clients could be an asthmatic."

"Boss, this was wrapped around the smoke bomb." Bette handed him a piece of paper.

Alex gingerly opened the folded origami-like page. He silently read it, then handed it to me. I glanced at the writing. Yes, this could definitely be called a hate letter. And also a threat.

*Alex, if you think I'm going to let you and your little fuck-a-cunt enjoy yourselves after you threw me over, you're wrong. Tell the dragon she'd better get over her sob story because when I'm done with the two of you, you'll both know what REAL humiliation is like.*

Bette, who was reading over my shoulder, let out a sharp whistle. "The bitch is back, that's for sure."

Alex's expression was dead serious. "I think it's time Glenda and I had a talk." He glanced over at me. "I'm sorry, Shimmer. I never meant for you to become a target."

I shook my head. "She has no clue . . . absolutely no clue . . . what hell I went through growing up. I learned how to play hardball. She wants to rumble, let her come. I think she might find that I come equipped with a few surprises."

"Like me." Chai appeared behind me.

"Damn it, dude, you do that one more time and I'm going to smack you!" But I laughed. I couldn't stay mad at him. As I swatted his arm, he pulled me into an easy embrace.

"Anybody threatens my Little Sister, they have to deal with Big Brother." His eyes twinkled. "I think your ex-girlfriend might find a djinn more than she can handle. *In every way.*"

Alex let out a snort. "Don't be too sure of that. The woman's a succubus. She's insatiable."

Chai raised his eyebrows. "And I am a djinn. One of the Efreet. I could twist her words in such knots that she would never get out of the tangle. If she sets one hand on Shimmer, I swear, I don't promise to leave her in one piece."

Alex gave Chai an odd look. "Not if I get to her first."

"I'm quicker than you, vampire." Chai had a smile on his face, but to my dismay, I heard a growl of a threat there. What the hell?

"You want to make a bet, genie-in-a-bottle?" Again, said with a smile, but also a show of fangs.

Hell, we were in the middle of a testosterone match. I glanced over at Bette, and she must have seen the look of horror on my face because she broke in loud and clear.

"Put away the measuring tape, boys. You both care about Shimmer. We know that. It's not a competition. We're all on the lookout now, so calm down. Chai, why don't you go search the neighborhood and see if Glenda's still around? Shimmer, come on, you and I are heading to the shore." And just like that, she swept us out of the office, away from the chaos.

# CHAPTER 7

"You know Glenda's" not going to be anywhere near the office. Why did you tell Chai to go look for her?" As we stepped out into the night air, I turned to Bette, confused.

"Sugar lips, those boys were about to get into a tussle. I thought it prudent to misdirect the energy, and Chai's so willing to help out that he'll do it before he realizes the futility of it." Frowning, she cocked her head. "What *was* that, anyway?"

"Hell if I know. Chai's always been protective of me, but he likes Alex, so I'm not sure what was going on. I've never seen either one of them puff up like that."

Then, at the very edge of my hearing range, I heard a shout from the building. "Hell, come on. I think something else is happening."

We rushed back inside to find Ralph scuffling with Alex. "I can't believe you stole her out from under my nose!" Ralph was growling. His parents looked horrified.

Chai snorted. "Little Wolf has big shoes to fill if he thinks he can seduce *my* sister!"

Alex rolled Ralph over, pinning him down, but it was obvious the pair were well matched. "Like you ever stood a chance, you mutt!"

Suddenly, everything crystallized. Alex and Ralph were close friends. Neither would *ever* treat the other like a punching bag without outside interference. And Chai had a level head—he wouldn't egg either of them on without good reason.

"Bette! That smoke bomb—it wasn't just an annoyance, it was a spell. These guys are under a spell."

"Of course—that makes perfect sense." She waded in and grabbed hold of Alex's shoulders. The Melusine was far stronger than she looked, because within a moment, Alex slumped in her hands, glaring at her. "It has to be in the residue smoke. You—the Spanglers—grab your son and get him outside. Shimmer, you tackle Chai."

I grasped Chai's wrist. "Come on, dude. Outside. Come with me, Big Brother." I flashed him a warm smile and he relaxed, following me.

As we all trooped outside, keeping the men apart, the crisp night air began to clear out a vague scent lodged in my nose that I hadn't realized was there.

Coughing, I turned to Chai. "Breathe. Breathe deep." Again, he complied.

Bette turned to Alex, still holding on to his wrist. "I know you don't have to, but do me a favor, sugar pants, and breathe. Take a long, deep breath and get some of the night air into you. That smoke seeped into your body—and don't give me crap about *'I didn't inhale'* . . . it managed to take root in those atrophied lungs of yours."

Alex glared at her, but he did as told and took a few very slow, very long breaths, sputtering as the shaky air left his lungs. Ralph was panting but finally composed himself.

A few minutes later, we were all staring at one another.

The three men looked sheepish. Ralph's parents looked confused. Bette and I were just irritated. After another moment, Alex broke into an embarrassed laugh.

"Ralph, I'm sorry, mate. You, too, Chai. I didn't mean anything I said." He sidled over and glanced at me. "Good call, Shimmer. Glenda had one up on all of us, it seems."

Ralph shrugged. "I know. Same here, Alex. I have no clue what the hell happened."

"Spell," Bette said. "The smoke bomb? Was a spell."

"Damn that woman." Alex glanced over his shoulder at the building. "Well, we have to clear out the dregs of it before the three of us go back in there."

Chai let out a low belch, then covered his mouth. "My apologies as well. I'm just glad I didn't let loose with any magic. I could have seriously harmed the both of you." He shot a look at me. "Shimmer, the best thing to clear that out would be a magical wind. I can do it, but you need to go open all the doors in the offices. I'll stand outside a window and send the spell through after you open them. It should be enough to clear away any residue."

I nodded. "You know . . . yeah, good idea."

"What happened? Why were you so upset, Ralph?" Emily Spangler was looking more confused by the moment.

"Don't sweat it, Mom. Just . . . someone who doesn't like us very much tried to trick Alex, Chai, and me into hurting each other. Part of the job." The look on Ralph's face told me that he was pissed off about something, and when I focused on him, I had the feeling it went deeper than any spell Glenda had cast. There was something going on, and by the way he pulled away from his parents, I had the feeling this wasn't a pleasure trip on the elder Spanglers' part.

Bette stayed outside with everyone while I went in and opened every window I could find in the office. The smoke hadn't filtered through the rest of the building—it had been localized from what I could tell. I leaned against the bars, staring down at them from the window in the reception area.

"Windows are open. Blast away."

Chai gave me a wave. "You might want to get out of there."

As he spoke, a gust sprang up and if I hadn't been holding on to the bars, I might have toppled over backward. I was about to shout down for him to give me a chance to move away from the window but then decided *what the hell*, and loped out of the office, the wind pushing at my back. A flurry of sparks—not actual flame, but flickering lights—glimmered through the rooms as I peeked in from the foyer of the building. Another few minutes and the wind suddenly died, and everything felt eerily calm. Another couple of minutes and we deemed it safe enough for everyone to troop back inside.

Bette and I kept an eye on the three men, but they seemed back to normal, and there were no more outbursts. The Spanglers whispered something to Ralph, and then—with a faint wave to the rest of us—they left the building. Alex put up the CLOSED sign and we all gathered around the break room table.

"So, Glenda's not going to let this rest, is she?" Alex fetched a bottle of blood from the refrigerator, then stared at it. "I don't think we should trust any food in here. For all we know, she may have come in and poisoned something. Toss everything edible, including any lunches you brought with you. I don't care if it's prepackaged. Get rid of the food."

We cleared out the cupboards and fridge.

Ralph finally asked the question that was going through all of our minds. "What are we going to do about her?"

"We've had the locks changed, and I've got a call into Ysella. I guess . . . maybe I should have a talk with her. Find out why she's doing this." Alex frowned as he waved away the protest I was about to lodge. "I don't want to, but I think that's the only way we'll get any resolution."

I wanted to argue, but he looked tired. "Fine, if you think it's wise."

He shrugged. "I think it's necessary. Shimmer, you go ahead and go swimming. I'll figure out something. Ralph, we'll just keep the doors shut tonight. Can you do me a favor and see if you can find out whether anybody has spotted that salamander yet? You're good at digging up info like that online. Twitter or whatever the newest social networking site is."

Ralph let out a short laugh. "Twitter's not the place for most Supes. We tend to use DragonTongue."

Chai cleared his throat. "I'm going to head out for now. I'll be back later. Shimmer, if you need me, call." He gave everyone a short wave, then vanished.

I glanced at the clock. "Tonya is supposed to be here around two A.M. We'll be back before then. It's only eleven fifteen."

As Bette and I left the building and locked the front door behind us, I was feeling more and more restless. Glenda's attack hadn't helped my agitation any, and now all I wanted to do was dive deep and go swimming. "I really need this, Bette. You don't know how much I need this."

"I can tell you're itching to be out in the water, Shimmer. Come on, get in the car."

We headed out toward West Seattle. Alex and I had scouted around until we found one of the best places for me to head out into the water—a point off Duwamish Head. Alki Trail curved around the point. There was a parking lot right before Harbor Ave SW turned into Alki Avenue SW, but Bette passed it by, stopping a block or so later as we came to the pier overlooking the water.

From here, at night I could climb over the guardrail, dive in, and swim out to where I could dive deep enough to change shape. As long as I didn't cause too much of a ruckus, the area provided me with a place to shift without needing to take a ferry toward one of the islands, or without having to drive up north a ways to find a turnout along Puget Sound.

Bette eased into a parking space along the street. The

street was empty. Nobody else was around, thanks to both the time and the weather. It was a chilly night, and rain was threatening. She turned off the engine and sat back in her seat, unbuckling her seat belt.

"I may be a couple of hours. If you want to come pick me up later, that's fine." I squirmed out of my jeans, tossing them in her backseat.

"Don't worry yourself. I need some time to think and this will give me a breather from Alex's hovering. He knows how much I cared about Marlene, and while I appreciate his concern, having him check on me every ten minutes isn't helping." She paused, grinning at my bathing suit. "I see you came prepared."

"Yeah, I did. I have no desire to run around the streets of Seattle naked. All right then, I'll leave my purse and everything here with you, then. I'll try to make it short."

"Take all the time you need."

"Yeah, except I want to be there when Tonya arrives. Okay, I'm off." Wearing only my bathing suit—a one-piece blue affair—I quietly shut the car door behind me and darted across the short advance to the pier, grateful no one else was around. Benches lined the pier, which was nice and wide with a strip of grass in the center. The guardrail was actually a series of nine thick metal cables that fed through evenly spaced posts surrounding the wooden platform. I peered over the edge. The tide was in, and the water was high, so it was an easy matter of climbing over the cables to jump in. As long as I didn't take too long, climbing back out shouldn't be a problem, either.

As I swung over the cables, holding on to the post for balance, the smell of the brine rose up to encompass my senses and I closed my eyes, every cell in my body aching to be in the water. I took a deep breath, then eased down into it, wary because I knew there were rocks below. The shock of the temperature raced through me, but then, taking a deep breath, I pushed off as my body adjusted to the frigid chill. Humans would have started going into hypothermia within a few minutes, but I wasn't human. I might look it, but my dragon nature gave me far more resilience than any mortal.

As I swam with broad, strong strokes, I estimated my distance from shore. I was fast and sturdy. When submerged, even if it wasn't deep enough to change shape near the shore, I could swim like a fish, and by now I knew the quickest route to take in order to reach deep water. Fifteen minutes later, I was at the proper depth to handle my dragon self, and I dove down, shifting as I did so.

As my body seamlessly transformed, a surge of power and joy washed through me. There was nothing so wonderful as being back in my normal shape. How I missed the freedom to change form at will. Blue dragons could fly, like all dragons, but I was bound to the water, bound to be in my natural form only when I was fully submerged. I longed to go shooting out of the inlet, to rise into the sky and circle round, stretching my wings, and then nosedive back down. But if I tried, I'd immediately lose control of my shape and fall back to the water in human form.

Letting go of thought, I gave myself over to the joy of playing. I barrel-rolled, over and over, the weightless sensation of playing with my element making me laugh, which came out in a stream of bubbles. Then, just as swiftly, I headed toward the bottom of the inlet. Here, I was able to touch bottom fairly easily, but a few minutes of strong swimming had me in deeper water. Four hundred feet and counting, and now I could truly let go and dive deep, the waves rocking around me like a welcome cradle.

A sudden shift in the current surprised me and I swiftly turned as a large shape, about twenty feet long—as large as me—swam past. The waters were dark, but in my dragon form, I could easily see below the surface, and what I saw was what looked like a very large fish. White and black, the creature glided effortlessly near me, and I let out a soft rumble. An orca. Killer whale.

The orcas of the Salish Sea were a single clan of whales, separated into three pods. Not all whales within a pod were necessarily related, but the bond between podmates was a strong one. I had met whales in the oceans up in the Dragon Reaches, but this was the first time I had encountered anything bigger than a jellyfish or a salmon here. I slowed, cautiously turning to meet the whale. One thing most humans did not realize about fish was that telepathy was a very real factor in undersea communication, but it tended to work more on intent and emotion than thought. Words did not make up the language of ocean dwellers, but emotions? Intentions? They carried just as much energy as the spoken word when directed toward those who were sensitive to picking them up.

I gathered my thoughts, then projected the sensation of friendliness—of welcoming energy. I was in the orca's territory and I had no intention on sending out hostile vibes—the whale could do some serious damage to me if it wanted to.

A moment passed, then another, and then the sense of curiosity flowed toward me.

*What are you? Not two-legged . . .* The orcas knew what humans were, all right. *Not food . . .*

*No, not food. Friend. Visitor.*

Another beat, then, very hesitant—*Play?*

Not wanting to be rude, and actually curious about how this would work out, I agreed. *Play!*

The orca circled me, then headed out toward still-deeper water. I followed. Within minutes, we were playing chase. There was a dangerous edge to the game—we were both predators—but it was as if the orca sensed that I could do as much damage to it as it could to me, and the knowledge produced a mutual détente, leaving us free to explore the possibility of friendship. We dove deep, then shot up toward the surface, chased each other in circles, and then dove again. A few minutes later, the orca rose to the surface and breached the water, then leaped out to glide into the air and then back beneath the waves.

*You, too?*

It was waiting for me to follow suit, but I couldn't. *Cannot leave the water.*

Curiosity played strong. *Why?*

How could I explain? It didn't know exactly what I was, and I had the feeling it would be wise not to give it the knowledge that I could take shape as a human. There was something about the thought that held me back—some inner guidance that whispered, *You might not want to tell it that.*

*Must be in the water. Cannot leave the water.*

The orca shrugged—or rather, attitude-wise it shrugged—and we went back to chasing each other. After a time, I sensed it was getting bored, so I backed away.

*Fun. Friend. Go find food.*

*Eat. Play again soon?*

*Soon. Yes.*

And we went our separate ways, the orca heading out toward open water as I began to swim back toward the shore. I wasn't sure how long it had been, but the play with the whale had drained away some of my restless energy. I let the water cradle me for a little bit, rocking in the currents below the surface, and then began to swim toward shore. At the point where the water would soon be too shallow, I shifted form and—with long strokes—returned to the dock and tiredly pulled myself out. The water was still high enough around the posts for me to haul ass on the dock and climb over the guard wires.

As I landed barefoot on the wood, I stopped short. A man was sitting there, staring out into the water. He looked at me, and in the dim glow of the streetlamps I could see that he was stoned, a joint in one hand, a water bottle in the other.

"Are you a mermaid?" He cocked his head to one side, his voice lazy and dream-laden.

"Yes, I'm a mermaid. You go back to watching and, who knows, maybe you'll see a dragon next." I gave him a soft smile. Sometimes, humans could be so wonder-filled that it warmed me.

"No dragons in these waters, but maybe a cousin of Nessie." And then he focused on the water again and seemed to forget I was standing there.

I padded along the wooden dock, back to the street. Bette was reading on her e-reader, and as I opened the car, she waved to a towel that was on my seat.

"Dry off before you climb in."

I did so, suddenly shivering. The wind picked up and fat raindrops began to splatter along the street. I spread the towel on the seat, then slid in and fastened my seat belt as Bette put away her tablet.

"Feel better?" She smiled, catching my eye.

I nodded, brushing my hair back from where it was plastering itself against my face. "I do, actually. A lot better."

"Now and then I need to get myself into the water, too. Melusines are water spirits, you know—we bond as deeply with it as you do. That's why I live on a houseboat. I can take a quick dip over the side whenever I like without being noticed, though I'm cautious about who sees me when I'm in my snake form. Humans don't like snakes, especially poisonous ones, and I'm always leery that somebody is going to try to finish me off."

I laughed. "We have a lot in common, when you think about it. I need to visit you more often. I've only been on your boat a couple of times. I could keep watch on you while you're in snake form so you don't get hit by some well-meaning mortal. Return the favor, so to speak."

"It's a deal. And yes, I really need to invite people over more often. There's so much to do, though . . . time seems to fly." She started up the car and turned on the heater. "Let's get back to the office. It's one forty-five and if Tonya's ferry arrives on time, she may be there already."

"She said her ferry docks at one forty, so chances are she's on her way. She was going to go to a hotel but I told her forget it, she can stay with Chai and me." I paused. "Bette, how are you, really?"

"You mean, because of Marlene? Alex told you to ask, didn't he?" At my silence, she added, "Never mind. I appreciate the concern. How am I? Sad, child. Sad. But in the time I've lived, I've lost many friends—most of them human. Each time, I swear I'll stick to my own kind. To Supes, you know. And each time, I meet someone new who has a heart of gold, or who is smart as a switch. And I forget my resolve. It's like loving a dog or a cat, in some ways. They leave far too soon, but you go ahead and take another in, because you can't not share your life with them. They're too wonderful, too sweet, too loving, to turn away from. And some people are like that. But I didn't expect Marlene to . . . she still had several hundred years to go, even if her clock was winding down."

I thought about what she said, then thought back to the cat in my apartment. Marlene's cat. Which meant . . . I made a decision right there. "Marlene's cat—Snookums. He's homeless now unless . . ."

"We can't give him to a shelter—I don't trust them and he'd be too confused." Bette kept her eyes on the road, but I could tell the wheels were turning. "Either you or I take him. I just worry about living on a houseboat. And there's my smoking, you know . . ."

I knew when I was being played. But I also couldn't stomach the thought of the poor creature being stuck in a cage. I knew what that was like, and Snookums wouldn't understand. "Right, which didn't bother you earlier. But never mind. All right, I guess I have a cat. But if he eats my fish, I'm going to be awfully pissed."

"He won't eat your fish. Not if you don't let him get to them. That aquarium of yours has bulletproof glass, doesn't it?" She let out a snort.

"Don't push it. It's strong, but . . . you never know. Snookums should be fine, except for the fact that I've never had a cat and I have no idea what to do for him. You're going to have to clue me in on how to take care of him. And you get to buy the cat toys. You're his godmother, like it or not."

Despite the fact that she had reeled me in, hook, line, and sinker, I was actually a little excited. Getting a cat seemed a very human thing to do, and I was trying to assimilate as much as I could. Plus, I had to admit, since Chai had moved in, I was a lot happier. I hadn't realized just how lonely I had been, and while I liked my space, having somebody around to talk to could be a good thing. And unlike Chai, Snookums wouldn't talk my ear off and I could tell him all my secrets without the danger of him betraying me.

"You're gonna love the little guy. He's a sweetheart. Make a list of what we picked up for him and I'll get whatever else he needs and bring it over later."

"No, you don't—not without me. If I'm going to have a cat, I want to pick out some of the stuff. But you can go with me and show me what I need."

And so we play-argued all the way back to the office.

B y the time we arrived back at headquarters, Tonya was there. She was talking to Ralph and Alex, both of whom appeared to have fully recovered from Glenda's surprise attack.

Tonya jumped up as soon as she saw me and gave me a long hug. "Shimmer! I missed you!"

"Oh, it's good to see you!" I spun her around. "How was your trip?"

"You're wet." She stood back, eyeing me up and down. "And in a bathing suit. Were you out in the sound swimming? In this weather?"

"Remember . . . dragon. Cold? Not such a problem. I needed to work off some stress." I grabbed my clothes. "And now, I'm going to go change clothes and warm up."

"Grab a shower while you're at it to wash off the brine." Alex motioned toward the back. We had a full bath at work, because—as Alex put it—you never knew when you might want to clean off the blood. "Ralph has some info on Chase's serial killer case, so when you get back, we'll have an honest-to-God meeting."

I stuck out my tongue at him, then hit the shower.

When I returned, clean, warm, and dressed, they had moved everything into the conference room. Tonya was leaning back in a chair, and the look on her face when I entered the room told me that whatever the conversation had been about, it wasn't all that pleasant.

"Is everything all right?" I slid into a chair and accepted a cup of hot coffee, heavily laden with cream.

Tonya shrugged. "I'll tell you later. I don't want to interrupt your office hours with my problems. Besides, what you're working on sounds like a serious case."

Ralph set up his laptop while Alex, Bette, and I got out our tablets. Before we could get started, Chai shimmered into the room. He was carrying Snookums in his arms.

"He was lonely." The look on his face told me that Snookums was going to end up his cat, not mine, and the look on Snookums's face said the same thing. The cat was snuggled in Chai's arms, purring so loudly we could hear it all through the room. Chai cooed to the cat as he stroked him under the chin. "Isn't that right, little guy? You need a buddy to play with. I think we should get you a pal."

I smiled at Bette, who was staring at the pair, a tear in the corner of her eye. "I think we should start the meeting. Chai, you take Snookums home right now and get back here."

Bette let out a soft snicker, and then the mood shifted as Chai, grumbling, vanished and reappeared a moment later, sans cat.

"Don't blame me when he complains about needing attention while you're trying to get to sleep." But he flashed us a grin. "He's comfortably perched on the sofa, watching Cat TV, otherwise known as your aquarium."

Ralph cleared his throat. "I pulled up everything I could find about the victims, and dug into a few places that . . . well . . . put it this way. The website devs think they've got their security down, but for someone like me? Not so much. One: I verified that all of our victims have had—at one time or another—dealings with the Supe Community Action Council. They've all taken classes there, participated in meetings, and—perhaps most importantly—they all participated in the once-a-month potluck dances. Not the council *meetings*, but an actual social event the agency holds every month."

"Why would that be an important factor?" Tonya asked.

Ralph glanced at her. "Think about it this way: You have a group of people in a social situation. Add in food and booze, and things can get chummy. If a person is lonely, they may talk more freely than usual. The alcohol would potentially lower their guards. We're not talking human beer and wine, either. These events are rife with Fae brandy and Elfin wine, and those are strong spirits. Also, members tend to dress up for the dances, so out comes the jewelry and the finery. It would be pretty easy for someone picking targets to separate those who are rich from those who are not."

That made perfect sense. "Right. And if we are dealing with a doppelgänger, then the creature can change shape every dinner. But if these events are held once a month, and all the victims come from within a six-week period . . . is that right? Six weeks?" All of a sudden, I stopped. "Oh hell. I forgot to tell you. Chase called."

Alex frowned. "What did he want? When was this?"

"When Ralph's parents were here—right before Glenda showed up. Things got so chaotic, I forgot to say anything. Chase said that he thinks they have another victim. Someone went missing and he said there was some tie-in to Marlene. They took the same classes or something." I rubbed my forehead. That I could have forgotten the most important part of his phone call . . . I let out a long, slow breath. "He asked if Bette could call him—he is looking for any scrap of information. I'm sorry. I really am."

"Did you tell him we think we're on the trail of a doppelgänger?" Alex merely raised his eyebrows, but he looked ticked.

"I told him we had a theory, but . . ." Knowing I had screwed up, I lowered my head. "No. I'm sorry."

Alex motioned to Bette. "Get Johnson on the phone now, would you?"

As she put in a call to Chase, I turned to Alex. "I'm still not used to the details on this job. I screwed up. I'm sorry."

He held my gaze, and I could feel the conflicting emotions emanating from him.

"Be more careful next time. Make certain you don't forget anything like this again. This time? It might not matter. But someday it's going to be a life-or-death situation, and a lapse like this? It will stay with you, Shimmer. I guarantee it, because I've had it happen to me. Once, because I forgot to pass along a warning, two people lost their lives. Two men who had families, both of whom should have lived long, happy lives. I still live with that memory, and they—they didn't get to live at all. I don't want you to have to ever go through that."

Embarrassed, feeling miserable, I stared at the table. Alex was right—and he wasn't even being mean about it. But what he said made a hell of a lot of sense. I had been so focused on going swimming that I had let business slide. *Important business.*

"Come now, just pay attention next time." His voice was soft. I raised my gaze to meet his and saw—not irritation, but compassion lurking behind those frosty eyes. "We all know how different this life is for you. You're adjusting, love."

Another moment and Bette returned, her face ashen. "Stone Weaver, a Fae connected with the Cascade Elemental

Fae, has vanished. Nobody's heard from him in two days. Chase was wondering if we could go scout around and see if we can find him. Stone doesn't like humans and if a bunch of cops go up there—even from the FH-CSI—he'll hide. That is, *if* he can hide."

Alex glanced at the clock. "Three fifteen. Where does he live and how far is it?"

"He lives up near North Sultan near Kellogg Lake." She turned to Ralph. "How far according to the maps?"

Ralph tapped out an address on his laptop. "About a forty-minute drive each way without traffic just to Sultan, but then after that, it will probably take another hour on the back roads to get to his house. At this time in the morning? There shouldn't be a problem with gridlock anywhere, but I'm not sure we want to start out this close to sunrise. And if we really take our time to look for him, it's going to add a couple hours. There's no way we can guarantee being home in time to avoid sunrise."

Damn it. If I hadn't insisted on going swimming, if I'd remembered to tell them about the call, we could have been on our way. I wanted to thump the wall, but in my frustration I'd probably put a hole in it. But I made up my mind—this was the last time I'd fuck up and forget to relay a message.

Alex stood, then folded his tablet cover closed. "Well then, we'll go first thing come evening. Meanwhile, Shimmer, why don't you take Tonya home? Ralph, I need you here. We should go over some of the system commands on the new security system I've decided to install. After Glenda's little visit, I don't want to leave anything to chance. I'm not just consulting Ysella, but I've decided to install a magical system as well. It's going to cost a pretty penny, but it's worth it. Bette, we need you here, too. Tonya, you brought your car—can you drive Shimmer home?"

"Damn it, I can't wait to get my license. One more week and I'll go test for it." I hated having to be chauffeured around.

"No problem. Since I'm staying with her, that will be fine. And I'll tell her what I told you."

"Good. We all need to discuss it later on. Shimmer, can I talk to you a moment?" Alex motioned me into his office. Once there, he shut the door and turned to me. "I'm sorry I yelled at you."

"You were right to. I screwed up and I feel horrible about it. But Alex, really . . . is this a good idea? *Us?* It's tricky, blending a work and personal relationship together." I hated bringing it up again, but I didn't want him to feel like he had to compromise his work ethic for me.

But he stroked my cheek. "I know you say it's too soon to promise exclusivity. I accept that. But Shimmer, I don't want to go back to being friends. You mean too much to me." The heat in his eyes belied the chill of his hands. "It's been a long time since I felt this way about someone. I can't say the words yet . . . I *won't* say them yet because I don't want to jinx it, but . . ."

I pressed my finger to his lips. "Shush. Don't. I'm not ready to say them either."

And then I leaned in and kissed him, softly at first, then deeper until we were wrapped in one another's arms. All of a sudden, I realized I was right where I wanted to be—in his arms. He wanted me, he wanted to be with me, he . . . and in the back corner of my mind, a little voice whispered out the words neither one of us could yet say.

Without thinking, I blurted out, "Alex, I'll be your girlfriend—exclusively. But I'm going to slip up now and then. I make mistakes, like I did tonight with forgetting to tell you about Chase's call. I'm not used to being part of a team, let alone a relationship. Can you accept that? That I'll make mistakes and maybe screw up bad enough for you to get pissed at me? And when it happens, can you make certain you don't treat me with kid gloves, as Bette says? I don't want you to give me leeway on standards that you hold Bette and Ralph to."

He pulled me close, whispering roughly in my ear. "Trust me, when you screw up, I'll yell at you. And we'll probably fight. But no matter what, we'll work it out. Can you accept that?" His voice was husky, and the scent of his cologne made my knees go weak.

I melted against him, wanting to slide my hands under his shirt. "Yes. I can accept that."

"Then get out of here. Take Tonya home, before I toss you on my desk and fuck you so hard you scream." And with that, he slapped me on the butt, and grinned. "You lovely dragon wench."

# CHAPTER 8

With it being three thirty, I still had quite a while before bedtime, but then I realized that Tonya wasn't on a nocturnal schedule like the rest of us were. She might need to get some sleep.

"You want to go to bed?" I directed her to my house, but mostly the GPS did the work.

She seemed preoccupied. "No, actually, I've had a lot of late nights lately and have been sleeping late. I have a lot to tell you." She pulled into the driveway, killing the lights as we got out of the car. Abruptly, she turned to face the house across the street, craning her neck. "Say, what the hell is going on with your neighbor? The energy over there is like a beacon shooting out fireworks."

I sighed. "That's Mary's house. Mary's a ghost. Mary has apparently decided that she is the guardian of the block and wants me to find someone to take over the house to help her keep it safe." As I lifted Tonya's suitcase out of the car—for me, it was an easy carry—I told her about what had happened over there. "So, she almost threw me down the stairs but she said it wasn't her fault."

"I don't know how much I'd believe her. Some ghosts do a damned good job lying. Let me read the cards for you while I'm here. I wouldn't mind taking a look for myself, either." She followed me into the house, with a last glance over her shoulder. As we entered the living room, the first thing we saw was Chai, stretched out in a chair, asleep. Snookums was wedged under his chin, also snoring up a storm.

I pressed my lips together, trying not to laugh, and motioned for Tonya to follow me up the stairs and down the hall. "Chai lives with me, but I have a fold-out love seat that makes for a comfy bed in the third bedroom. I use it as a library right now. Will that do?"

"That's fine. I can go to a hotel if it makes it easier on you—" But the catch in Tonya's voice sounded like it was the last thing she wanted to do.

"Nonsense. You'll stay with us. Here we go." The third bedroom was small, but the perfect size for bookshelves, a little writing desk, a rocking chair, and a love seat. I had picked up a love seat that folded out into a double bed, and it was surprisingly comfortable. The room was one of my favorites in my house. I had painted it a deep blue with white trim, and even though Bette told me it was *so '80s*, I had affixed a seashell border around the top of the room. I liked it, even though it was out of date and no longer the trend. I had found a banker's lamp in bronze and cream, and a floor lamp to match, and the room felt cozy and welcoming to me every time I set foot in it.

Tonya looked around as I set down her suitcase. "This is lovely, Shimmer. Your house is wonderful."

"Well, it was the right price. It's in the Greenbelt Park District—the most haunted neighborhood in Seattle. A lot of heavy stuff can go on here, from what I gather. But I'm a dragon. I can deal with it."

"Seriously, though—your ghost next door? I want to go

over there with you and check out the situation. I have a lot of experience with ghosts. And, dragon or not, they can harm you. They aren't like normal mortals, even if they were human to begin with. Ghosts take on a special type of power when they're dead. I just don't want to see you hurt."

I nodded. "You want to head over there after you get situated?"

"Sure." She glanced around. "I guess I'll lay out a few things I don't want to wrinkle. Can I use the closet?" She pointed to the door against the opposite wall. "Or at least, I assume that's a closet?"

"Yeah, it is. There are even a few hangers in it. I'll meet you downstairs in the kitchen." And with that, I withdrew, giving her time to get settled.

D ownstairs, Chai was cooking something that smelled hearty and slightly spicy. "Tonya getting settled?"

I heard something in his voice. "Chai . . . you're really happy to see her, aren't you?"

He went back to frying the sausages. "If you want to help, you can crack the eggs into a bowl and add that little dish of seasoning to them. The whole dozen, please. I'm hungry, you're always hungry, and I imagine Tonya could use something to eat."

As I did as he asked, I casually mentioned, "Tonya is going to go across the street with me and check out the house over there. To see if Mary's really the spirit she says she is or if I'm being played."

Chai's shoulders stiffened. "I'll come along."

"That's all right, you don't need to."

"No, and that's final. You're a dragon, Little Sister. You can take care of yourself. But Tonya, she's human and she might need some watching after." He cleared his throat. "Hand me the eggs, please. There's French bread in the oven, warming with parmesan and butter."

"I can smell it. I'm hungry." And indeed, the yeasty, buttery smell wafted up to fill my senses. My stomach rumbled. I decided to tease him a little. "But Chai, you seemed worried enough about me back at the office."

"Don't even try to start a fight. I tell you one thing for sure: That succubus is going to get her ass whipped. First, nobody attacks *you* and gets away with it. Not on my watch. Second, she's nasty, that one. She's got a spiteful nature that won't listen to reason." He stopped, putting down the spatula after pouring the eggs into a large skillet and turning down the heat. "Shimmer, that succubus is dangerous, and she's not all wrapped up right. I'm worried that she'll do more than just try to cause havoc. I think she has it in her mind to go after you—to try to harm you. She may be lashing out at Alex, but you're her real target. You're the one whom Alex loves—"

"*Loves?* He doesn't—"

He held up his hand. "Little Sister, you are the only one who can't see it, and if you'd only open your eyes, you wouldn't be blind either. Alex is head-over-heels nuts about you. And you are treating this like a summer fling."

I stared at him, and once more, the wall I'd erected began to crack. "Chai, you know my background. Blue dragons . . . we feel things very deeply. And I spent most of my life alone, once I got out of the Lost and Foundling. I was able to push my emotions away—to ignore them. Truth is, I haven't ever had to cope with the onslaught of emotions that surround me here. The past few months have been like an overload for me. I'm trying to process and learn how to deal with all of this."

"I know, Little Sister, but the only thing you can do is learn how to allow yourself to feel without getting overwhelmed."

"There are a few other things she can do, Chai. I'm pretty sure there must be support groups for Supes trying to come to terms with living here." Tonya peeked around the arch leading into the kitchen. "I love your house, Shimmer. I love the aquarium!"

As she entered, Chai swung around, a wide grin on his face. Speaking of emotions, he was wearing his heart on his sleeve. Trouble was, Tonya had a thing for a spiritwalker named Degoba. I thought Chai realized that when we had first met Tonya in Port Townsend, but now I wasn't so sure.

"I hope you're hungry because I've been cooking." Chai began fluffing the scrambled eggs, softly folding them over until they were done.

The smell from the food set off my stomach and it growled. I blushed, but laughed. "Well, I'm ready for food."

Tonya nodded. "I could eat something." But though she was smiling, I still sensed that something was off.

I motioned for her to follow me. "While you're helping me set the table, tell me why you're here. What's wrong, Tonya?"

As we laid out the plates and silverware, Tonya took several deep breaths, like she was gearing up to perform a high dive into a pool of water. Finally, she put down the butter dish and rested her hands on the back of one of the chairs. "Degoba . . . he's getting married."

I blinked. "*Married?* To . . ."

"To someone who isn't me." She choked back a sob and then, dropping into the chair, propped her elbows on the table, folding her arms. Tears glistened in her eyes. "I didn't even know he was dating anybody. We went out once and I had a great time, but he seemed pretty quiet during the date and after that, he kind of avoided me. Now our friendship's all messed up and I feel like a fool."

I quickly slipped around back of her and rested my hands on her shoulder. "It's okay . . . it's going to be okay." I wanted to hug her but wasn't sure that was the right thing to do. I glanced over at Chai. It was obvious he had been listening, but he pretended not to notice. After a moment, though, he carried a platter of eggs and sausages and the basket of bread over to the table and set them down.

"Eat. It will help." He smiled softly at Tonya. He deftly began to dish out the food, nodding for me to sit down. "Heartaches are a pain in the ass, aren't they?"

A ghost of a smile flickered at the corner of her lips. "Yeah, they are. And I can't even claim that he led me on. He really didn't. I just . . . I like him so much."

"Do you know who he's marrying?" I forked a bite of scrambled eggs into my mouth, salivating. Chai was a damned good cook, that was for sure.

She sniffled, pulling a tissue out of her pocket to wipe her eyes. "Vaguely. I mean, I know *who* she is. Her name is Beatrice, and she's around his age. I guess . . . if he had just mentioned at some point that he was seeing someone, I would have backed off sooner. Now I'm wondering how long he's known her. Was he going out with her when we went on our date? He had to have been, unless they had a whirlwind romance. I know that can happen, but . . ."

"Chances are, they had a fight around the time he went out with you. And then . . ." I lingered over the last.

"Made up? Yeah, that's what I thought, too. I guess I can't complain. He didn't string me along. He didn't ask me out again or even suggest the idea of it. On the date, I was having a great time but he didn't say anything to make me think he was interested in anything more than the evening out. I tried to tell myself he was just being a gentleman, but . . . I just . . . I like him so damned much. And I wanted to believe that he felt more for me than he said." And once again, a flurry of tears raced down her cheeks.

"So you came here to get away for a little while?" I was starting to piece things together.

She sniffled, then hiccupped. "Yes. They get married on Friday. I figured I'd stay here for a week. I don't want to be at the wedding. I don't even want to be in town."

"What did he say?"

"I have no idea." She blushed again. "I sent him an e-mail before I left Port Townsend. I haven't bothered to check if he's answered. I suppose I should, just to be grown-up about this."

I murmured a note of sympathy. "Humans have so many concerns about being grown-up. Emotions are emotions, whether you're an adult or a child. If you really want to, you can use my laptop to check your e-mail after breakfast."

"I brought mine." She let out a sigh. "But that's not the only reason I came down, Shimmer. Hell, I could have just driven down to Bainbridge Island for the week, if I only wanted to get away. No, I have a problem, and I'm hoping you and Alex can help me figure out if I'm imagining things, or if I'm really being stalked."

I blinked. This was out of the blue. "What? You're being stalked?"

The tears dried as a look of wariness crossed her face. "I think I might be. I was hoping that I could talk to you and everybody at the agency. Maybe hire you guys to find out if this is just my imagination or if I really do have a problem."

I nodded, sobering. "Yes, I think you'd better. Stalking is a dangerous crime, and if you really do have some creep following you, we need to figure out what we can do about it. Do you know who it is?"

She nodded. "Yeah, but I have never met him. I have no clue as to where he knows me from. I'll tell you about it tonight at the office, if that's all right?"

"I'll leave a note with Bette to schedule out the first hour for you so that she won't book any appointments until after." I pulled out my phone and texted Bette, then went back to my food.

We finished eating in silence, with Tonya yawning her way through the meal. I glanced at the clock. Four A.M. "Why don't you finish eating and then go to bed? The way you're yawning, I'm afraid you're going to keel over in your plate."

"Actually, I feel like I could, except that I'm also still

hyper from the trip and my mind is whirling. Why don't you show me your haunted house and then I'll go to bed after that? You're still awake, right?"

I nodded. "Given my bedtime is around two o'clock and I wake up at six or seven, yeah, I'm up for a while." I dug out a flashlight and strapped my dagger to my thigh, and, with Chai in tow, we headed across the street.

As we approached, Mary's house seemed so silent that my stomach lurched—too silent. *Unnaturally silent.* But the moment we stepped into the yard, the energy rose, whirling around us. The willow was restless—I could sense its wariness. A rustling through the undergrowth startled me, but when I closed my eyes, reaching out, I knew that neither human nor animal was responsible for the noise.

Tonya's tears had vanished, and she looked wide awake and alert. She glanced around the yard, pausing just past the gate. "There is so much going on here. I've never been in the Greenbelt Park District before, though it has a reputation with all the witches and psychics in the area. But the activity is amazing." She turned to the swing and gasped. "There's a child's ghost here—on the swing."

Chai and I both turned to look. I could see a wispy outline. Beside me, Chai stiffened. I had the feeling that, regardless of whether he could see the same thing I was, he knew something was there.

Another moment and he let out a long breath. "How young?"

"Ten . . . maybe twelve?" Tonya tilted her head to the side, watching the mist. "I don't know what you can see, but she's wearing a dress that I'd place . . . oh, pre-1940. Brown hair, braids, sad look on her face. She looks lonely."

I frowned. The image felt *heavy*, would be the best way I could describe it. Dark with an outline of light. And the sadness went so deep that it threatened to swallow me up. There was something behind the sadness, though. Beneath the surface . . . *close eyes, tune in, listen . . .*

*A hunter.* I jerked back as it flared, angry and hurt—like a wounded animal. As I jerked around, Tonya started forward. Her brown eyes were glassy, pools of coffee.

"Stop! It's not—"

But Chai was faster. He had hold of her arm, dragging her back from the swirl of mist. It rose up like a snake, let out a long hiss, and then vanished. Tonya blinked.

"What . . . crap!" She shook her head. "That thing got past my wards, and I thought they were pretty damned strong. What the hell?"

"Don't feel too bad. The Greenbelt Park District is a nest of strong spirits. More powerful people than you have been taken down here. I've heard some pretty frightening stories, and Alex has a few of his own." I motioned toward the porch. "Let's go find Mary. I hope that wasn't her."

Tonya raised her eyebrows, grinning. "If it was, I'd say we're in for a hell of a ride." She swung around me and resolutely marched up the stairs. Shapely, she was fit but curvy. Tonya was wearing jeans and a pale blue tank top beneath a denim jacket. Her dark blond hair was braided back into the French braid she'd been wearing the first time I met her. But what really set her apart was her energy. When Tonya walked into a room, if she wanted to she could own the place and everyone in it. I'd seen her take control of situations on a magical level, and it was pretty damned dramatic.

We followed her up the stairs, but Chai hit one of the soft spots at the top and his leg went straight through the boards. He let out a curse, but before we could get to him, he was out and on the porch proper, glaring at the broken wood.

"Be cautious—this whole place could fall down around our heads." He held out his hand and a soft glow of light emanated from his fingers. He blew on it and it grew to encompass the area around the door. "Let me check for weak spots before you go any farther."

"I was just here—"

"No, Little Sister." Most definitely a *Shut up and let me*

*do this* tone. When Chai was determined, there was no stopping him. So I stood back as he examined the wood for any further weak spots. After a moment, he nodded to the door. "Now, you may."

I opened the door and entered the narrow hallway. Tonya and Chai followed. I pointed to my right. "Living room, I think, or parlor. Not much in there. Tonya, can you sense anything?"

She peeked in, glancing around in the glow of Chai's light. "Nope—nothing that seems willing to show itself."

"The kitchen was where I met Mary. And the basement is where she tried to shove me. The creature behind her supposedly forced her to do it, but now . . ." I fell silent as we entered the kitchen. One glance around told me Mary wasn't around. Or at least, she wasn't showing herself. But as Tonya entered, the floor began to shake as knickknacks rattled against the walls.

"Earthquake?" Tonya turned to run back toward the door, but Chai caught hold of her.

"No, this is something supernatural. Stay here—don't get separated."

At that moment, the door to the basement swung open and out lurched the head of a giant anaconda, except that it was rumbling with a low roar. I then noticed its head also had a dragonlike look to it.

"Oh, hell. What the—" My question was cut off as the creature rammed forward and, with a quick thrust, hit my stomach with its head. It was in midair, propelling along with no legs, and felt far more solid than any ghost had a right to be.

It slammed me through the door, into the kitchen, lodging me against the corner of the range. The impact was so brutal that I couldn't even scream. Hell, I could barely breathe. As the shock of the metal meeting my back registered, Chai lunged, grabbing the creature around the middle. It twisted and—like a cat whipping its tail—volleyed the djinn against the wall.

At that moment, a noise from the front door took us all by surprise, the monster included.

Alex stood there, eyes blazing crimson. He launched himself down the hall, leaping to land astride the serpent. The creature let out another rumble as Alex clung to it, swinging down to face its underbelly. It tried to shake him off but he hung tight, climbing along its length like he might climb across a bridge made of a single rope. Chai caught hold of its tail and tried to hold it steady.

Tonya knelt beside me, helping me stand. The blow had been strong enough to knock the breath out of me, and my back had taken a beating when I hit the corner of the stove. I knew I was bleeding from where a sharp edge had cut me.

As Tonya dragged me aside, Alex leaned his head back as his fangs descended and he plunged them into the throat of the serpent. As he held on, his eyes blazing crimson, the creature tried to throw him, but Chai yanked on the tail—hard. He held up one hand and his scimitar appeared. I'd seen it once before, when we were in Port Townsend, when I had learned something disturbing about the djinn, but I hadn't asked him about it because the subject definitely had *Do not approach* written all over it.

Chai brought the huge blade down, slashing into the tail, and the serpent let out a loud hiss, struggling. But Alex held firm to the throat. As he pulled away, blood dripped down his chin, but it wasn't red—it was a pale green liquid, and it had a neon glow to it.

Tonya caught her breath. "Oh my Goddess . . ."

Another slash from Chai, this time more toward the center of the creature, and the blade went completely through, severing it in half. The serpent let out another sound, like that of air escaping from tires, and vanished from sight, including all of its blood, or whatever it had been dripping.

Alex landed on the floor and Chai reached down to give him a hand.

"Alex, are you . . . what was that stuff?" I hobbled over

to him, my side aching. If I had been human, I probably would be dead—or close to it.

Alex answered by turning to the side. He doubled over, vomiting up the fluid that had apparently passed for blood. As he clutched his stomach, I landed on my knees beside him, wrapping my arm around his shoulders as he choked up the rest of it.

Chai and Tonya approached, Chai keeping a close eye around us for any more surprise attacks. Tonya motioned for me to move to the side, and as I did, she placed a hand on the back of Alex's neck, and one on his forehead.

> *Clear the body, clear the blood,*
> *Clear the poison, clear the muck,*
> *Cleanse the aura, cleanse the air,*
> *Chase the toxins out of here.*

As her voice softened, Alex began to relax. One last cough and he hacked up a small ball—it was the same neon green as the serpent's blood, but it looked like an egg. As we stared at it, the shell began to fracture and then cracked fully, releasing a miniature version of the serpent. With one swift motion, Alex smashed it flat and then leaned back against the wall, shaking his head.

"You really have to be careful around here." The voice startled all of us, but as I turned, I knew who was there. "You never know what's going to pop up to take you off guard."

Mary, in all her ghostly flesh. She was smiling softly. "Thank you. I've been trying to evict that critter for some time, but I couldn't get to it because it was dawdling along over in the astral realm, while I exist in the spirit realm."

I smiled weakly at her, praying she wasn't going to go all psycho on us, but she just stood there, translucent and looking cheerful. I turned back to Alex. He pushed himself off the floor and pulled out a handkerchief, wiping his mouth.

"I'd kiss you but . . ." Somehow, the thought of kissing

him and getting some of that ectoplasmic goo in my mouth just didn't do much for me.

"Yeah, don't sweat it. Boy, do I need some mouthwash to rinse my mouth out with. Or real blood to wash the taste of that crap out of my mouth." He shook his head. "Wasn't expecting that, tell you for certain."

"Why are you here?" Now that the immediate danger was over, it occurred to me that Alex hadn't said a word about dropping over.

"I had a feeling . . . call it intuition. Plus, you left your tablet and notes at the office and I thought you might need them. I decided to drop them off on my way home." But his look told me there was another reason, one he didn't want to talk about in front of the others.

I nodded. "All right. But for now . . . this is Mary. She owned this house. I told you all about her."

As we turned to the ghost, she tilted her head to one side, smiling. She still looked like the welcoming, sweet old grandmother, but now I was wary. One: She still had tried to shove me down the stairs, even though she said it was the dark shadow that made her do it. And two: After that serpent? I didn't trust anything in this house. But Tonya stepped forward, staring straight at her.

"Mary," she said. "That's your name, isn't it?"

Mary nodded, staring at her as though she was surprised to be seen. "Yes, that's my name. Who are you?"

Tonya hesitated, a thoughtful look on her face, as though considering what to say. After a moment, she carefully edged a step closer to the ghost. "My name is Tonya. I'm a friend of Shimmer's." She pointed to the splatter of green plaid on the floor that Alex had upchucked. "Do you know what that creature was?"

For a moment I thought Mary wasn't going to answer, but after a long pause the ghost let out what sounded like a rustling sigh. "There are so many monsters in the area that it's hard to count them all. I've seen this creature around, though until now it has never bothered me. But it crosses through the yard at night, and I know it feeds on small animals. Which is why, if you have a pet, you should always keep it inside if you live in the Greenbelt Park District."

"Mary, is it true that you are here to help guard against the negative entities that make this place their home?" Tanya was being blunt, all right. I wondered how Mary would take it, but the ghost simply smiled and gave a brisk bob of the head.

"Oh yes, I consider it my civic duty."

Tonya turned to me. "Can we talk about this outside for a moment?"

It seemed odd to me that she would say this in front of Mary, but as I looked at the ghost, there was no sign on Mary's face that Tonya's comment had registered in any way. I shrugged. "All right. Alex and Chai, can you come with us?" I really didn't trust going out in the yard after dark, especially with what we had just encountered.

Alex glanced at my back. "Can you walk okay?"

I stretched gently, trying to ease the sharp ache under my shoulder blade. "I'll be fine. Dra— I'm tough, I'll heal up fast."

"If you're sure. Just all of you, be careful on the porch, I noticed a large hole in the middle of it when I came up the steps."

Chai laughed. "Yeah, we found out on the way in—the hard way." He led, followed by Tonya, then me, and lastly— Alex. When we were on the porch Tonya carefully shut the door behind us.

"Mary is the real deal, except . . . there's something wrong with her and she doesn't know it. There's a darker spirit behind her and I think it's playing her. I think you're right—she's trapped. Whether it's because she trapped herself, or whether this darker spirit is keeping her here, I'd like to set her free. She may think she's a spiritual warrior, placed here to fight against darker entities, but honestly, I think that she's the only one who believes that."

Alex cocked his eyebrow and looked at her, a quizzical

expression on his face. "Do you mean that spirits can be . . . kidnapped?"

Tonya bit her lip, then shook her head. "Not exactly, but . . . in a way. She's not free to leave—something seems to be holding her here. It wasn't that snake . . . dragon . . . whatever. But the creature was a manifestation of a darker evil that's lurking in there. At first I thought Mary was being possessed by a walk-in, but now . . . I am pretty sure she isn't being possessed by anything."

"Walk-in?" I had never heard the term before.

"The term is commonly used when a spirit possesses a living being and affects their behavior. But it can also happen to other ghosts. Especially ones who feel like they never did enough in life, or who feel they must stay around to protect others. These guilt-ridden feelings make them vulnerable to attack—spiritual attack, that is." Tonya cautiously walked over to the edge of the railing, avoiding soft spots in the porch. She leaned against one of the columns and stared out into the night. "Mary seems like a sweet person, so what could she have done that would make her feel guilty enough so that she felt she had to stay here?"

Alex cleared his throat. "We can do a little research and find out. After all, we are a PI firm."

"I'd like that, if we can." I stood beside Tonya, also staring out into the vast yard. Across the street, my house glowed with ambient light from the aquariums inside. As I looked up the block, I began to realize just how isolated I was from other people. Few of the houses on my street were occupied, and I hadn't bothered to get to know anyone who lived in my neighborhood even though I had been here for over five months.

Tonya must have caught my mood, because she looked at me and placed a hand lightly on my shoulder. "This neighborhood feels so deserted. There aren't many people around here, are there?"

I shook my head. "No, but this is the only area of the city

that I could afford to live in. And truly, it suits me in many ways. I like having friends, but it's better if I keep to myself so that others don't find out exactly what I am." I knew what kind of trouble it would cause if word got out that I was a dragon. Better to let the neighbors—such as they were— think that I was Fae. I was working on building up my cover as a water sprite, although that seemed ludicrous given my size, but none of the humans had to know.

Alex turned back to look at the door. "So what do we do about Mary? Do you need to perform some sort of exorcism? And if she is being restrained, whatever is keeping her here isn't going to like having you try to break his . . . her . . . its hold, now are they?"

Tonya laughed. It was one of the first real laughs I had heard from her since she arrived. "I need to think about this for a little bit. I'm actually not entirely sure how to go about it. But I know there has to be some way around this. I just have to figure it out."

"Mary is very adamant about having someone who loves the house here," I said. "I wish we could clear it and find someone to live in it. But I don't even know if the house is for sale. I found an old sign, but the print has worn away and the house was unlocked when I came over to check it out." Pausing, I glanced at Tonya. "Do you think that Mary knows you're a witch?"

She paused. "That, I don't know. I'm not sure if she was able to see through me or not. I suppose, if there's something restraining her, then when I come back it might show itself. I wonder what it would do if I decided to buy this house?" She said it offhandedly, but I jumped.

"Do you think you might want to? I'd love having you for a neighbor."

Tonya laughed again, shaking her head. "I was just thinking aloud. I have a house, even though I'm uncomfortable there right now."

"Well, whatever you decide to do," Alex said, "can we

make it quick? There's something I want to discuss with Shimmer before I have to leave for home. Sun will rise in a bit."

I decided to make an arbitrary decision. "Let's see what happens if we tell Mary that Tonya is thinking of buying the house. Maybe it will prod her captor into coming out of hiding if he . . . it . . . thinks a human's going to take over here again."

"Sounds good to me." Tonya opened the door. "I'm always up for a psychic experiment."

I entered the house, ignoring Chai's pleas that I stop.

"I can't wait to see what this does," Alex said, rolling his eyes. But he swung in behind, following us in. Chai grumbled but acceded.

We traipsed into the kitchen. Mary was still there, shimmering in the dim room. Her hands were folded in front of her, and she looked like she had all the time in the world. Which, I suppose, was true enough.

"Mary?"

Mary turned to me and smiled. "Shimmer, you haven't introduced your other friends to me."

I suddenly realized that a ghost was berating my manners and broke out laughing. The situation seemed so surreal that, for a moment, I wasn't sure exactly what to say. Finally, I motioned to Alex.

"May I introduce you to Alex? He's my boss. Tonya is a friend of ours; she lives in Port Townsend. And this is Chai. He's my brother."

She tilted her head, studying us. "There isn't much of a family resemblance."

I repressed a snicker. "That's because he's my brother in all but blood. He watches out for me. Mary, I wanted to let you know that Tonya will be buying this house. She is going to live here and take care of it." Now to see how Mary reacted.

*One beat. Two.*

Then Mary slowly turned to Tonya, beaming. "How

lovely. I think you'll do nicely, and it will be so nice to have company again."

Tonya met Mary's gaze. I swore that I could see the wheels turning in her mind. "I'm glad you approve. I would hate to think of moving in here and upsetting you."

Mary just let out a tinkle of laughter. In that moment a chill ran up my spine and I realized that there was far more to her than we knew. But she smiled, and said, "Oh, child. I'm not upset at all. In fact, I think we're going to have a *wonderful* time together as roommates."

A simple sentence, but it shook me to the core and Tonya's face went white. I murmured a quick good-bye, and we headed for the door. As we crossed the street back to my house, I knew then that Mary—or whatever spirit might be lurking in the shadows pulling her strings—was a dangerous predator. And we were walking right into her lair.

# CHAPTER 9

Once we were back at my house I locked the door and closed the curtains, but I still couldn't get rid of the feeling that we were being watched. The realization that my neighbor across the street was a dangerous spirit really threw a damper into my evening. As we sat around the kitchen table, Chai fretted. Snookums jumped into his lap, and Chai absently petted the cat.

Alex drummed his fingers on the table. "I'm not sure where you wrestled that thing up from, but it needs to go back wherever it came from. She might look like a friendly old grandma, but I can guarantee you she's not."

"He's right." Tonya rummaged through my cupboards and finally came out with a package of cookies. "I'm beginning to think that Mary has secrets we have no clue about. She feels like a predator, but I don't think she sees herself that way. And usually, the people who are dangerous but truly don't think they are tend to be psychopaths."

"Can a spirit be a psychopath?" Alex asked.

"Oh yeah, they most certainly can be." Tonya opened the package of Oreos.

"What do you need to go up against her?" I had seen Tonya in action up in Port Townsend, and even though she was human, her magic was powerful. She worshipped the goddess Hecate, and that magic was nothing to mess around with.

Tonya bit into the cookie, then leaned back in her chair and chewed thoughtfully. After a moment she swallowed. "What makes you think I'm going to go up against her?"

I blinked. "I . . . I . . ." Truth was, she had never said she was willing to take on Mary. "I guess I just assumed . . ." I felt like a fool now.

But Tonya let out a laugh. "I'll do what I can to help you. But first, I need to understand what it is that we are actually dealing with. I'll have to lay out a spread with my tarot cards and see what I can find out. And we need somebody to research the house and land. Find out what was there before and what might still be there now. But right now, I'm exhausted. Whatever that snake-thing was that came at us did nothing to help. The adrenaline is wearing off, and I really need to sleep. Do you mind if I go to bed? I don't want to be rude."

"Please, go to sleep. Can you find your way up to the library? The blankets are in the sideboard that's against the window. Do you need me to show you the way again?" I started to stand, but she waved for me to sit down again.

"No, it's not like you live in a mansion where I could get lost." With a smile, she gave Alex a wave. "I'll see you tonight at the office." Turning to Chai, she winked. "Night, Chai. Sleep well."

He smiled back, watching as she left the room. As she trudged up the stairs, sounding as tired as she looked, I wondered whether it was safe to have her here, considering the spirit across the street. Mary seemed to have taken a fascination with her. But whether Tonya was here or in a hotel probably made no difference. If the ghost had latched hold of her, it wouldn't matter where she was.

I turned to Chai, thinking of how best to phrase my thoughts. "I think it would be best if we keep a close eye on Tonya. It occurs to me that Mary—whatever she is—might have tried to attach to her. I'm remembering the land wight and how it corded into Degoba."

The djinn gave me a thoughtful nod. "Good point. And since you need your sleep, I am going to keep watch over her. And no"—he laughed with a wink—"I'm not doing you a favor. I want to do this."

"I love how well you understand me." I glanced over at Alex, who looked preoccupied. "You wanted to talk to me about something?"

Alex glanced at Chai. "I do, but it's rather private."

Chai took the hint. "I'm going to go keep a watch on Tonya. I promise not to peek when she's undressing." He headed out of the kitchen and up the stairs.

After he left, I turned to Alex and leaned across the table, taking his hands in mine. "So, what's so important that you had to come over here at this time in the morning? I know I'm charming but I'm not *that* much fun." I laughed as I said it, but he didn't join in.

"After you left the office, I got a call from Glenda. She wants to see me. She says she knows she went too far, and that she did it because she still loves me." He was watching me closely and I knew he was waiting for me to react.

My gut twisted, tying itself up in a knot. I tried to read his expression but it was guarded. I managed to keep calm, however. "And what are your thoughts about that?" was all I said, when I actually wanted to shout, *Are you crazy?*

My expression must've shown in my face because Alex started to laugh. "Oh love, you don't think I am going to fall for her hijinks, do you? I just need to talk to her and make her understand it's over between us."

"Hijinks? Hijinks? The woman's a flaming lunatic.

What's she going to do next time? Burn the building down? She left a silver stake on your desk, for the sake of the gods!" I stared at him, unable to believe he was being so blind.

Alex frowned. "I know she is reckless, but I don't think she'd try to deliberately harm us—"

"Really? We are seriously having this conversation? And why do you need to see her at all? You *know* she's just going to try something else." As much as I cared for Alex, sometimes I thought he was a lot more gullible than he'd ever admit to being. That was not a word I would usually apply to a vampire, but when it came to Alex and women, he seemed to have a blind spot.

"I need to see her because I know I can talk sense into her if we sit down and talk face to face." He sounded a little put out. "You might be a little more enthusiastic that she's willing to talk at all."

"Enthusiastic? Alex . . ." But I couldn't even continue the thought. There was no way in hell that I would ever trust Glenda to be anything but trouble. Succubi had volatile natures as it was; they didn't need a reason to lash out. There were a few exceptions, of course, but Glenda wasn't one of them.

I took a deep breath, letting it out slowly, then tried again.

"You seriously believe you can calm her down with a little chat? Alex, you *know* what she's like. How many things of yours has she broken over just the past few months? How many temper tantrums has she thrown? You were in a relationship with the woman for years. By now I think you should have a pretty good idea of what her reaction is going to be."

Alex just stared at me, the smile vanishing from his face. "Shimmer, I know you're trying to help, but I think you're underestimating my influence. It's obvious that Glenda's still in love with me. Yes, we had a rocky relationship, and yes, it went south months ago. Neither she nor I was able to admit it. And now, she's angry and hurt, even though deep inside, she knows it was for the best. The least I can do is meet her in person and talk her through this."

And that was that. There was nothing more I could say. But the fact that Alex could brush off what she had done so quickly pissed me off. I jumped to my feet, striding over to the sink because I couldn't sit there and face him when he was being so stupid. After a moment, I turned to face him, leaning back against the counter.

"Get real, Alex. Open your eyes. Glenda's out for revenge. She's not upset that you broke up with her, she's upset that *any* man broke up with her. She doesn't want you, but she doesn't want me to have you either. And she's going to make trouble for both of us. Mark my words."

Pushing his chair back, Alex came to his feet. "When you're in this sort of a mood I can't deal with you. I have to go. It's getting close to sunrise. But, like it or not, Shimmer—I *am* going to talk to Glenda." He glanced at the clock. "And I don't want to hear any arguments over my decision."

As he headed for the door, I shot out, "Then you'd better be wearing a spike-proof vest, because trust me—she's going to be ready when you come."

He glanced over his shoulder, shaking his head. "Shimmer, you've got a lot to learn about relationships. I'll talk to you later." He didn't even blow me a kiss on his way out.

As **Alex left,** I realized I was shaking. This was the first big fight we had had since we had paired up. When I had been with Carter, he and I had never fought. Not until the sorcerer charmed me, but even then, Carter and I both knew that we weren't in it for the long haul. I thought about giving him a call—we were still good friends and maybe he could help me make sense of everything. But if I did, Alex might misinterpret it. My thoughts were interrupted by the phone.

I glanced at the Caller ID on my cell. Stacy. Relieved to

see her name, I answered. "Hey, Stacy, how are you? How's the bronchitis? I miss you."

Stacy's voice was raw, but she sounded stronger than she had the last time I had talked to her. "Shimmer, I miss you, too. I'm trying to stick to my usual schedule so it isn't so much of an adjustment when I go back to work. I'm sick of being sick. I thought I'd give you a call and see how things are going. I had a feeling something is wrong and I wanted to make sure you're doing okay."

"Yeah, I'm okay. Alex and I just had a fight thanks to Glenda. She's being a pain in the ass. And I've got a ghost living across the street who is turning out to be a trouble-maker, as well. My friend Tonya, from Port Townsend—remember I told you about her? She's here visiting. I'd like for you to meet her—I think you would get along well."

"Men always bring headaches with them, whether they're human or vampire. That's why I don't date right now. The last boyfriend I had was a leech and I kicked his ass to the curb. I'd like to meet your friend, too. If she still here when I get well, we can get together and have a girls' night. I figure I'll be up and running again in a couple days. The antibiotics the doctor gave me kicked in and I can already tell they're going to do the trick. It drives me nuts to be flat on my back and not working, and Mama is doing her best to help out, but I hate putting her to the trouble because she has enough problems of her own."

Stacy's mother was disabled, and Stacy did her best to help. Emily had multiple sclerosis; she had apparently developed it shortly after Stacy's brother was born. He was in his early twenties now and going to college, but Emily's disease was beginning to progress at a rapid pace. So Stacy worked two jobs and lived at home to help out her mother. She also helped put her brother through school. He was on a full-tuition scholarship and worked after class. Without that, Stacy had confided in me, there was no way they could have paid for him to go.

"Do you need anything? I can run over there if you need me to get some groceries for you. Bette will drive me." Stacy worked her butt off, and now that she was sick, I wanted to help if I could.

She paused to cough. "Are you sure?"

I could hear the hesitation in her voice. "Of course I'm sure. I'd love to help and it's no trouble at all. I promise."

Sounding almost on the verge of tears, she agreed. "That would be wonderful, I would appreciate that so much. My brother is so busy right now with exams and his job. I don't want to bother him any more than I need to. If you could pick up some soup and some prepackaged frozen dinners, it would help a lot. That way we can pop them in the oven and Mama won't have to try to cook."

I smiled. "I'll be there in a couple of hours. You just get some rest and I'll call you before I arrive." As I dialed Bette's number, I wished I could make *all* our problems go away with a shopping trip.

Bette came right over. "I needed to get away from Dent, so this solves that little issue. And I'm happy to help. Stacy's a good girl," she reassured me. "I don't think I'm going to be keeping Dent around much longer."

I slid into the passenger seat, looking longingly at the steering wheel. She caught my look.

"Oh, no you don't. You finish getting your license in Ralph's car. I'm not trusting you with my baby." Bette was exceptionally protective of her car, and she would only ever say that it was a gift from someone who had been very dear to her.

I sighed. "Fine. I'll be getting my license in a week, and then you and Ralph can go car shopping with me." I leaned back against the leather, which was smooth as a baby's bottom. I had no clue what a baby's bottom felt like, but I'd heard the expression and it sounded good. "So, why are you done with Dent?"

"He's nice enough, but he's clingy and he's starting to

talk marriage. And that's when I skedaddle." She grinned at me, her cigarette hanging low on her lip as she puffed and talked at the same time.

"You really aren't ever getting married, are you?"

Bette snorted. "Me? I'm a Melusine. It's a wonder we bother with relationships at all, but I admit—I like having a man to hang around with. But then they get all possessive and they start to talk about the altar and at that point, I'm done. Because once a man has it in his head he wants to marry you, it's hard to ever maintain the status quo. They may say they can handle a casual relationship, but truth is, men need women more than we need them."

"Alex and I had a fight." I didn't like admitting it, but Bette had been around the block more times than I could even imagine and I trusted her judgment. "Glenda wants to meet with him, to *talk things over* as she put it. She told him she's still in love with him. He fell for it and we got in an argument. He thinks she's on the up-and-up and that he can talk some sense into her."

"He's a man. No man I ever knew could talk sense into a succubus. Just like no woman can ever control an incubus. They always have the upper hand because they can manipulate your hormones." She shrugged. "He's going to be in a world of hurt if he lets her worm her way back in with some sob story."

I stared at the dash. "You think . . . do you think he still . . ." Even thinking the words made me cringe.

"Has feelings for her?" She cast a quick glance my way. "No, sugar pie, I don't. But I think Alex's Achilles' heel is his sympathy. If she can get him to feel sorry for her, he'll let her back into his life and she can work on him subliminally."

My stomach sank like a lead balloon.

"Damn it." I pressed my lips together and looked out the window. It was nearly six A.M. and the daylight world was just beginning to wake up. Bette let me stew in silence as we pulled into the local Wholemart Grocery. As we headed into the store, I grabbed a cart. If Alex was stupid enough to let Glenda have that much influence on him, then nothing I could say would do any good.

Bette, a cart of her own in hand, joined me. As we strolled through the aisles, I tossed cans of soup and boxed meals into the cart, trying to focus on the job at hand. Stacy wasn't up to cooking and her mother wasn't strong enough to do a lot anymore. But heating up prepared foods? Easy enough. Baked beans, soup, boxed mac 'n' cheese, rice pilaf mix, prepared hamburger patties and stuffed chicken breasts that just needed to be fried up or roasted . . . some frozen entrées—lasagna and the like.

Bette, on the other hand, was filling her cart with the makings of what appeared to be a sumptuous Italian dinner. Wide flat noodles, tomatoes, basil, ground beef and lamb, French bread, olive oil spread, ricotta, mozzarella, parmesan . . .

"You going to invite Tonya and me over to help you eat all that?" I grinned at her.

Her eyes crinkled. "Actually, this is my prebreakup dinner for Dent. He loves my cooking. Might as well give him one last nosh. But I'll be happy to make up a second batch for you to take home tomorrow morning."

My mouth watered. Bette could cook. Bette could cook like a champ. "Yeah, that would be awesome. Not too much garlic, though. Alex can smell it on me a mile away."

"You'll notice I don't have any in my cart. Onions, I will use, but because I work with Alex, I long ago gave up on garlic." She paused, in the middle of the baking aisle, and turned to me. "You need to understand something about Alex. It's frustrating and kind of makes you want to kill the guy, but the fact is, he loves women. I am not saying he's a horndog. Actually, it's the opposite. Alex has a hero complex. He likes to rescue women. It's in his nature and he doesn't realize it. In fact, he'd deny it if you told him. But I've seen it time and again. That's how we met."

I hadn't heard this story before. "How so?"

She started pushing her cart forward again. "You know I'm from Greece, right?"

I nodded. Bette had mentioned that she was originally from the Greek islands, and the way she hinted, she had been alive for a lot longer than Alex. Other than that, she never spoke of her past.

"I was traveling the world when I met Alex. I had taken a boat to Australia after a spate of bad luck. When I arrived in Sydney, I met Alex one night in a bar. He was hanging out with some friends when I came in. Some perv tried to force me to kiss him, and before I could, Alex decked him a good one. We got to talking, and ended up walking all night long and getting to know one another. But I think . . . the fact that he 'rescued' me set us up to talk in the first place."

I stopped at the deli to grab chicken and jo-jo potatoes for dinner. I added some coleslaw for Tonya and a lemon meringue pie. Then, realizing we'd need something when we woke up in the evening, I added a box of doughnuts and several pints of berries. I had bacon and sausage at home, so that would be perfect.

"Do you think . . . do you think he feels he rescued me?" The thought nagged at me. Yes, the Wing-Liege had dumped me on Alex's doorstep, but that wasn't quite the same as rescuing. Was it? My thoughts must have been apparent on my face, because Bette turned to me.

"You don't owe Alex your life, if that's what you think— and he doesn't for the moment believe anything of the sort. Yes, he agreed to take you on, but the Wing-Liege wouldn't have forced the issue if he had said no. And you pull your weight around the office, girl. Never think that you don't. Alex respects you." She added a tub of whipped topping to my cart. "But the problem is that Alex still feels responsible for Glenda. She managed to brainwash him at the start, and I imagine she's going to try to reinforce that. Once she gets him off guard, she'll be out to do whatever she can to make *you* miserable."

"Chai thinks I'm her target, too." We headed toward the cashier.

"You are. Listen to him." And with that, the conversation was over and we checked out, then headed to Stacy's.

The house Stacy shared with her mother and brother was up in Shoreline—which, while it was its own incorporated city, was still part of Seattle as far as general opinion was concerned. They lived on 202nd Place, off Richmond Road, in a house that her family had owned for forty-five years.

Bette and I carried the bags to the front door. A moment later, Stacy answered, a shawl wrapped tightly around her shoulders. She looked like hell and her cough was deep and phlegmy.

We carried the food into the kitchen. "No, you don't. You sit down and tell me where you want these," I said as Stacy moved to unpack the bags.

"Fine, bossy. How much do I owe you?"

I shrugged. "I have no idea. I already owed you for two dinners and a bunch of coffees. Call it even?"

She frowned, but then, with a soft sigh, gave in. "I'm too tired to argue it. And truth is, with me being off work—and with no sick leave—this is taking a bite out of my pay. Thanks, Shimmer. But I get to buy dinner next time."

"Deal." I tucked the groceries in the cupboards, fridge, and freezer. "What do you want to eat? While we're here, we might as well heat something up for you."

Bette shooed us into the living room. "She needs some good hot soup and tea. The pair of you leave it to me and go talk."

I glanced around. I had been to Stacy's house once, but

only briefly. She usually stopped in at my house when she got off work, so we wouldn't disturb her mother. Speaking of . . .

"Where's Emily?"

"She's still asleep. She had a rough night." She glanced at the clock. It was seven thirty.

"Right." I waited until Stacy had curled up in the rocking chair, then handed her a blanket. She wrapped it over her, leaning her head back against the cushion. Her coughs were jarring, but I knew that was the nature of bronchitis.

I wandered over to the mantel. The living room felt weathered, but it was cozy, and the fireplace mantel was covered with family pictures. One was a picture of three women. I recognized one as a much younger Stacy. The second woman was, I thought, Emily. The third was an elderly woman with dark, rich skin and salt-and-pepper hair. "Who's the older woman?"

"That's Grandma Hailey. Hailey Noble—she was the first woman in our family to own property of her own. Grandpa Jack died young. I think Mom said he died in 1968—a bad car crash. Grandma Hailey took their savings and the insurance money and bought this house. Mom's sister, Crystal, is married to a lawyer and living in New York."

"Is your grandmother still alive?"

Stacy nodded, interrupting with a coughing fit. After a drink of water, she continued.

"Grandma Hailey decided she wanted to travel the world. When Mom was pregnant with Martin and began to develop multiple sclerosis, our father ran off. So Grandma deeded the house over to Mom in a trust that stipulates it will always remain in Mom's name. When she passes it down to one of us, we have to agree that if we are married, our spouse—or any fiancé—has to sign a prenup excluding it from community property. The house is paid for, and Grandma Hailey pays the property taxes, so Mom will always have a place to live." She frowned, toying with the edge of the blanket.

Her mother's condition weighed heavy on her mind. That, I had known from the first day we met.

"I wish I knew more about my relatives." Once again, the feeling of being isolated—a random blip in the universe—stole over me. "How far back can you trace your family?"

Stacy glanced over at me. "Back to 1840. Great-Great-Great-Great-Grandmother Hessie—4G Hessie we call her, to make it easier—was a slave in South Carolina. After the Civil War, she and her husband made their way up to New York. It wasn't until 1935 that my Great-Great-Grandpa Thomas got a job out here in Seattle, working on the docks as the city began to grow as a major port. He brought his family west, and our family has been here ever since."

I let out a slow breath. I wasn't sure how to approach the fact that her ancestor had been a slave. I knew that among humans, race was still a touchy issue—though the influx of Fae and Supes had kind of eclipsed it. A number of the hate brigade found it easier to target the Supes than the blacks or Asians or Hispanics. The differences were more obvious, and the *us-versus-them* mentality liked to latch onto those things. Then again, when I looked at my own kind, prejudice wasn't so much based on color—though that played a distinct part in the hierarchy—but lineage.

"Actually, when I think about it, my kind are as racist as humans. Though it's a bit different, it's still based on color and lineage. Whites are the low dragons on the ladder . . . silver at the top." Shaking my head, I shrugged.

At that moment, Bette carried in a tray with a steaming mug of soup on it, along with some buttered toast and a cup of peppermint tea. "Here you go." She edged it down onto a TV tray, then pulled it to where Stacy could reach it. "Get some of the broth in you, at least. And the tea."

Stacy gave her a wan smile. "Thank you. I really didn't expect you guys to wait on me hand and foot."

"Of course you didn't. But we're doing it anyway." I motioned to Bette and she settled in on the other end of the sofa. "Tell us if we're keeping you from sleeping. You need to rest."

"The company does me good. I love my mother but to be honest, we're very different people and I need somebody else to talk to. And Martin is so busy with his schoolwork that I don't want to take up his time." She ladled up a spoonful of the soup and tasted it, then smiled. "I love this brand—it always reminds me of my childhood."

As Stacy set to eating, Bette asked, "What is your brother studying?"

"He wants to be a lawyer—he's studying law and politics. And that's not cheap. He's on a full scholarship right now at the University of Washington, going for his degree in criminal justice. Then he'll apply to law school at the UW. By then, we're hoping he'll qualify for some sort of internship or scholarship or some way to help him pay for it. He's a straight-A student." She ate one piece of the toast, coughing as she swallowed, and then finished the soup. "I think I'm getting sleepy now."

"That's because you should be in bed." The voice from the door echoed through the room—a rich, throaty voice. The woman it belonged to was in a wheelchair. She was dressed in a pair of olive green trousers and a rust-colored V-neck sweater. It was Emily, Stacy's mother.

She was a handsome woman, stately, with short curly hair cropped close to her head, and she looked tired but still had a smile on her face. "Shimmer, good morning." Her gaze traveled over Bette, and I caught the faintest glimpse of disapproval, but she merely nodded and extended her hand. "I'm Emily, Stacy's mother."

Bette crossed to meet her. "I'm Bette. I work with Shimmer."

"Mom, you should have called me—" Stacy started to say, but Emily cut her off.

"Nonsense. If I needed you, I would have called you. I

had a rough night, but I'm feeling a bit better now." She sniffed. "Do I smell soup?"

"Would you like some? We brought over some groceries so Stacy wouldn't have to go shopping." I started to stand but she waved me back into my chair.

"Relax. I can get it myself." She glanced over at Stacy, then held her finger to her lips and nodded. Stacy had dozed off. "I wish I could get her into bed without waking her."

While Emily didn't know I was a dragon, she did know I wasn't human. "I can take care of that, if you'll let me." I carefully lifted Stacy and carried her back to her bedroom— the house was ranch style, all on one level—and tucked her in. Stacy must have been exhausted because she didn't even flutter her eyes.

When I returned to the living room, Bette was deep in conversation with Emily. They were discussing some TV show I'd never heard of, with a fierceness that made me wonder if I shouldn't be watching it.

"I tell you right now, they never should have gotten rid of Agent Gideon." Emily's voice was firm, and she shot Bette a cool, scathing look.

"He wanted to leave the show—it wasn't like they could hog-tie him to the set. And you have to admit, Rossi isn't all that hard on the eyes," Bette parried, winking.

"Whoever Rossi and Gideon are, they need to wait. Bette, we have to go. I should get my groceries home before anything goes bad. Emily, it's always wonderful to talk to you. Call if you need anything. We all want Stacy up and running around again, and it's no trouble to drop over if you need help." I jerked my head toward Bette. "Move it, woman."

Bette snorted. "Hold your britches, sugar pie." To Emily, she said, "It was nice to meet you. Maybe we should have a *Criminal Minds* marathon sometime. Watch from the beginning."

"I'd like that. Stacy has no time for TV, and my son . . .

he's immersed in his schoolwork. None of my book club members share my interest in crime shows." By the tinge in her voice, I could tell that Emily didn't get much company.

Bette handed her one of her business cards. "Absolutely. Call me when you're interested. I own all the seasons so far on DVD. We can settle ourselves in front of television with something good to eat and continue debating the merits of Rossi versus Gideon."

And with that, we were off. As we headed back toward my house, I thought about the friends I had made since I had been exiled Earthside, and was suddenly very glad I had stolen from Greanfyr, even if it had put me in danger.

# CHAPTER 10

By the time I woke up and began getting ready for work, Tonya was awake. She had slept well and was nose-deep in her laptop, waiting at the table. Chai had made breakfast out of the food I'd brought—sliced strawberries and whipped cream with doughnuts. My mouth watered. Mostly, I preferred meat; but now and then sweets caught my fancy. I slid into a chair and snagged a strawberry from the plate, popping it into my mouth.

Tonya looked up. "I've been looking up the past of the house across the street. There are some interesting facts I found out about Mary that she didn't tell us."

"Who was she? There really was a Mary?" I began filling my plate as Chai brought me a cup of coffee. He refilled Tonya's mug and then sat down with us.

"Oh, there was a Mary all right, but the story she gave you isn't quite the story that actually played out. Mary Smith—yes, I know, laugh." She paused, grinning.

"Why should I laugh?" I was confused as to what was so funny.

"*Mary Smith?* Oh, right . . . over here, at least in this country, Smith is one of the most common surnames there is and a lot of people use it as an alias when they don't want people to know who they are. Mary's also a common name for a girl. So Mary Smith is . . ."

"Like an assumed name. Got it." I filed the information away for future reference. It wasn't so much the big differences that caught me up, but the small ones.

"Right. Anyway, Mary Smith lived in that house, all right, and she did have children there, but in 1938, when she was forty, she killed her husband and her children with an axe. The baby boy was never found, but they assume she killed him, too. Mary Smith is a lovely, sweet axe murderer. She claimed that they were demons in disguise and that she had to kill them to save their lives. She managed to cop an insanity plea, though most researchers are fairly sure she was sane as you or I."

"So our ghost was an axe murderess? Shades of Lizzie Borden." Chai shook his head.

I wasn't sure who Lizzie Borden was but kept my mouth shut.

Tonya nodded, scanning the article. "According to this, Mary was committed to the Greenbelt Park Asylum and kept in the ward for the criminally insane. Which is smack central in your Greenbelt Park District—37501 Sythica Street. Apparently the asylum owner and his son spent fifty years tormenting the patients until there was a revolt. A group of patients seized control of the institution, killed the administrator, and slaughtered a bunch of other inmates. Then one of them, Silas Johanson, who was also a murderer, managed to burn the place to the ground by . . . well, it looks like he screwed around with the boiler in the basement and it blew up. Massive gas explosion. Three hundred fifty-seven patients died, along with twenty-five guards and twenty-four staff members. This took place in 1959, so Mary would have been sixty-one, but she probably didn't age well."

I tried to imagine the mayhem, but the images didn't set well. "So Mary either burned to death or was killed by another inmate."

"Right."

"Do you think she remembers what happened? Maybe she's tried to blot it out because she realized what she did to her family and it pushed her over the edge. I'm not sure if ghosts can have PTSD, but . . ."

"I don't know," Tonya said, scanning the rest of the article. "She maintained to the very end that she didn't kill her baby boy. But she couldn't tell them where to find him."

I thought over what she said. "So does it stand to pass that all people who are dangerous or psychopathic in life remain that way after death? There's so much to this that I don't understand."

Chai shrugged. "That, I would like to know, too. I make it a point to have as little to do with spirits as I can. But I will tell you this: I feel like you just uncovered the tip of the iceberg about what's going on over there. I don't often get spooked, but right now I'm spooked."

I turned to Tonya. "How far away are we from the Greenbelt Park Asylum? I never heard about it till now."

Tonya pulled up Mapsi—one of the newest, best maps programs on the Internet. "You are seven blocks away from what's left. The place was pretty much destroyed. Not very far from here, really. As to your questions about spirits keeping their natures after death, I don't think anybody knows the answer to that. Unfortunately, this isn't *Beetlejuice* and we don't have a handbook to the afterlife."

I glanced at the clock. "I have to get to work. You were going to come with me to tell us about your stalker?"

She closed her laptop. "Yeah, but can we take breakfast with us? It was too good not to have another doughnut." As she gathered her things, Chai made up a boxed lunch for us, along with more doughnuts, berries, and cream, and I slid into my jacket and made sure I had everything I needed.

"Bring your laptop. You can always hang out in the office and use our Wi-Fi."

A honking from out front told us Bette had arrived and we dashed out of the door. As we jammed ourselves in the car, I wondered what kind of mood Alex would be in, and I hoped our argument was over and done with. I really didn't want to deal with a testy vampire tonight.

Ralph and Alex were waiting in the conference room. As Bette and I headed in, followed by Tonya, I saw that they were dressed to head out.

"What gives?"

"We thought we had a lead on the salamander, but it ducked back in the sewers. That thing is going to eat somebody before we can catch it." Ralph sounded pissed—so much so that I had the feeling it was over something beyond just losing track of a big fiery lizard.

I chanced a sideways glance at Alex. He returned my look rather coolly, I thought, but it could have just been my imagination. Whatever the case, we needed to get some work done and we had to be on speaking terms to manage it.

"So what next? We head out to Sultan to check on Stone Weaver, before it gets pitch-black?"

"Right. Let's get the daily meeting over with first." Alex motioned for us to sit down, nodding at Tonya. "All right, you mentioned you had a problem when you first arrived. Have a seat and tell us about it. Ralph—notes, please."

"Will do." Ralph began to type as she talked.

"As I told Chai and Shimmer, I think I'm being stalked, but I'm not sure. Maybe it's my imagination but one way or another, I need to find out. If I am, then I need to put a stop to it. If not? Then I can rest my mind. But you guys have a pressing matter, it sounds like. I'd rather you take care of it first. I'll be in town several days, so there's always tomorrow night if we run out of time tonight." She smiled, then added, "And I wanted to ask if you minded if I tag along? I really don't feel like sitting alone with my thoughts."

I glanced up, realizing that Alex didn't know about Degoba's marriage. I'd fill him in later.

Alex glanced at the clock. "Since it's going to take so long to get out there, fine by me. We have nothing else on the slate tonight except the salamander and that's at a standstill for now, so let's head out to Sultan and track down the Elemental Fae." He picked up his tablet and notebook. "Bette, hold down the fort while we're gone. If anybody wants to talk business, make an appointment for tomorrow night."

She nodded. "I hope you find him. Stone's a good man. He's shy, and not very forthcoming, but he's a good-hearted soul."

And with that, we were off, into the Range Rover, and on our way to North Sultan.

Rather than take the freeway, since it was past rush hour, we decided to take the more direct route. From our office, which was also on the outskirts of the Greenbelt Park District, we pulled onto Highway 522 and headed east, around the northern edge of Lake Washington. Though it was rainy and dark, the traffic was light and we made good time. We passed through the upper Eastside—a group of Seattle bedroom communities composed of a number of suburbs. The drive was about forty-five minutes during light traffic, and we were making decent time.

As we reached Woodinville, Ralph let out a sigh from the backseat he was sharing with Tonya.

"I have to get something off my chest." He didn't sound happy at all.

I glanced over my shoulder. "What's up?"

"Remember my parents came to visit? Well, they've

given me an ultimatum." He shifted uncomfortably. "My brother ran off—he left his wife and kids for another woman. He turned against the Pack, and he's shamed our family. My parents disowned him, but there's only one thing that can be done to restore honor for the family."

Alex let out a low grunt. "If it's what I think it is, then yes, you are in a pickle."

I frowned. "I know nothing of werewolf hierarchy or rules. What's going on?"

Ralph pursed his lips. "Alex knows. Since I'm not married, and I'm the oldest son, I'm expected to marry his wife and take responsibility for her and my nephews."

I blinked. For some reason, that possibility hadn't crossed my mind. In the Dragon Reaches, divorce and abandonment happened, but the *community* rallied around the injured party if there was nothing to spur on the abandonment and made sure they were properly cared for.

Tonya cleared her throat. "Do you want to marry the woman?"

Ralph shot her an incredulous look. "I don't even know if I want to *get married*, period. I mean, I like her—she's always been a sweetheart, and yes, my brother was a cad. But me? A father? With a wife who I didn't choose? I'm not sure I'm up to it." He sounded miserable.

"What happens if you refuse?" I asked.

Ralph shrugged. "My parents will take her and the children in—that's what they would do if she were widowed and there were no other sons. But I'd be seen as a disgrace and shunned by the Pack for not doing my duty. Essentially, like my brother, I'll be considered pathetic and useless." He let out a soft groan. "I don't know what to do. I love my family, I love my Pack, but damn, what if I meet someone who I fall head over heels for? What if I'm stuck forever in an arranged marriage?"

Tonya reached out and patted his arm. "I'm sorry, Ralph."

Alex stared at the road as the asphalt disappeared beneath

our car. We were past Woodinville now, headed northeast toward Maltby. After a while we'd pass through the town of Monroe, then turn right onto Highway 2, leading toward Sultan on the way to Stevens Pass.

"What does your heart tell you to do?" Alex asked after a brief silence.

Ralph hesitated, then, "Marry her. There's a reason we have rules in the Pack. And if we can't abide by them, it's out you go. The Pack looks after its members. We're all responsible for doing so. And if I shirk this, then I shirk more than duty. I shirk my honor. My brother fucked up. He had no complaints against Shayla, but instead of divorcing her the proper way and making certain his children were supported, he just up and ran off, leaving her to file for divorce and scrounge to make ends meet. Hell, I'm ashamed of him. I never want anything to do with Freddy again."

The conflict was roiling in him—I could feel it like I could feel the turmoil of ocean waves. He wanted to do the right thing, but that meant sacrificing his freedom and hopes for the future.

"You won't resent her, though? I mean, how will she feel if she knows you're taking her and the kids on just because the Pack says you have to? Just so you won't be thrown out? I can't imagine that's going to help her self-esteem any more than it did when your brother left her high and dry. Alex got stuck with me but it was business. With you, we're talking about *marriage*." The thought of being saddled with someone like a ball and chain when they didn't love me made me queasy.

"No matter what, Ralph will do the right thing. He's not going to punish Shayla for his brother's stupidity." Alex sounded so sure of himself that I wondered if he knew something I didn't.

Ralph straightened up and shrugged. "Alex is right. If I marry her, it will be my choice. Once a decision is made, it's sealed and you move on. That's the thing—if you belong to the Pack, once you make a promise you keep it. You throw yourself into the work. There's no looking back, no wondering if you made the right decision. You commit to it."

He slowly let out a long breath. "I'm going to do it. I realize, talking to you, that I can't disappoint my parents. My brother took care of that. And I can't turn my back on Shayla and the kids—they didn't ask for this. They're good kids, she's a good woman. I have more than enough to take care of her and my nephews. They'll have to move here, of course, but this will give her a fresh start."

Surprised that he actually was going to take this on, I turned back to face the road. It was honorable, yes, but still—the level of commitment that he had for his Pack and family startled me. And it made me think . . . would I be able to do the same, if I were in his shoes?

Alex eased into the turn lane at the juncture of Highway 522 and Highway 2. A moment later, we had turned right and were on the way to Sultan.

Sultan was a small town—as in five thousand people small—located along the Skykomish River. We turned left onto Sultan Basin Road, a two-lane rural street that led out into the wilds. It was dark and winding and the trees overshadowed us on both sides.

Tonya shifted in her seat. "There's a lot of feral energy out here. Be cautious—I don't care if you're dragon or vampire, there are old spirits out this way. The closer we get to the Cascades, the more you'll find the native energies are restless. And I'm not talking Native American. I'm talking earth energies."

"She's right. These mountains have a life and essence of their own, and being volcanic, that makes them even more volatile." Ralph pressed his face against the back window, staring into the darkness.

I said nothing, but now that they mentioned it, I could feel the presences all around me. Oh, humans lived out here, and Fae, but the earth itself was the one who ruled.

We eventually came to a fork in the road, and Alex idled the Range Rover as he consulted the GPS. "We turn right onto Kellogg Lake Road, and it will lead toward Kellogg Lake. Shortly after the lake, there's a turnoff to the left onto a gravel road, and that's where Stone Weaver lives."

I glanced at the clock. "It's amazing he ever makes it into Seattle. This is quite a drive."

"Well, it says in his dossier that he's very active in the Supe Community Action Council—he's quite political, even if he lives like a hermit. And he's also quite wealthy. He's very attuned to his element, which is earth. Which means he has an affinity for gold and silver and gems." Ralph was busy tapping away on his tablet. "The records say that he's got a good-sized fortune accumulated, though most of it's in land and metal. Apparently, he decided to beat the humans at their own game and start buying up land when he realized that the developers had their eyes on this area. He owns over two hundred acres here, and then another thousand up north of Bellingham. He set up several renewable resources—a Christmas tree farm, some actual farming as in berries during the summer, holly during the winter. He also funds a number of small eco-businesses."

"Smart man. But . . . lonely? Isolated and worth a lot of money? Perfect territory for the doppelgänger to move in. If it could impersonate him, then it could liquidate his holdings before anybody found out and probably have several million dollars at its disposal." I frowned. "Are doppelgängers male or female?"

"Nobody knows," Tonya said. "I studied them, along with the other creatures in my bestiary. They're mutable and gender neutral at birth, so hard to track."

"If they're gender neutral, how do they breed?" Ralph sounded confused.

Tonya laughed. "Well, it takes a little more thought than humans, that's for sure. First, they must find a mate. Then they have a battle—of sorts. The winner shifts to female, the loser to male, and they mate. They don't stay paired up, though. Doppelgängers work alone and are solitary by nature."

"Having you along is better than having an encyclopedia." I flashed her a quick grin over my shoulder. "Somehow I doubt they reproduce at a rapid rate."

"No, and they don't usually hang out in the wilds. They're a predatory species, and they congregate where humans are." Tonya pressed against the window. "They shun each other's company when they aren't in breeding season. The female doppelgänger claims the young. The males just wander off after they've done their job at impregnating the females."

"Like my brother," Ralph muttered.

I repressed a laugh. Ralph didn't need us making any sort of jabs at his situation. "At least we aren't dealing with a colony of them."

Tonya shook her head. "You'll never find them in those numbers."

"Okay, heads up." Alex slowed the car. "Start looking for the road to the left. It will be gravel—we are nearing it according to the GPS."

Ralph shaded his eyes as he stared out the window behind Alex. After a moment, both he and Alex let out a shout and Alex slowly eased the Range Rover onto the gravel road.

We were really into the wilds now. The trees closed in from either side, and the road was so narrow that we would have a hard time passing if another car came from the opposite direction. Also, it occurred to me that even though the Range Rover was geared toward this type of terrain, we could still end up sinking in mud along the way. And I couldn't change into dragon form to help yank it out if it got stuck. But then, given the combined strengths of a vampire, a werewolf, and a dragonshifter, we could probably pry it loose if that happened.

Up ahead, faint lights glimmered off to the right among the trees, and then we were suddenly at a driveway leading into the woods. Alex eased onto the graveled road. A few minutes later, we were at our destination. The house was beautiful. It was a log cabin by style but looked updated with solar panels lining the roof. It sat in the middle of a clearing. The lights we had seen were streetlights, also solar powered, I assumed, and they lined the walkway from the drive to the house. A windmill sat a ways behind the house, and a stream that trickled near had a waterwheel on it.

"Stone Weaver is sure into renewable energy." Tonya opened her door. I followed suit, joining her. Alex and Ralph also emerged from the car.

Alex made certain the Range Rover was locked after we were all out. "I don't want anything getting inside that doesn't belong there." He looked around, gauging the situation. "I *think* we're alone. I don't sense any movement or presence beyond what animals might be in the surrounding forest."

As he fell silent, I listened, closing my eyes. I assumed the others were doing the same.

The first thing I noticed was the wind—steady and brisk, it turned the blades of the windmill. From where we were standing the sound was concussive, a rhythmic *whoosh whoosh* as the blades sailed around. I let the pattern lull me. It was loud, but the susurration reminded me of white noise.

Then I cast out, searching for emotions. Ralph's raw worries were on the surface, as was Tonya's curiosity. Alex—I couldn't read him. But beyond that . . . hunger and . . . concern told me there was something around. Maybe a bobcat or cougar nearby. If it was a big cat or a bear, it would stay away, though, because Ralph's scent—that of werewolf— would be as good as a signature.

"I don't think . . . there's anybody on two feet near here. Now, I don't know whether doppelgängers have any sense of emotion, but as far as I can tell, we're out here on our own." I folded my arms and stared at the house. "Shall we go in?"

A sprinkling of rain started up, and then the clouds

opened and a steady downpour began. Thanks to the sudden drenching, we broke into a run and headed to the house.

Ralph quickly picked the lock and we were in. Another moment and he found the light switch. A pale, bluish-tinted light flooded the room. Energy-efficient bulbs, I thought. Of course Stone Weaver wouldn't use incandescent lights. The house itself was built for function and form. Everything looked usable, but wherever you looked, there was art in the function. A large geode that had been split in half formed the kitchen sink. Holes had been drilled in the bottom to drain the water, and a clear coating filled the crystal hollows so that nothing would be damaged by putting it inside what were essentially crystal bowls. All the furniture was wood, smoothly carved and polished. And yet when I looked close, I realized the wood used had been tree trunks that were hollowed out for seats, or driftwood. Flotsam given new life.

Stone Weaver had created bookcases out of old wooden pallets and while there were a few nods to modern technology—a laptop, TV, a range and refrigerator, to name a few—I had a feeling he had somehow managed to make them as eco-friendly as he could.

We spread out, looking for any sign of the man.

"I'll check the bedroom," I said, heading toward a door that was ajar enough for me to see the corner of a bed in it. As I entered the room, I thought I heard something swish, but shook my head. As far as we knew, we were alone in the house.

The wardrobe was ajar and as I opened it, I saw a jumble of clothes, which conflicted totally with how neat the rest of his house was. I picked through them, but there was no way to tell what might be missing. And the bed hadn't been slept in—it was still made up.

Another sound—though I couldn't make out what it

was—alerted me and I cautiously reached for the dagger I kept strapped to my belt. Slowly, I edged back, glancing around the room. A large window looked out into the forest. Crossing to it, I stared out into the night. At first, it was all shadow and darkness, but then I saw a pair of pale yellow eyes gleaming in the forest. But as I watched them, I knew this wasn't what I had heard. The feeling that something was in the room with me was growing stronger, and whatever it was, it *wasn't* coming from whatever animal might be outside.

Swallowing my nerves, I crossed to the bathroom and pushed the door open, going so far as to check behind the shower curtain. Nothing. The room was empty.

I returned to the bed, where the feeling was strongest. Then I knew. Easing down on my hands and knees, I peeked under the bed. A suitcase rested to one side, and then—what the hell? A small clear box was sitting there, with a frog inside. The energy suddenly increased and I realized that—whatever it was—the sense of being watched came directly from the frog.

Rather than pull the box out on my own, I inched away from the bed to call the others in. Whatever was down there knew I was here; there wasn't any use in being sly about it.

"Let me—if the bugger drains life energy it's not going to get juiced from me. And if it has poison, then again—not going to hurt me." Alex reached under the bed and pulled the box out.

I stared at it. "That's no ordinary frog."

"Obviously not. Tonya, you seem versed on creatures. Any idea of what we have here?" Alex carried the box over to the nightstand. "It feels about the right weight for a frog."

She hesitantly approached it, cocking her head. After a moment, she shrugged. "I have no idea. It's not like any frog I've ever seen. See the crest and spines on its back?"

I leaned closer and sure enough, she was right. For one thing, the frog almost glowed—it was neon green with gold leopard spots, each surrounded by a nimbus of black. Along its back were a row of spines. Rather than porcupine quills, they looked more like a horse's mane cut into a Mohawk and slathered with setting gel. The spines were mottled, green and red. The frog's eyes were a deep black, glistening, and I sensed a very strong intelligence behind them.

"Should we try talking to it?" Ralph scratched his head, looking puzzled.

"Hey, frog. Do you by chance speak English?" Tonya spoke directly to it. The frog stared back, and—with the slightest shift of its eyes—I could have sworn it understood her. But no response.

"Should we open the box? It doesn't look locked." I wasn't sure it was a good idea, but one of us had to ask it.

"Are you insane? What if it's dangerous? What if it's . . . Well, now, what are we doing?" Alex spoke very softly and the rest of us looked back at the frog.

The creature was puffing up, very much like a blowfish. In fact, another inch and it would fill the box, which meant either it would have a hell of a lot of pressure bearing down on it or—

The *or*, it was.

As the sides of its skin touched the plastic cover, the lid blew off—like it had been on a spring, and the frog hopped past us, into the middle of the room, where it stopped. But it was still growing, though now it looked nothing like a frog. No, it was mutating. And then, before we could say a word, a young girl stood there, with eyes so dark you could fall into them, and hair the color of spring grass. She was odd looking—very Elfin in some regards, with a pointed chin and very sharp ears. But this was no elf.

"What . . . who are you?" I asked out of habit, unable to take my eyes off her. There was something transfixing about her—almost mesmerizing.

"Oh good gods, I think she's one of the Elder Fae." Alex

was backing away. "Be very careful. They're a tricky lot, even for dragons, Shimmer."

"Thanks, you just outed me." I shot him a quick glare. Sometimes, keeping the truth of my identity was a good idea,. especially when facing what could potentially be a dangerous foe.

The girl—though I quickly realized I needed to stop referring to her as a girl . . . chances were she was as old as or older than I was—was barely four feet high, and her arms were thin and insubstantial, while her legs looked muscled and ready to run. She was stocky, with ruddy skin.

"Who are you?" Tonya stayed where she was, focusing on the girl.

The frogshifter cocked her head to one side, as though she were deciding whether to answer. After a moment, in a throaty voice, she said, "Who I am is none of your concern, human. But I owe you a favor for freeing me from my prison."

The word *prison* worried me. Who had locked her up, and why?

Alex must have been thinking along the same lines because he asked, "Why were you in the box?"

"An enemy locked me in to prevent me from helping my friend." She frowned, looking around. "He's gone, isn't he?"

"Are you talking about Stone Weaver? We came out here to find out if he was all right. There are reports he's missing." I paused, a thought crossing my mind. What if *this* was the doppelgänger? But then, no, it wouldn't have shut itself in a box, and surely doppelgängers couldn't assume the air of the Elder Fae. Plus, Alex seemed so certain about her.

"Stone Weaver is a friend of the Elder Fae—and yes, you are right, vampire, I am one of them." Her eyes narrowed and a cunning look stole over her face. "I warned him not to trust the woman, but he was infatuated. I warned him that she wasn't who she seemed to be, but his ego got the best of him and now he's gone. The creature came in here, sniffing around for gold. I could see the greed in her eyes—but the Weaver only heard the flattery. He was hungry for praise, and his need blinded him."

As she was speaking, I focused on her emotions but couldn't sense a thing. She must have powerful protection and warding up. Either that, or I just couldn't read the Elder Fae. But jealousy and anger rang clear in her voice. For a brief moment the thought she might have killed him in a jealous rage ran through my mind, but I pushed it aside. And right then, a flash of understanding hit me.

"You *saw* her kill him, didn't you? She trapped you because she thought you were a danger and there was nothing you could do to stop it?" As I spoke, the girl turned to me and the cunning look vanished as pale gold tears streamed down her face and fell to the floor, solidifying into coins.

As the coins clattered to the floor, she hung her head. "I tried to stop her, but she caught me in the box. Even though he didn't love me, I would have protected him with my life."

# CHAPTER 11

Alex and Ralph stared at the coins. Tonya was focused on the girl's face.

"You want them, don't you?" the Elder Fae asked. "You see my coins and you're like all the others. You want them." She sounded angry and defeated.

Alex shook his head. "I don't need treasure. Neither does Ralph. But I've never seen . . . *What are you*, if I may ask? I know you're one of the Elder Fae."

Quick as a cat, she moved past him and sat on the bed, crossing her legs. "I'm known as Gerta, the Golden Frog. Mortals have chased me for my tears since I can first remember."

"Stone Weaver . . ."

"He kept me around for my tears. I didn't want to stay, but there was always the hope he might return my feelings. That he might want me for more than my wealth." Her voice was wistful and I realized she was very young, as far as the Elder Fae went. I found myself tearing up, empathizing with the loneliness in her voice.

"You don't have many friends, do you?" Before I could stop myself, I was by her side kneeling down. I reached out to touch her arm, but she jerked out of my reach.

"Don't touch me or you'll hurt yourself." The words were hoarse, and she gave me a wide-eyed look that told me she had been hurt one too many times.

I stayed my hand. "How so?"

"My skin . . . it oozes a poison that can paralyze and stop the heart."

"I'm a dragon. I'm immune to most poisons."

"I'm one of the Elder Fae. I wouldn't count yourself clear of my dangers so easily." She held up her arm. "Look closely."

I leaned in for a better look. Sure enough, there were pale drops—tiny, the size of pinheads, welling up on her skin. The opaque liquid was murky, and I caught the faint hint of something acrid. "Do you always have that sheen on you?"

She nodded. "Always. There are some who can touch me, who are immune to the poison. Stone Weaver was. He was one of the few who could take my hand."

"Will you tell us what you know? We're trying to catch the . . ." I paused. She hadn't mentioned the word *doppelgänger* yet and I wasn't sure if we should tell her. "*Killer.* She's killed more than once and we're trying to stop her before she finds another victim."

Alex pulled up a chair. "We don't want your tears, we don't want to hurt you. All we want is to find the . . ." He glanced at me and seemed to come to the same conclusion I had. "We are looking for Stone's murderer. You can help us find her." He glanced at Ralph and Tonya. "Make certain the front door is locked. We don't want anybody surprising us while we're in here."

They headed out of the room. I pulled a second chair over next to Alex. "Please help us, Gerta."

The Elder Fae thought for a moment, then said, "All right. I will tell you what I know. Stone Weaver and I have been friends for years. I know he mostly wanted my tears, but he was kind to me, and he made me feel less alone. About three weeks ago, he came home from a meeting of the Supe Community Action Council, and he seemed . . . off. Not his usual self."

"How so?"

"He was humming—and Stone never hums. I asked him what was up and he said that he had met someone, that he thought maybe he finally had met someone who could be his match." She let out a long breath. "I wasn't happy for him. How could I be? But I tried to accept it, and I tried to support him. Then, she came to visit."

"Would a description do us any good?" I asked, mostly to Alex.

He shook his head. "I doubt it."

"Stone Weaver was enthralled—he seemed intoxicated by her. I swear she was feeding him some sort of drug because every time I mentioned even the littlest thing that seemed off, he would fly into a rage, defending her. But then she saw me crying once, and the light in her eyes told me that she coveted my tears. She was after money." Gerta stared harshly at the bed. "She did everything he wanted, and he followed her around like a slave."

"When did you first begin to think it was a doppelgänger and not just some gold digger?" Tonya appeared in the doorway again. "Everything is tight as a drum."

I groaned. Tonya had just given away our theory.

Gerta jerked slightly, then frowned. "*Doppelgänger?* You think she was a . . . that would make sense, though. Because I do remember walking into the bedroom after Stone went outside to check on the wind machine, and I found him standing in front of the mirror. I thought he just doubled back really quickly but maybe I was wrong. That was a few days back. Then, a day or so later, I found her rummaging through his desk. I managed to back out of the room without being seen—or at least I thought she . . . *it* didn't see me. I turned

into my frog shape in order to spy on her, but I guess she was
on to me. Before Stone got home from town, she slapped a
pan over me. The next thing I knew, she had me in that box.
I couldn't change form in there. She shoved me under the
bed and I figured she was going to steal me to force my tears
to come."

"What happened next?" Alex was taking notes.

"Well, an hour or so later, Stone and she had an argument
in the bedroom. She told him that I stomped off in a huff.
He started yelling at her and the next thing, I heard crashes
and a loud thump. After that, I never heard his voice again.
I expected her to come back for me, but so far—no go."

Alex leaned back in his chair. "So there might still be a
chance she—it—will return. The doppelgänger knows you
have golden tears, right?"

Gerta nodded. "Yes, Stone made me cry to show her. He
was proud of being able to show me off like a trained seal."
She sounded so glum that I wanted to hug her.

"Why didn't you leave? He treated you so badly."

She looked up at me and shook her head, a pained look
on her face. "I loved him. I always thought he would finally
realize that and love me back."

I wanted to say something but kept my mouth shut. Abuse
was rampant in all realms, and Gerta was still in the phase
where she was making excuses for her abuser. She wouldn't
be able to see clearly until she was ready to really look at
herself. For all her golden tears, she probably thought she was
worthless.

Alex flashed me a question with his eyes and I shook my
head. With an imperceptible nod, he smiled at the frogshifter. "The creature is out for money, so it may return. It
locked you away so you couldn't warn Stone Weaver, but it
knows that you are a source of wealth. Unless it's convinced
the danger is too great, I doubt it will be able to resist the lure
of easy money."

He hesitated for a moment, then cautiously added, "I

don't want to intrude, Gerta, but if I were you, I'd keep your ability to yourself until you truly know you can trust someone. Stone Weaver made you cry for money—and that's a rotten thing to do. But there are plenty of people who would hurt you far more and enjoy it, to capitalize on your assets. Do you understand what I'm saying?"

Wide-eyed, she nodded. "I've met a few in my life. They hurt me badly and laughed while I cried for them."

"Where do you live? Where's your home?" I wanted to get her back to her family, to find a safe place for her because it was rapidly becoming clear that Gerta made the perfect victim. And with her low self-esteem and such a great desire to be loved, she was headed for a disaster far greater than losing an unrequited love.

She shrugged. "The realm of the Elder Fae, but I like it over here." Sadly, she said, "I like humans. I like their laughter and the fun they seem to have. I don't like my own kind much."

Ralph cocked his head, a look of understanding crossing his face. "You're still quite young, aren't you?"

Again, she shrugged. "Yes, I suppose so, among the Elder Fae I'm practically a newborn."

That was it. *A newborn.* Gerta wasn't looking for a lover, she was looking for a parent—for someone to watch over her. I turned to Alex. "We can't leave her here on her own."

"I'll be fine. Don't worry about me!" Gerta was quick to protest.

Alex motioned for me to follow him out of the room, while Ralph kept watch over her. "What do we do with her? She could probably take us both on. She's Elder Fae, but she's also a sprout. There's no Department of Social Services for the lot of them. Who do we talk to about her?"

"Maybe Chai has some advice. Or Bette. Please, let's take her back to headquarters with us? We can't leave her here. If that freak returns, it will enslave her and probably torture the coins out of her eyes." I wanted to say I was sorry, that I didn't like arguing and that I just wanted things to be calm between us. Instead, I focused on Gerta. But Alex surprised me.

"I'm sorry, love. I didn't mean to slam out like I did this morning. We'll have to figure something out about Glenda, but I don't want to hurt you." He held out his arms and I slipped into them, enjoying the feel of my head against his shoulder. "We'll take her back," he whispered in my ear. "We'll figure out something to help her."

And then we returned to the bedroom.

"So, if she killed Stone Weaver, where did she put the body?" Ralph asked.

Gerta let out a little sob but managed not to break into tears again. "I don't think she cared about hiding him, not any more than it would take to loot his accounts. If she . . . it . . . thought that nobody knew Stone was missing, I imagine that his . . . that he . . . is out there in the woods somewhere."

Ralph cleared his throat. "I can probably find him. If I shift into my wolf shape, I'm going to be able to track down the scent of decay—" As Gerta made a strangled sound, he stopped. "Crap. I'm sorry. But I think I could pick up on his scent since it's probably been a couple days since Stone's been seen."

Alex frowned. "All right, but it's dangerous out there. We're going out with you, and we'll wait near the edge of the trees." He motioned to me. "Bring Gerta. Tonya, you help Shimmer."

Still protesting she would be fine on her own, Gerta finally consented to go with us.

As we headed out toward the edge of the yard, the trees loomed tall against a dark sky. Ralph moved to one side and transformed into a beautiful white wolf. He shimmered, his clothes becoming a bandana around his neck. I always wondered about Weres and their clothing until I came to work at the agency. When Dragonkin shifted, our clothes shifted, too, and I could never figure out how it worked.

Tonya and I flanked Gerta's side cautiously, to avoid touching her, while Alex followed Ralph to the edge of the trees. Ralph padded off into the woods, his white fur waving in the breeze. The rain had stopped, but it was chilly, and I noticed Tonya starting to shiver.

"Take Gerta and get into the car. Lock the doors." I moved over to Alex. "Unlock the door for them, would you? Tonya can't take the cold like we can."

He glanced over his shoulder. "Right," he said, and beeped the key fob. As Tonya and Gerta settled themselves in the backseat, he locked it from where we were standing. "Do you think Ralph will find anything?"

"If there's a body to find, my guess is that yes, Ralph will be able to hunt it down." I let out a long sigh. "What do you think about Ralph's ultimatum? That he marry his sister-in-law? He said he's going to do it and you know he'll follow through. He won't go against his parents. He respects them too much."

"He may respect them, but he's making a mistake if he accepts the responsibility. You don't get married if you don't love someone. It might have worked in the old days when love was a luxury, but now? There are too many other options. He could set them up in an apartment, pay for their rent and keep. He's rich and has plenty of money. He doesn't have to marry the woman." Alex frowned. "I'm not against marriage, but you have to admit, this has too many shades of disaster painted on it."

"Yeah, I know. Though, in the Dragon Reaches, matches are made politically more than anything else. It matters *who* you marry, there." I stared into the dark thicket of trees. "But honestly? This is Ralph's affair. It's his choice and he has to do what he feels is right. And we aren't very good friends if we don't support his choice."

That probably wasn't what Alex wanted to hear, but he kept quiet, scanning the yard. After a moment, he said, "So you think I should keep my mouth shut about how I feel?"

"I think that our opinion doesn't matter. Or it shouldn't. I don't want to put him in the position of feeling like . . ."

"Like we expect him to follow what we say or we'll ditch him?" Alex relaxed then, his shoulders losing that "at attention" look that he had been sporting. "I don't want that either. All right, I'll drop the subject and if we end up pressed into attending a wedding, we'll go and smile. But you know, as well as I do, that it will be a shotgun wedding."

I didn't recognize the expression but it was pretty self-explanatory when I thought about it. I was about to say something when the bushes parted. We readied ourselves, but it was just Ralph. He shifted back into human form and ran his hands through his hair.

"I found him. He's out there, all right, about a quarter mile into the trees. It's not pretty, and the animals have been at him. You'd better call . . . well, who *do* we call? The locals or Chase?"

Alex narrowed his eyes. "The local cops will be pissed if we go over their heads. I'll call Chase and let him decide how to proceed. Meanwhile, you two get back in the car. We know the doppelgänger is likely to come back for Gerta—unless he's been watching us tonight—and we don't want to get caught off guard."

While he made the call, Ralph and I headed over to the car.

"Be cautious in what you say. Gerta has it bad for Stone Weaver, and you don't want to upset her." I glanced over at Ralph, who nodded. "And, Ralph . . . whatever you choose to do about your sister-in-law, you know Alex and I will support you."

He snorted. "You had a talk with him, didn't you? I know what you both think about this, but thank you for having my back. I can't leave my Pack, Shimmer. They're my blood, my family. I am bonded to them in a way neither you nor Alex can understand. We are born into the Pack. The Pack is our family, our blood, and we are bound by loyalty and heart. My brother turned his back on us, and he dishonored everything we stand for. I can't let that act go without making reparations. And by Pack law, this is the way I can put it to right. I owe it to my family name, I owe it to my parents. I owe it to my sister-in-law."

My hand on the door handle, I paused. "Will you be happy?"

He shrugged. "One thing I've come to learn in life—happiness isn't a gift. You have to seek it out, to cultivate it. There's never any guarantee in life, and joy? It's not a right. And to be honest, there are far more unhappy ways to spend my life than married to a lovely woman and playing father to my nephews."

His fatalism startled me—I had always thought he was a dreamer. But he sounded a lot like me right now. As I opened the car door, I shot him a smile. "You're right. And your sister-in-law is a lucky woman to have such an honorable man in the family. I hope you're going to be happy, Ralph. I want you to be happy. And she deserves to be, too."

We settled into the Range Rover—me riding shotgun, Ralph sitting next to Gerta. Tonya was on the other side.

Gerta let out a soft breath. "Did you . . . did you find him?"

Ralph nodded, mutely. Gerta began to cry, silently, and we sat there, quietly, staring into the darkness as Alex returned to the car and we waited for the police.

Chase must have smoothed things over with the local PD because he and his men joined the Snohomish County police at the site. Ralph led them to the body while Alex and I waited with the FH-CSI team. Chase glanced at the Range Rover, where Tonya and Gerta were still waiting.

"I'd like to question her. I asked Chief Sanders to let me do the talking. I told him she was Elder Fae and he didn't want anything to do with the business. He's frightened of all the Fae, Elder or Earthside, or Otherworld born, but he won't admit it."

"Frightened of, or prejudiced against?" Alex asked.

Chase let out a snort. "Is there much of a difference?" Then, answering himself, he said, "Well, actually, there is a difference. And Sanders isn't prejudiced. He just doesn't know enough about the Fae to be certain of how to act around them. He asked me to question Gerta so that he wouldn't upset her by inadvertently saying the wrong thing. I told him what Ralph told me, that she was sweet on the victim."

"How did he die? Could you tell?" I didn't want to go look, but I was curious.

"Do you really want to know?" By the tone of his voice, Chase told me it wasn't pretty.

"No, I guess not."

But Alex interrupted. "We need to know if we're going to do our job right. Give us the bare-bones details and spare the gore."

Chase ducked his head, his slicked-back hair gleaming in the light of the floodlights the men were setting up around the area. "Stone Weaver's throat was sliced from ear to ear. Like the others, he was missing his eyes and tongue."

I winced, although I had to admit to myself, I felt less sorry for Stone Weaver than the others. He had been cruel to Gerta, stringing her along in order to satisfy his greed for her gold. He hadn't been a very nice man, Fae or otherwise, and if the doppelgänger hadn't come along, he would have continued to extort money from the Elder Fae.

Alex must have caught my train of thought, because he shrugged. "The man was not without his own sins, that's for certain. I don't think the world is terribly worse off for his loss, at least as an ethical person. He was a genius, however, and it's sad his work on the environment will stop."

"How are you going to work this with the locals?" I turned to Chase. "I know how territorial the human police can get."

"We've had a talk. Since this connects with the ongoing serial killer case I'm working on, they'll report to me about the case. They asked if we should call in the FBI. I had to tell him what we're up against. That the FBI won't be able to help."

"Is there a federal version of the FH-CSI?" I was surprised that the Earthside governments hadn't formed something of that very nature yet.

Chase gave me a long look. "I haven't told anybody this yet, and I'd appreciate it if you'd keep it quiet—though it's not secret—but I've been tapped to help create one. They want me to move to Washington, D.C., on a temporary basis, and oversee the formation of a governmental Federal Supe Bureau of Investigation. The FSBI, it would be called. I have asked them to hold off for at least a few months, but I can't tell them—or you—why. There's so much the higher-ups don't really know about, for everybody's good, and I can't talk to them yet. But in a few months, I'll be flying down to Quantico."

I blinked. Chase seemed to be a fixture in Seattle. I wondered how his unit would get along without him. "Isn't your wife the Queen of Elqaneve?"

His eyes flashed and, although he still smiled, I had the feeling I had stepped hip-deep into a mud pit. "Sharah is not my wife, unfortunately. Not yet. But yes, she is my girl-friend and we have a child together. As I said, this will be a temporary situation, for six months or less. And really, it's vital. They need someone who has been in the trenches. Someone who's interacted with the Fae and the goblins and the bone-walkers every day, if they're going to fully understand the cultural differences, the expectations, and the issues that can arise when humans interact with Supes, especially in the legal arena."

He paused as a couple of the local police walked by. They were headed toward the house with evidence bags. After they were out of earshot, he continued. "Anyway, the local boys are working hand in hand with us and they understand that they need to handle this case with kid gloves. Even if it's not something the FBI could handle, the fact is that the doppelgänger could easily decide to start picking human victims, and then it would hit the papers."

I thought about what he said. "So most crime by the Fae . . . or other Supes . . . doesn't get written up?"

Chase froze, then let out a long grumble. "By the papers? No, it doesn't. We have an agreement with Elqaneve and Y'Elestrial to do our best to keep events out of the news that are Supe-on-Supe. Unfortunately, the tabloids pick up on things ten times faster than the regular news agencies, and they always exploit it. But I agreed, when I helped create this agency, that we would . . ."

"Whitewash Fae activities?" Alex let out a snort. "It's always the same, isn't it?"

"No, it's not, and I'll thank you to keep your judgments to yourself. The fact is, it would be ten times worse for Other-world citizens if humans thought there were Fae serial killers and dem—" He stopped abruptly. "Let's just say that it's in everybody's best interests if mortals don't know everything that goes on behind the scenes. Hell, the hate groups are all over the vampires. And the Weres? They lump them in with the 'if you're not Earthborn, you must be a devil' mind-set. What we are doing actually protects the Fae who come here to visit, as well as the ones who were born Earthside."

"Doesn't protect vampires, though, does it?" Alex seemed determined to needle the detective and I wasn't sure why. But then, it seemed like the type of night where anything could be taken as an offense.

Chase stared him down. "I would like nothing better than to see vampire rights pass the legislature. I suggest instead of bitching about it, you put your energy toward making it happen. Because, Radcliffe, I don't have time to play tes-tosterone games. In the beginning, I might have. Now? I just want to catch this damned serial killer." And with that, he stomped off toward the Range Rover.

"Don't antagonize him." I glanced at Alex. "Why does he bother you so much?"

Alex watched him for a moment. "I think he's hiding something. I don't know what, but I have the feeling . . ." He paused, then shrugged, shaking his head. "Eh, just call me a conspiracy theorist. I always think the government's out to hide things from the public." With that, he motioned for me to follow him and we headed over to the car.

Chase—very gently—questioned Gerta. After she had told him everything, the detective pressed his lips together and slowly walked away from the car. Alex and I joined him.

"The bastard kept her around for her tears, didn't he?" He spoke softly, and I realized he was used to being around the Fae, whose hearing was extremely heightened.

Alex, softening, nodded. "Yeah, he did. We aren't sure what to do with her. She seems . . . very young, if you know what I mean."

"She's Elder Fae, but I suppose even they have to be born. I'm used to dealings with ones who would soon as eat you alive as make a daisy chain." Chase's lips twisted into a sad frown. "What are your options? I don't think the safe houses would be the best place for her."

I snapped my fingers. "Bette. Bette would know. She's been around a long, long time, and I think she would be the best person to ask. She's the only one I can think of." That wasn't saying much, given the short time I'd lived over Earthside, but it was the best I could do.

Alex gave me a nod. "I think you're right. I don't have much truck with the majority of the Fae, except those who come to me as clients. But Bette might be able to come up with an idea. We'll take Gerta back to the office with us and ask her when we get there. What time is it, by the way?"

We had started out for Stone Weaver's place around eight

thirty and it was now almost twelve thirty—given we had had to wait for Chase and his men to come out. They were still examining the crime scene, but there wasn't anything more we could do there. With the detective's permission, we returned to the Range Rover and Alex slowly began to ease out of the driveway and down the road. Chase had promised to call us first thing with any information that might help us on the case.

On the drive back to the office, Gerta stared out the window, saying nothing. She looked lost, and afraid, and I couldn't help but wonder how she had first met Stone Weaver. But that was a question better left for later, for when the grief had had a chance to settle. I still didn't fully understand why she had loved him—as I had told Alex, I was new to relationships, and the thought of loving someone who hurt me didn't make sense to me, but then again, I wasn't even sure I knew what love was.

By the time we reached Seattle and eased into the parking lot next door to the office, I could sense Tonya's weariness. Even though she had slept, she seemed tired. Alex and Ralph escorted Gerta inside, but I hung back, motioning to the witch.

"Are you all right? You seem . . ."

"Don't mind me." She flashed me a mirthless smile. "I've been thinking about love and relationships all the way back from Stone Weaver's place. Gerta's story struck a chord. She's in love with someone who didn't love her back. Kind of sounds familiar, doesn't it?"

Of course—Degoba. I was about to say that the circumstances were different, though—that she wasn't like Gerta—but she beat me to the punch.

"I realize that whatever hell I've been in over this, I made it myself. Degoba never once led me on. He never told me he loved me, and while we hung out, he never encouraged me to stay and he certainly didn't hurt me. He was always good to me. I feel bad now . . . like I let him down by not attending his wedding, but that's my own feelings of insecurity eating at me. He had to have known how I felt, but he didn't lead me on. What happened to Gerta—*that's* truly heartbreaking. And how will she ever know if someone wants to be with her because of who she is, or because of the gold that falls from her eyes?" Tonya hung her head. "I feel sorry for her."

"So do I. She has a long, hard road ahead. I'm hoping Bette might get through to her. Bette . . . once you get to know her, you'll see she has a way of cutting through the layers. She can get straight to the point and somehow she makes the situation seem very clear." I noticed Tonya was shivering. "Come on, it's misty and cold out here. Let's go inside."

But as we headed into the building, I couldn't help but wonder: Was I clear on my relationship with Alex? I really didn't know how I felt. I cared about him, but now I wondered if I was even capable of love. And if I was, would I know what it was when I felt it? With those thoughts and others running through my mind, I followed Tonya through the door, into the building.

# CHAPTER 12

Gerta seemed tired, so Bette led her to one of the conference rooms where she could rest on a sofa, then returned as we discussed the situation. As she slid into the chair, the Melusine had a determined look on her face. "You have no idea how to catch this creature, do you?"

Alex played with a bottle of blood, sliding it back and forth on the table. He looked grumpy, but then again, we hadn't been running a winning streak lately.

"No, to be honest. And I don't think Chase does either. How do you catch somebody who can—whenever they want—transform to look like someone else? I called Johnson a few minutes ago. They're wrapping up out at Stone Weaver's place, and he said that he's going to notify the banks Weaver frequented. He'll tell them that if someone purporting to be Stone Weaver tries to make a withdrawal or transfer, to call the FH-CSI immediately. He can't very well tell them it's a doppelgänger, they wouldn't understand, so he's telling them there's an impersonator defrauding wealthy Fae. But chances are the creature has already been there and wiped out every account it can. We'll know more when the offices open, so Bette, love, will you do us a favor and get that information before you leave work in the morning?"

She jotted down a note. "Sure thing. I've been thinking. The doppelgänger will move on pretty soon, so if we want to have a chance of catching it, we have to move now. I suggest . . . bait."

"Bait?" I glanced at her, not sure I liked the sound of that.

"Yes, bait. This doppelgänger goes after wealthy older Fae. We know he—she—it . . . travels in the circles I do. I suggest that I let it be known I just came into an inheritance. I look older, let's face it, I look like a grandma—"

Alex and Ralph both snorted.

"You look as much like a grandma as Glenda did," Alex said.

I shot him a long look. Just how much was he thinking of Glenda, lately? But the flare of irritation passed as Bette let out a loud chuckle.

"Sugar, you're blind. Truth is, I do look like an elderly Fae. Not an Elder Fae, but an elderly one. Melusines don't retain their physical looks quite so much as they retain the power to charm. We have it where it counts, but the wrinkles and gray hair are there from fairly early on. If the doppelgänger is still around—and I suspect it may try one or two more catches before it moves on to new territory—then I'll set myself up to be right smack in plain sight. And truth is, I have more than a pretty penny set by, so if the critter checks me out, it will see money in the bank."

The silence was worthy of a pin drop. Ralph cleared his throat, speaking first. "Nope. We can't let you do that, Bette. What if something goes wrong? And doesn't everybody know you work for Alex? If the doppelgänger is smart, it won't dare try anything."

"There's the kicker, sugar butt." Bette flashed him a bright smile. "I don't tell anybody down there what I do. I figure it's best if they don't know. Oh, they know I have a job, but most of them assume that I work in a brothel. I let them think that."

Alex choked on his blood, spitting a bright red patch of liquid on the table in front of him. He immediately grabbed a napkin and wiped it up. "My apologies, but . . . *What the hell?* You let them think you work in a brothel? As a hooker?"

She stuck out her tongue. "As the madam, I'll have you know. The men are too embarrassed to ask about it—they don't want me knowing they're interested. The women aren't all that interested. It's the perfect cover and it fits a lot more than trying to pass as working as a medical receptionist or something equally inane. I'd never be able to pull off that disguise."

I hated to agree with her. The idea seemed too dangerous, but it was the only one we had to go on. "Bette may have something. We need to engage the doppelgänger before it moves on. This might be the way to do it. At least it's a plan, and if we can attract its attention, then it won't be hunting some unwary victim. Bette knows what to look out for. It's not like she's going to be taken in by a smooth-talking charmer. But what about Dent? Don't your friends know you have a . . ." I paused, about to say *boy toy*, but I didn't want to offend her.

But she just laughed. "My young stud? Hunk-a-hunk-a burning love? I told you, I was going to break up with him. I don't want anything long term and he does. I'm planning on dropping by his apartment in the morning. So I can put a spin on it and play it out like he broke up with me. I can play the dumped girlfriend to the hilt, and make it out that he thought I was too old for him and how horrible I feel and insecure. If the doppelgänger is around, that will give it the perfect opening."

Ralph frowned, rapping his knuckles on the table. "It does make sense."

"I hate to admit it, but I concur." Alex rubbed his head. "But don't you go playing heroine. You keep us fully informed. If this does draw the doppelgänger out, we need to know the minute you think he—it—has made a move. We have to walk a fine line here."

"Sure thing, sugar." Bette took a long drag on her cigarette. Ralph coughed as she breathed out the smoke in a long plume. Just then, my cell phone jangled.

I glanced at the Caller ID. *Chai.* "Hello?"

"You at the office, Little Sister?" The sound of traffic roared past in the background. Where was he, given the streets were fairly empty during this time of night?

"Yes, I am. What's up and what's that noise?"

"There appears to be a bit of a road race going on, and the cops have just shown up to put a stop to it. But I called you because I was out for a stroll and smelled the salamander. I know where it is and thought if you guys were up for a rumble, maybe we can take the sucker down. He's got himself trapped inside a fenced-in schoolyard and I slammed the gate on him. He doesn't realize it yet, but if you get over here, maybe we can take care of the problem. Though I'm pretty certain he's probably eaten a transient or two by now." Chai let out a snort. "He looks fat and sassy to me."

"Do you think you can gate him back to the plane of Fire?"

"Only if I have somebody to distract him while I'm setting up the gate. So get over here pronto." He hung up. I had put him on my cell phone plan and he wasn't shy about making use of it, even though he knew very few people. He liked playing games on the thing.

I glanced up. "Salamander is caged and Chai thinks we can take it down if we get over there. Or rather, that he can gate it back to the Elemental plane of Fire if we distract it while he sets up the gate." At the *ding* of my phone, I glanced at it. "He just texted me directions. Not far from here, actually—the creature's got itself stuck in an abandoned schoolyard."

Ralph and Alex were on their feet immediately.

"Tonya, you stay here with Bette and Gerta." I slipped on my jacket. "Let's go, boys."

As we headed toward the Range Rover, I glanced back

at the clock. Four o'clock and all was ready for hell to break loose in the shape of a giant lizard.


By the time we reached the enclosure, Chai had managed to prop the gate shut on it and trap the salamander inside. The lizard was slamming around against the chain link, and it wouldn't be long before it managed to smash its way out.

"We've got to do something soon," Alex said. "What's our next move? I have no clue how to control one of these beasties."

Chai eyed the flailing lizard. "I need to open a gate to the Elemental plane of Fire. Chances are, the creature will dive straight through it once it senses it. Usually, Elementals who have been summoned don't really want to hang around, so it should want to go home. But I can't get close enough to open the gate without getting hurt, unless you distract it. So I guess . . . act as bait while I open the gate?"

"You're a poet—" Ralph started to say, but Chai cut him off.

"Yeah, yeah . . . just don't get near its mouth. It might not be a Komodo and have the bacteria they do, but those teeth could sever you in two, wolf boy."

Ralph grinned. "Then we play a game of keep-away. Alex and Shimmer and I will take turns distracting it while you set up the gate."

*Oh, lovely*, I thought. Just what I wanted to do with the rest of my evening, but we really didn't have a choice, so I steeled myself and—as Chai opened the chain-link fence— we swung in behind him. Alex immediately raced over to the right of the salamander, yelling at the top of his lungs and waving his hands. It swung on him, and Chai slipped past it and began setting up for the gate. As the salamander charged on Alex, Ralph ran to the middle and set up a racket. The giant lizard stopped, then turned and lunged at him. I immediately picked up on what they meant by *keep-away* and—as the salamander careened toward Ralph—I took the left side and pelted it with a nasty rock that was near my foot. And so we went—back and forth, taking turns keeping the thing distracted. I knew this lull wouldn't last long, though. Pretty soon the creature would get so frustrated it would charge one of us and not pull back. I had the feeling we were rapidly reaching that state.

I spied a two-by-four and darted forward to smack the hindquarters of the salamander as it nearly caught Ralph in its teeth. As it spun on me, Chai let out a yell. He was standing by a fiery-looking gate—flames were shooting out of the portal. I dashed toward him, the salamander on my tail. At the last minute, I leaped to the side. The lizard paused for a moment, glancing at me, then at Chai, then back at the flames. It flicked out its tongue, eyeing us as if it were deciding whether we were crunchy enough to stick around for, but then apparently decided we weren't worth the bother and lurched through the gate. Chai shouted some sort of incantation—guttural and harsh—and the gate slammed shut and disappeared with a wisp of smoke.

"What do you know about that?" The voice took us all by surprise.

As we all whirled around, a man staggered into view. He was holding a bottle of what looked like whiskey, with a bemused look on his face. "I didn't realize this stuff was so pow . . . pow . . . strong." His words were slurred, and I realized he was drunk. He looked like a college frat boy.

Ralph hurried over to him. "What are you doing here, dude?"

"I . . . I'm sorry, sir . . ." The college boy fell back, landing on his ass. It was only then that I realized he was wearing what looked like a toga, and from the open slit on the side, I could see a pair of pink panties. I coughed, not knowing what to say.

"You're being hazed, right? Pledging to a fraternity?" Ralph let out a long sigh.

With a nod, our frat boy leaned to the side and vomited on the pavement. I grimaced.

Ralph glanced over at us. "We can't leave him out here. He'll get himself killed."

Alex was frowning. "I hate this sort of crap. These organizations think the way to induct members is to make them humiliate themselves, or to put them in outright danger. Look, mate, where are you from? Where do you live?" He made the mistake of smiling, and his fangs peeped out.

The college kid freaked. "Vampire!" He tried to scramble to his feet, but only tripped over his toga and went sprawling face first. Alex reached down and grabbed him by the arm, hauling him to his feet. He forced the sodden frat boy to stare at him. A moment later, the kid relaxed in his grip.

"Mate, I just asked you where you're from and what's your name?"

"Westminster House. Western Washington College of the Arts. I'm . . . Curry . . . Curt."

"I know where that is," Ralph said. "It's a new, very private, very exclusive conservatory. In West Seattle near Alki. Ask him what he's supposed to be doing?"

Alex asked him.

"I . . . I . . . drink the bottle and find my way back." The boy hiccupped.

Alex snorted. "I say we take him back and drop him off at the dean's house."

"He'll get in trouble, and so will the fraternity." Ralph frowned.

"Too bad. They deserve to be upbraided for this stunt. Haul him over to the Range Rover, Shimmer, while Ralph and I make sure there are no remaining signs of the lizard."

Chai joined me. He picked up Curt and gently tossed him over his shoulder. "I'll never understand humans and their need to degrade their own kind."

"Dragons are good at that, too." I hated to admit it, but

humans had nothing on my kind when it came to games of humiliation.

"I know, Little Sister."

We situated Curt in the backseat, and Chai crawled in next to him. By that point, Alex and Ralph returned. Alex eased out of the dead-end street and we headed toward West Seattle.

"At least the salamander is taken care of. One case closed."

"For all the good ten dollars a month will do." Alex laughed ruefully. "But we'll consider it our good deed for the month." He sobered. "What do you all think about Bette's plan? I have a really bad feeling about it."

"Yes, Han," Ralph said.

"I'm more of a rogue than he was, and my bike is way cooler than the *Millennium Falcon*."

Suddenly getting the reference—I had been watching a lot of movies as of late—I laughed. "You may be more of a rogue, but you aren't as mercenary." But then, I, too, sobered. "I don't like Bette putting herself out on the line, but she's right. We don't have a clue as to what to do other than this. There's no way to find the doppelgänger without luring it in."

Ralph let out a long sigh. "Shimmer's right, Alex. Otherwise, this thing will kill again, and then move on to fresh fields."

Chai narrowed his brow. "What are you talking about?"

I explained Bette's plan.

"Dangerous, definitely. The woman is brave. But truly, what else can you do at this point? Ralph is correct—the creature will move on to a different city and try the same game. No matter how much you warn people, when someone is lonely, they don't want to believe that the person who is offering them love is a fraud." The djinn shrugged. "Let her try it—we can keep a close eye on her."

And with that, we were decided. We delivered Curt to the security at the conservatory, with a plausible story that we had found him running around outside a bar. As he spun his tale of a giant lizard to the man, I put on a wide-eyed *have-no-clue* look, and the security guard just shook his head and hauled him off to his frat house, muttering something about rich kids.

After that, we headed back to the office. There, we found that Bette had sent Gerta packing out to the Fae Sovereign Nation known as Talamh Lonrach Oll.

"I put her in a taxi. I thought that would be the safest place for her at this point. Tonya's out picking up takeout for us. Well, not for you, sugar lips, but then, you drink your meals." She winked at Alex.

"You sure Gerta will be okay with the Fae Queens?" He ignored her taunting.

"Yeah, they'll take care of her and hopefully snap her out of moping. What about the lizard?"

"Sent back to its home." Chai joined us in the break room.

Bette nodded. "Then I can close it out on the books and contact Lydia?"

"Go ahead. Tell her we took care of it." Alex dropped into the chair at the head of the table, his legs stretched out in front of him. He dropped his head back for a moment, then straightened up and pulled himself close to the table. "Bette, we talked over your plan to bait the doppelgänger."

"Don't you say no—" she started, but he interrupted.

"It would seem, after much discussion, that we agree it's the best option." He gave us a pointed stare. "Some of us agree more reluctantly than others. Provided the creature's still in the area. We have no way of knowing that. So, if you could set it in motion, maybe we'll see results. But I want you to promise me . . . to promise *all of us* . . . that you won't go anywhere with anybody without checking in. Promise me you'll be extra cautious. I know you can take care of yourself, woman, but the doppelgänger is smart."

Bette stared at him for a moment. "You wouldn't be so worried if you didn't think I might be taken in by it. I assure you, I'm not that susceptible to flattery." She sounded almost insulted.

He shook his head. "No, you aren't. But there are other ways to worm yourself into someone's life. You've shown yourself in the Community Center to be someone who can take care of herself, but you also have shown yourself to be someone who has a soft spot for people in need. I'm just thinking this creature may attempt to get to you in some other way . . . through your desire to help out friends in need."

Bette frowned, but didn't contradict him. "Yeah, yeah. I get your drift. I'll watch myself. Meanwhile, I called Dent and told him we needed to chill things down. I was going to go over there for breakfast, but really, it's just . . . it's done. Tomorrow, I'll have lunch at the center and put our plan into motion."

Alex gave her a slow nod. "Until then, what do we have on the docket?"

Bette tossed a clipboard on the table. "Not much, we've closed out most of our current caseload."

At that moment, Tonya entered the room, carrying two big bags of food. "I couldn't decide what to get, so I stopped at a couple all-night joints. We have tacos, and fish and chips. I also picked up a box of doughnuts."

Ralph jumped up to take the bags from her. He set them on the table. As Bette and I began unpacking the food, Ralph brought out paper plates and napkins from one of the cupboards.

I glanced at Alex. "Does it ever bother you to sit and watch us eat?"

He shrugged. "Once in a while. I do miss food, but it's been long enough that I don't give it much thought anymore, love." With a wink, he added, "Not for you to worry yourself over."

Tonya slipped out of her jacket and hung it over one of the chairs, then settled in beside us. "I heard what you were saying. Since you don't have anything pressing, would you mind hearing me out?"

"Be my guest, love." Alex pulled out his tablet and prepared to take notes.

She filled her plate with a couple of tacos and a fish fillet and fries. "I think I'm being stalked, but I'm not sure."

Ralph frowned. "What do you mean, you're not sure?"

Tonya took a bite of her fish, then—after swallowing—said, "I'm not sure. I'm not sure if I'm reading the situation wrong, or if there's really a problem."

Alex flashed her a warm smile. "Why don't you start at the beginning? Maybe we can figure it out."

After a moment, Tonya took a long sip of her soda and then let out a long, slow breath. "It started before we met—before you came up to Port Townsend to help Patrick. I have a MyFriend page, like half of America, and I started getting friend requests from people I didn't know. Some I accepted, because they sounded interesting and we had mutual friends. Others, I didn't know—they were smarmy guys, or people who wanted me to teach them magic. I refused those. But then, I got a friend request from someone who said he knew my mother. He said that while I was gone—when I moved away—he became friends with her. He told me how sorry he was that she died, and said that he missed her. That she had been like a second mother to him. The whole spiel. So I accepted his friend request. His profile places him at around my age, and he doesn't have much personal information listed. Mostly that he lives in Gig Harbor, and that he runs a chicken farm."

I didn't know much about social networking, though it seemed to be a huge thing among humans. I did know enough that, if I had decided to create a profile on any site, I would probably be overly paranoid about accepting friend requests. In fact, given my nature, I rather doubted I'd allow anybody on there, so it would be pointless.

Alex was jotting down notes. "What's his name?"

"Jack Skelton. S-K-E-L-T-O-N. At first it made me think of *The Nightmare Before Christmas*, but that's Skellington, not Skelton." She frowned. "His middle initial is P, but I'm not sure what it stands for."

"Got it. Go on."

"Anyway, so shortly after I friended him, he sent me a direct message. He told me I was beautiful, like my mother had been, and that he really appreciated all she did for him. It was a little . . . it wasn't crude or anything, but it implied a lot. I thought maybe it was my imagination, though, thanked him, and left it at that. After that, the messages started in earnest. He began sending me at least two or three messages a week. We should meet for coffee, or he would come up to Port Townsend and take me out to dinner. Again, nothing rude, but I began to cringe when I saw his name. Something just felt . . . pushy?" She shrugged, looking both confused and irritated.

Bette leaned forward. "It sounds like you felt crowded?"

"Yeah, sort of like . . . every time I turned around, there he was. Again, the messages weren't overtly sexual, but they were . . . *insistent*, I guess the word would be."

Alex nodded. "What did you say to him? How did you answer them?"

"Most of them, I didn't. At first, before I realized I might have a problem on my hands, I said sure, that a meet-up would be fun. But then I began to get nervous. I started avoiding MyFriend. After a couple weeks when I didn't go on there, the e-mails started. Now here's the thing: I don't have my private e-mail address listed online. I have the one for the shop, yes, but nowhere have I listed my private e-mail addy. I keep that for a few good friends. I have a separate e-mail for online shopping, newsletters, that sort of thing."

"And let me guess. He sent his letters to your private address?" I was beginning to get the gist of the problem. The guy had gone out of his way to find info on her.

She let out a soft sigh. "Yes. He asked where I was—said he missed me on MyFriend. He asked if I was mad at him. I didn't answer him, but I posted a note on my profile that I was taking an Internet break and that nobody should worry. He stepped up his e-mail campaign then. Was I okay? Was somebody bothering me—it took everything I had to not respond and say, 'Yes, *you* are.' But I didn't. A week or so after that, he began to get abusive. His language devolved from polite to crude. He said I was a cocktease, and that he didn't like to be strung along."

Ralph opened his laptop and began tapping in information. "Did he post anything on your profile?"

"Yeah, here . . . let me friend you and then you can see." She gave him her profile name, he sent her a friend request, and then she pulled out her phone and accepted it. "I haven't been on there in a couple days so I haven't . . . oh crap."

"I see it." The smile slid off Ralph's face. He turned the laptop around so the rest of us could see the picture. Somebody by the name of Dr. Jack had posted a picture of a bouquet of dead roses on her page. A knife pinned one of the roses to the background and blood streamed out of the rose. The caption read, WAYS TO KILL A ROMANCE.

"Is he a real doctor?" I asked.

Tonya shook her head. "I don't know. I doubt it. But yeah, that's his profile."

Ralph clicked on the man's avatar—which was an animated skull—and up came a page filled with mostly memes. Most of the posts were pictures of television stills—all characters from horror movies or crime shows who were female, and who had been either battered or murdered. Or both.

"This dude is running some seriously sick energy," Ralph said, grimacing. He turned the laptop back to him and began his search again.

Tonya paled. "I haven't seen his page in a while. It wasn't like this when he first contacted me." She wrapped her arms around her shoulders. "I'm scared. I should be scared, right?"

"I think you've got damned good reason to be. Let me find out something . . ." Ralph muttered away as his fingers danced quickly over the keys.

Alex leaned forward. "Do you know for sure that he lives in Gig Harbor?"

Tonya shook her head. "No. His profile said Gig Harbor, but people can lie. I do know that. And I never asked him—I didn't want him to think I was interested in him, so I tried to keep things on a superficial level, especially once he began messaging me so much."

Bette pushed the food across the table to her. "You've only picked at your food. Eat something more—it will help ground you. Get a good meal inside you."

Tonya mutely obeyed. I crossed to behind Ralph and leaned over his shoulder, watching what he was doing. After a moment, he glanced up at me.

"Would you mind not doing that? I don't like it when people stare over my shoulder. I feel crowded."

"That's how I felt with his messages, like he wasn't giving me room to breathe." Tonya finished another taco. She opened her bag and pulled out a stack of what looked like already-opened mail. "After he began bombarding me with e-mail, these started coming."

As she tossed the letters on the table, I shivered. Something felt really off about them, and I realized that I was feeling the residual energy that belonged to the sender. And it made me want to take a shower.

Bette looked at the letters. "Has anybody else handled these besides you and the mailman?"

Tonya frowned. "Whoever sorted them out at the post office, I guess."

"Wait a moment . . ." Bette crossed to the counter for a pair of latex gloves. She slid them onto her hands and then began sorting them out. "Didn't you notice that none of these have a postmark? Nor are the stamps canceled."

"That means he could have put them in my box directly." As the full implication of this hit home, Tonya paled even further. "He's been to my house, hasn't he?" she stuttered.

"I'm not sure, but I think I'll take these back and run

some print tests on them. If he's human, he's going to have fingerprints." Carrying them carefully, Bette headed out the door.

We had a mini–fingerprint lab in the back, and somehow— I wasn't sure of the particulars and had never bothered to ask—Alex seemed to have access to the IAFIS, the FBI's fingerprint database. I had the feeling that not even Chase Johnson knew about *that*, and the less said, the better. That was one thing I had learned early on: In this line of business, you learned to keep your mouth shut. And luckily, I wasn't one to spill secrets.

As a rule, dragons were private individuals. We all had a true name, spoken to us at birth by our mother, and only the child, the mother, and the record's keeper ever knew a dragon's true name, because if you knew a dragon's true name, you could cast a spell to summon or control them.

Unfortunately, I didn't have one—there was no record of my birth, with me being a foundling. And without my true name and lineage entered into the Hall of Records, it meant that I had no legal existence in the Dragon Reaches. It also meant that nobody could magically make me toe the line, at least not in the way of normal dragons. Hmm, now that I thought of it, maybe there was an upside to being orphaned.

Tonya was looking frantic. She leaned her hands on the table. "He's been to my house. I know he has." She looked up, fear creasing her face. "What if . . . what if he's been *inside* my house?"

Ralph let out a shout and jumped to his feet. "Found him. Or at least, I found out more about him! Good old Jack seems to have a criminal record for domestic violence. Apparently, he had a girlfriend named Wendy who took out a restraining order on him after he put her in the hospital. She's disappeared, though . . ." He sat back down, a worried expression on his face.

"Jack served three months in jail for . . . oh lovely. Not only did he beat up his girlfriend but, after she took out a restraining order and started dating a man named Ken, our boy Jack didn't take it very well. Seems Jack also beat Ken to a pulp, and served another five months in jail for that assault. I can't find any further mention of Wendy, but Ken was left with a permanent limp from Jack's assault. Ken moved away to the East Coast shortly after he recovered enough to leave the hospital."

Tonya let out a frightened yelp. "He's violent? I wonder if he really ever knew my mother. I have no recollection of ever meeting him . . ."

"Let me cross-check your names to see if I can find out more. What was your mother's name?" Ralph's fingers were flying over the keys.

"Penelope. She went by Penny, mostly."

"Penelope . . . Harris. Penelope Carol Harris?" Ralph's voice took on a strange tone.

"Right." Tonya jerked her head up. "Why? You find something?"

"Yeah. Okay, your mother never left Port Townsend, right?"

"Correct. I left for several years—seven, in fact. I moved to Aberdeen after my mother and I had a huge blowout. When I came back, we made up." Tonya brushed a stray hair back from her face. "Why?"

"Did your mother ever tell you that she had gotten married while you were gone? For a very brief time, right after you left. The marriage only lasted three months, but here's the record. She married George Skelton . . . who happens to be Jack's father." Ralph sat back in his chair as the room fell silent.

# CHAPTER 13

After a moment, Tonya let out a strangled "What the fuck?"

"Your mother married Jack's father. Didn't she ever tell you?" Ralph motioned for us to crowd around the laptop. Tonya and I peered over his shoulder. There, on the screen, was a copy of a marriage license for one George Skelton to Penelope Harris. Tonya glanced at the date and sputtered.

"She got married to him three months after I left home. We had a horrendous fight and I stomped off." She rubbed her forehead. "I'm beginning to get a horrible headache. My mother was spontaneous to say the least. I have no doubt that she did this as a reaction to me leaving."

"I take it your father wasn't around," I said.

"No, he abandoned us when I was five years old. He wasn't the type to stick around. To tell the truth, my mother and he were fuck buddies, according to what she told me when I was old enough to understand. I was the result of a ruptured condom, and my mother decided that I was her one chance to have a child. Since they were good friends, they decided to try to give it a go, and they managed to stick it out for five years. Trouble was, Clinton, my father, wasn't a stable man in terms of relationships. And to be honest, neither was my mother. It was the perfect storm. Total disaster, according to her. But I'll say this for him. Clinton sent child support every month until I hit eighteen."

An odd look swept over her face and she lowered her voice. "But he didn't have the daddy gene. He didn't take any interest in my life. Never wanted to talk to me on the phone or take me for the summer . . . or even a weekend. We haven't spoken since my graduation from high school."

Ralph gave an almost imperceptible shake of the head. "That must have been difficult."

Tonya shrugged. "It would've been worse if they'd stayed together and started arguing. At least they gave it a try, and they knew enough to get out before it got really bad. I wasn't traumatized—Clinton seemed more like a friend than a father to me. My mother had to play both good cop and bad cop."

"And you had no idea that she had hooked up with George?"

Tonya twisted her lip to one side, then made a *tsk-tsk* sound. "Not in the least. As I said, we had a big blowout and I left home. I moved to Aberdeen and it was seven years before we spoke again. You say the marriage only lasted for three months?"

Ralph tapped away at the keys. A moment later, he brought up another screen, this one with a listing of divorce decrees on it. A quick search and we had the answer.

"Right. They were married for three months. And—" Another furious flurry of the keys and he pointed to the screen. "During the time they were married the cops were called out to the house five times for domestic violence complaints. Your mother reported George for trying to strangle her, for giving her a black eye, for pointing a gun at her, and two other reports that don't go into detail. Each time George was hauled away to jail, but your mother posted bail the next day."

Tonya let out a disgusted sigh. "Good grief. But that would be exactly what my mother would do. She could be a hard-edged bitch when she wanted to be, but underneath it all, Penelope was pretty insecure. After I returned home, she went through men like used tissues, discarding them as soon as she found a problem with them."

"Including Patrick," Alex said.

"Yeah," Tonya said, "including your friend Patrick. I have to admit that, for a vamp, he was remarkably patient with her. I wonder if her marriage to George caused some of that. He sounds like a horrible man. But now for the million-dollar question—did Jack live with them at the time? He never once mentioned that his father and my mother were together."

Ralph started searching again. I returned to my seat and glanced over at Alex. He was frowning. I knew part of the frown related to the news about what George had done to Penelope. If there was one thing Alex couldn't stand, it was rough treatment of women. I caught his eye and gave him a soft smile, which he returned.

A few minutes later, Ralph sat back in his chair. "Like you, Jack was an adult when these two got together. I don't find anything about whether he lived with them, but I do find an old address for him during that time period. He apparently lived in Port Townsend at the time. I am *not* finding an address for him in Gig Harbor. I did find one for a Jack Skelton in Tacoma, but he moved away from there two months ago and seems to have dropped off the grid. I am guessing that he is staying in Port Townsend somewhere."

"Does his father still live there?" I asked.

"Good question." Once again, Ralph hit the search engines. A few minutes later he looked up beaming. "That was a good call. His father actually died a year ago, but he left his house to Jack. And that house is in Port Townsend.

I don't see any record that Jack actually took possession of the house, but that doesn't mean anything. Oddly enough, though I found death records for George, the electricity, water, and sewer still haven't been turned off to the house."

Alex rested his elbows on the table. "Then it's a good bet that's where we'll find Jack. Now for the million-dollar question: Why is he stalking Tonya?" He turned to her. "I need you to give Ralph access to your e-mail account so he can look at every single e-mail that Jack has sent you. You did keep them, didn't you?"

Tonya nodded. "The first few I may have deleted, but since I use Smart Mail, it keeps a record of everything that I receive, so it should be in my web archives if nowhere else."

"Good girl. We will also need every letter that you received in your mailbox. Now, have you noticed anything else? Have you seen anybody hanging around your house or your shop who doesn't belong there? Any strange cars that seem to pop up wherever you are?"

Tanya thought for a moment, and then she snapped her fingers. "Yes! I knew something felt off! There have been several times when I've gone out to do errands that it felt like I was being followed. And I seemed to notice something, but I couldn't ever put my finger on it. But now that you mention cars . . . A red convertible. Once it was parked near me at the drugstore. Another time at the supermarket. Several times. I figured it was just somebody around town who shopped at the same places I was. I wouldn't have paid any attention except red convertibles are rather rare around Port Townsend. *Any* convertibles are rather rare, actually. The weather just isn't geared for them."

Alex motioned to Ralph. "Do your thing."

Another few minutes and Ralph turned the screen around again. We were staring at a fancy little red sports car, top down. "Is this the car you remember?"

Tonya nodded. "Yeah, that looks about right. Why?"

"The same model of car is registered to Jack Skelton." He looked over to Alex. "What do we do next, boss?"

Alex thought for a moment. "We figure out why Jack is stalking Tonya, and then we head up to Port Townsend and have a talk with the police."

At that point, the door to the conference room opened again and Bette entered, a strange look on her face. She tossed the letters on the table and shook her head.

"I have a bit of a conundrum here," she said. "The only prints on here are Tonya's. Whoever else handled these letters left no prints. Either he was wearing gloves or he's not human."

At that moment the phone rang. Bette answered from the phone in the conference room. Another moment, and she handed it to Alex, mouthing *Chase Johnson on the line*. Alex took the receiver and listened for a moment, then grunted. He handed the phone back to Bette.

"Well, it's confirmed that Stone Weaver's death fits the same MO as those of the others. No doubt about it, our serial killer has struck again. Also, Chase managed to get the bank manager of Weaver's main branch to check through the records. Luckily, the doppelgänger hasn't gotten to the bank yet and most of the assets are still there. They froze every account, so that nobody can siphon off any money. My guess is that this is going to make the doppelgänger really pissed when it realizes that it went to all that trouble for nothing."

Bette snorted. "All the better to fall into my trap. As long as we don't scare it away before we're able to find it."

"I have a question." A thought had occurred to me. "When we do find it—given we do—what do we do with it? If it can change shape, we obviously can't lock it up. I don't think we want to deport a serial killer to Otherworld. That wouldn't exactly be what I'd call being a good neighbor."

"Only one thing we can do," Ralph said. "Kill the thing."

"I have no problem with that, but what do you think

Chase will say?" I wasn't entirely sure how the legal system was set up to deal with something like this. Matters would be different if it were a human suspect we were after. But a doppelgänger? An entirely different situation.

"I think Chase will be grateful for anything we can do in this situation," Alex said with a shrug. "That's why he came to us in the first place. He knows that the FH-CSI is not set up for this sort of criminal. We're dealing with a monster here. This isn't exactly Ted Bundy or Jeffrey Dahmer. They were monsters, too, but they could be locked up without fear of them imitating the guards and escaping."

I glanced at the clock. It was getting on toward morning. "So where are we at for now?"

Alex looked over his notes. "First, Bette needs to contact Lydia and give her the news that we have eliminated her little salamander problem. Second, Bette will put into motion this cockamamie plan to catch the doppelgänger. I still don't like this plan," he said, leaning forward, his hands pressed on the table. "But I suppose it's the only idea we have at the moment. But Bette"—he gave her a long stare—"once again, you be careful. No playing heroine here. Your safety comes first. Do you understand?"

She nodded. "Loud and clear, sugar lips."

"As long as you do. Ralph, why don't you start researching Jack Skelton more? I don't want to move on Tonya's issue until we know what we're dealing with, but it won't hurt us to get a jump on things. All right, is there anything else on the table?"

I raised my hand. He laughed and nodded to me. "What is it, Shimmer?"

"I'd like to do a little more research into Mary, the ghost next door. That whole thing has me rattled."

"Use whatever resources you need." He stood. "I suppose we better get to it. Shimmer, will you join me in my office?"

The others grinned and I suddenly felt self-conscious, but I nodded. "Sure thing."

* * *

Once Alex and I were alone in his office, I turned to him. "Before you say anything, we have to clarify office protocol here."

"Is something wrong?" He set down his tablet and leaned against the front of his desk, his long legs stretching out in a deliciously long line.

"I really like you, Alex. And I really enjoy our time together." I wasn't sure how to continue without sounding prudish.

"Are you breaking up with me?" The hurt in his eyes hit me hard.

I rushed to say, "*No*, that's not what this is about. Remember I said that I'm uncomfortable having sex in your office? Well, I've thought about it, and I mean it. I really want to make this relationship work, and in order to do that, we have to work on both the business level and the personal level. The fact that you are, in essence, my parole officer confuses the matter even more. And I just feel weird when we make out here. I feel like we're acting like teenagers who can't keep their pants on."

A look of relief washed over his face. "Is that all? No problem. Like I said, I find you irresistible, and I admit that it's hard to keep my hands off you. But I promise, I'll be good. This may mean I'll be spending more time at your place, though—or you at mine."

Relieved, I slipped into his arms. The pale chill of his body washed over me as I rested my head on his shoulder. We were about the same height, so when I raised my head it was to look him straight in the face. I leaned in and gave him a gentle kiss on the lips.

"I still think we're walking a dangerous line, but it's one I'm willing to walk. I'm learning what it means to be in a relationship, but there's still so much that I'm not familiar with. I honestly don't know how to act at times. Nobody's ever given a damn about me before, except Chai, and he's my brother."

Alex brushed the hair back from my face. He stroked my cheek, gently playing one finger over my lips. "Have you ever wondered about your parents? Or is that a stupid question?"

"Every day. I wonder who they were. I wonder why my mother abandoned me. I wonder how many brothers and sisters I have. Are they still alive? There's *so much* I want to know. And yet . . . and yet, if I were to meet my parents today, what would I say? *Why did you throw me away?* That's the only question I can think of."

I broke away and paced over to the giant palm tree in the corner. "When I was little, I would have given anything for my mother to show up and claim me. Now, having lived with the stigma of being nameless, I'm not sure how easy it would be if that happened. Sure, they could put me on the record books then, and everything would be *normal*, but . . . I would never forget how I've been treated. Once you've been cast away by a society, it's not exactly easy to imagine becoming part of that society. Especially when I think the way I'm treated is unjust and archaic."

Alex was nodding. "I understand. It may not be exactly the same thing, but I wonder, when we manage to achieve vampire rights here, what group are they going to oppress next? It seems some societies always have to have someone to look down on."

"Exactly!" I turned, smiling. "You understand. Sometimes, I wish I could go back to the Dragon Reaches and adopt every little dragonette from the Lost and Foundling. I hated that orphanage and I sure as hell feel for the dragonettes who are still there."

Just then, the intercom buzzed. Alex answered. "Yes?"

It was Bette. "I'm sorry to interrupt you, boss, but I have a new client on the phone who would like to talk to you. I've taken their information, but figured since it's so late, you might want to schedule an appointment for them later on?"

Alex glanced at the clock. It was going on four thirty. "Why don't you have them come by tonight. Schedule them first thing."

"Will do."

I let out a long sigh. "Thanks for understanding. And for listening."

"I understand, and it's okay. Listen, why don't you drop by my place after work? We can leave in a few minutes. I'm sure Tonya wouldn't mind driving herself back to your place. Chai can go with her." A glimmer of a smile crossed his face and by the glint in his eye, I knew what he was thinking.

"If you think we have enough time, I'd like that."

As we left the building, leaving Bette to lock up, the rain started in earnest. The drops pounded around us as we headed toward the Range Rover, pelting the street with a heavy hand. I closed my eyes, letting them stream over my face, the water washing away the growing headache. And for the first time in a while, I was able to leave work behind me as we headed toward Alex's condo.

"**O**h good gods," I said, falling back against the sheets, my body slick with sweat. "That was wonderful." I closed my eyes, drifting in the shower of mist that sprinkled down on us. It had started in Port Townsend, with the first time we had sex. A sparkling web of dewdrops had showered over us as I came, magical and beautiful. It didn't happen every time, but when it did, it usually meant I was thoroughly sated.

"Feel good?" Alex leaned back against the pillows, one arm under his head, a goofy smile on his face. But it was an adorable goofy smile.

I rested my head on his shoulder. "Yeah, I really do. I could get used to this, you know. Sleeping in this bed, beside you." As I said it, I realized I meant every word. It felt comforting to sleep beside someone, to know there was someone else on the other side of the bed.

He pulled the covers up as I shivered, the glistening drops of sweat chilling against the air. "I forgot to turn up the thermostat for you, love. I'm sorry." Vampires didn't need heat, and Alex kept his place at sixty-five degrees, warm enough to prevent mold.

I tucked the blanket under my chin, yawning. Even though I wasn't ready to go to sleep yet, sex always relaxed me into a dozy state. "That's all right. I'm not fragile. Besides, the Dragon Reaches aren't warm—not where I'm from. Oh, when you head into the southern climes, where the golds and the reds live, yes—it gets downright steamy. But we're at the top of the world. There's not much room there for heat, you know. And on the edge of the ocean, it's always windy and cool."

He stroked my back, kissing my forehead. "You really have led an isolated life, haven't you?"

I nodded. "The culture shock, coming here, was incredibly difficult. There are people everywhere." I pushed myself up, sitting against the headboard, my knees up to my chest as I wrapped my arms around them. "I think what surprised me most was how gregarious humans are. Even when dragons congregate, there's this sense of isolationism. Aloofness, I suppose."

Alex eased up till he was sitting cross-legged beside me. "Did you mean what you said about being exclusive? Or was that just . . . said under duress?" He softly touched my arm, his fingers cool against my skin. "It's okay if you say yes. I just want to know the truth."

I gazed at him, realizing how safe and comfortable I felt. We weren't at the office; it didn't feel like a game here. This . . . this felt real. "I meant it," I said softly. "I don't know . . . long term, how we will do together. But for now, while we're good . . . I mean it."

He thought over my words, his gaze never leaving mine. "That's good enough for me. I have something for you I'd like you to wear." As he spoke, he reached over to the night-stand and handed me a velvet box. It was a ring box.

"Alex . . ."

"Not an engagement ring—not at all. But while we're together, as long as you want to be with me, will you wear this?"

I opened the box, slowly, and found myself staring at a beautiful ring. Platinum, it was a simple band with three stones. The center was sapphire, and the two to either side, diamond. The sapphire was dark as ocean water on a cold day. But there was more to it than the eye could see—I sensed the rush of ocean waves, the siren song of the water calling.

"What magic does this ring hold?" I held it up, gazing at it.

"I had it enchanted. The ring is aligned to the plane of Water. It will enhance your water magic and always tell you when you're near the ocean or a lake or river." His smile was so genuine, so caring, that I found tears welling up in my eyes.

"You are a special man, you know that?" I held out the ring and, as I stared at it, it was as though a dam that I hadn't known was there in my heart began to shatter. Mutely, I leaned in and kissed him gently on the lips.

"You like it, then?"

I nodded, unsure of speaking. Finally, I found my voice. "I've never . . . felt this way before." I searched his face. How could I shift from being uncertain to knowing—absolutely knowing—in a matter of seconds? It wasn't the ring, it wasn't the jewels . . . no, it was that he had cared enough to have something made for me, something that would make my life better.

He took it and, holding my hand, he slid the band on my left index finger. "This means you're my girlfriend, you know."

"I know." And then, before I could help myself, I blurted out, "Alex, I think I love you."

With a soft laugh, he pulled me into his arms and laid me back against the sheets. "I love you, too, Shimmer. I love you, too." And then, once more, he entered me, and the world fell away.

By the time I slipped out of the satin sheets that Alex kept on his bed, he had fallen into that sunrise slumber all vampires fall into. I wandered through his apartment. Leather furniture, heavy wood . . . Alex liked traditional styles. The books were evenly spaced on the bookshelves, the shelves thoroughly dust-free. His desk was neat and tidy, and the kitchen clean. Bottles of blood lined the shelves in the fridge, but he had also stocked food, for me.

I made toast and eggs, then washed the pan and my plate. All the while, the ring felt heavy on my finger. I loved jewelry, but this one—it meant something. As I washed my face and brushed my hair, getting ready to leave for the day, I stared at myself in the mirror.

"I can love . . . I can feel love . . ." I had been afraid the feeling would slip away, would vanish the moment I said the words, but it was more surprising to me that it didn't. A part of myself that I'd kept walled off for so very long had broken wide open, and now I was stark raving terrified.

What if it didn't work out? What if he hurt me? What if I hurt him?

*What if the world blows up with you and everybody else on it? Anything can happen. Just let it be. Accept it, and let it be. Life will sort itself out if you allow it to.*

Tired of worrying, I decided to embrace the new feelings that had opened up. Bette had said Alex liked crossword puzzle books. It seemed a poor gift in exchange for the ring, but if it was what he loved, I'd buy him several on my way home.

I was about to let myself out of his apartment when his phone rang. He had left it on the living room table and at first I was about to ignore it, but then thought that maybe the call was important. Whoever was calling might not realize sunrise had already happened from behind the cover of heavy gray clouds that filled the sky. I picked up his phone and glanced at the Caller ID.

*Glenda.*

Oh, hell. Should I answer it? Should I let it go to voice mail? After a moment, I set the phone down and let it continue to ring; another couple of rings later it fell silent. Wondering what she wanted, half wishing I had answered, I let myself out, making sure everything was locked tight.

The doorman nodded and opened the door for me as I left. He was from the Supe Community Action Council and I knew he was a werewolf. They had ironed out a treaty with the Seattle Vampire Nexus to exchange guard duties when necessary. The Shrouded Grove Towers was an upscale complex, and Alex paid a pretty penny to live there. I thought about stopping in at Ralph's place, given he lived next door, to find out if he had discovered anything else about either Jack Skelton or Mary, my ghost. But for the moment, I wanted to just let the newness of my feelings settle in, so I discarded the idea and headed for the bus stop.

I could have called Tonya to come pick me up, but I didn't want to bother her. Instead, I hopped the bus and was relieved to see that most of the seats were empty.

My thoughts wandered back to the discussion Alex and I had had in his office, about whether I had ever tried to find my parents. Throughout the centuries after I left the orphanage, I had looked for them. But truth was, I had no real clue of where to start. The Lost and Foundling refused to give me any information about where they had found me, or anything surrounding how I came to be at the orphanage. I had asked time and again, coming up against a brick wall each time. Now, I wondered if there was any way I could break into their records. It would have to be legally, given that I couldn't even go back to the Dragon Reaches at this point. But maybe, just maybe, someone could help me.

I hated owing favors, but Camille D'Artigo was married to a dragon who was considered almost a prince in the realm. Lord Iampaatar and his mother had a tremendous amount of clout with the Council. If I appealed to them, they might just help me. I had a feeling that Iampaatar would be far more understanding than most of the dragons I had met. For one thing, he was married to a half-Fae, half-human woman. That alone set him apart.

I decided that I would give them a call later on. The worst thing that could happen was he could say no and then I would be no worse off than I was now. Feeling somewhat more settled, I leaned back and stared out at the silvery morning sky as the rain washed down to clean the streets.

A s I walked through the door, Chai took one look at me and smiled. "What happened?"

I blinked. "I can't get anything by you, can I?"

He shook his head. "Spill it, Little Sister."

Tonya came up behind him. "Spill what? Shimmer's got a secret?"

I let out a long sigh. "I guess it shows on my face, huh?"

"Your face, your aura—you're positively glowing. What happened?" Chai glanced over his shoulder. "We have waffles and bacon, but you don't get a bite until you level with us."

With a soft smile, I said, "I told Alex . . . that I love him."

And that, of course, called for a celebration with a second breakfast. They weren't nosy about it, but I finally explained how the dam had broken open, and showed them the ring.

"That has some pretty heavy-duty magic on it, Little Sister," Chai said.

Tonya agreed. "Oh, by the way, Stacy called. She said

thanks again for the food. She's headed to the doctor's again today."

We settled ourselves in the living room with our food. Feeling slightly overwhelmed, I said, "Let's talk about something other than me and my feelings, okay? Why didn't you tell us about Jack while we were up in Port Townsend? Maybe we could have helped you at that point." I shoved a forkful of waffles into my mouth and smiled as a burst of maple syrup trickled down my throat. While I preferred protein to any other food, I had to admit—waffles were nature's perfect sweet.

Tonya looked up from her book. "Because at that point, I wasn't sure it was a serious issue. I was uneasy, but I thought it might just be my imagination, or that I might just be exaggerating things." She placed the bookmark between the pages and closed the volume, setting it on the side table. "Human women are often trained to accept bad behavior like that. A lot of men try to get away with it, telling us we're imagining things, when in fact they're actually being jerks. I thought I was immune to falling into old patterns, but apparently not. I still don't understand why my mother didn't tell me that she had gotten married while I was gone."

"If you don't mind my opinion," Chai interjected, "she might have been embarrassed about it. Or she might have thought you would think she was stupid. Your mother sounds like she was a strong-willed woman, and to mistake an abusive man for a good person might have made her feel like she had failed."

"You probably have something there." Tonya let out a little sigh. "Penelope was a very strong-willed woman; that's why we argued so much. I'm just as stubborn as she is. I doubt if she'd want me to know that she had actually gotten involved with someone who was that abusive. And that she had stayed with him after the first time he hit her. I suppose she was lonely."

"Loneliness can make us do a lot of strange things." I

shrugged. "When I was back in the orphanage, a lot of the dragonettes let themselves be bullied just because they were so lonely. Friendships were discouraged, and Ser-Rigel encouraged us to turn in any suspect activity. The Ser used the divide-and-conquer method with us. As long as we didn't unite, we were at risk and more tractable."

Chai shook his head. "The more I hear about your childhood, the more I want to go back there and break some heads."

I laughed, the mood breaking. "Sometimes I wish I could say yes, go ahead. But I think even a djinn would have trouble against a dragon. You're definitely tough enough, but when you're facing an entire organization of my kind, I doubt you'd have much of a chance."

He shrugged. "To be honest, Little Sister, you've seen very little of my powers. I don't think you are aware of how capable I am of taking on adversaries much larger than myself. I keep cloaked for many reasons."

This wasn't the first time that I wondered about Chai's background. When we were in Port Townsend he had mentioned being an executioner at one point. I had refrained from asking about that part of his life, partially because the whole thought frightened me and partially because it felt like it would be intrusive. But now and then, Chai came out with something that made me think we should have a long talk. He knew a lot about my background but I really didn't know much about him.

Tonya seemed to sense the unease and cleared her throat. "My mother had an abusive childhood and I think there were some things she just couldn't let go of. Whatever the case, I knew nothing about her marriage to George and she didn't tell me. But that does give me some idea of how Jack got hold of my information. She must've talked about me while I was gone, and I left a number of my personal papers there from high school. Chances are, Jack knows far more about me than I thought."

I could tell that the worry from before had now turned into active fear. I didn't blame her, either. Obsession was a dangerous thing. It blinded people to reality and made them believe the damnedest things. In some ways, love was more dangerous than hate.

I wanted to take her mind off the subject and I thought I knew just the thing to do that. "Want to go see Mary again?"

Tonya blinked. "Do you really think it safe?"

"Of course it isn't, that's part of the fun." I shook my head at Chai, who gave me a dirty look. I really didn't think it was terribly risky, not if we were careful and maybe stayed outside the house and looked around the yard. It would take Tonya's mind off her stalker, and it would take my mind off my morning with Alex, and Bette's upcoming plan. I had a bad feeling that it would go south, but we didn't have many options. If we didn't catch the doppelgänger soon, it would move on, killing its way across the country. That we might be able to prevent further deaths outweighed the risk. Besides which, we could watch out for Bette. She was one of our own and we wouldn't let anything happen to her.

I waved at the window. "It's light outside. For some reason, I always think that ghosts have more power in the dark."

"That's never been proven," Tonya said.

"No, but we can hope. Chai, if you're so worried you can come with us."

Chai grumbled but pushed himself to his feet. "All right, I'll come with you. But I don't see the fascination with a grungy bunch of spirits in a dilapidated house." He was smiling, though, and I knew he was teasing us.

Tonya winked at him. "I'm glad you're coming with us. It never hurts to have a powerful djinn on your side."

"You're just saying that because you want backup." But he laughed, joining us.

I shrugged into a jacket. It was pouring out, the rain rushing in rivulets down the sidewalk, clogging the storm drains with cast-off leaves and debris from the trees and gutters.

The Greenbelt Park District was old enough that it still had sidewalks running along the curbs, rather than driveways pulling directly into the houses. I had noticed that in a number of modern suburbs, the notion of *sidewalk* seemed to be outmoded. I liked my neighborhood, ghosts or not, and it made me sad to see so many houses standing empty. But the aura of decay and abandonment seemed to fill the air around here, and the entire district reminded me of old mausoleums covered in ivy, with oaks hanging low, dripping with moss and bracken.

As we crossed the street I glanced back at my snug little cottage, and once again the sensation that I had found my home hit me. The Dragon Reaches had abandoned me before I ever abandoned them. And I realized that deep in my heart, I hoped it would never be the same over here, Earthside.

# CHAPTER 14

**I wasn't sure** what I hoped to gain, but now that we knew Mary was the deeply disturbed spirit of a murderess, I hoped we could find a way to put her to rest. Although, she *had* killed her children and her husband. Was she here as a punishment? Was she supposed to remember what she had done? Or were we missing some other possibility? Perhaps she already did remember her actions and was playing on our sympathies. Perhaps the demons she blamed for the killings had never really existed. Evil was very real, and quite often, extremely conscious and cunning. Whatever the case, I felt drawn to the old house.

Tonya had brought her bag of tricks. She was a powerful witch and had faced down far more spirits than I had. I glanced over at Chai. He had paused by the gate and was staring past the back of the house. There was no real delineation between the backyard and the front yard, no fence to mark the division. The swing hanging on the tree was moving softly, but I put the motion down to the wind.

"Where did they find the bodies?" I turned to Tonya.

She nodded toward the top story of the house. "They found three of her children and her husband up in their bedrooms. The baby, well, they never found the body. But they assume that she killed her baby boy and disposed of him. The cops made a few halfhearted attempts to dig up the yard, but nobody really believed he was alive."

"It must have been terrifying . . . to be one of her neighbors and discover what had happened. If I had children I would've been terrified. Hell, even without children, I would've been terrified. Finding out you have a mass murderer in your neighborhood wouldn't exactly make for peace of mind."

"There were very few who took her side. Most of them thought the whole demon story was just that—a story. There were quite a few protesters outside the courthouse when she was on trial. Most of them were calling for her life." Tonya skirted the house and headed toward the back. Chai and I followed her. "I'm not sure how the trial went, story I read wasn't all that involved, but it ended with a hung jury, and the judge sentenced Mary to life at the Greenbelt Park Asylum. The thing is, don't you have to be just a little bit crazy to kill your entire family?"

"To be honest, I can't answer that. I never met my family, and among my kind things are very different. Ancestry is extremely important. If you dishonor your family, your parents have every right to kill you. I suppose it's very much like an honor killing. And if a spouse dishonors his family and his partner, well—that happened not too long ago and ended up with a white dragon being destroyed. You know who the D'Artigos are?"

Tonya shook her head. "I don't think I ever heard of them."

"I guess it doesn't matter. They're half Fae from Otherworld. I think their mother was human. But anyway, one of the sisters is married to a dragon. His father was excommunicated and executed because he kidnapped and tortured her, dishonoring his wife and his son and abusing family relations. Even those of us who don't live in the mainstream society of the Dragon Reaches heard about *that*."

There was no easy way to explain the complicated rules of my society to her, especially when I wasn't entirely sure of all of them myself.

"I suppose sometimes not having a family is a blessing in disguise," I said, after a moment.

By that time we had reached the back of the house. I was surprised to see how big the yard was. It spanned at least three full-size lots. Heavily wooded, the yard was pretty, even in its abandoned state. Of course the gardens were overgrown, and the grass was knee high. The trees needed a good pruning, and the old shed out back was leaning precariously, about to fall down. But otherwise, the lot and the house had once been beautiful.

"You know, this really is a lovely place. Or it could be," Tonya said. She cocked her head to the side. "I wonder what it would take to clear this land of the ghosts."

"You mean the entire neighborhood? The district is pretty large—"

She interrupted with a shake of the head. "No, I just mean this house and the yard. Maybe it would be a good thing if I got out of Port Townsend. I would probably do much better business down here with my shop than up there, and now that my mother is dead there's really nothing to hold me there."

After a pause, she added, "Not even Degoba."

Chai cleared his throat. He looked distinctly uncomfortable, and I almost teased him by saying, *Well, you wanted to come along with the girls.* But I kept my mouth shut. It felt like we were walking on eggshells with our conversation and I wondered how much of that was because of our surroundings. It made me slightly nervous knowing that Mary might be listening to us, now that I knew the truth about her.

"Do you think there's anything we *can* do about Mary?"

Tonya shrugged. "I've been thinking about that. We need

to know whether she really understands why she's here. I'm beginning to think that all the monsters in the house are the parts of herself that she's pushed away and that she's denying. Almost like having MPD. Only instead of fragmenting into separate identities, she fragmented into separate entities."

"MPD? I'm not familiar with the term."

"It stands for *multiple personality disorder.* Sometimes when a human is traumatized, a part of their identity will splinter off, in order to cope with the traumatic event. There are people who have hundreds of personalities and each might as well be a separate, distinct individual. They all coexist within the same body. In a few cases, the person is actually possessed by other spirits, but mostly this happens in cases of severe abuse." She stopped abruptly.

"What is it? Do you see something?"

Slowly, Tonya shook her head. "No. It just occurred to me that . . . I wonder. Do you think that perhaps Mary was abused by her husband? Back in that day, it wasn't against the law—nobody looked into domestic violence cases. And nothing in the articles I read ever mentioned it, but I doubt if they would have. If she was the victim of traumatic domestic violence, that might account for what happened to her."

I wandered over to a dilapidated picnic table and gingerly sat on the bench. What Tonya proposed made sense. Or maybe I just wanted it to make sense, because I didn't want to believe that Mary could deliberately destroy her family. Tonya must've noticed the expression on my face.

"You want her to be innocent, don't you? You want her to be everything she says she is." She rested a hand on my shoulder.

After a moment, I shrugged. "I suppose you're right. I guess I do prefer happy endings. I haven't had very many of them in my lifetime, and that spans a hell of a lot of years. I know not everything is going to work out the way I want, and maybe Mary is just the spirit of a cold-blooded killer, out to play us even from the spirit world. But I hope she's not. I hope that—if she *did* kill her family—she was truly possessed by demons. Not everyone is strong, and that's something I've had to learn since I came here. I had to be, I had to push my emotions to the side, to fight for everything I got. And now I'm learning that some people just can't do that. Sometimes, they just don't have the ability to fight off the darkness."

"Come over here," Chai called.

We turned to see him examining something near the back hedge. The foliage had grown up to crowd out the sky, at least thirty feet tall. I wasn't sure if they were trees or bushes, but they provided a dense barrier to the lot behind Mary's house. Tonya and I cautiously crossed the yard. He was kneeling in the grass, brushing a tangle of the tall weeds to one side. As we approached, he held out his hand and a globe of light flickered above his fingers, bright enough so that we could see what he was doing. Dawn was streaking across the sky, but here in the shadow of the hedge, it was still dark.

"I found a flagstone that doesn't seem to belong here. There aren't any others, so I doubt that it marks a path through the yard. And I sense something here. A presence, although it's faint, and I can't hear anything."

Tonya joined him, kneeling in the grass. She placed her hands against the stone and closed her eyes, cocking her head to one side as she listened. I had the distinct impression that she was hearing something that we couldn't. After a few moments, she pulled back, resting her hands on her knees, staring at the flagstone.

"You're right. There's something here. I can hear a faint cry in the wind and I felt a great sadness when I touched the stone. I think we should dig this up. Is there anyone who would care? Who owns this house, now? I know you said that Mary told you that her children did, but her children are dead."

"That, I can't tell you. We should check into it. If the city owns it, then they sure haven't done anything with it." When

I had been searching for a house to buy, Mary's had not been on the list of available ones. Again, I wondered if Tonya really was interested in the house. "You're really thinking of buying this, aren't you?"

She gave a slight shrug as she attempted to pry the flagstone out from the dirt. "Maybe. As I said, it might be time for me to leave Port Townsend."

Setting the globe of light to float in the air, Chai motioned for her to move aside. He took hold of the flagstone, digging his fingers into the dirt, curling them beneath the wide stone. With seeming ease, he jostled the rock until he had pried it loose. The heavy stone gave way with the sucking noise and Chai turned to set it aside. The light lowered itself until we could see that we were staring into a small chamber dug into the ground. It was lined with brick and about the size of a violin case, and about two feet deep. There was something at the bottom wrapped in what looked to be a tattered cloth.

A sinking feeling hit my stomach. I didn't want to know what was inside the shrouded cloth.

Tonya glanced first at Chai and then at me. In a hushed voice, she asked, "What do you think it is? Do you think it's—"

"I don't know, and I'm not sure I want to know. But since we've come this far, we might as well go all the way." I started to lean down to gather the cloth in my arms, but Chai stopped me, resting his fingers on my wrist.

"Let me do it, Little Sister." His voice gentle, he motioned for both Tonya and me to back away. As he lifted the bundle out of the chamber, I thought I heard a faint cry go whooshing past. Tonya let out a gasp and I knew that she had heard what I had heard. Chai very carefully placed the cloth on the ground and began to pull back the cloth, corner by corner. He motioned for the globe of light to hover over the bundle so that we could see. The cloth gave way, exposing the gleam of ivory bones. They were the bones of a child—a baby.

"Mary's lost son." I knew that, without a doubt, we had found the bones of her baby boy.

Tonya glanced up, looking beyond me toward the front yard. Her eyes widened and she let out an "Oh!" as she slowly rose to her feet. I quickly turned to find myself staring at Mary. This was the first time I had ever seen her out of the house, and instead of the cheery smile she was staring in horror at the bundle of bones on the ground.

"No, no . . . No, no, no!" Her voice grew progressively louder, culminating in a shriek as she raised her hands to her face, disbelief giving way to horror. "I don't want to remember. Please don't make me remember!"

I half expected her to turn violent and attack us. But instead, the spirit moved forward and knelt by the fragile bones. She lowered her head and reached out one ghostly hand to run them over the rib cage of what had been her child. "He wouldn't let me keep him. He couldn't stand that I was happy. He threatened to take everything away from me."

She spoke as if we weren't there. Leaning forward, she brushed the forehead of the little skull. "I'm so sorry. I tried to stop him, but I couldn't. I never meant for any of this to happen."

And then, slowly, Mary rose and softly passed by us back toward the house, where she vanished through the wall. The early morning fell unnaturally silent. I had the feeling that we had witnessed something terribly private and intimate.

Tonya was the first to speak. "I think there's a lot more here than meets the eye. I know ghosts can lie, and I've dealt with some pretty skeevy characters, but in my gut something tells me that this is no open-and-closed case. Something happened here—more than a demon possessing Mary. More than her going berserk and killing her family. I don't think she's the one who put the baby in this chamber."

"I think you're right. I know that whatever happened here took place decades ago. But it feels like it's still going on. I haven't been able to decide whether Mary is benign and under attack, or whether she's the instigator. But now I think that she was the original victim in all of this." I brushed the wet leaves and dirt that stuck to my knees off my jeans and arched my back, stretching. "So what do we do? Do we take these bones to the police?"

"Remember what happened at Patrick's. We had to turn over the skeleton we found. But first, I'd like to do a little scrying over these bones. I want to see what I can pick up. Who knows, maybe I'll come up with some of the answers that we're looking for." Tonya turned to Chai. "Is there a way we can protect these bones without appearing to have disturbed them too much? I don't want the cops asking what we were doing with them."

Chai frowned. "If I bury them again, who knows what's going to happen? If something is out to protect a secret, it might decide to get rid of the bones. Whatever you're going to do, I would do it now so that Shimmer can call the authorities."

The last thing I wanted to do was put in another call to Chase Johnson, but he was the only one I could think of. I wondered if I should contact Alex first, but then realized that would take all day—until sunset. Reluctantly, I pulled out my phone and scrolled through my contacts. Finding Chase's name, I hit the Call button.

"Faerie-Human Crime Scene Investigation unit, Yugi speaking. How may I help you?"

I remembered that Yugi was Chase's right-hand man. I wasn't sure exactly how he figured into the hierarchy at the station, but I knew he was fairly high up. "Hi, this is Shimmer, and I work with Alex Radcliffe at the Fly by Night Magical Investigations Agency. We've talked before."

"Oh yes, hello. What can I do for you?"

"I'm calling about the house across the street from mine. We have a situation here." I explained to him what was going on. I knew that he and his men were all well aware of the ghostly activity in the Greenbelt Park District, and so I felt comfortable telling him all we had found out about Mary and the house. In fact, this seemed a good enough time to ask who owned the place.

After listening to everything, Yugi asked me to stay put and said he would send out a patrol car. "In fact, I'll come myself because this sounds a little complicated to explain to my men. I'll be there in about fifteen minutes. Until then try not to disturb anything else about the scene."

After I hung up, I told Chai and Tonya what he had said. Tonya sat down by the bones, careful to avoid disturbing them, and pulled a crystal ball out of her bag.

"I guess I'd better get busy before they get here," she said.

Tonya didn't have time to tell us what she found out, although the look on her face told me she had discovered something. Before she could say anything, the lights of the prowl car flashed from the curb in front. Tonya jumped to her feet, slipping the crystal ball back into her bag. She backed away from the bones. I went to meet the officers.

A muscled but lean blond-haired man reached out to shake my hand. "How do you do? I'm Yugi and this is Officer Lawrence. If you could take us to where you found the skeleton?" The man beside him was obviously Fae, dark and short, with a wild, feral look about him.

I led them to the backyard and pointed toward the brick chamber. "We found it under a flagstone. I'm pretty sure the bones are the missing son from the Mary Smith case. She supposedly killed her family in 1938 with an axe, but the body of her baby boy was never found. We think these are his remains."

Yugi somberly knelt by the skeleton. "And you found him in that enclosure?"

"Yes sir." Tonya moved forward. "My name is Tonya Harris and I'm a witch. I'm from Port Townsend and I'm down here visiting Shimmer and Alex. We've been investigating the haunting in this house, and I was drawn to come out here tonight; I could hear someone crying in the wind. I had the feeling something was under the flagstone."

Yugi stared Chai for a moment, smiling softly. "I'll ask you no favors as long as you offer none in return."

Chai laughed, his eyes crinkling. The pair understood each other perfectly. "Ask your questions; they won't be considered favors."

"I'm going to assume you're the one who pried up the flagstone?"

"Yes. Shimmer is strong enough, but I'm stronger."

That was true enough while I was in human form, but part of me wanted to say, *Let me just shift into my dragon form and we'll see who's stronger*. But I had the feeling it wouldn't be diplomatic, and it sounded too flippant when we were standing over the skeleton of a baby.

"I see the child is wrapped in a blanket. Was the skeleton originally in that blanket?" Yugi was jotting down notes in a small notebook. Chai's globe of light dove down to cast a glow over the paper so Yugi could see what he was writing. The officer flickered a glance at the djinn and smiled faintly.

I decided I would answer this one. "Yes, it was wrapped—fully. We didn't know what it was until we lifted it out of the enclosure. Although, to be honest, we all had the feeling that it wasn't going to be any treasure chest or anything."

The officer laughed at that. "I wish it *were* a treasure chest, for all our sakes. It would save us a whole lot of trouble. And you think the bones are those belonging to a baby boy who lived here in 1938?"

"We're fairly certain they are. We decided we had better call you, even though I'm not sure what exactly you can do at this point." I stared at the bundle again, feeling wistful and sad.

"We'll run some tests on it, but I have the feeling you're right. It's an old skeleton. Even I can feel the energy surrounding it, and it reeks of years gone by, forgotten and neglected." There was a tone to his voice that made me glance a second time at him. This was no ordinary human, but neither was he Fae, nor elf. "We're going to be here for a little while, and I'm pretty sure we're going to have to search the house again. You say you've been inside?"

"Yeah, and I have to tell you there are some dangerous spirits lurking around inside, so be careful. I don't mean to sound forward, but if you need our help, we don't mind sticking around." I looked into his eyes, and I could see a spark of fear behind those cool blue irises. But he merely shook his head.

"Thank you for the offer, but I think you should go home for now. You say you live right across the street? All of you?"

I pointed to my house. "I own that house, and Chai is my roommate. Tonya is staying with us for the moment. If you need to ask us any questions, feel free to come over. I work nights so I'll be up for a while yet."

As we walked back across the street, I glanced at the house behind me and thought, just for a moment, that I saw Mary peeking from one of the top-floor windows. But then the faint light was gone and I wasn't sure if I had seen anything at all.

B y the time we got into my house, Tonya was shivering. I motioned to Chai. "Why don't you get her a blanket? I'll put on the kettle for some tea."

I hurried into the kitchen and set the kettle on the burner, turning it on full blast. And then, because I remembered the way Tonya had been up in Port Townsend after we had exorcised ghosts from a bed-and-breakfast, I took cheese out of the refrigerator, and bread, and roast beef, and began to make several sandwiches. They would give her necessary energy. Carrying them into the living room along with a bag of cookies, I set them on the coffee table. Chai wrapped a throw around her shoulders. By then, she was visibly shivering, her teeth chattering.

"Are you all right? Is there anything we can do?" I sat

down beside her and took her hands in mine, rubbing them briskly to warm them up.

Chai stood behind the sofa and held out his hands, not touching her but close enough so that when he began to generate heat it wrapped around her like a gentle wave. I could feel it from where I was sitting, and it was more than welcome.

"I'll be all right, if I can just get something to eat and something warm to drink inside me."

I stuffed a sandwich in her hands and she began to devour it. Halfway through, she slowed, a relieved look spreading across her face. By the time she finished off the sandwich, the kettle was whistling. I hustled into the kitchen and made a pot of tea. As I carried it out on a tea tray, along with cups and saucers, Tonya had moved on to the cookies. Chai was doing his best to help her finish them off.

"Save one for me!" I held out my hand after I set the tea tray on the coffee table. They handed me the bag, Chai giving me a scolded-puppy look. "Oh stop that, I know you're not sorry. I know how much you love Oreos." Turning to Tonya, I asked, "Are you up to telling us what happened?"

She let out a long sigh and nodded. "If I could get a cup of that tea, yes."

Chai poured tea for all of us. I found it amusing to watch the seven-foot djinn gracefully handling china cups without breaking them. He was extremely graceful and somehow managed to get tea to all of us without spilling a single drop. After she had managed several sips, Tonya set down her cup and leaned back, shrugging the throw tighter around her shoulders.

"While I was using my crystal ball, I was dragged into a very dark place. At first, I couldn't see anything around me. Then a light appeared and I realized I was in the kitchen of Mary's house. I saw her standing there, crying as an angry man loomed over her. As she pulled her hands away from her face I could see that she had a black eye. I wasn't sure what the man was angry about—I couldn't hear them. But he raised his fists, and I had the feeling he was threatening her. And then the scene changed. I was seeing a bedroom, and she was sitting in a chair, holding a baby to her chest. The child was crying and she seemed to be trying to get him to stop, patting his back as tears poured down her face. The same man was there. He pointed at the child and said something. Mary shied away, looking like she was trying to shield the baby. Again—this was all silent, like some silent movie."

"Ten to one, it was her husband you saw." I had a very bad feeling about how this was going to end, and the look on Tonya's face did nothing to calm that feeling.

"Oh, I'm sure you're right," she said. Her voice was tired, and she stared down at the cup and saucer in her hands. "You know, sometimes I hate having the Sight. Sometimes I hate being able to peer into business that's none of my own. I feel like a peeping Tom, or voyeur. And half the time, I don't want to see what I'm forced to. But I can't help what I am, and if I can help put someone to rest or calm someone's fears, then I feel I have no choice."

Chai left off playing heater and joined us on the sofa. He reached out and softly brushed Tonya's shoulder and right then, I knew that he was falling for her. There was something about his touch—a gentleness that I had never seen in him before. He was gentle with me, but in a brotherly way.

"You do what you have to do," he said.

She nodded. "I know, and that's why I forced myself to stay, to watch. Mary was still holding the baby—and oh, she looked so much younger there, and so fragile. The man suddenly yanked the child out of her arms. She began to scream, but he turned and . . . and . . . he shook the baby so hard that even in silence, I could see that he snapped the child's neck. Mary fell to her knees, still screaming, as he dumped the child in front of her on the floor and barked some sort of an order. I think he was ordering her to get rid of it." She spoke so flatly that at first the words didn't register, and then I realized what she'd said.

"He killed their baby. I wonder if that's what sent her over the edge? Why didn't she call the police?"

Tonya shrugged. "My guess is he threatened that if she did, he would tell them she was the one who killed the baby. Back then, nobody believed the woman. I'm not sure exactly whether that was what broke her, but I have a feeling we're going to find out. When Mary saw the bones, I could see the look of recognition cross her face—as if she were waking up from a dream. I think we have to be very careful. This may drive her over the edge, and who knows how powerful a spirit she really is?"

"I think you're right." I picked up the cookie bag and shook out the last three into my hand. As I bit into one, the chocolate filled my mouth, but it couldn't take away the sour taste that Tonya's revelation had left in it. I knew how cruel people could be; I grew up with cruelty. But I wanted to believe in goodness, and I wanted to believe that there were parents who loved their children. Tonight had shaken both hopes.

Chai seemed to sense my mood, and he patted the seat next to him. As I slipped in beside him, he wrapped his arm around me and I leaned my head on his shoulder, finishing the cookies. He held out his other arm and Tonya stared at him for a moment, then slid into his embrace as well, leaning against his other side. We sat that way for a long time, still as statues, unspeaking, as the tea cooled, and the flash of police lights flickered through the front window.

# CHAPTER 15

It was ten A.M. before Yugi rang the front doorbell. By then, Tonya had taken a shower. She was wearing down, exhausted from the night. I was still running on adrenaline, although I had the feeling I would go to sleep early—perhaps even sleeping a full seven hours. Chai was cleaning house. He knew how much a clutter-free environment helped me think.

I ushered the officer in. He glanced at the aquarium against the wall and smiled softly. "That's quite a setup you've got there. I take it you like fish?"

I gave him a soft smile. "I'm particularly fond of jellyfish. But yes, I love everything to do with the ocean." I wasn't sure if he was aware that I was a dragon—a water dragon at that—but chances were good that Chase had told him. "Please, have a seat. Would you like some coffee or tea?"

He shook his head. "No, thank you. I have to get back to the station. I just wanted to let you know that we've gone through the house. You're right, it's extremely creepy and I have to agree that it's haunted. Of course, that won't go in my official report but I will be sure to tell Chase about it. He should be in the office by the time I get back there. I also had one of my men do a little research while we were waiting for the coroner. It appears that the house actually belongs to a distant relative of Mary Smith. I have her name if you would like it. Elena Johnson lives in Maine. Her mother was Mary's niece, Cordelia. Cordelia passed the house on to her daughter. Elena has never been out to claim it. She pays the property taxes but she said that every time she thought about selling it, something bad happened to one of her family members. I have a feeling she thinks it's cursed."

"In a sense, she's right. Please do leave us her name and number. I think my friend Tonya might be interested in talking to her." I paused, trying to think of how to phrase my next question. "What happens next? Who claims the body of the child? Did Mary have any other relatives around here?"

"That, I don't have an answer for. At least not at this point. You should ask Chase later on, if you want to know. Or you can call me in a few days and I might be able to give you more information." He stood, and with a bob of his head added, "It's been nice to meet you, Shimmer. I wish it were under better circumstances. And now, if you'll excuse me, I have to get back to headquarters."

I ushered him out the door, watching as he walked down the sidewalk to his cruiser. As I closed the door and turned back, pressing my back against it, Tonya appeared in the living room, a terry-cloth robe wrapped around her. She was carrying Snookums, who was draped over her shoulder, looking extremely relaxed. Tonya, on the other hand, just looked tired.

"I have the name of the person who owns Mary's house. If you're really interested . . ." I let my words drift off. While I was excited at the thought that she might move down to Seattle, I didn't want to seem pushy.

"Yes, but first I have to figure out if I can clear the house and land. And I need to check my e-mail before I turn in for the day." She moved toward the table holding her laptop. Chai popped out of the kitchen, another tray of tea in hand. He cleared a space on the table and carefully set the tray down. Then, without a word, he returned to the kitchen and I heard the sound of dishes rattling as he filled the dishwasher.

Tonya fired up her computer and I sat beside her.

"Bette will be heading toward the community center soon." I glanced at the clock. "I believe her class starts at one P.M. I just hope she's careful. The doppelgänger is terribly dangerous."

"What *is* Bette?" Tonya typed in her password.

I had forgotten that Tonya didn't know. Bette hadn't been with us when we were up in Port Townsend. And apparently she hadn't had time to fill Tonya in on her background.

"Bette is what is known as a Melusine. She's a Greek water spirit and can turn into a water moccasin. Melusines are extremely sensuous and can turn the head of just about any human. But I think there's more to her than meets the eye. She won't talk about her past. Or, at least, she never has to me. In fact, I kind of get the impression she's not really sure about her past. In a sense, we have that in common."

"She and Alex were a couple at one time, weren't they?" Tonya brought up her Smart Mail account and clicked on the inbox.

"Yes, they were, but it was quite a while ago. They're pretty much best friends at this point. In fact, that was part of the problem with Glenda, Alex's ex. Glenda was jealous of Bette."

But Tonya wasn't listening. She was staring at an e-mail. "Crap. I can't believe he wrote to me again."

Another moment and she gasped, then turned her laptop so I could see what she was looking at. There was an e-mail there from Jack Skelton. The only thing in it was an image. The picture was graphic, the colors heightened. It had obviously been Photoshopped, but that didn't make it any less disturbing. It was a picture of a woman lying on her back, naked with a knife stuck through her heart. She was bleeding and obviously had been stabbed multiple times. And the woman's face had been replaced with an image of Tonya's face.

As I stared at the picture, a wave of anger swept over me. How dare someone do this? What right did he think he had?

Tonya was shaking as she raised one hand to cover her mouth. "Why is he doing this? What does he want from me?"

"I don't know, but I'm calling Ralph and getting him over here right now to take a look at this." I jumped up and headed into the living room, where I had left my cell phone. As I pulled up my contacts and tapped on Ralph's name, I decided that one way or another, we were going to find Jack Skelton and put an end to this.

While Ralph examined the e-mail, I headed into the living room, where I picked up Elena's number. After a moment, I decided that I might as well give her a call. Tonya didn't *have* to buy the house, but we might as well know what the terms would be. That is, if Elena would even sell, considering she had decided the place was cursed.

After three rings, a woman's voice answered. It was a pleasant voice, light and tinkling like chimes. "Elena Johnson speaking, how may I help you?"

"Hi, my name is Shimmer. Officer Yugi gave me your number. I live in the house across the street from Mary Smith's house. My friend is visiting from out of town, and she's taken an interest in the property. We were wondering if there was any chance you might be willing to sell?"

There was silence on the other end for a moment, and I half expected her to hang up. But then, in a slow voice, Elena said, "I'm not sure. The house has been in the family for a while, but none of us have ever lived there. Not since Mary owned it." A pause, and then she added, "Can I assume you know the story behind the house?"

"If you're asking if I know what happened regarding Mary and her family, yes—actually I do. And so does my friend. But the house has great potential, and it's on a very pretty lot. There's a lot that can be done with it."

"I'm sure there is. I've never seen it in person, but I've seen pictures." Another pause.

I had a sneaking suspicion of what she was trying to say, without actually saying it. I decided maybe I could make things easier for her. "Just in case you're wondering, we do know that the house is haunted."

Elena let out a little laugh, but it sounded strained. "I wasn't sure how to approach the subject. In some states you have to declare whether a house is known to have ghosts. I'm not sure if Washington is one of those states. But the fact is, we tried to rent it out several times. Or rather, my mother did. Each time the family left abruptly and refused to go back. I believe there were three leases broken in the first two years. Finally, my mother gave up trying to rent it."

"Trust me, there's a reason they left."

She let out a soft laugh. "I don't know if I believe in ghosts, but I know that our renters did and they were so scared that they were willing to fork over the remainder of the money to get out of the lease. We didn't ask them to—we released them without penalty. But each time, someone in my family got terribly ill. I don't know if there's any correlation, but I suppose that I am superstitious enough to be wary."

I bit my lip, unsure how to answer her. "The house is definitely haunted. But my friend and I believe there's a lot more to the story. Things about Mary that nobody else knew. We think . . . we believe that she had a rough life. In fact, to be honest I think the demons she thought were haunting her were very real and very mortal."

"What you mean?"

"We have reason to believe that she may have suffered terrible abuse from her husband. Some of the things we've seen and found corroborate that. It's nothing that we could take into a court to clear her name, and the truth is, I think that she actually did murder her husband and three of her children. But we think that something happened to drive her over the edge. You see, early this morning we discovered the skeleton of her missing baby on the property."

"That's what Officer Yugi told me. It's hard to believe that after all these years they found him." Elena sighed. "I suppose I can't just ignore that the house exists. As much as I'd like to pretend that that blot on our family name never happened, I guess I have to deal with it. If your friend wants to buy the house, have her call me and we'll talk numbers. Maybe it's time to clear away the past. I'll be home all day, as well as tomorrow." And with that, she quietly said good-bye.

**returned to** the kitchen to find Ralph chugging down a mug of coffee. His drink of choice was Flying Horse—an energy drink that was so caffeine rich it made espresso look like Kool-Aid. But I never kept any around because I didn't like the taste of it, so he'd have to make do with old-fashioned caffeine.

"I just talked to Elena, the woman who owns Mary's house. She might be interested in selling and I think it would do her family good to get rid of that place." I had already made up my mind that whether or not Tonya bought the house, it was time to clear out the ghosts. And if she didn't want it, I thought I might buy it. We could clear the land, fix it up, and rent it out. In fact, if Tonya didn't want to live there, I could use it for a second income property.

Ralph was mumbling to himself. He took another swig of caffeine and set down the mug on the coaster. "There's nothing I can find out about this except that yes—he did alter the photo. One of the problems is that Tonya doesn't remember anyone taking a picture of her recently."

"But it's just your face. Would you recognize where this picture was from?"

Tonya gingerly pointed to the earrings that she was wearing in the photo. "I bought those a week and half ago. I haven't had a picture taken of me since, and I'm not in the habit of taking selfies. So somebody else had to take this picture."

I realized what they were saying. "Jack took it, didn't he?"

"Yeah . . . He took it all right." Ralph sounded furious. "I can't stand these freaks."

"What do we do now? Is there a way we can have him arrested?"

"Well, this e-mail is as good as a threat. I'm going to call the police in Port Townsend and see if they'll pick him up for questioning. Stalking laws are still nebulous, and it all depends on where you live and whether the authorities take it seriously. I also suggested to Tonya that she have a friend go over and check on her house. Stalkers can get pretty freaky when the object of their obsession vanishes. And since Tonya just took off, there's no telling what Skelton might do." Ralph cast a pointed look at Tonya.

"All right, all right. I hear you. I'll call Patrick. He and I've been talking a lot since you guys cleared out his bed-and-breakfast. I'll call him tonight and ask him to go over and check. I'd ask Alice, one of my friends, but I don't want to put any other women in danger. It seems safer to ask a vampire to go check. And you're right, I think it's time to talk to the police. I was hoping that this would all turn out to be my imagination—that I would be exaggerating things. But I guess I'm not."

"It's so much easier to think it might be our imagination. By the way, Elena wants you to call her if you're interested in the house. And if you're not, I might be." I explained my reasoning.

"Well, either way then, I guess we should call her." Tonya paced around the dining room. "You know, when I went home, after I had climbed down from my high horse that sent me careening over to Aberdeen, I hoped that my mother and I could pick up our relationship without too much of a problem. I was pretty naïve, expecting her to just ignore the fact that I had walked out on her and cut her out of my life. It took a while but we became friends again, but it was never the same. I hurt her pretty badly."

Chai vocalized a question that I was thinking but hadn't wanted to ask. "What was your argument about?"

Tonya shrugged. "Does it really matter?" After a moment, she added, "My mother wanted me to go to college. Something she had never been able to do. I wanted to get married to my boyfriend. He was a pretty rough character and I was caught up in the excitement of being a rebel. And then he was caught trying to rob a bank and went to prison. I tried to defend him to Penelope, but she rubbed it in my face. I hated that she was right. I didn't want to admit that she had seen through him and that I hadn't. So I picked a fight and it escalated."

"Family dynamics are never easy," Ralph said, frowning. "I know, I'm going through a situation right now."

"Family dynamics make for damned rough complications. Anyway, Penelope told me that I had to decide how I wanted to live my life. I could straighten up and take responsibility, or I could live it as a reactionary, rebelling against authority just for the sake of rebelling. I got pissed, and she told me to make a choice, so I packed a suitcase and took off. I crashed on a friend's couch in Aberdeen until I could find a job. Over the next few years I tried to sort out my feelings. Finally, I realized what an ass I had been and that Penelope had just wanted to make my life a little easier. So I went home, expecting her to jump for joy. When she didn't, I realized that some fences are hard to mend."

As I listened to Tonya speak, it occurred to me that quite a lot of people had bad relationships with their parents. I had always assumed that it was easier among humans and Fae than among dragons, but apparently I was wrong. Family drama was family drama no matter where you were.

Tonya let out a soft laugh, then shrugged. "At least we ended on decent terms, even if things were never the way they had been before I left. In fact, if I'm honest with myself, they weren't all that great, so I guess we ended better than we started. I always blamed her for driving my father away, but the truth is he just wasn't cut out to be a parent or a husband. He didn't even come to her funeral, although I notified him when she died. He sent me a sympathy card, but he didn't offer to come. I guess I'm alone, really."

I realized Tonya was as lonely as I had been. Oh, she had friends in Port Townsend, but I had the feeling that, deep down, she felt isolated.

Wanting to change the mood, needing to lighten things up a little, I glanced at the clock again. It was eleven thirty. "I kind of want to go spy on Bette, to see if anybody takes the bait today."

"I don't advise that," said Ralph. "We have no way of knowing if he's going to be there today—the doppelgänger, that is. And frankly, I don't trust you to spy on the situation without giving yourself away."

Tonya let out a sigh. "I don't know about the rest of you, but I'm feeling tired. Ralph, if you would call the police in Port Townsend, I would appreciate it. You have my permission to forward any of the e-mails and the letters to them that they might need. Jack is scaring me." She gave me a quick hug and a kiss on the cheek, then waved at Chai and Ralph before disappearing up the stairs to her bedroom.

After she was gone, Ralph motioned for me to sit down. "I didn't want to scare her while she was here, but the truth is this guy is a real nut job. I'm afraid for her life. I'm going to call the cops, and fill them in on everything. But for now, she needs to stay here."

I could tell he wanted to say something else, and I thought I knew what it was. "You think he might have followed her down here? Do you think he knows she's here?"

Slowly, Ralph nodded. "I'm pretty sure that he's kept close tabs on her. I doubt if she made a move over the past month that he hasn't noticed. In fact, I'm going to talk to Patrick and suggest that he sweep her house. I'm not a betting man, but I'll give you good odds that Skelton has bugged her house, if not installed a secret camera somewhere. From the nuances in the letters, I think he has erotomania. And that hardly ever ends well."

"What's erotomania?" I wasn't familiar with all of the terms for stalkers and perverts.

Chai broke into the conversation. He had been listening from the door to the kitchen. "Someone who believes that the object of their affection is in love with them, when in fact the person may not even know they exist."

"Oh, lovely."

I yawned. Normally I didn't go to bed until around one thirty or two P.M., but lately, things hadn't been all that normal. I found myself rubbing my eyes, as Chai leaned down behind my chair, his hands resting lightly on my shoulders.

"Little Sister, why don't you get some sleep? Go to bed early and rest. Ralph and I will finish up here, and then he can go home and sleep, too. Everything will be okay, wait and see." His hands were warm against the tops of my shoulders and I found myself starting to drift.

"I think I might do that. If anybody calls and it's important, wake me up. Otherwise I'm going to set my alarm for six P.M. and get some extra sleep."

As I dragged myself up the stairs to my bedroom, I tried to sort out my feelings. I was worried about Tonya; I was upset over what had happened to Mary. I was mourning the bones of a child that I had never known. I was in a relationship with someone and feeling the first pangs of love, and had no clue of how to handle them. All the emotions swept in like a towering wave to wash over me and as I crawled beneath the covers, the sheets smooth against my skin, I wanted nothing more than to be wandering alone on the shore, unfettered by all these feelings.

* * *

Chai woke me up. At first, I wasn't sure what was going on because I wasn't used to seeing him in my bedroom. Normally, I woke from sleep as quickly as I fell into it. Head on the pillow, eyes closed. But I felt groggy and out of sorts as his voice penetrated the layers of fog in my mind.

"Shimmer, it's time to wake up. You need to come downstairs. Glenda's here and she wants to talk to you."

*Glenda?* Glenda who? And then the name pierced the fog and I realized who he was talking about. I shot up out of bed so fast that I almost knocked him over. It didn't even occur to me that I was standing there naked until Chai raked his gaze over me, a peculiar grin on his face.

"Oh, stop that. I know you don't think about me that way." I pushed past him and stomped over to my dresser, yanking out a pair of panties. As I slipped them on, snapping them tight around my hips, Chai let out a low chuckle.

"No, in truth I don't. But that doesn't stop me from looking. Face it, Shimmer. You're a gorgeous woman—dragon—and it's not my fault that my parts stand at attention when I see you naked. But you can trust that I'll never make an effort to act on it."

We stood there staring at each other, an awkward silence suddenly filling the room. Chai had never really remarked on my looks before, other than to tell me I was pretty or that the outfit I was wearing looked good. He swallowed, blushing.

"Well, then . . . I'd better get dressed."

Looking relieved, he headed for the door. "I think that's best. I don't think the bitch from hell is going away until she talks to you. I could probably take care of her, if you wanted. But somehow I think that might make more trouble than it would be worth." Abruptly, he turned and strode out of the room, shutting the door behind him.

Muttering a few choice curses, I shoved my feet through the leg holes of my jeans and drew them up, fastening the snap and zipping them quickly. I hurriedly hooked my bra and then slipped on a sweater, adjusting the cowl so that it wasn't choking me. I ran a brush through my hair to smooth it back, and thought about putting on boots, but I decided that it was my house, damn it, and if I wanted to go barefoot I would.

As I dashed down the staircase, I heard Tonya moving around in her room. I wanted to get Glenda out of there before she came down because I didn't trust Glenda around humans. I hurried into the living room, and sure enough—there she was. Decked out in her finest leather pants and halter top, wearing snakeskin ankle boots with heels a mile high, and carrying what looked like a high-end designer bag, Glenda was leaning against the back of the sofa, staring around the room with a smirk.

"What do you want?" I wasn't awake enough to be friendly, and I wasn't friendly enough to be polite.

"Is that how you greet all your houseguests?" She flashed me a smile but I could sense the bared teeth behind it. "I think we need to have a little talk."

"Make an appointment at the office." I shoved my hands in my pockets and leaned against the wall, looking her up and down. When I really took the time to look at her, her beauty felt just a little too jaded. The expression in her eyes was a little too weary. I realized that Glenda wasn't just angry, she was tired.

"You'd like that, wouldn't you? I'm going to tell you this once: Break it off with Alex. He's coming back to me sooner or later, and the quicker you let go of him, the less it's going to hurt."

"For your information, Alex and I have agreed to be exclusive. That doesn't sound like someone who wants to run back to their ex. And that's something you, as a succubus, can never, ever give him." Two could play the snarky game. And I could play it better than she could.

"And I suppose like a good little dragon you said yes. That's all well and good, but he's going to get bored. I know Alex, and he needs more excitement in this life than you can provide. I wanted to give you the chance to withdraw gracefully, but I see that you're not interested in listening to reason."

I wondered if she really believed what she was saying. There had to be a part of her that knew Alex was done with her. "Are you serious? Do you really believe what you're saying? I don't understand you, Glenda. You weren't happy with him. He was miserable, so why do you want him back?"

"Who gives a damn about whether we were *happy*? Happiness is an illusion. The only thing that matters is that Alex is *mine* and you're trespassing on private property." Her voice was so bitter that I knew there had to be something else behind this.

"Why are you so pissed off at me? I didn't steal him from you." I shifted, wanting the conversation to be over with as soon as possible.

"What you did was worse. You encouraged him to leave me. And so did Bette, that old bitch. You're both going to be sorry." And with that, she reached into her purse and pulled out something wrapped in her hand. With a quick flick of the wrist, she sent it flying. *A rock. Damn.* And then, before I could make a move, the rock smashed through the central glass in my aquarium.

I let out a scream as hundreds of gallons of water began to pour into my living room along with all my fish, including Coolray, my pet jellyfish. Glenda laughed as the rush of water rapidly began to saturate my floors, carpeting, and furniture. Then, before I could attack her, she vanished.

At that moment Tonya appeared on the stairs, her eyes wide. "What the hell is going on?" And then she saw what was happening and stopped in her tracks.

Chai had already sprung into action, grabbing a pan as he tried valiantly to save some of my fish. With relief, I saw him scoop up Coolray, but there were so many other fish swimming around my living room that I knew we wouldn't be able to catch them all before they died.

Anger ricocheted through me, breaking my paralysis. I headed to the kitchen in search of another pan. And then there was a zap as a jolt ran through me. The water had managed to short out some of the electronics in the room, splashing against the outlets that were placed lower on the wall. The jolt didn't hurt me, and it certainly wouldn't affect Chai, but I yelled for Tonya to stay where she was. I crawled on the sofa to get away from the ankle-deep water that was now spreading into the kitchen.

"Motherfucking son of a bitch," I shouted as fish began to float to the surface. The electrical shorts had apparently been enough to kill some of them. "I am going to kill that bitch of a succubus, if it's the last thing I do."

At that moment, my cell phone rang and I pulled it out of my pocket. It was Ralph. As I jabbed the Talk button, Chai let out another shout and I glanced over in his direction. He had managed to reach the stairs, where my octopus was trying to pull itself out of the water. Grateful that Wriggly had survived, I brought the phone to my ear.

"Ralph, I'm going to have to talk to you later. We have something of an emergency going on here."

"Unless somebody's dead, you need to get to the office *now*. I just stopped by Bette's houseboat. Somebody tore up the place, and I can't find her anywhere. Her cell phone was on the floor, smashed to bits. I have a feeling our doppelgänger figured out our plan. I think it abducted her."

I stared at the phone, panic washing over me. Suddenly, nothing else mattered. Setting down the pan, I turned to Chai and Tonya. "The doppelgänger has Bette." And then, overwhelmed by everything that had happened, I burst into tears.

# CHAPTER 16

Chai was the first to speak. "Get moving. Tonya and I will take care of this mess, and then I will meet you at the office. Just go."

"I can't drive, I don't have my license yet and I don't have a car." Furious that I had let it go this long, I waded through the ankle-deep water toward the front door. I had no clue where my purse was and I didn't have time to look for it.

"Let me grab my purse, I'll drive you." Tonya raced back up the stairs.

I yanked open the front door and a rush of water flooded out and down the stairs, swirling around my ankles as it flowed out of the living room. I ignored the fact that my fish were splashing around, trying to breathe, and that my jeans were soaked through, and took the porch stairs in a single jump, landing on the sidewalk below. Tonya was right behind me, keys in one hand, my purse in the other. As she tossed me the bag, she held out her key fob, unlocking the car doors. I slid into the passenger side and fastened my seat

belt. She slammed the door, jamming the keys into the ignition as she turned the engine. Without another word, she
eased out of the driveway and we headed toward the office.

We were halfway there when I managed to find my voice.
"I knew it was a bad idea. I knew we shouldn't have let her
go ahead with it. Alex won't be able to wake up for hours.
What the hell are we going to do?"

"We'll take things one step at a time. First, you'll call
Chase Johnson. You tell him what's going on. They will probably meet you over at her boat, to make sure that it wasn't
some run-of-the-mill burglar. You should check the community center as well. Someone there might have seen something. But you need to stay calm because panic isn't going to
help anything."

She was right, all panic would do would be to make
things worse. I did my best to calm my breathing and clear
my head.

"I don't understand how the creature knew what we were
up to. If Bette never said who she worked for, why would it
be suspicious? Or was it just in a panic, looking for a new
victim as soon as possible?"

"I don't know, and there's no way to tell at this point. We
just have to focus on finding her." She paused. "I should
have brought my cards with me. Maybe Chai can bring them
down to the office?"

"I'll give him a call. He can just lock up the house and
we'll deal with the mess later." All my anger at Glenda had
vanished for the moment, overwhelmed by my sorrow over
my fish and my worry about Bette. I pulled out my phone.
Chai answered almost immediately. "Hey, lock the doors
and bring Tonya's cards to the office, would you?"

"Of course. I'll meet you there." He hung up before I
could say anything else.

Unfortunately, traffic was thick, and there had been a
nasty fender bender in the middle of an intersection. As we
sat there waiting for the tow trucks to clear the area, I began

to fret. We were still far enough from the office that it would take me a while to get there if I ran, but there was no way of knowing how long it was going to take for us to get through the quagmire of traffic.

"Some days it feels like everything is just falling apart," Tonya said. "Just breathe, and we'll get through this as soon as we can."

"Does this happen to humans a lot? Everything happening at the same time?" Right now, Earthside looked far less glamorous than it had twenty-four hours ago.

Tonya gave me a sideways look. "I know you're grumpy, and I know it's because you're scared for Bette and you're mad at Glenda. But sometimes, shit just happens. It's part of living in the human world. Don't dragons have the same problem?"

I didn't want to admit it, but finally I nodded. "I guess we do. I've just never been part of society enough to notice. Whenever anything went wrong after I left the orphanage, it was easy enough to just pick up stakes and move on, to leave the chaos behind."

"You really didn't have any roots back in the Dragon Reaches, did you?"

I ducked my head, staring at my hands. After a few minutes, I answered. "Not really. Once the Lost and Foundling releases you, you're on your own. And if you have no background and no relatives, you're really and truly alone. I would sometimes wander the countryside for months without speaking to a single person. I kept to myself and kept away from the populated areas. I didn't mind so much, usually. I'm good with my own company. But sometimes, I would pass by an isolated house or a dreyerie and I would see the lights inside, and it would hit me how much I wanted a home of my own. Just to gather around a table with a group of people who wanted me there. Those times, they were hard."

Tonya said nothing and I glanced over at her. I was surprised to see a single tear trickling down her cheek. "Are you all right?"

She sniffled and dashed away the tear. "I'm just sorry that you had to go through that. And given the life span of dragons, even though you're young, it sounds like you have spent so many years alone. I'm glad you're here now, and I'm glad that you have friends. People you care enough about drop everything and run to help. And you know, if something happened to you, we would come running."

The tow trucks eased the cars out of the center of the road as we sat there. Another couple of minutes and the congestion began to thin out as we edged forward, turning onto a side street. Another five minutes and we were traveling at a decent clip down a back road. And a few minutes after that, Tonya pulled into the parking lot at the office. We dashed out of the car and into the building.

Ralph was waiting at the front desk. He glanced at us—both Tonya and I had jeans that were soaked up past our knees. Chai was leaning against Bette's desk, Tonya's cards in hand. He thrust them at her and she grabbed them and headed into one of the conference rooms. Ralph and I followed, with Chai behind us.

"Chai told me what happened at your house. I'm sorry. Glenda's off her rocker for sure. Will insurance cover the damage?"

"I have no idea. I don't exactly have insurance against an angry succubus." I shrugged. "But leave that for later. It doesn't matter right now. Tell us what happened with Bette."

"I headed over to her houseboat. I knew she was supposed to leave for the community center before I got there, but I had borrowed a book from her that she asked me to return. She told me just to leave it in the box she set out for packages next to her door. But when I got there the door was ajar, and I knew something was wrong. Bette never leaves her houseboat unlocked when she's gone. When I peeked in, I saw the place was trashed."

"How do you know it was the doppelgänger? How do you know it wasn't some burglar that broke in?"

"Her cell phone was on the floor and it had been smashed. I called down to the community center and asked if she was there. They said she never showed up. I looked everywhere in the boat and she was nowhere to be found. Her purse was missing, as well. I know, because she's very attached to that leopard-print satchel and never goes anywhere without it. I couldn't find it anywhere. I also found a roll of duct tape on the floor. It wasn't new—about half of it looks to be missing."

"Have you called Chase yet?"

Ralph nodded. "He and his men are on their way to her boat. I didn't want to leave the office without someone here. Tonya, do you mind staying here in case someone calls? Shimmer and I should head over to Bette's boat and meet the cops there."

"Not at all. Go. Take Chai with you, since Alex is still asleep." She glanced at the clock. "When is sunset tonight?"

"Around seven fifty. Damn daylight saving time." Ralph pushed back his chair. "Chai, Shimmer, let's get moving. Tonya, in case anybody calls about Bette, or on the off chance that she manages to get a call through to us, let us know immediately."

As we headed out the door, I found myself praying that a burglar had found Bette at home. Because she stood a better chance against a thief than against the doppelgänger.


Chase Johnson and his men were waiting at the boat for us. I had been to Bette's houseboat a few times, and had seriously thought about buying one for myself. But I needed more space, and I would never be happy being cramped inside such a small vessel. On the other hand, it would be nice to have a boat that I could take out into the sound to make it easier when I wanted to go swimming in my natural form.

"I'll wait on the dock—that place looks too small to fit me along with everybody else," Chai said.

We nodded, leaving him right outside as the rest of us cautiously entered the boat, trying not to disturb anything.

Chase motioned us in. "Come on in. We've taken all the evidence we can find. There are so many fingerprints in here that it would be useless to check them all. Anyway, we're pretty sure it's the doppelgänger."

My blood froze. "Why do you say that?"

"First thing, I called the bank. Her savings account has been wiped clean, at least the one attached to her checking. Apparently she had several other accounts, and those are still safe. I told the bank to freeze all of her other assets."

"Then the creature was looking for money as quick as he could get it. How the hell did he work so fast? Wait . . . she never made it to the Community Action Council. So . . . it had to be waiting for her." We explained to Chase what our plan had been.

"I wish you had checked with me first. But then again, I'm not sure what else we could've done. Are you sure that she wasn't in contact with the doppelgänger before this and didn't know it? That it didn't overhear her talking about the case?"

I thought it over. Who had been around when we had been making plans? Tonya, but there was no worry with her. No, there had been somebody else . . . someone who . . .

"There's only been one person that I can think of who knows about all of this. And who might know that Bette was going to try to lure the creature out. But there is no way that she would betray us." I glanced over at Ralph. "I'm thinking of Gerta, the Golden Frog. She was there when we were talking about this, although I think that Bette had taken her in the back to lie down."

Ralph paled. "I think I'm having the beginnings of a horrible thought. We need to contact Talamh Lonrach Oll. We need to find out if Gerta is still out there."

"What's going on?" I wasn't tracking his thought process.

"What if the doppelgänger was still there when we got

to Stone Weaver's house? What if it had killed not only Stone Weaver, but Gerta?"

I felt like he had punched me in the gut. Slowly lowering myself into a chair, I whispered, "Oh no. You're thinking that we brought back the doppelgänger instead of Gerta? Please don't tell me that we could have made such a huge mistake. How could she have cried golden tears? I didn't think that doppelgängers could assume the powers of the creatures they kill and mimic."

"There's a whole lot we don't know about them." Ralph was growing more pale by the second. "And when you think about it, we jumped to the idea that we're dealing with the doppelgänger. Suppose there are more types than one? Suppose that we are dealing with a creature that has powers similar to a doppelgänger but isn't the same? What then?"

His suppositions ricocheted through me. He was right. We hadn't even bothered to think of any other possibilities. We had jumped directly on the idea that we were dealing with a doppelgänger, and even then—we had assumed we knew everything that doppelgängers were capable of. I let out a sigh and stared at the table, not knowing what to say.

Chase was listening to us, and now he leaned his hands on the table, staring into my eyes. "Do you mean to tell me that you might have made a mistake? That we might not be dealing with a doppelgänger at all?"

"It appears that might be the case. I'm not sure." I stumbled over my words. If only Alex were here to take control of the situation. He knew how to talk to humans better than I did. And Ralph wasn't being much help. While the man was brilliant, he was socially awkward and right now he seemed wrapped up in tapping away on that stupid tablet of his. I swallowed, trying to think of something to say.

"One thing is obvious," Chase said, his voice softening. "Whatever we are facing, it can take on the visage of its victims. And it's dangerous, and greedy."

"Do you think Bette's phone was broken by accident, or

on purpose?" I tried to think of some practical question that could give us some sort of information or lead.

"Oh, I'm pretty sure that it was broken on purpose. It looks like something heavy and hard stepped on it. I'm guessing somebody wearing boots." He relented then, sitting down opposite me. "So tell me, if it's not a doppelgänger, then what else could it be?"

That was a question to which I had no answer. I looked over at Ralph. "Do you have any idea?"

He shrugged. "Offhand, no. But you know what? Tonya, who is back at the office, has that wonderful bestiary. Remember? The book she had up in Port Townsend?"

"Of course!" I snapped my fingers. The volume was huge and magical. It had also been bound with a cover made of dragon leather, which gave me the creeps, but there wasn't much I could do about that.

"She had to have brought it with her, it's one of her most prized possessions." I looked around the living room. Bette had an eye for decoration, and as garish and flamboyant as her clothes were, her house was equally snug and cozy. "Let's head back to the office, if there's nothing else we can do here. Chase, do you want to come with us?"

"I might as well, if you think Tonya can help." As we stood and headed to the door, he glanced over his shoulder. "You know we'll do all we can to find her before . . . well, before anything happens."

"We know," I said. "We know."

Tonya was waiting for us on our return. As we came through the door, she jumped to her feet where she was sitting behind Bette's desk.

"Did you find anything? Did you find her?" She scanned our faces, then slowly sat down again. "I guess not."

"Since you are sitting back there, can you figure out where Bette keeps her phone numbers? We need to find the phone number for the Fae Sovereign Nation. Its actual name is Talamh Lonrach Oll. We need to contact them and ask them if Gerta is still out there." I leaned across the counter as Tonya began to search through the papers on Bette's desk. A moment later she came up with an old-fashioned Rolodex.

"Here it is," she said as she flipped through the cards. "Do you want me to call them? I'm not sure what to tell them or who to ask for."

Ralph reached for the phone. "Hand the receiver to me and punch in the number. I'll talk to them." Tonya did as he asked. A moment later, they must've come on the line because Ralph shifted, straightening his shoulders as if he were talking to a teacher. "My name is Ralph Spangler, and I'm with the Fly by Night Magical Investigations Agency. We sent a member of the Elder Fae out there earlier. Her name is Gerta, the Golden Frog. We were wondering if she is still there and if we can talk to her?"

After a pause, the smile vanished from his face. "I see. Well, thank you. Can you tell us anything else—it's extremely important, a matter of life and death." Another moment passed, and then another, and finally he murmured good-bye and hung up the phone. We waited as he stood there, shaking his head.

Finally, I had to ask. "What did they say?"

"Gerta appears to have murdered a couple members of the guard and then vanished. They have cast out magical nets to dispel illusions. Nobody appears to be out of place, so there's a good chance that she's no longer within the confines of the land. This happened early this morning. That would have given her enough time to reach Bette's place."

I explained what we suspected to Tonya. "We need to know if you can tell us anything. Do you have your bestiary with you?" I was praying she would say yes.

After a moment, Tonya nodded. "I'd never leave that behind. It's too valuable. It's actually in my suitcase at your place."

"I'll be right back." Chai turned and then vanished.

Ralph paced back and forth. "The creature is devolving, whatever it is. But there has to be a reason why it took Bette with it. Otherwise, I would've expected to just find her body. The duct tape actually gives me hope."

"What do we know about Bette? Besides the fact that she probably has quite a bit of cash accumulated? Is there any other reason why it would have taken her hostage?"

Ralph paused, as if unsure whether to answer. After a moment, he said, "I haven't even talked to Alex about this. I didn't want to alarm him or to stir up something that is better left alone. But I think there's more to Bette than meets the eye."

"What you mean? Why do you say that?" He seemed pretty sure of himself, so I knew that he must know something.

"One time, oh—about a year ago—I happened to come back early from investigating a case. Alex asked me to start writing up our reports while he finished up at the scene. The door was locked, which was strange because we were open for business. So I unlocked it, but I guess I was pretty quiet, because when I came in, Bette was sitting at her desk in a trance. I saw a tall glowing figure standing in back of her with its hands on her shoulders. The figure was shining so bright I had to shade my eyes. I guess I startled it, because the next moment there was a flash and it vanished. The shock wave from it knocked me off my feet, and when I stood up Bette was going about her business as usual. She glanced over at me, and asked what I had tripped over when I came to the door. I started to ask her what the hell was going on, but something kept me from speaking. I physically could not ask the question. So I tiptoed around the subject and realized that she had no clue about what had happened. I started thinking maybe I had imagined the whole thing."

"Why didn't you tell Alex?"

He shrugged. "I don't know. Honestly, I was going to and then . . . I never did. Every time I thought about it, something came up to distract me. Until now."

"You mean, we're the first people you've told about this? You never once mentioned this to Bette?" Tonya was frowning.

"No. And now that I think about it, that's really strange, isn't it?" Ralph looked perturbed at this point. "In fact, now that I've actually said something, I can't believe I never mentioned this before."

A funny feeling tickled the back of my brain. "I think something prevented you from talking about the matter. Or, *someone*."

Tonya nodded. "I think Shimmer's right. Whatever it was that had its hands on Bette's shoulders, it didn't want you to tell anybody. In fact, my spidey-sense is tingling. I know I'm right about this."

"Then why can I talk about it now? What's so different?"

I knew the answer to that. "The difference is, Bette's life is in danger. So what could the creature be that had its hands on her shoulders? You said it was brilliantly lit—was it ambient lighting, or was the light coming from the figure itself?"

Ralph twisted his lips as he thought. After a moment, he said, "The light was coming from the figure. It emanated out from . . . Wait, I remember more. While I couldn't tell whether it was a man or a woman, the figure was wearing something like a Greek dress or toga. It was draped and white, very Grecian. And the figure had . . . I want to say it had wings of some sort. They may have been vestigial, because they were extremely small, but I remember them now."

This was just getting more and more confusing. But then a thought crossed my mind.

"Melusines are Greek, aren't they? I seem to remember Bette saying that she was originally from Athens or Cyprus or someplace like that. And if she is Greek, and you saw someone wearing something like that toga, it seems to me that would be a connection?" I frowned, trying to piece together several thoughts that were tapping at the edge of my brain. Puzzles weren't my strong point, but I was trying to learn because in the PI business, being able to piece together disparate facts often led to a solution.

Ralph nodded. "Yes, she is originally from Greece. I think she once mentioned that she was born near Parnassus, a sacred mountain near the Castalian Spring."

Tonya perked up. "I know something about that area, considering that I worship Hecate. That's near where the Oracle of Delphi was located. Apollo took over the shrine from a dragon named Python. It was the guardian of the Oracle until he supposedly killed it."

I felt like I was on the verge of making some sort of connection. "Bette is a Melusine, and she can turn into a water moccasin. That's a snake. Could there be some sort of connection here?"

"I'm not sure," said Ralph. "But I've got a funny feeling in my stomach that we are standing on the edge of a very big secret about our friend. And I have no clue whether Alex knows anything about this. But could this creature, whatever it is, have recognized something about Bette?"

At that moment Chai appeared, the bestiary in hand. He passed the book to Tonya, then turned to me. "I took a moment to make sure that all the fish we had managed to save were in enough water. Coolray is bopping around just fine. I'm afraid that you're going to lose some of your possessions—there's going to be quite a bit of water damage."

I shrugged. "Things are things, I can always buy new toys. I'm just sorry to have lost some of my fish. And that aquarium is not going to be cheap to replace. But right now, I'm just worried about Bette."

Tonya was flipping through the pages, with Ralph looking over her shoulder. "So we're looking for something like a doppelgänger, which might have more capabilities than just changing shape?"

"Right. The fact that it was able to mimic shedding golden tears . . . Or *was* it mimicking? I suppose the question is, was there ever really a Gerta, the Golden Frog, to begin with?

And if not, how on earth did it come up with something so specific?" I glanced over at Ralph. "If so, do you think it killed Gerta, too?"

He went back to pacing. I was beginning to recognize that this was a common habit of his, when he was thinking. It probably had to do with his werewolf side. "Honestly? I think there *is* a Gerta, and given the creature's greed, I would think she's still alive, hidden somewhere to be its own private bank. But to be able to subdue one of the Elder Fae? That denotes a creature of some strength and power. We're dealing with a creature that is not only cunning but strong."

"I think Gerta's young, though, given the way the creature portrayed her. Although that could have been an act, as well. That might have made it easier to subdue her. Do you still have any of the golden coins that fell from her eyes?" I wanted to examine them. Were they truly gold?

Frowning, Ralph held up one finger. "Let me go check. I think a few rolled on the floor when she was crying in the conference room."

As he left the room, Tonya kept flipping through the pages. Suddenly, she stopped. "What do you think about this? The diatrofymata?" She scooted to one side so I could see the picture of the creature.

The creature seemed rather amorphous, although bipedal, and had teeth that looked like tiny needles. It made me shudder. It looked worse than the land wight we had fought up in Port Townsend.

"The diatrofymata is a shapeshifting creature that can mimic not only its victims but others it comes in contact with," Tonya read aloud. "In fact, it resembles the doppelgänger. However, unlike typical doppelgängers, this creature feeds on eyes and tongues when it makes a kill. This feeding is believed to be part of a magical ritual that strengthens the diatrofymata. Greedy in nature, it will hoard gold and jewels and other expensive goods. It establishes its hoard in an isolated area. With brilliant intelligence, this is a highly danger-ous and skilled hunter. Like some amphibians, this creature can change sex depending on what form it takes. In its natural state, it is genderless, and develops sexual organs only when it comes together with another of its kind to reproduce. A scuffle for dominance will ensue, and the victor will assume the female genitalia and bear the offspring."

"That sounds terrifying. But it sounds like what we're up against, given that the eyes and tongues of victims have been missing. Does it say where it's likely to keep its hoard? That might help us to find it." I had no desire to find out, to be honest, but we had to know everything we could.

"Let me read further." She scanned down the page. "Okay, the diatrofymata is very rare. It usually creates a home base in the area of its kills. You know—" She looked up from the book. "It occurs to me that if it *does* have a lair of some sorts nearby, that's where it might be keeping its victims till it kills them. And maybe that's where Bette and Gerta are. Since it can take the shape of those it comes in contact with as well as just its victims, I would agree that it's probably keeping Gerta alive in order to force her tears." Tonya skimmed the rest of the page.

At that point, Ralph returned. He tossed the coins on the counter. "They aren't gold. I'm not sure what they are; they remind me of amber resin." He was right—they still had the basic shape of the coins, but they had altered in looks.

"Then while the creature was able to mimic Gerta, it couldn't fully reproduce her abilities. Tonya," I said, heading toward Alex's office, "why don't you fill Ralph in on what you found out? I'm going to see if there's anything in Alex's files about Bette. He'll probably be pissed that I've rifled through his papers, but given the circumstances, I'm going to chance it."

As I entered Alex's office, I wasn't sure what I was look-ing for. But anything I could find that would tell us why the diatrofymata had captured Bette instead of harming her would be of help. I glanced at the clock. Three thirty. Still far too long until Alex was able to wake.

I sat down at his desk, feeling awkward, and began opening the drawers. There were five, and the bottom right appeared to be locked. In the center drawer, I found basic supplies and what looked to be a spare set of keys. The top left drawer contained paper and notebooks. The top right drawer had various bric-a-brac, a few small figurines, a wire mesh tray that held a deck of playing cards, some dice, a few coins, and other assorted trinkets. The bottom left drawer opened with ease and I found several bottles of blood in it, a big box of tissue, and some travel brochures that looked fairly old.

But the bottom right drawer was locked. I jiggled it, and then remembered the keys. Hunting through them till I found one that looked about the right size, I tried it in the lock. A perfect fit. I was feeling more and more like a burglar—or worse yet, a voyeur—but I turned the key and the drawer silently slid open.

Feeling vaguely guilty, I rifled through. There were several file folders and I recognized them as dossiers on Ralph, Bette, and me. There was another file folder there—unlabeled. Hesitating, my fingers hovered over the file as I debated on whether to look in it. After all I was looking for information on Bette, no one else. And it felt extremely disloyal to even think about peeking inside the file folder. But then, before I could second-guess myself, I pulled out all of the files and opened the unlabeled one.

"Oh hell." I immediately wished I'd kept my nose out of it. I found myself staring at several pictures of Glenda, stark naked and spread out on the bed. She was obviously comfortable with herself being photographed, I gave her that much. I glanced at the date on the back of the prints. They had been taken a year ago. Well, at least they weren't new. But the fact that Alex had kept them made me uncomfortable. My cheeks flaming, I flipped the folder shut and put the file back in place.

"Moving on," I whispered to myself. "Let's see what he has to say about Bette." I opened the file folder. Inside were printouts with her address on it, and a list of all the men she had been involved with for the past five years. Next to each name was a checkmark. As I flipped through the rest of the file, I realized he had done a credit check and a background check on every man she had been with. Or at least, I thought, every man he *knew* she had been with. On several of the background checks, incidents where they had been incarcerated for assault or other potentially dangerous activities were highlighted.

*He has to be making sure that she's okay*, I thought. Alex loved Bette like a sister. No, that wasn't exactly true. Their friendship ran deeper than that. I flipped through the rest of the papers and realized that whatever I was looking for, Alex didn't have it in his desk.

I hesitated over my file and then decided that I didn't really want to see what was in there. Quietly, I replaced everything as it had been and locked the drawer. I put the keys back in the center drawer, hoping that nothing looked out of place. As I rose and headed toward the door, I couldn't decide whether to tell Alex what I had done. I had a lot of thinking to do before he woke up, and I just hoped I could come to the right decision.

# CHAPTER 17

Chai glanced at me and I swear he could read my mind. But he said nothing, simply nodded me over to where Ralph and Tonya were staring at the Mapsi program on the web. I noticed that they were searching the area around Stone Weaver's house.

"What are you looking for?"

"It occurred to us that the land surrounding his house would be the perfect hiding place for the diatrofymata's lair. It's private, set out a ways, and it's not public land someone can just stumble over. Stone Weaver owns a lot of acreage out there. The creature could have decided to hole up on the land long before it made him its victim. After all, if it has been trolling the Fae at the community center, then it probably knew all of its victims long before it decided to kill them." Ralph looked up at me, waiting for my reaction.

"That makes a lot of sense. And since people come and go from those groups, newcomers wouldn't be unexpected or out of place. I wonder . . ." A thought struck me. "Do you think it might have set up a persona down there other than as bait? I mean, nobody ever mentioned the boyfriends or girlfriends of the victims showing up at the meetings. Even Bette, when she met Marlene's boyfriend, she met him away from the community center. Maybe, just maybe, this creature has a separate persona who attends meetings, gets to know the people there, and then chooses the best pick. That way it could come and go without being a suspect." I knew I was on to something.

Tonya seemed to think so, too. "That makes perfect sense. You don't shit where you drink. It would only make sense for it to keep a cover there that was separate from those it used to lure in its victims. Chances are, once it picked a victim, it met them off site—to avoid suspicion. And since, as you say, all the murders have happened in the past few weeks, it would make sense that whoever the creature is masquerading as probably showed up shortly before then. I have a feeling the diatrofymata doesn't hang around long before it strikes. It has to get in and get out."

"Yes, except this time it found a gold mine. You find this many rich Fae together, it's a temptation to something like the diatrofymata. I did a little extra searching while you were in Alex's office, Shimmer. Even though this is an extremely rare critter, rumor has it that it's getting braver and creeping into cities more. There is a clan of demon hunters near here. The Hunters Glen clan, and they come from the Old Country. They tend to hunt down things like this. I want to get in touch with them. They might have some information on this."

"Do you have a contact name?"

He nodded. "Tanne Baum appears to be the front man. I have his number and I'll give him a call directly. Regardless if he can help us on this case, I think they might be good contacts for the future." He paused and glanced up at me from where he was sitting. "Did you find anything in Alex's office?"

Even though he didn't say anything else, I detected a tone of disapproval in his question.

"No, nothing relevant. And yes, I will tell Alex that I looked through his desk." Until that moment, I hadn't made up my mind what I was going to do, but I realized I had to. And I'd tell him I saw Glenda's pictures. Getting it out in the open seemed the best idea. Meanwhile . . . I pointed to the screen. "So do you have any idea of where the diatrofymata might be hiding?"

Ralph zoomed in on an area near a hill. "They tend to prefer underground lairs. I'm thinking it may have found a cave in the side of the hill. For all the contacts Stone Weaver had with the Elementals, considering he was an Elemental Fae, I don't think the earth energy around there would necessarily suspect the creature was out of its element. Anyway, since the diatrofymata are also aligned with earth energy, because of their connection to metals and gems, nothing would seem amiss to set off the wards. Or at least that's the way I'm reading it."

"Should we head out?" I glanced up at the clock. It still seemed far too long until Alex woke up. "Every minute that it has Bette in its grasp is another minute she's in danger."

Chai cleared his throat. "Why don't I go? I can take a look around. I promise I won't do anything without checking in."

I realized I had to make an executive decision. Chai was my friend, and although I valued his offer, I wasn't sure if he could hold to his promise. And if he went in after this creature, there was no telling whether it would kill Bette if it saw him coming. Plus, there was another reason to hold back.

"I think you better wait. You're from the realm of Fire. Going into earth Elemental territory means your presence will be noticed. And you were with us the other night, so if the creature sees you, it's going to know we're on to it and it might kill Bette." I almost added *if she's still alive* but then stopped. We had to hold out hope, because hope was all we had at this point.

"Unfortunately, she's right." Ralph printed off the maps and sent the coordinates to his phone. "From what I can tell, these creatures are so connected to the earth, they're bound to notice energies from other planes coming in."

"It kind of reminds me of dwarves," I said. "Dwarves are often mistaken for being part of the Fae, but they aren't. They're actually Elemental earth spirits. Not many humans realize that. They lump all the creatures of legend and lore together under one or two labels."

I had met several dwarves in my life. Once in a while a few hardy souls—rather, a few *foolhardy* souls—trekked into the Dragon Reaches, hunting treasure. Most of them never made it home if they actually managed to find a drey-erie filled with treasure. The majority of dragons were wealthy, but white dragons were the ones who truly hoarded gold and gems. And white dragons would think no more of crisping up a dwarf or human who came to pilfer their stash than they would a cow when they were hungry. Attempt to part a white dragon from his treasure and you were writing your own death warrant. And I knew that from experience. The more I thought about it, the more I realized just how stupid I had been. And the more grateful I was to the Wing-Liege for saving my ass.

Chai patted my shoulder. "Thinking of old times?"

I rolled my eyes at him. "I wish I weren't. Greanfyr will be hunting me for years. What I took didn't amount to a backpack full of coins, a silver chalice, and a platinum belt. But in his eyes, I raided his vault and stole every penny from him. The chamber was filled with coins and treasures and goods. I didn't really want his stuff, you know. I just wanted some sort of revenge."

"And that was the only way you could think of getting it." It wasn't a question. Chai knew my situation inside out.

"Pretty much. Anyway, I think it's best we wait for Alex to wake up, so we can go out there as a team."

"What should we do until then?" Ralph asked.

"You contact Tanne Baum. I'm going to call the director of the Supe Community Center and ask for a list of any new members in the past two months. Maybe we can figure out the name of the cover persona the diatrofymata has been using."

Ralph put in a call to the Hunter's Glen clan, but all he got was an answering machine. He left his number and a brief message, then hung up.

At that moment, Chase Johnson arrived. "I'm sorry it took me so long. We've had several pressing matters that I had to attend to. Emergencies." He didn't elaborate and we didn't ask. I knew there were things about his job that he couldn't tell us. I did ask if they had any new information, but he shook his head. "I wish I did, but I'm sorry. No."

"Well, we have some for you." At that moment, I noticed Tonya was yawning. I realized she hadn't had any sleep in well over twenty-four hours. "Tonya, why don't you go in the back for a while and rest. There's a couple rooms that have daybeds in them. You need sleep. The rest of us can manage for a while longer without it, but you're human. You need to get some rest, especially if we're going hunting for Bette tonight." I motioned to Ralph and he nodded, leading her off to the back. I turned back to Chase and filled him in on everything we had discovered.

"So it looks like we're dealing with a creature that's not quite a doppelgänger. It's actually worse. I was about to put in a call to the Supe Community Center to find out if they've had any new members in the past two months. We think that the diatrofymata set up a cover persona there to gather information on potential victims. Then it could masquerade as a love interest, once it knew all about them."

"Why don't you go ahead and do that while I check in at the station." He pulled out his phone and moved off to the side.

I flipped through Bette's contacts and found the number. I called the contact listed, hoping that I wouldn't get hold of the diatrofymata.

"Supe Community Action Council, Donna speaking." A brisk voice answered me—female.

I realized I wasn't exactly sure what to say. "My name is Shimmer, and I'm from the Fly by Night Magical Investigations Agency. We are working on a case involving several of your members who have been murdered." I knew that Chase had given us this case on the QT, but now was not the time to pussyfoot around. "Can you tell me how long you've been with the Council?"

"Five years, why?"

I supposed the diatrofymata could be lying, but I decided to chance it.

"We need to know if you have had any new members in the past two months. This particular member would be someone who would probably show up at every meeting, and who might have taken an overt interest in several of the elderly members."

There was a pause, and then Donna cleared her throat. "Actually, yes we do have a couple members who fit that description." There was something about her voice that made me take notice.

"One of them strikes you as odd, don't they? We need as much detail as you can remember. If you would like to verify that I am who I say I am, I can have Chase Johnson, director of the FH-CSI, call you."

A pause, and then she said, "No, I trust you are who you say you are. I have the ability to sense these things. And you're right. One of them has never sat well with me. She makes me uneasy. She kept asking about their mental state—whether they were lonely and lived alone."

"Did she get the information she was looking for?"

"I imagine she did, but not from me. She signed up as a volunteer during an art class led by one of our other members. She also signed up to volunteer during our community dances. I asked her if she would like to work with some of our more indigent members, those who need help but can't afford it. Basically, our homeless Fae and Supes. But she said she wasn't geared for that kind of work. I turned her over to another board member who is more diplomatic than I am."

I could read between the lines. "In other words, she didn't want to work with the poor and hungry. Can you give me her name? Do you have a home address for her?"

"She goes by the name Estelle, and she said she was rooming with a friend until she could afford an apartment. She did give me a cell phone number. Let me get it for you." After a moment Donna rattled off a number and I wrote it down on a pad of paper next to the phone. I had the feeling the number would be a no-go, but there was always a chance.

"When was the last time you saw her?"

"Let me think . . . I'd have to say that it was last week. She showed up for a short time, and then took off again before I could say anything to her. I haven't seen her since then." A pause, and then Donna asked, "Do you think she's the one who murdered our members?"

"I can't answer that, but I will say this: If she shows up again today, will you please call me or Chase Johnson? And whatever you do, don't let on we were asking about her. This is extremely important." After giving Chase's number to Donna, I hung up.

As Ralph came back, Chase finished his conversation and I told them both what I had found out.

"We have the cover persona, that much is for sure. Chase, can you marshal together a group of officers to go with us? They need to be Supes—strong ones. The diatrofymata tend to be exceptionally strong, and they're resistant to all attacks from metal because it's part of their element. Which means I doubt if bullets will do any damage. We're going to need a different way to attack it. I wish I could just turn into my dragon self while we're out there, but I can't unless I'm underwater. So we need brawn and plenty of it. And I don't think Ralph and Alex will provide enough muscle to take the thing down."

"Don't forget I'll be there," Chai laughed, but there was

a seriousness behind his levity. "She's right. Creatures that are from an Elemental plane tend to be overtly strong on a physical level. And because this creature's from the Elemental plane of Earth, it's going to be exceptionally muscular in its natural form."

"I know just the men you need." Chase headed for the door. "I'll be back with the cavalry shortly before sunset. We'll be ready to roll. We cannot allow this creature to get away or it's just going to move on to new fields. Damn it, we just don't have enough of a national communications network when it comes to things like this. When we're dealing with human victims, the FBI can reach out on a nationwide level to spread information throughout law enforcement agencies. And *this* is why I'm headed to Washington, D.C. Everything has to change, given there are so many Supes and Fae in the world today."

As he closed the door behind him, I turned back to the others. "Get everything ready, Ralph. Chai, I really should go home and make certain Glenda hasn't struck again. It just sucks that I have to walk there because it will take me too long to find a ride." I gave him a soft smile.

"I can take you—" Ralph started to say, but Chai interrupted.

"I get your meaning," he said. "I'll go home and make sure everything's all right. I'll be back before you can blink." And with that, he was gone.

I looked up at the clock. One more hour until Alex woke up. Realizing that I was hungry—my stomach was rumbling—I put in a call to the closest pizza place and ordered four pizzas. Between Ralph, Chai, Tonya, and me, we would finish them off in no time flat.

As hard as it was to sit and do nothing, we forced ourselves to rest and eat. I waited until the last minute to wake up Tonya. Ralph handed her a Flying Horse, and she was groggily starting in on the pizza when Alex walked through the door. He took one look at us and dropped his backpack into a chair.

"What's going on?" He looked wary.

I glanced at Ralph. This was going to be one of the toughest things I'd ever had to tell Alex—probably one of the toughest things he had ever had to hear.

"We have a situation. Sit down and we'll tell you everything."

Without a word, he slid into a chair. "Talk."

"First, we have figured out we're not dealing with a doppelgänger. Not exactly. As far as we can tell, we are dealing with a creature called a diatrofymata. It's similar, but it's a creature from the Elemental plane of Earth. It not only mimics its victims, but it can mimic others it has simply met. And it can manifest some of their abilities, although not perfectly. Gerta, the Golden Frog? That was the creature. We think that it has actually captured the real Gerta and is hiding her in its lair to force gold coins from her eyes. And now, it's also captured Bette."

Alex let out a string of curses and jumped to his feet. "Do you know where the hell this creature is?"

"We have a good idea. We were just waiting for you to get here. We've narrowed it down to an area on Stone Weaver's property. Chase will be here shortly with reinforcements. This creature is strong, Alex. Strong in a sense that I don't think we have the upper hand. It's from the plane of Earth, and it's going to have the strength of the earth behind it."

Ralph cleared his throat. "I stopped at Bette's houseboat to drop off something and found it had been trashed. We found enough circumstantial evidence to tell us that the creature has captured her."

As we filled him in on the day, and Tonya showed him the passage in her bestiary, the look on Alex's face grew more and more troubled. I had expected him to be angry, and I knew he was, but instead of lashing out and running amok, he seemed to withdraw. And when Ralph told him about what he had seen with Bette and the figure bathed in light, he seemed even more thoughtful.

"If there's any reason you can think of why it would be holding Bette hostage other than money, it would be good if you would tell us now. We know she has cash, but there's something else about her. Am I right?"

Alex stared at the table for a moment. "There's a great deal I know about Bette that she doesn't even know." He glanced at me. "I seem to be the caretaker type. Not only am I your parole officer, but I was assigned to watch over Bette. You ask if there's any reason why this creature might want her besides money? I can't tell you why, because if I do it will cause a great deal of trouble. But yes, I do know of a reason. Bette is worth a great deal to the right person. She doesn't know who they are, she doesn't know anything about this . . . but we have to get her back alive and intact."

I had always known there was a special connection between Alex and Bette and it didn't bother me in the slightest, but now I had the feeling that it went far deeper than anything any of us could imagine. "Did you know all of this about her when you first met her?"

He shook his head. "No," he said. "I only found out after she and I had been together for a while. As I said, I cannot tell you anything about this right now. And Bette must never know we've had this discussion. But we have to get her back safely."

At that point the soft chime of the bell announced a visitor to the office. Alex jumped up and headed out of the conference room, leaving the door open. I could hear Chase's voice from the waiting room. Our reinforcements were here. Ralph and I locked gazes, but we said nothing. Whatever was going on, it was obvious we weren't going to find out about it tonight.

I stood up and stretched. "Tonya, I want you to stay here. You're still tired, and it would help if we had someone here to watch over the phones just in case Bette manages to call."

"You're just worried about me because I'm human. Trust me, I can take care of myself. I'm tired but another good jolt of caffeine will help. I want to go. I want to see this creature for myself, and I'd like to help if I can." She folded her arms across her chest and I had the feeling she wasn't going to budge.

"If Alex says you can go, fine. I just want you to be careful."

"Trust me, I'm not going to risk my neck." She yawned and Ralph silently handed her another can of Flying Horse. She chugged it down, blinking at the taste. "Oh man, give me a latte any day, but this will do for now."

We tripped out into the main waiting room. Chase was there and he had with him four brawny-looking men.

Ralph let out a little growl. "Werewolves."

"That's right," one of them said. "I think we've met at Supe Community meetings before. I'm Frank Willows. I'm the leader of the Supe militia. These are a few of my buddies—José, George, and Thomas. We're at your disposal this evening. Tell us what you need done, and we'll do it."

"Unfortunately, I can't come with you." Chase looked rather uncomfortable. "I have yet another fire that needs putting out. I hesitate to send any of my men with you, at least on an official basis. There are certain aspects to this case that I'm not sure I want written into the books. Although, once we get the federal agency going, it would make a good case study for it." He suddenly stopped, glancing at Frank, and I realized he had said more than he wanted to in front of the werewolf. But Frank just looked the other way, as if he sensed Chase had made a slip of the tongue. I had a feeling that Willows was good at keeping his mouth shut. None of the other werewolves seemed to have noticed.

"I suppose we better get moving. We need to brief the four of you on what we're dealing with, and make certain you understand the risks. Ralph, if you could go with the werewolves, I'll take Shimmer, Tonya, and Chai." Alex turned to the werewolves. "Do you have a large enough vehicle to handle the back roads? We're not off-road per se, but I'd rather not have you take a sedan or town car out there."

Frank laughed. "I got the perfect vehicle. If Ralph can navigate, I'll drive. I'm used to off-roading."

"Then let's head out. Chase." Alex turned to the detective. "We'll let you know what happens. And . . . Thanks. I mean it."

As we all headed out the door, I prayed that we could find Bette while she was still alive. And I couldn't help but wonder what the hell secrets Alex had on her.

I hadn't yet told Alex that I had been through his drawers, and I decided the car, with three other sets of ears, wasn't exactly the place to do it. At least I had enough sense to recognize potentially volatile situations, and I didn't want to make our friends uncomfortable if he decided to pick a fight over it. I did, however, fill him in on what Glenda had been up to.

"One thing I forgot to tell you is that your ex-girlfriend trashed my house. And that includes killing a bunch of my fish." I told him exactly what had happened. "I have no idea how much damage has been done. We had to drop everything because of the situation with Bette. I dread going home and dealing with a waterlogged living room."

Alex was silent for a moment. He switched on the turn signal, and, as we edged out onto the freeway, he gruffly said, "I'll take care of it. I'll take care of any damage done, and I'll replace your fish and aquarium. Don't even bother going through your house insurance. You don't need them to raise your rates because of what Glenda did. And trust me," he said in an icy voice, "I'll take care of Glenda as well."

I was about to tell him not to worry but decided that, no, everything wasn't all right. It was time he faced exactly what kind of person she was.

"Thank you," was all I said.

"Not all succubi are like her. I hope you realize that. I've met some over the years who were absolute gems. Unfortunately, it looks like I ended up with the bad apple in the barrel." He looked so unhappy that I realized he truly hadn't believed she was dangerous. I had just shattered his illusions.

After a moment, Tonya broke the awkward silence. "I'm glad that my bestiary could come in handy." When we were in Port Townsend, she had told us the story about how she found it. It seemed more than fortuitous and made me wonder if destiny had forced her hand.

"As soon as we take care of the matter with Bette and have her home safe, we'll see what we can do about Jack Skelton. I don't like the idea of you returning to Port Townsend while Jack is still up there. He's far too dangerous. Shimmer, Ralph, and I will be worried sick about you if you go home while he's still prowling around the town." A pale smile flashed across Alex's face, and I realized just how much he cared about all of us. Even vampires had to deal with stress.

"I'd really appreciate that. To be honest, I'm scared to go home now. When I came down here, it was mostly to get away from Degoba's wedding. But I think I was secretly hoping you guys would tell me I had nothing to worry about and that I was just imagining things. Instead, I'm going to be jumping at shadows until Jack stops bothering me." Tonya leaned forward to stare over the front seat. "I sent Degoba a note this morning. I congratulated him, and told him I wished him and his wife all the happiness in the world." Her voice was strained, but I could tell she meant every word of it. "I realized, I don't want him to ever think that I'm doing anything like Jack is doing to me. I like Degoba, and I would miss his friendship so much if he felt he had to distance himself from me. I don't want that to happen."

"Nobody could ever mistake you for a stalker," I said. "And you just wait, you'll find someone better suited to you.

I know it." I was starting to understand what it meant to reassure a friend, even if you weren't sure of what you were saying. I didn't know if she would find love, but she needed to hear that now.

Chai shifted in the seat next to her. "Sometimes, the person you're waiting for might be right next door."

I restrained a snicker. Oh yes, Chai had a crush on her. But Tonya was too absorbed in her worries to notice. I didn't know if that was a good thing or a bad thing.

As the miles passed, the road grew darker and the traffic was almost nonexistent. Early April in the Seattle area was still chilly and overcast, with a lot of rainstorms and wind coming through. Spring in western Washington wasn't like spring in the Dragon Reaches, where the sun shone cool but bright most of the days. Of course, the sun often was shining down on a pile of melting snow, but the days were brighter than here.

As if reading my thoughts, Tonya asked, "Tell me what it's like in the Dragon Reaches. I'd like to get my mind off Skelton and stalkers and monsters lurking in the dark."

I let out a short sigh. "Well, this time of year, snows are still melting over a vast area of the Dragon Reaches. You have to understand that we live at the top of the world, above the Northlands. Oh, the red and gold dragons tend to gather more in the southern areas where the temperatures are warmer and the winter is milder. And my kind—the blue dragons—almost always live next to the ocean. But for the most part, the Dragon Reaches are mountainous and craggy, and the snows flow thick and heavy throughout most of the winter. There aren't vast forests there. There are in the Northlands, but the tree line grows thin up in the Dragon Reaches and most of the timber is scrub, short and stubby from the constant winds. It's beautiful, but it's difficult for humans to live up there, and even the Northmen have difficulty when they work their way up into the mountains of the Dragon Reaches. In fact, most of them are afraid to stray too far into our territory. They are afraid they'll get eaten."

"Is there validity to that fear?" Alex asked.

I shrugged. "Perhaps, although most dragons prefer to eat livestock. In fact, there are a number of Northmen who make their earnings by farming livestock for the Dragonkin. It's a mutually advantageous situation." I paused. We were finally near the road that led to Stone Weaver's house. Ralph, riding with the werewolves, was right behind us.

As we edged into the forested drive, once again the mood in the car fell into an uneasy silence. Would we find Bette, alive? And was the diatrofymata keeping Gerta hostage as well? Would we really be able to stop this creature before it vanished only to pop up in another place, seeking other victims? As the Range Rover bumped along the gravel drive, all these questions and more raced through my mind.

# CHAPTER 18

Alex pulled to the side as we entered the drive in front of the house. Ralph knew the way, so he and the werewolves took the front and we followed the narrow dirt road behind them. From what I remembered of the map, we were headed through the woods along an access road that led toward the hill bordering Stone Weaver's property. Chances were, the diatrofymata wouldn't have chosen a lair that was too remote. After all, it needed to get its treasure that it stole back to the hoard without having to trudge miles through the forest.

I wondered where the thing had come from—doppelgängers were Germanic in origin, but the diatrofymata seemed an odd variant. Elemental creatures tended to congregate in areas that reminded them of their plane of origin. Very few djinn would ever be found in the Arctic or Antarctica. By the same token, Elemental creatures from the plane of Air tended to stick near mountaintops, and creatures from the Elemental plane of Water weren't found inland. It made perfect sense that a creature from the Elemental plane of Earth would make its home in a cavern or even a cabin deep in the woods.

As we followed Frank's massive SUV, Tonya suddenly asked, "So you think the creature is planning to hold Bette for ransom?"

For a moment, I thought Alex wasn't going to answer, but then he said, "I cannot tell you what I know about Bette and her past, but if the diatrofymata found out the truth about what she is, yes, I think that's likely. But we're not the ones it would approach for ransom."

Once again, a sense of foreboding swept over me. Alex's reticence was contagious and I felt myself shying away from the discussion, although in the back of my mind I couldn't help but ask, *What is she? What's her secret?*

After another pause, Alex continued. "The good news is that if the creature does know what she is, she's probably safe for the moment. I'm clinging to that hope."

We were deep into the woods, and the access road had become a road in name only. The dirt was bumpy with deep ruts running through it, and the rain had created puddles that accumulated in the tire tracks, forming muddy ruts.

The road wasn't big enough for logging trucks, but something big and heavy enough to create the ruts had been through here recently, and it made me wonder what Stone Weaver had been up to. This was still his property, but what reason would such a strong environmentalist have to bring in heavy machinery? Especially machinery heavy enough to leave deep impressions in the dirt road?

Frank's SUV made a sudden jog to the left and then eased off the road into a turnout. They turned off their headlights. We followed suit. Quietly, we slipped out of the Range Rover and joined Ralph and the four werewolves.

Around us, the sounds of raindrops echoed in a soft, steady cadence, dropping the branches to the ground below. Mist rose around us, and overhead the clouds had pulled back to let the pale sliver of moonlight shine through. The light was faint but reflected off the rising fog, casting an eerie glow, as all around us the forest crackled and snapped with the sounds of the night. Small animals rustled through the undergrowth, through the fern and bracken and brambles that covered the ground. In the forests around here, there was no such thing as flat open ground. Detritus and moss spread in a thick blanket, and it was easy to trip over hidden roots, or twist an ankle on a buried rock, or sink to your knees in the mulch that covered the woodland floor.

We spoke in hushed whispers. Voices echoed all too easily through the mist, and the last thing we wanted to do was to give away our presence to the diatrofymata.

"The cavern we're looking for is about a quarter mile through the woods here. It's not very far, but the going won't be easy. If it were daylight, we could look for the trail that the creature has most likely blazed. But since it's night, I don't think we should waste time looking for its path. We could be out here all night searching. It's easier to just follow my GPS to the cavern itself." Ralph turned and pointed into the forest. "This way. Be cautious, and if you need, find a stick now to balance yourself with. Tonya, I suggest that you stay here, but if you insist on coming with us, let's find you a walking stick."

"I'm not staying behind. I promise to keep up the best I can." She started looking around where we were standing for a branch. I spotted one behind me and, taking hold of it, finished breaking it off the fallen snag. About five feet tall, the branch was an inch and a half in diameter. To my relief, it felt solid. Wood rotted quickly in these forests.

Tonya tested it, tapping it firmly against the ground several times. "This will work fine. Thank you, Shimmer."

Alex, Ralph, and I took the lead. Chai and Tonya came next, the djinn keeping an eye on her. Frank and his werewolves followed behind. As we entered the heart of the forest, I could feel creatures and beings watching us. And somehow, I didn't think all of them were friendly. Stone

Weaver had been an Elemental Fae, and he had no doubt some powerful and questionable company.

As we made our way through the tangle of undergrowth, our journey took on a surreal sense. I had been in some odd places throughout my life, but trudging through a forest with a vampire, a djinn, a human, and a bunch of werewolves had to be one of the strangest adventures I'd had yet. As something slithered past my feet I jumped, then caught myself. Just a snake, disturbed by our passing. Probably a garter snake. Rattlesnakes were usually found east of the mountains, and most of the reptiles over here on the coastal side of the state were relatively harmless.

Behind me, Tonya whispered something in a soft voice to Chai, and he answered her just as softly. I couldn't quite catch what they were saying and I didn't try. If it was something that we all needed to know about, they would tell us.

Ralph moved ahead, consulting his phone. While the cell reception here wasn't great, he had taken an image of the map and we were following directions from that. We continued uphill for about fifteen minutes, and then Ralph held up his hand for us to stop. He turned around and, finger to lips, pointed to the right of where we were standing. Then he turned off his phone and the pale light from the screen vanished, leaving us in the dark, our only illumination coming from the sliver of moon reflected through the clouds. If the sky closed in again and the rain returned, we would be left in the dark.

Once more, Ralph began to forge on, this time toward the right. We followed, trying to keep our footsteps light. The werewolves and Alex were exceptionally good at walking silently, but Tonya, Chai, and I couldn't help but make noise. Every time I stepped on a branch and it cracked, I held my breath, wondering if the diatrofymata would hear us. My heart was pounding, more from nerves than from fear.

And then we were at the bottom of a ravine. Ralph pointed up the side to where a dark patch opened against the hill. The grade wasn't terribly steep, but it would be tricky and I realized Tonya might have a hard time of it. But there was nothing we could do about that now. She would have to keep up as best as she could.

Ralph began to ascend the side of the hill, and even though he moved as silent as the night, leaves and branches still scattered beneath his feet, creating a soft cadence of their own. I glanced over my shoulder to see that Chai was helping Tonya. She held her walking stick in her right hand, and he was holding her left elbow, bracing her as they ascended the hill. Relieved, I returned my attention to my own footing. The leaves were slick with mold and mildew and raindrops, and it was easy to go sliding. I tripped over a hidden root once, landing on my knees, but scrambled back to my feet the next moment, unhurt and smelling of the forest floor.

We were about five yards below the opening when I realized that we had reached a ledge. In fact, the ledge merged with a path that must have started somewhere below. If we had seen it, our jaunt would have been far easier, but we were here now, and we paused, spreading out along the trail to regroup.

Ralph motioned to Alex to join him, then signaled for the rest of us to stay put. The two of them searched along the path until they found a narrow trail leading up to the opening of the cave. Alex held up his hand to Ralph, and then in the blink of an eye, he transformed into a bat and vanished into the cave.

We waited, and I found myself staring intently at the cave, trying to fathom what was inside. I strained, listening for the sound of voices, but all I could hear was the continual *drip, drip, drip* as the raindrops fell from the tall fir trees. After what seemed like an interminable time, Alex reappeared and flew down, transforming back into himself. Ralph scrambled back down the trail to the main path.

"The chamber is illuminated. I'm not sure by what, but there's light in there. And yes, Bette is there," Alex whispered. "And so is Gerta. They're both tied up and off to one

side. You are right on that. And what I assume is the diatrofymata is there, but it's not alone. The creature has reinforcements and I'm not sure what they are." He frowned,
shaking his head. "They're rather terrifying, actually. I saw
three of them. They . . . well, take a giant spider and mush
it together with a human torso . . ."

"*Werespiders!* I really didn't believe they existed. I didn't
*want* to believe they existed." Horrified, Tonya leaned closer
to Chai. "I read about them in my bestiary. I was hoping
they were a myth, even though they have been rumored to
inhabit the forests around this area."

The concept of a werespider turned my stomach. I wasn't
afraid of spiders, especially in the way many humans were.
But the idea of an actual shapeshifter who could turn into
a spider made me queasy. It was all sorts of wrong.

The werewolves didn't look too happy either.

Frank let out a curse under his breath. "Are you positive?"

"I know what I saw," Alex said. "I only wish I hadn't."

"Do you think they're poisonous?" Again, the question
made me feel queasy. I could handle the thought of just about
any Were creature, but when it came to insects, again . . .
just wrong.

"I certainly hope not, but I'm not gonna bet on it." Alex
looked over at Chai. "You wouldn't happen to have any
thoughts on the subject, would you?"

Chai shook his head. "I have seen many monsters in my
life, some which make the thought of a werespider sound
downright chummy. But I've never dealt with werespiders
before. I guess we'll find out what they're like. I would recommend, however, that you, Shimmer, and I go first. We're the
most likely to be immune to any venom they might have."

"I hate to agree, but you make a good point. We're going
to have to take out those werespiders before we get to the
diatrofymata." Alex looked downright irritated at this point.
"Whatever you do, keep Bette out of the crossfire. And try
to keep Gerta from being hurt as well." He paused, staring

at the werewolves. "There's something you need to know about Gerta. We believe she's one of the Elder Fae. And she has a unique ability that might catch your notice. But the first person to lay hands on her will feel the point of my fangs. I won't have her being abused."

Frank nodded. "I take it this . . . ability . . . is enticing in some way?"

Alex rubbed his chin. "You can say that. And if the diatrofymata was telling the truth, Gerta has poison skin. I suggest you let me untie her. The passage into the chamber is short, but the cavern is far larger than I thought it would be. I didn't go all the way to the back—the actual cave tunnels deep into the hill. I'm not sure what's back there, so be prepared in case there are other horrors waiting for us."

"Right." Frank glanced at his men. "You getting all this?" They nodded.

"All right," Alex continued, "so here's what we do. Chai, you immediately blast a light in the cave. Even though there's dim illumination, a bright flash will give us an edge."

"Got it. Everybody needs to be prepared to close their eyes, though, because it will be sunlight bright for a second."

Alex glanced around. "Everybody got that? All right, after the flash, Chai and I will take on the werespiders. Shimmer, you free Bette. Ralph, transform into your werewolf shape. You know why. Attack whatever you can. Frank, you and your men go after the diatrofymata. It appears to be a tall, lanky creature, bipedal and muscular. Its muscles look like gnarled wood. In some ways it looks like a walking skeleton with a thin layer of skin stretched over it, but don't let that fool you. The energy coming off that thing? So strong I could feel it radiating like a beacon. And since it *is* from the Elemental plane of Earth, my guess is that its magic will be Earth-based. Which brings to mind a potential scenario. It might just be able to cause an earthquake. If it does, get the hell out. We can't afford to be trapped inside there. Any other thoughts?"

"What do you want me to do?" Tonya asked.

"You stay here. No arguments. There's nothing you can do in there to help and we'd probably end up having to rescue you, which would dilute our focus. I don't mean to sound harsh, but you have to wait here. If for some reason we don't return in twenty minutes, or if one of the other creatures comes out, get the hell out of here. If you have to hide in the woods, hide until morning and then get back to the Range Rover. There's a spare key beneath the front left tire well."

Tonya was about to protest, then stopped. "I understand."

Ralph transformed into his werewolf shape, and once again I marveled at the beautiful white wolf. We shifted positions, Chai and I moving up front with Alex, and Ralph falling back with the werewolves. We were as ready as we were going to get. It was time to go rescue our friend.

The entrance to the cave was narrow; there was only room for two of us to walk side by side. Alex had told us that it would widen out into the main chamber only a few yards in.

Alex and Chai went first and I followed directly after, Ralph padding at my side. Next came Frank and José, and then George and Thomas. Tonya fretted but did as Alex requested and stayed outside.

It was difficult to see, but true to what Alex had said, a faint light filtering in from up ahead dimly illuminated the passage. But even though we moved as quietly as we could and didn't have a light source, chances were good that they knew we were here. Creatures like werespiders and other Supes tended to have an uncanny sense when something was trying to sneak up on them.

Suddenly, Alex held up his hand.

He had been correct about the passage being short. The opening loomed ahead, leading to the main chamber. Alex counted down from five using his fingers. Five, four, three, two, *one*.

As we swung into the room Chai let out an incantation, his voice booming through the silence. As his words crackled in the air I closed my eyes, guarding against the intense flash of light that shimmered through the chamber. I sucked in a deep breath and opened my eyes.

It was as if the sunlight had found its way into the depths of the earth. Suddenly worried, I glanced over at Alex, but he seemed unaffected and I realized that, as bright as the light was, there was no heat coming from it and it wasn't a captured sunbeam.

The werespiders were shading their eyes, trying to avoid the light. They were hideous creatures—huge and bloated, looking for all the world like giant black widows with male torsos attached to them. Their legs ended in what looked like razor-sharp points, and protruding fangs glistened from their mouths. They had arms like men, but their heads were more spiderlike, with multiple eyes encircling them, and no hair to speak of.

I have seen some hideous things in my life, but these felt like a freakish mockery of both spider and man.

"They're constructs," Chai said. As he raced toward them, his scimitar appeared in his hand.

"What do you mean?" Alex called as he followed, holding Juanita—his wickedly sharp bowie knife.

"They are magical creatures; they aren't natural." Chai was already taking on the nearest one. As he swept the scimitar down, the creature lunged forward toward him and they were engaged in battle.

I forced myself to turn away from the fight and turned to look for Bette, but instead, I found myself staring into the face of the diatrofymata.

Alex was right. The thing reminded me of a walking skeleton with a thin, stretched sheet of skin clinging to the bones. Its eyes were pinpoints of light glowing within deep black sockets. The mouth was round, and razor-sharp teeth glistened like tiny needles encircling the orifice. It was standing right over me, a good eight feet tall, and before I realized what was happening, it swept one arm forward, connecting with my shoulder to knock me off balance. I went sprawling back on my butt, unprepared for the attack.

As it leaned over me, Frank and one of the other were-wolves attacked, diverting its attention away from me. I scrambled to my feet again and, as I looked around, I saw Bette and Gerta tied up against one wall. They were sitting on the ground, their hands and feet duct-taped together.

I darted through the fighting, dropping to my knees as I unsheathed my dagger. I sawed at the duct tape, glancing over my shoulder to make sure no one was behind me. Within seconds, I had freed Bette. As she struggled to her feet, she grimaced and I realized she had been in that position for far too long. Melusine or not, muscles were muscles.

"Give me your dagger, and I'll cut Gerta loose. You go help them." Bette held out her hand and I slapped the dagger into her palm.

I jumped up and turned around, trying to figure out where I could do the most good. Chai was still fighting with his werespider, trying to dodge the razor-sharp tips of its legs as it stabbed at him. Alex was on the back of another one, trying to get hold of its throat. Frank and José were fighting the diatrofymata. Thomas was curled up on the floor, down for the count. And George was being backed into a corner by the other werespider. I raced across the cavern floor to help him.

I didn't have any weapons, but the werespider didn't see me coming. As I approached the bloated abdomen, I let loose with a punch that could have broken through a wall. My hand met its exoskeleton, and the reverberation almost knocked me back. The damn thing was as hard as armor. But I had made enough of an impact that it left off attacking George and turned toward me.

Oh, hell. Now what was I supposed to do? Bette had my dagger. I was strong, but somehow I didn't think I could pull off a Samwise Gamgee move. This wasn't a movie, and the werespider wasn't Shelob. As it closed in, I did the only thing I could think of. I turned and ran like hell. It followed me, which was what I was hoping it would do, giving George enough time to get out a weapon.

"This is the last time I go into battle with just a dagger," I shouted to no one in particular.

Suddenly, a white wolf leaped past me. Oh hell, Ralph. I didn't want him getting in the way because this creature could take us both on and come out unharmed. But Ralph growled, loudly, and drew the attention of the werespider away from me. Frantic to prevent him from getting hurt, I looked around for anything that I could use as a weapon.

Over in the corner, I spotted a broken stalactite lying on the floor. It must have been two feet long, and it looked wicked sharp at the tip. I dashed over and grabbed it up, hefting the weight in my hands. It was solid and heavy enough to have a good knockback potential.

I whirled around just in time to see the werespider looming down on Ralph. He was backing away, whimpering in fear. I took aim, targeting in on the werespider's chest, hoping that its heart was in approximately the same place as a human's.

With a deep breath, I hurled the stalactite, sending it spinning toward the monster. The werespider didn't notice the approaching missile until too late. As the stalactite drove itself through its chest, it let out a tremendous roar, arms flailing as it reared back. As I watched, it lurched to one side, scrabbling to pull the stalactite out of its chest.

Ralph took the opportunity to get away, running toward Bette.

Another roar echoed against the cavern walls. Alex had managed to slit the throat of the werespider he was riding. It tried to claw at him, but it couldn't reach behind its neck, and Alex stabbed the eyes in the back of its head as a dark viscous blood began to spurt out of its severed jugular.

Chai was making headway with his opponent. He had

managed to sever several of its legs and it was leaning precariously to the left. The djinn had several long deep scratches along his arms, and I realized the creature had managed to attack him, but if it had venom, Chai didn't seem to be affected.

Frank was embroiled in a wrestling match with the diatrofymata. The creature was holding him down, clawing for his eyes with its long, bony fingers. I was close enough to join in, and I wrapped one arm around the diatrofymata's neck, yanking hard to pull it away. We went sprawling to the ground, and the creature grabbed hold of my ankle and bit down, its needle-sharp teeth digging into my boot. I kicked it with my other foot as Frank came in behind, brandishing a wicked-looking dagger. He stabbed at the diatrofymata's back, and I heard the impact as metal screeched against bone.

The werespider I had been fighting staggered, finally crashing to the floor. Alex's werespider followed suit. Alex leaped to Frank's side and neatly brought Juanita across the diatrofymata's throat as he grabbed hold of its head and yanked backward. Frank placed his hands against Alex's and, together, they ripped the head clean away. No blood flowed, but the body fell to the floor, arms flailing, and then was still. Another moment, and it melted into a sludgelike goo, soaking into the dirt of the cavern floor.

Chai finished off his werespider and propped his scimitar against the floor, point first. He leaned on the pommel. "We better get out of here because where there's one werespider, I assume there are more. And I don't want to be here when they arrive."

Silently, glancing over the carnage, I crossed to Bette and Gerta to make certain they were okay. Frank and José carried Thomas out of the cave. We had managed to finish what we had set out to do, but I couldn't help but wonder what else lurked inside these mountains.

* * *

Tonya was waiting for us. When she saw Bette, she broke into a wide smile. "I take it everything is all right?"

"Thomas is severely injured, but I think he'll live. We all took our lumps and bruises," I said. "But the diatrofymata is dead, along with three werespiders. Later on, I want a look at your bestiary to see if it talks about what they are." I motioned to Bette. "Are you sure you're okay? You're not hurt?"

She shook her head. "Takes more than a few giant arachnids to harm me. Seriously, though, I have a feeling by morning I wouldn't have had my eyes or my tongue."

Alex almost said something, then caught himself. "Well, luckily we won't find out." But he glanced at me, and I could see the wariness in his eyes. I gave him a silent nod, a promise that I would keep my mouth shut about what he had told us. But as I watched her, I realized my curiosity was eventually going to get the better of me. I would have to watch myself.

As we approached the vehicles, Gerta remained silent and suspicious. It occurred to me that the real Gerta had never met us. We had been talking to the diatrofymata the entire time. I motioned to Alex and we stepped one side.

"What should we do about Gerta? She doesn't know any of us except Bette, and she only knows Bette from what little she saw her in the cavern. Should we ask her if she even wants to go with us?"

Alex glanced at the Elder Fae. Hell, come to think of it, we really didn't know if she even *was* Elder Fae. "You make a good point. The last thing I want is for her to feel like we're kidnapping her, too."

He motioned for everybody to stop, then turned to Gerta. "You don't know who we are, but we have an idea of who you are. The diatrofymata was imitating you. What do you want to do now that you're free? Do you want to go with us?

We're headed back into the city—into Seattle. It would help if you could answer some questions for us, but we understand if you don't want to. We have the general idea of what happened with you, Stone Weaver, and the diatrofymata."

She held his gaze for a moment, unsmiling. Then, in a voice that sounded like she was speaking through wind chimes, she said, "I don't like cities. They unsettle me. I just want to return to my home."

"Where do you live?"

"The realm of the Elder Fae. I know there's a portal near here. I can find it on my own." She paused, then asked, "Is it true that Stone Weaver is dead?" Her voice wavered ever so slightly, enough to tell me that the diatrofymata had it right. Gerta had truly loved the Elemental Fae. That was one thing the creature hadn't lied about.

In a soft voice, Alex said, "Yes, it's true. I'm sorry."

"Then I'll go home. There's nothing left here for me now." And a stream of tears trickled down her face, falling to the ground in the shape of golden coins. She looked at them, then looked at us. "Consider them my ransom fee, paid in full." And with that Gerta, the Golden Frog, turned and vanished into the forest without a sound. I wondered if we would ever see her again.

The return trip was silent. Thomas had been seriously injured, but he would survive, and he was in the back of Frank's vehicle. Bette leaned against the left backseat door, her feet up and resting on Chai's lap. Tonya was on Chai's right, and Ralph rode home with us, in the back with all our supplies. Chai was rubbing Bette's ankles, which still bore the marks of the duct tape that had bound her.

"I suppose Chase will be happy to hear that the serial killer is dead. And trust me, that creature *was* the killer." Bette sounded discouraged. "I suppose you're wondering what happened?"

"Well, yes. Ralph went to the boat to drop off something and found the mess there. But we know what happened." I went on to explain what we had figured out about how the diatrofymata had created a persona to mingle with the others, and how it had imitated Gerta. "So it managed to pinpoint its marks well ahead of time. As Estelle, the creature was able to dig into the background of everybody there. It wouldn't take much spying to find out that you work for a private investigator. And, as Gerta, it listened in to our plan to set you as bait." That explanation was true, yet skirted anything that might expose what Alex had told us.

"Damn thing thought of everything, didn't it? I hope to hell they're a rare breed because I don't ever want to go up against another one. Anyway, I was getting ready to go down to the center when Estelle came knocking on my door. Of course I let her in because, hey—it was Estelle. Once she was inside the boat . . ." Bette's voice drifted off. "You know, I don't remember anything else until I woke up in the cave, strapped up tighter than a hog on butchering day. I don't know what happened."

Something about her memory loss made me nervous, but I kept my mouth shut. It could be that the creature had knocked her out with some sedative, or cast a spell that it managed to get from somewhere. Whatever the case, we could figure it out later. At least Bette was safe, we had freed Gerta, and our serial killer was dead. And that was as much as we could ask for, when I really thought about it.

# CHAPTER 19

On the way home, I put in a call to Chase to let him know we had caught the serial killer. I got hold of Yugi, and he promised to call Chase as soon as he was off the phone with me.

"So is it what you thought it was? Chase told me it was some sort of doppelgänger."

"It was even stranger than that, but you don't have to worry about it anymore. We took care of the situation." I wasn't sure exactly how far to go in terms of telling Yugi what had happened. I figured Alex would decide how much we should tell the cops. I was still finding my way around interacting with humans and human authorities, and I didn't want to overstep my bounds. But I did have a question. "Do you know anything new about that baby's skeleton?"

Alex jerked his head, flashing me a puzzled look. But he kept his mouth shut and went back to focusing on the road.

"Given the circumstances, we had one of our Otherworld specialists look into it. She determined that the baby was human, and yes, the bones are those of Mary's missing son. Of course, we'll run them through testing with the medical examiner, but I guarantee you the results will be the same. The child had a broken neck." Yugi was silent for a moment, then let out a soft breath. "Mary will probably get blamed for the death, but somehow I don't think she did it."

"She didn't. Her husband did. Who will take possession of the body?"

"Probably Mary's relative—Elena. One way or another, the child will be properly buried." He paused again, then asked, "That's what you are wondering, isn't it?"

"You nailed it on the head." As I punched the End Talk button, I wondered about Yugi and exactly who he was. I knew he was human, but he was a very special human.

"The skeleton *was* Mary's baby." I let out a sigh and leaned back in my seat. "I want to cleanse that house. I want to put her to rest. I wonder, do you think she's there, searching for her lost child?"

"You might be right." Tonya leaned forward, peeking between the seats. "Even though we know her husband drove her over the edge and that she killed her family, we also know that he's the one that killed the boy. It could be that when she finds out that we know the truth, it might set her free."

I glanced at the dashboard clock. It was just past one A.M. "I know it's been a long night already, but what do you think about telling her?" I suddenly had a strong need to clear that space as soon as possible. "I don't know how to explain this, but I'm actually afraid of letting it go for another night."

"What do you think might happen?" Ralph asked.

"I don't know, but it feels like we stirred up things when we found the child's body. I'm nervous." And then a thought hit me, and my stomach curled in that way that told me I was right on key. "I know something—I know whatever that creature is we met in the house, and that's still there, is her husband's ghost. He's still abusing her from the spirit world. He drove her into insanity and now he's punishing her."

"You're right. I know you're right!" Tonya shifted in her seat. "I'll go with you. I've got my tool bag with me. I didn't want to leave it in the house in case—" She paused, glancing over at Alex. "I didn't want to leave it there in case Glenda returned and took it in her head to destroy anything else."

Alex let out a low growl. "Rest assured, I'll take care of the bitch."

That startled me. Alex seldom cursed in front of women.

He flashed me another look. "By the way, are you going to tell me what you're talking about? What skeleton did you find and where?"

We filled in both Alex and Bette on what had happened early in the morning. "So much has gone on today that it's hard to remember who knows what."

"As soon as we make sure that Thomas is all right, we'll head over to your place. We might as well tie up as many loose ends as we can before the night's over." As Alex eased the car onto the freeway and we headed west toward Seattle, Tonya and Chai and I discussed how we were going to tackle Mary. And Ralph, he just stared out the window. I had the feeling he was thinking about his upcoming marriage.

We reached the FH-CSI shortly after Frank and his men arrived. The medics brought out a stretcher to carry Thomas inside. As we followed them in, Tonya craned her neck. I had only been here a few times, but I did my best to explain to her how the organization was set up, even though I didn't know all that much about it. Yugi met us and led us back to the medic unit, where we sat in the waiting room, along with Frank and his men.

"I want to thank you. You really helped us out tonight and we appreciate it." Alex leaned over and held out his hand to the werewolf. I knew it was difficult for him; vampires and werewolves usually didn't get along very well.

Ralph and Alex were an exception. But Frank returned the smile and then accepted the proffered handshake.

"My pleasure. It takes a united effort at times to overcome a common enemy. That creature wouldn't have stopped with Fae. It would have gone on to wealthy Supes. But I am concerned about the werespiders. They aren't unnatural. And your friend here, he said they were magical constructs. If that's true, then who created them and why?"

"That's an extremely good question and not one I have any answers for at this point. But I suppose we should look into it. I'm concerned about what else might be lurking out there." Alex usually didn't make it his business to look into matters we weren't hired to investigate, but I could tell the werespiders had unsettled him in a way I had never before seen.

"Why don't you give me a call tomorrow night around nine P.M.? I'll do a little digging and see what I can come up with. I know some friends of mine had a problem with hobo werespiders a couple years ago, and there were coyoteshifters involved. I don't know much more than that, but the rumor mill gets around." Frank rubbed his chin, then jumped up as one of the medics approached.

The elf looked barely old enough to vote, let alone be a doctor, but I knew the Elfin race, and they usually were far older than most people thought. Most of them were ancient, although not as old as Dragonkin.

"My name is Mallen. I'm the head medic here. We've done a cursory examination on your friend Thomas. I don't think there's any internal bleeding, but he suffered multiple broken bones. I know werewolves heal quickly so I wanted to talk to you about the best way to proceed. If you could follow me, you can give me information on his background."

Frank stood, but before he left he turned to Alex. "So I'll talk to you tomorrow night? Nine P.M.?"

Alex nodded. "I'll expect your call. Go take care of your buddy. And wish him swift healing from us, if you will. Send the bill to Chase Johnson."

As Frank followed Mallen into a private office, Chai, Bette, Ralph, Alex, and I all stood. We made our good-byes to the remaining werewolves and headed out the door.

"Can you drop me off at my boat? I'm tired and I want a shower. And from what it sounds like, I need to clean up my place and see what's broken." Bette let out a long sigh. "You'll forgive me if I don't go ghost hunting with you tonight."

"Do you want some company?" Alex lightly placed a hand on her elbow, looking worried.

She bit her lip, glancing at me, and I realized she was worried what I might think.

"Go ahead. You can come over later. Tonya, Chai, and I can take care of the ghost." I glanced at Ralph. "Do you want to come with us?"

He shook his head. "I'm sorry, I'm wiped. I'd like to help out but I just don't have any oomph left in me tonight."

"Then go home and rest. And, I guess, start planning your wedding." I winked at him, wanting him to know that we supported him.

"Yeah, I guess there is that."

Bette tapped him on the shoulder. "You're going to need someone to help you. Geek boys don't make the best wedding planners. Why don't you come over to my place? I've got beer, and that way Alex can go with Shimmer and the others." She held up her hand as I started to speak. "No, sugar. It's all right. Ralph can watch after me. Not that I *need* watching after. And I'll look after him."

She wouldn't take no for an answer, so Alex dropped them off at her houseboat. Ralph assured us that he could pick up his car from the office later on, and the rest of us headed to my house.

* * *

By the time we reached my neighborhood, it was almost three. With a heavy heart, I climbed the stairs to the front porch, hoping that somehow Coolray and Wriggly had managed to survive in their interim tanks. I hesitantly unlocked the door and we entered. I hadn't set the alarm when we left because I wasn't sure of how much water damage there was and whether it had affected any of the wiring. Chai struck up a light without being asked, a soft glow that illuminated the entire room.

Alex stared in silence at the shattered aquarium and the glass that covered the floor. The standing water was gone, having saturated the carpet, drained out the open door when we left, and—I feared—soaked into the floor. There was a grimy line around the wall about six inches off the floor and the room smelled vaguely of mildew. I cringed as I saw dead fish everywhere. And even though things mattered to me a whole lot less than my fish, the sight of my ruined furniture disheartened me. My books on the bottom shelf were goners. Feeling helpless, I stood there shaking my head.

Alex slowly walked into the room, and when he turned, the look on his face almost broke my heart. "I'm sorry. I'm so sorry this happened. I promise, I'll make it right. I'll pay for all the repairs and I'll replace anything that got damaged. I can't do much about the fish that were killed, but you'll have new fish. And Glenda will cease to be a problem."

There wasn't much I could say. I knew he meant well, but until Glenda was long gone, it would be hard for me to trust that she wouldn't come back to make matters worse. "Why don't we head over to take care of Mary?"

As we trooped back outside and across the street, I wasn't sure why I felt so confident this was going to work. But something inside whispered that all she needed to do, all she needed to hear, was that we knew she hadn't killed her baby. Somebody needed to believe that she hadn't killed the infant.

We cautiously skirted the holes on the porch and I opened the front door, letting myself in. Tonya followed, and then Chai and Alex behind us.

"Mary? Mary are you here?" I glanced around, hoping she would just show up.

A noise from the kitchen alerted us, and I headed in that direction. But I had no more than reached the doorway leading into the dining area when something came sailing through the air at me. I screamed, "Duck!" as I dropped to the floor.

Luckily, the others reacted just as quickly as a cleaver went sailing over our heads.

"So you want to play?" Chai whispered as he quickly moved to the front and motioned for us to stay back. "Wait for my signal."

Another loud noise crashed in the kitchen and I heard Chai yell, "Get in here but be careful!"

We rushed in just in time to see a menacing figure standing there. A large man, and I knew from Tonya's description of her vision that it was probably Mary's husband. He turned to us and let out a thundering roar that shook the house.

"Get out of here or I'll kill you!" His voice reverberated through the walls, and I heard someone cry out.

I turned to see Mary standing in the corner of the kitchen, holding her head as she rocked back and forth. "Make him stop, make him stop, *please* make him stop!" She was screaming and he turned to her and held out his hand. A dark plume of smoke engulfed her and she began to scream louder.

"Shut up, you bitch! I should have killed you when I had the chance." His voice ricocheted along the walls, knocking bric-a-brac to the floor.

"Mary, listen to me!" Tonya moved forward, fumbling in her bag until she found what she was looking for. She pulled out a silver dagger and Alex flinched to the side.

"Mary, hear me!" Tonya drew a pentagram in the air and as we watched, it took on a faint blue light. "We *know* you didn't kill your son! We know that it was your husband who killed your baby. We know he made you bury it in the yard, and we know that his abuse drove you insane. We found your baby."

There was a sudden hush as both Mary and her husband turned toward us. The look on her husband's face was terrifying, like some grotesque mask or demon's face. But Mary heard us. She slowly lowered her hands and straightened her shoulders.

"You found him?" Her focus was solely on Tonya, ignoring her husband as if he didn't exist.

"We found him. He's going to be properly buried. We know how hard your life must have been. We're so sorry." Tonya slowly moved forward, her dagger outstretched, moving the pentagram along in front. "By the powers of Hecate, I free you from your torture. I free you from your memories. I free you from the spirit of your husband. You can go now, Mary. He can't keep you here anymore."

Mary's eyes grew clear and the cunning look that I had seen on her face was gone, along with the fear. She hesitantly stepped toward Tonya. "You mean I can leave? It's okay for me to leave? I can rest?"

The spirit of Mary's husband roared and he charged toward Tonya. Chai let out a shout and within the blink of an eye was between them. The spirit froze, a look of fear crossing his face as Chai blazed with a brilliant, fiery light and held out his hands.

"You will harm her no more!" As Chai's words reverberated through the kitchen, Mary silently moved toward Tonya, who closed her eyes and whispered something that I could not hear. The pentagram of blue light expanded, and Mary entered it, vanishing as she touched the edges of the energy. All we heard was a soft "thank you," and Mary was gone.

Mary's husband was apparently pissed off because the

walls began to rattle, and it felt like we were in the middle of an earthquake. But then Tonya held her dagger over her head and began an incantation.

"O mighty Hecate, Guardian of the Crossroads, I call to thee! I summon your power, O Mother of Ghosts. I ask that you consign this spirit, this demon to the Netherworld! Punish him for his deeds and prevent him from crossing back to the land of the living! O mighty Hecate, hear my prayer!"

And then the earthquake stopped.

Mary's husband froze, and the next moment, his form broke down, flooding into a pillar of black smoke. A portal opened in the middle of the kitchen ceiling. The vortex reminded me of a spinning kaleidoscope. A sudden gust of wind sprang up, and the smoke was sucked through the portal as if into a giant vacuum. The vortex slammed shut and vanished.

The house felt remarkably quiet, as if it had taken a deep breath and exhaled all the bad memories.

"They're both gone." Tonya looked over at me and shook her head. "Mary just needed someone to know that she didn't kill the baby, and she needed to be freed from her husband's tyranny. Imagine, being trapped with your abuser in the spirit world. How horrible."

I closed my eyes, but the house truly felt empty. A soft wind started to blow through the broken window. "It's over. They won't be back."

"I think when morning comes, we'll call Elena Johnson, and I'll make an offer on the house. Maybe it's time I left Port Townsend. And somebody ought to love this place. It has good bones, even with a few skeletons in the closet. Besides, until we catch Jack and make him stop, I don't feel like returning home." Tonya smiled, but tears were running down her face.

We headed back across the street. "I don't really want to stay in my house tonight. It stinks and we need to clean it up before we can move back in."

"I can go to a hotel for the night. It won't hurt me any." Tonya shrugged. "Just let me get my suitcase."

"You can stay at my apartment, Shimmer." Alex headed toward the Range Rover. "I'd like that."

"Chai can crash in my room," Tonya said. "Considering Skelton is still out there, it would make me feel safer to have someone else around. I doubt if he knows what's going on here, but right now I'm a little bit paranoid."

"Understandable. I'd be happy to spend the night." Chai glanced at me and glared as a smirk crossed my face. "And I'll be a perfect gentleman. No worries there."

Tonya gave him a puzzled look, then shrugged. "If I were worried, I wouldn't have offered."

We drove back to the office, where Tonya picked up her car. She and Chai drove off to find a hotel as Alex and I headed toward his condo. It had been a long night, and I hoped that nothing else was going to drop in our lap until we had all had a good sleep.

Alex and I finished taking our showers, and then we curled up in his bed together. I knew it was now or never, and I knew that I had to say something.

"Alex, I have to tell you something. When we were trying to figure out how to help Bette, before you woke up . . . Well, we were frantic, searching for any information we could find that might help us. Ralph had told us about the figure of light he saw, and we needed to know if you had anything that might shed light on what it was or if it might relate to her being kidnapped." I pulled out of his embrace and straightened up, crossing my legs on the bed.

He frowned, pushing himself up to sit against the headboard. He crossed his hands over that rock-hard abdomen of his and asked, "What's going on?"

"I looked through your desk." I waited to see if he would understand what I was saying.

After a moment, understanding dawned in his eyes. "I see. Did you find what you're looking for?"

"No. Oh, hell." I was tired of pussyfooting around. "I saw the pictures of Glenda. And I looked through Bette's file, but I didn't look through mine. I only saw the pictures because I was trying to find anything that might help us with Bette."

He nodded, chewing on his lip. At least his fangs hadn't descended and his eyes weren't crimson, so he couldn't be terribly angry. "What do you want me to do with them?"

Flustered, I shrugged. "I'm not sure; after all, they're not my pictures. I just wanted you to know." But that wasn't true. I wanted to ask, *What are you still doing with them?* But I felt embarrassed for having snooped.

Alex leaned forward, rubbing the ever-present stubble on his chin. After a moment, he said, "To be honest, I had almost forgotten they were there. I'll get rid of them. I'll shred them." He cocked his head, giving me a sideways glance. "You say that you didn't look in your file?"

I shook my head. "No, I didn't. I thought about it, to be honest. But I wasn't sure that I'd like seeing what you might have written in it. And I want you to know, I never would have touched your desk if we hadn't been so frantic."

"I believe you. Shimmer, if there's one thing I know about you, it's that you don't poke yourself in where you think you don't belong. Tomorrow night, after I've talked to Frank, I want you to come to my office and I'm going to show you everything in your file. I want you to see that there's nothing there to hurt you. And I'll shred Glenda's pictures while you're there. I told you, I want us to work. I don't know what we have here, either, but I want to see where it goes. I don't want you to have doubts about me. I wouldn't have given you a ring if I thought that I might want to go back to that bitch."

I smiled then, turning the ring on my finger. "I love it, you know."

"I'm so glad." His eyes were cool, but a sparkle in them

told me he truly was happy. "Speaking of Glenda, tomorrow night I'll have a talk with a couple buddies of mine. They have influence with her. They owe me a big favor and I'm going to call it in. I'll get Glenda off our backs."

I exhaled deeply, letting the tension drain with the breath.

"I won't ask about Bette. If I'm supposed to know, good. Until then, I won't say a word. But if you need help, you know I'm here. I love that bad-assed broad, and I don't have many people that I can say that about. And for what it's worth, I'm not jealous of her. I'm not jealous of what you had with her, and I'm not jealous of the friendship that you still have. I trust Bette, and I trust you."

That was what it came down to. *Trust.* I had never thought I could say those words to anybody in my life, but I realized that I *did* trust Alex. And I trusted Bette and Ralph and Chai and Tonya and Stacy. I had gone from having no one to having a circle of friends.

Alex must have sensed the shift because he held out his arms. "Shimmer, let me make love to you. I want to feel your skin under my fingers; I want to taste you. I want to slide inside you and move so slowly that it feels like time stops."

He folded me in his embrace, his hand trailing down to caress my nipples, to cup my breasts and then slide down toward the V between my legs. I let him touch me, holding very still as he fingered my sex, stroking gently until I ached with desire. I moaned, shifting so he had easier access. As he slid two fingers inside me, thrusting gently, I wrapped my hand around his erect penis, squeezing as two drops of pre-cum trickled out of the head.

"I want you," I whispered, lowering my lips to fasten around him. I slid down his length, gripping him with my mouth as I stroked his rock-hard cock with my tongue. And right then, I realized that this was the only place I wanted to be.

Alex gently pulled me up to face him. "Let me love you, Shimmer. Let me prove myself to you. Let me make you happy."

"Love me, then. Love me, because I meant what I said. I *do* love you." The words echoed strong in my heart.

And then Alex made love to me until the sun rose and dragged him into his deep slumber.

As I quietly showered again and then curled up in the spare bedroom, drifting as the weariness of the past few days took hold, I thought about my life. We would repair the damage done to my house, and Chai and I would move back in. Tonya would buy the house across the street, and I would introduce her to Stacy. I thought they would make great friends. And Ralph . . . dear Ralph would soon be married with a family of his own.

And one day, when it was time, we would find out what Bette's secret was.

As I drifted off to sleep, it occurred to me that—for the first time in my life—I had a family. And that was a treasure greater than any dragon hoard I could ever accumulate.

# THE PLAYLIST

I write to music a good share of the time, and so I always put my playlists in the back of each book so you can see which artists/songs I listened to during the writing. Here's the playlist for *Flight from Mayhem*:

**AC/DC:** "Back in Black"

**Air:** "Playground Love"; "Moon Fever"

**Android Lust:** "Here and Now"; "Saint Over"; "Stained"; "Dragonfly"

**The Animals:** "Bury My Body"; "House of the Rising Sun"; "We Gotta Get Out of This Place"

**Arcade Fire:** "Abraham's Daughter"

**Arch Leaves:** "Nowhere to Go"

**The Black Angels:** "You on the Run"; "Evil Things"; "Don't Play with Guns"; "Holland"; "Always Maybe"; "Broken Soldier"

**Black Mountain:** "Wild Wind"; "Queens Will Play"; "Buried by the Blues"

**Black Rebel Motorcycle Club:** "Feel It Now"

**Black Sabbath:** "Paranoid"

**Bobbie Gentry:** "Ode to Billy Joe"

**Boom! Bap! Pow!:** "Suit"

**Broken Bells:** "The Ghost Inside"

**Cher:** "The Beat Goes On"

**Cobra Verde:** "Play with Fire"

**Commodores:** "Brick House"

**Crazy Town:** "Butterfly"

**Dire Straits:** "Money for Nothing"

**The Doors:** "People Are Strange"; "Hello, I Love You"; "Roadhouse Blues"

**Eastern Sun:** "Beautiful Being"

**Eels:** "Souljacker Part One"

**Fatboy Slim:** "Praise You"

**FC Kahuna:** "Hayling"

**The Feeling:** "Sewn"

**Fluke:** "Absurd"

**Garbage:** "Queer"; "#1 Crush"; "Push It"; "I Think I'm Paranoid"; "Bleed Like Me"

**Gary Numan:** "I Am Dust"; "Sleep by Windows"; "Here in the Black"; "Love Hurt Bleed"; "Remember I Was Vapour"; "Petals"

**The Guess Who:** "No Sugar Tonight/New Mother Nature"; "American Woman"

**Harry Nilsson:** "Coconut"

**The Hollies:** "Long Cool Woman"

**Jace Everett:** "Bad Things"

**Jay Price:** "Something Bad"; "Baby Where Are You?"; "Boneshaker"; "I Don't Want You Anyway"; "Number 13"

**Jeannie C. Reilly:** "Harper Valley P.T.A."

**Jessica Bates:** "The Hanging Tree"

**Johnny Otis:** "Willie & the Hand Jive"

**Joy Division:** "Atmosphere"

**Julian Cope:** "Charlotte Anne"

**The Kills:** "Wait: You Don't Own the Road"; "Future Starts Slow"; "Satellite"; "Dead Road 7"; "Murdermile"

**King Black Acid:** "Rolling Under"

**Ladytron:** "Black Cat"; "Ghosts"; "I'm Not Scared"

**Little Big Town:** "Bones"

**Lorde:** "Yellow Flicker Beat"

**Low with Tomandandy:** "Half Light"

**Mark Lanegan:** "Riot in My House"; "Phantasmagoria Blues"; "Wedding Dress"

**Matt Corby:** "Breathe"

**Nancy Sinatra:** "These Boots Are Made for Walking"

**Nick Cave & the Bad Seeds:** "Right Red Hand"

**OneRepublic:** "Counting Stars"

**Orgy:** "Blue Monday"

**The Pierces:** "Secret"

**PJ Harvey:** "Let England Shake"; "The Words That Maketh Murder"; "In the Dark Places"

**Rachel Diggs:** "Hands of Time"

**R.E.M.:** "Drive"

**The Rolling Stones:** "Gimme Shelter"; "Little Red Rooster"; "19th Nervous Breakdown"; "Lady Jane"

**Screaming Trees:** "Where the Twain Shall Meet"; "Dime Western"; "Gospel Plow"

**Stealers Wheel:** "Stuck in the Middle with You"

**Syntax:** "Pride"

**Tamaryn:** "While You're Sleeping, I'm Dreaming"; "Violet's in a Pool"

**Three Dog Night:** "Mama Told Me"

**Tom Petty:** "Mary Jane's Last Dance"

**The Verve:** "Bitter Sweet Symphony"

**Voxhaul Broadcast:** "You Are the Wilderness"

**Wild Cherry:** "Play That Funky Music"

**Zero 7:** "In the Waiting Line"

Dear Reader:

I hope you've enjoyed *Flight from Mayhem*, the second Fly by Night book. Read on for an excerpt from *Shadow Silence*, the second Whisper Hollow book, coming out on September 27, 2016. Also, check out my website and sign up for my newsletter to keep informed of all my future releases!

Bright Blessings,
The Painted Panther
Yasmine Galenorn

The Cold Moon brought the winds, rushing in off the Strait of Juan de Fuca to whistle through tall fir and cedar and snake through the thick undergrowth, rattling the windows as they surrounded Whisper Hollow. Catching the town up in their icy embrace, they danced through the long December night. Up on Hurricane Ridge, the snow was clouding the Olympics, blanketing the peaks with a thick layer of powder. Down in the shadow of the mountains, the storms were bringing rain and sleet, and perpetual gray clouds that swept through on the atmospheric river.

I adjusted my coat and blew on my fingers, trying to warm them as I inscribed a band of runes in charcoal paste on the headstone. I was sitting on the grave, straddling the freshly mounded earth that covered the pine casket bearing Hudson Jacks's mortal remains. Saturday, he had left this world, dragged down into the lake by the Lady. She was ravenous lately, it seemed, and Hudson had been in the wrong place at the wrong time.

As I inscribed the runes, Ellia played in the background, her violin keening through the night as the wind picked up her notes and tossed them willy-nilly, almost as if the song and storm were doing battle. Her music strengthened my magic, as we bound the dead man to the deep dark of the graveyard. Penelope was waiting in her tomb to take his spirit with her into the Veil, my gruesome Gatekeeper who was terrifying and beautiful. *Death's maiden.*

To the side, Bryan stood watch. My protector and guardian shifter, he kept on guard for those who sought to disrupt me when I was too far into the magic to protect myself. He was also my lover. Fiercely protective, his arms were crossed as he surveyed the graveyard.

Behind me, the sound of the tomb opening told me Penelope was ready.

I stood and pointed my dagger at the headstone. Twin serpents coiled around the hilt in silver, and a crow was engraved on the pommel. The sigils on the blade began to glow as I whispered the chant of summoning I had found in my grandmother's journal.

*From the depths of your grave, I summon thee.*
*From the dark night of your death, I call thee.*
*From the icy grips of the Lady, I wrest thee.*
*Hudson Jacks, I command thee, stand forth in my*
    *presence.*

I shuddered, wondering if I'd ever get used to the weight of the dead pressing in on my shoulders. I could feel them watching through the Veil. Those who still walked this world watched silently from their graves, awaiting their own chance to wander.

A moment later, there was a rush of energy as Hudson shimmered into sight. His form was translucent, and he looked as he had in death. Coiling vines draped around his neck where the Lady had taken him into her arms and dragged him below her icy surface. Hudson had been wandering since his body had washed up on the shore, and twice now, he had appeared outside his brother's window. The Lady's spirits often turned into Haunts, dangerous and hungry. So Ellia and I needed to put him to rest before he became trouble.

I held out my hand to him. I had only been doing this for a little over a month, but I was learning fast. He gazed at my fingers, then at me, cocking his head to the side.

"You cannot refuse me. I am Kerris Fellwater, the spirit shaman of Whisper Hollow. I'm a Daughter of the Morrígan and you are bound to obey me. Let me lead you to the Veil, where the Gatekeeper awaits." The words themselves were a charm, strengthened by the strains of Ellia's song and the power of the Morrígan.

Hudson paused. If he bolted, we'd have our work cut out for us. But a glimmer of relief appeared in his eyes and he held out his hand, placing it in my own. His fingers were like bees stinging my palm, the energy crackled and snapped, sparking against my skin.

I held fast, ignoring the discomfort, and turned, leading him toward the tomb, where the double doors were open. Ellia fell in behind, still playing as her cloak fluttered in the wind, and Bryan followed, silently guarding our backs.

Penelope's mausoleum glowed from within, the blood of her chalice lighting the night. As the wind keened like a Bean Sidhe, merging with Ellia's violin to knife through the air, we approached the base of the knoll where Penelope had been laid to rest. Her crypt straddled the line dividing the modern graveyard from the Pest House Cemetery, where more dangerous shadows lurked. Built of cinder block buried deep into the shroud of grass and mounded dirt, the crypt was stained from time and weather.

A plaque affixed to the side of the door glimmered in the light emanating from inside. I knew the words by heart: HERE LIETH THE MORTAL REMAINS OF PENELOPE VOLKOV,

GUARDIAN OF THE VEIL, GATEKEEPER OF THE GRAVEYARD. ENTER AND DESPAIR.

As I entered the crypt, the crystal chalice stood on the dais, the crimson liquid within churning like a kaleidoscope. My own blood was in there, along with the blood of other spirit shamans, lament singers, and guardians who had held their posts during Whisper Hollow's history. It was rumored that every Gatekeeper's chalice contained a drop of the Morrígan's blood as well. This is what kept the glass intact and the liquid within, in a perpetual motion, a whirling vortex. I dipped one knee in front of the chalice, acknowledging the Gatekeeper.

And there she stood, to one side. Penelope in all her gruesome beauty. Dark veins of black blood trailed out from the raccoon mask that shrouded her eyes. She looked delicate as porcelain, fragile as a picture from long past, ready to dissolve at the first whisper that touched her. Her hair was upswept in a chignon, blond tendrils coiling down to her shoulders.

Penelope towered over me, six feet tall and gaunt in a black dress that fell to her ankles. The dress shimmered with sequins, the sheer material revealing the bones that thrust against her alabaster skin. But jutting out from her body from within, as if she were a voodoo doll turned inside out, were the tips of long nails, surrounded by glistening splotches of dried blood. She looked as though some crazed inner carpenter had gone mad with a nail gun.

She glanced at Hudson's spirit, a hungry look filling her eyes, then back at me. "He reeks of lake water and *her* scent. We will cleanse him and remove her binding."

"Yes, he was taken by the Lady a few days back. She gave up his body fairly quickly, though. I don't know why." Usually the Lady kept them longer, tying them to her while she fed on their spirits before she loosed them back into Whisper Hollow.

"Perhaps he was not to her taste." Penelope laughed,

making me shiver. I had gotten used to her appearance by now, but she still scared the hell out of me. I had no clue as to how extensive her powers were and I wasn't sure I wanted to know. The fact that she was Ellia's sister didn't help any, either.

I let go of Hudson's hand, and he glanced at me, a fearful light in his eyes.

"Go on, it will be all right." I gave him a gentle nod.

Penelope held out her own hand, and he reached out to touch the nails jutting out of her wrists. He glanced up at her—he was not a tall man—and she gave him a soft smile and took hold of his fingers.

"Welcome to the Veil, Hudson Jacks. Take my hand, love, and join my dark kingdom."

It was the same greeting each time, and each time, the spirit would smile dreamily and follow her into the Veil. As I watched, she gave me another nod. I turned and walked out of the crypt to where Ellia and Bryan waited for me. The doors behind us swept shut with a thud, and that was the end of Hudson Jacks.

We returned to his grave, Ellia still playing. I had one last spell to weave before we were done for the night.

I pressed my hand against the charcoal rune stream, and sprinkled Rest Easy powder on his grave. As I stood and circled the grave, deosil—clockwise—with my dagger pointing out, I invoked the charm that would, with all luck, keep Hudson by Penelope's side until he was ready to move on from the Veil to . . . wherever it was that spirits wandered after they left this world.

> Do not rise. Do not wake. Do not the Veil, now
>     forsake.
> Do not whisper. Do not walk. Do not dance and do
>     not talk.
> To the Veil, you shall remain, within the Gatekeeper's
>     domain.

As I finished, there was a hush, and then the sound of crows echoed through the graveyard. The charm had taken. The Crow Man was watching.

I turned to Ellia. She switched to a tune that made me weep no matter what mood I was in. I had learned over the past weeks that it was customary for the spirit shaman to weep over the dead, to mourn them even as she drove them to the Veil. It was an honor, my duty to remember them. I knelt, my tears falling on Hudson's grave, as I filled a little jar with graveyard dirt and labeled it. Then, we were done. I wiped my eyes and stowed the jar in my bag along with my dagger and other tools. Ellia slowly lowered her violin.

Bryan silently crossed to my side and held out his arms. I leaned into his embrace. Each spirit had their own story. Each spirit left a legacy and a family behind, even if we never knew what that legacy was. I was the last to bid them farewell as they crossed between the worlds. Sometimes, I would be the only one to *ever* remember them—*all* of them, whether beloved or lost and forlorn. Over the world, the spirit shamans were the last face the spirits would see from their mortal lives.

I rested my head on Bryan's shoulder. He was familiar, he smelled of safety and love and passion. Like myself, like Ellia, he was a child of the Morrígan. As he leaned down and pressed his lips to mine, I glanced over his shoulder. The moon had broken through the clouds. She was shimmering against the grass, and as I watched, a murder of crows flew past the silver orb, winging their way toward us and over our heads.

"The Crow Man is walking," I whispered. "Something's going to happen."

As I spoke, the clouds rolled in again and a hail of rain broke over our heads. As we raced for my car, I glanced back at Penelope's tomb, where a faint light shimmered from the knoll. The crows had landed on the tree over her mausoleum. Yes, something was up, and I had no doubt the Crow Man would make sure I was right in its path.

We sped through the night, our work done, to Lindsey's Diner, the hot spot for Whisper Hollow residents who wanted a late-night snack. Peggin, my best friend, and her new beau—Dr. Divine—would meet us there. I still wasn't sure what to think of Deev, as he had told us to call him, or D-D, as Peggin called him. An artist, he had been drawn to Whisper Hollow like a moth to a flame. The town was like that. If Whisper Hollow wanted you, you would somehow find your way here and stay. If the town *didn't* like you, it spit you up and out, and if you resisted going, it would feed you to the Lady or one of the other spirit beings that lurked in the shadows.

As we pulled into the parking lot, I saw Peggin's car. I eased into the spot next to it. As I turned off the ignition and stiffly stepped out of the driver's seat, I glanced down at my jeans. Dried splotches of mud dappled the denim, but at this point I didn't care. I just wanted something to eat, and to catch up with Peggin, who had been swamped at work the past week.

Bryan wrapped his arm around my waist as we headed into the diner. "You okay? You sure you're up for this? We could go home and I could make you something to eat there."

I caught my breath. His touch sparked me off no matter how tired I was, and I flushed just looking at him. He was five eleven, with dark brown eyes that shifted color depending on his mood, and his hair grazed the top of his shoulders, tousled strands the color of wheat. Bryan Tierney looked to be in his thirties, but he was actually over one hundred and forty years old—he was my protector, a wolfshifter guardian, a son of the Morrígan.

"No, I want to see Peggin. It's been over a week since we last got together."

He laughed. "You two are inseparable. I love that you have her for a best friend."

"She's your friend, too. You know that anybody who has my back is good as gold in her book. And vice versa." I glanced over my shoulder.

Ellia was two steps behind us as she checked her phone for texts. The older woman was over seventy but looked timeless and was as fit as anybody I knew. Tall, her long silver hair flowed over her shoulders, draping down her cape. She was wearing a pair of linen trousers, a button-down blouse, and the flowing floor-length green cape that she always wore when we went out to tend to the dead.

I pushed through the door as we came to the diner and the smell of burgers and fries assailed me, making my mouth water. The restaurant was open till two A.M., and Lindsey had remained true to her mother's vision. It was outfitted in retro-fifties style, but updated and clean. The menu had more choices, and they even made specialized dishes for allergy sufferers, but overall, it was still Mary Jane's Diner, under her daughter's name.

I started to look for Peggin but Debra-Su, who worked the night shift as a waitress, pointed me toward the back corner booth. She knew who I was looking for. She handed me three menus after seeing who I was with.

"I'll be there in a moment. They haven't ordered yet." She winked.

"Thanks, Deb." I took the menus and threaded my way through the tables toward the booth.

Peggin heard my voice and was instantly on her feet. My best friend—and the only one I had kept in touch with on my fifteen-year sabbatical from Whisper Hollow—she was a firecracker. At five seven, she was a few inches taller than me and stacked in all the right places with a plump hourglass figure. Her rich coppery hair was natural, and she was one of those wisecracking brainy women who caught you off guard, flaunting the stereotypes. She was about as athletic as my cats, she dressed like a fifties pinup girl, and she carried a gun with which she was a deadeye shot.

"Get your ass over here, *chica*." She hugged me first, then gave Bryan a quick hug. Ellia she did not touch. *Nobody* touched Ellia—it was too dangerous.

As we swung into the other side of the booth, I saw that Dr. Divine was there. He had lived all around the States, but could never seem to remember where. It was as if he had just appeared full-grown on Whisper Hollow's doorstep one day, ready to rock. He turned heads wherever he went, but for him, his appearance was as natural as breathing. Tonight was no exception.

Dr. Divine looked like a steampunk aficionado on steroids. He was probably about five nine, but he wore platform sneakers that sent him past six feet. His top hat was made of purple velvet, encircled by a black leather band with an intricate brass clockwork design on the front. Thin black braids dangled down past his ass—there must have been fifty of them.

Deev had amber-colored skin, but I wasn't sure what color his eyes were because he always wore clockwork goggles that looked out of some mad scientist's lair. He was in blue jeans and a button-up denim shirt, over which he wore a patchwork duster of denim and velvet and leather and a kaleidoscope of prints.

He also had an open-carry license and wore an antique flintlock pistol—a blunderbuss—strapped to his thigh. I asked him once if it really worked. He answered by pulling it out and promptly shooting a can of cola that was sitting on a picnic table. Apparently, he had put it together himself from antique parts, just like he had made the rest of his outfit.

But there was nothing precious or prima donna about him. He was dead serious about his art. When we had first met, I wasn't sure whether he was just odd or scary-crazy.

Turns out, a little bit of both. But, he was as sane as anybody who lived in Whisper Hollow.

"Hey, Deev," I said, sliding into the booth. Bryan followed, and Ellia swung a chair around from one of the tables to sit at the end. "How goes it?"

Deev cocked his head to the side. Somehow, he always managed to keep his hat on perfectly straight. "Jokney got out today. I still haven't found him."

Bryan cleared his throat and I could tell he was trying not to laugh. Jokney was a sculpture of a doglike creature that Deev had built from shiny chrome scraps, black leather, and some sort of fur that he'd found off an old coat from the vintage clothing shop.

At times, Dr. Divine's artwork took on a life of its own and went wandering around the town till he rounded it up and carted it back to his house. This usually didn't present a problem, except when it was some nightmarish vision he'd had. Those he kept locked away against the chance that they, too, might decide to wake up and go out for a little walk.

"Have you tried the dog pound?" Ellia asked, her eyes twinkling. She liked the man, that much I could tell from the very beginning.

"Not yet, but that's on my list for tomorrow if he hasn't come home." He leaned back, wrapping an arm around Peggin's shoulders. At first she'd been skeptical when Bryan offered to fix her up with Deev, but after the first date, they had become an item. They fit. Together they made for a startling duo. His crazy met her twisted in a wonderful, weird way.

I leaned back in my seat and opened the menu, staring at the choices. Everything looked so good. I was starving, as I always was after a night in the graveyard.

"You've been chasing down spirits in the graveyard?" Peggin was studying her own menu.

"Yeah, we had to make sure Hudson Jacks didn't go gallivanting around. You know what happens to the ones taken by the Lady. They tend to wander. Usually they become

Haunts, or in some cases the Unliving, and right now, we don't need any more of either type around town."

There were five paths of the dead.

My grandma Lila—the spirit shaman of Whisper Hollow before I took over when she died—had drilled me on the lessons from the time I was little.

The Resting Ones were those who had died, but not yet passed through the Veil. They quietly waited for Penelope to come for them and caused no trouble.

The Mournful Ones were more memory than anything else, reliving their deaths time and again as though on a movie screen. They could be disturbing to watch, but usually had no truck with mortals.

The Wandering Ones wandered far from their graves, traveling the byways, but they, too, ignored humans for the most part. All three of these were rarely a problem, although I did my best to release them so they wouldn't be caught forever on this side of the Veil.

The dangerous spirits, though, were another matter. Haunts were active troublemakers and liked to make life uncomfortable for human beings. They were the poltergeists and the spirits who could occasionally shove people down staircases.

And then, there were the Unliving. The Unliving returned on a corporeal level and could cause serious harm. They weren't zombies, not in the movie sense. No, the Unliving were smart and cunning and highly dangerous, especially when rogue. Veronica kept a tight rein over those she summoned, and at some point, I had to visit her lair. All spirit shamans had to make some sort of connection with the royalty of the Unliving.

"Honestly, your night sounds more fun than mine." Peggin made a face. "I've got to move in less than thirty days."

It was my turn to frown. "What's this? Why? I thought you loved your place?"

She shrugged. "I do, but the landlord called me last night.

She's going to move back into the house. I have until the end of the month to find a new place to live."

"Aren't you on a lease?"

"No," she said. "Once the initial lease was up the arrangement fell into a month-to-month agreement and I just forgot about it. My landlord is seventy-two, and up until this week, she seemed to be very happy living with her daughter. But apparently, the two had a major tiff—which I heard all about—and that sealed that. No warning, nothing. Just a big bomb dropping." She made a whistling sound, then, "Poooooof . . ."

"What are you going to do?" I knew how hard it could be to find real estate in Whisper Hollow, and I knew Peggin didn't have enough savings to buy a house.

She cleared her throat, staring at me over the top of her glasses. "I think I've found a place. I went out looking today and landed on a house that might be perfect for me. I haven't been inside, but I'm going to check it out tomorrow. It's a fixer-upper, but I'm not afraid of a little work."

The waitress returned. "Ready to order, folks?"

I handed her my menu. "Double cheeseburger, fries, and a chocolate shake. Also—coffee. Lots of it."

Peggin laughed. "It's almost midnight. But coffee for me, too, and I'll have the grilled cheese with bacon. Chips, pickles, and cherry pie."

"How you two can consume so much caffeine and still sleep at night confounds me," Bryan said. "I'll have chicken strips, fries, and no coffee. A Sprite, please."

Dr. Divine asked for loaded potato skins and a plate of calamari.

After the waitress left, I turned back to Peggin. "So, where is this house? I hope you have room for a garden. I know how much you love the hydrangeas at your place."

She gave me a long look. "Promise you won't argue?"

That rose the alarm right there. Peggin wouldn't say something like that unless she knew I wasn't going to like her answer. "All right, let's hear it. Where is it?"

Peggin glanced at Dr. Divine. He just stared at her silently. "On Fogwhistle Way, across from the pub. It's one of those abandoned houses near the Pier."

*Fucking hell.* "You have to be kidding. Are you *insane*? You can't move there." I leaned on the table, staring at her.

Ellia leaned in. "That's prime territory for the Lady. What on earth prompted you to think of moving into that subdivision? Or what there is left of it."

The Foggy Downs subdivision was all but abandoned. Too many people had met with accidents, been lured into the lake by the Lady, or had otherwise fallen into general misfortune of one sort or another. There were about ten houses in the little subdivision on the lakeshore near Fogwhistle Pier and most of them were abandoned now.

"Listen, you know as well as I do that there aren't many houses in Whistle Hollow that are up for rent. I can't live in an apartment—I can't stand the idea of being cooped up. And the houses in safer neighborhoods? Way too expensive. This house is rent to own, and if I fixed it up, I think it would be pretty."

Peggin could be pretty bull-headed when she thought she was being ganged up on, and if we continued to argue with her, it would only make her more determined.

I wanted to reach across the table and knock some sense into her, but since that wasn't an option, I decided to try another route. "Will you at least let me come look at it with you?"

She held my gaze for a moment, then relaxed. "All right. I've got an appointment with the Realtor tomorrow. Come with, if you like. As I said, it has a rent-to-own option and it's in my price range. I've had enough of people yanking my life out from under me, so I'm thinking of buying if it looks like I can reclaim the house."

Bryan turned to Deev. "What do you think about this plan? Have you seen the house?"

"I have." Deev regarded him from behind the clockwork goggles. "Peggin's an adult, she can make up her own mind."

But then, he glanced at Peggin, a frown forming. "I just want you to be careful. The Lady eats who she will, and she's been hungry lately."

Peggin laughed. "Don't think I'm unaware of that. But I promise you, I won't hang out at the lake. I'm not the sunbathing type, which is probably why I live here and haven't moved away." She sobered. "To be honest, I don't know what it is about this house, but I feel . . . it needs me. And I need a place to call my own."

"You can always move in with me till you find a safer home."

I blinked. That was a quick offer, considering how short of a time they had been together. But then again, if it were me, given the option of having Bryan move into a house next to a monster's lair and letting him come live with me, I'd pick the latter, too. And Bryan and I had only been together about five to six weeks, though it felt like so much longer.

But Peggin was having none of that. "Thanks, but I need my space. I learned the hard way that I have to make my own way in this world." She ducked her head. "I know you're trying to help, but I . . ." She paused, looking over at me for support. "*You* understand."

I let out a slow breath. "Yeah, I do."

And I did. Peggin's childhood had mostly consisted of ridicule for her choice of clothes, for her weight, for her lack of interest in getting married. Her older sister, Lisha, had become a family icon. The "normal" one, she was blond, trophy-wife thin, had gone to college, and—after earning a bachelor's degree in art history—had married into a family filled with lawyers and doctors. Peggin, on the other hand, was a size twelve, had no interest in joining the upwardly mobile society set, and so her parents told her she could either study law or business in college. Anything else and she'd have to pay for it herself. She had turned them down and found herself a job, saving enough to take an online medical transcription course.

A year after Peggin graduated from high school, Lisha got pregnant, and her parents moved to Seattle so they could see the baby more often. Peggin had stayed behind.

After she earned her certification, she had gone to work for the hospital. Now, she worked for Corbin Wallace, one of Whisper Hollow's best doctors. She had managed everything on her own. Peggin was used to taking care of herself and she was wary of anybody offering help, since it had always come with strings attached.

Deev seemed to sense her resistance because he gave her a little squeeze and backed off. "Well, if you need a place, you know you've got one. Just keep it in mind in case you don't like the house and can't find something suitable by the end of the month."

I decided to change the subject. Peggin was looking far too tense.

"Agent-H caught a mouse today and decided to drop it on my bed for when I woke up." Agent-H was one of my Maine coons. I had three. The other two were girls—Gabrielle, better known as Gabby, and Daphne, named after Daphne du Maurier, one of my favorite authors. They were all huge, basically walking Tribbles on legs.

Peggin snorted. "Sounds like Frith. He likes to bring me garter snakes that get in the house. Folly's too lazy."

"I love your ferrets." Dr. Divine grinned, then. He didn't smile often, but when he did, it was a trickster grin, a heady, sensual smile.

Bryan let out a laugh. "Have you ever let your ferrets visit Kerris's cats?" He slid an arm around me as the conversation eased into a comfortable chat and we wound down from the day.

**was standing** in the field near the lake. I recognized that I was dreaming—or rather, that I was out on the astral in my dreams. The field was open with no shrubs or trees except for the knee-length grass that whistled in the wind. As I stood there, my arms stretched to the moon that rode high in the night, the faint cawing of birds echoed through the air.

A murder of crows came winging in, landing around me. The vast flock settled, their blue-black feathers shimmering under the silver moonlight. They formed a circle, with me at the center. And then, I heard it. A slow processional filled the night, accompanied by violins and panpipes and the ever-present bodhrans beating the steady rhythm.

*The Crow Man is coming.*

I shivered, exposed and vulnerable in the Dream-Time. The ground around me quaked with his footsteps as the giant approached, clouds of blue fire swirling at his feet. An indigo cloak flared around him, the stars reflecting in its folds as he walked. A fur shawl encircled his shoulders, and atop his head rested a headdress—a giant crow's head with eyes that glowed red and a piercing beak. His hair was long and black, falling to his shoulders, and his eyes were slits of white fire. In one hand, he carried a wand of silver, with a glowing crystal on top.

I slowly settled to the ground, overwhelmed as I always was by his presence. Each time, his power seemed to have grown stronger, perhaps because I was far more attuned to his Mistress than I had been the first time we had met. Or perhaps he was just opening himself to me. Whatever the case, I just wanted to curl by his feet and stare at his beauty.

He did not speak, but held out his hands. As I looked into his palms, a mist began to rise, coiling like a serpent. It bade me to follow it, and I was flying through the night, the Crow Man by my side. He winked at me, but his smile vanished as we spun through the stars. Then, without a word, we landed again, by the shores of the lake. The Crow Man pointed to the waves and I gazed out over the dark surface of the water.

The winds rose as the flock of crows thundered overhead, shrieking their anger. I glanced back at the water and there she was. Rising from below the surface, a figure cloaked in pale white, dripping with water. She reminded me of a skeleton, clad in a layer of waxen skin. Her hair draped around her shoulders, long strands of seaweed and vines, and her skin was the color of gray mud. Out of hollow sockets, dark as the raging depths of the waters, she looked straight at us and began to laugh as she held out her arms.

"Come to me. I promise you peace of mind. You will find joy in my embrace, and all that you've ever longed for will be yours. Let me give you a taste of my magic." Her voice was as silken as smooth brandy, and my first instinct was to answer her call.

But the Crow Man clasped a hand on my shoulder. "Listen to her song, so you will recognize it when you hear it again. The words may not be there, but the call is always the same."

At that moment, a scream echoed through the clearing. *Peggin!*

I whirled, looking for her, but all I could see was the Lady, standing on the water, laughing as she held Peggin in her arms, unconscious. The water churned as the Lady began to slowly sink below the surface, dragging Peggin with her. I began to scream as I wrenched myself out of the Crow Man's grasp and raced forward. Overhead, the crows went winging by, screeching so loud their cries filled the night air, as the Lady and Peggin vanished from sight.

*New York Times* bestselling author **Yasmine Galenorn** writes urban fantasy, mystery, and metaphysical nonfiction. A graduate of Evergreen State College, she majored in theater and creative writing. Yasmine has been in the Craft for more than thirty-four years and is a shamanic witch. She describes her life as a blend of teacups and tattoos, and she lives in the Seattle area with her husband, Samwise, and their cats. Yasmine can be reached at her website at galenorn.com, via Twitter at twitter.com/yasminegalenorn, and via her publisher. If you send her snail mail, please enclose a self-addressed stamped envelope if you want a reply.

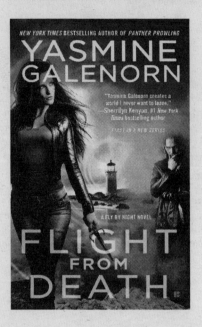